THE RUNAWAY

CATHERINE LAW

Boldwood

First published in 2018. This edition first published in Great Britain in 2023 by Boldwood Books Ltd.

Cover Design by Head Design Ltd

Cover Photography: Shutterstock

A CIP catalogue record for this book is available from the British Library.

Paperback ISBN 978-1-83751-601-8

Large Print ISBN 978-1-83751-602-5

Hardback ISBN 978-1-83751-600-1

Ebook ISBN 978-1-83751-603-2

Kindle ISBN 978-1-83751-604-9

Audio CD ISBN 978-1-83751-595-0

MP3 CD ISBN 978-1-83751-596-7

Digital audio download ISBN 978-1-83751-598-1

Boldwood Books Ltd
23 Bowerdean Street
London SW6 3TN
www.boldwoodbooks.com

For my mum.

PROLOGUE

MIDSUMMER'S EVE, 1930

Alexa got out of the back seat of the car and stood perfectly still on the gravel drive, clutching her fur stole over her shoulders.

Ferris House, high up on the Enys Point headland, had always been foreboding. The wind-buffeted granite was hard and severe against the often blissful, blue Cornish sky and, Alexa admitted, it had always scared her a little. But this evening, the house was transformed and softened by music, by laughter, by light. The towering front door, propped open by bay trees in copper pots, welcomed her, enticed her to walk to the top of the sweeping stone steps and enter its embrace. As a fleet of cars and taxis continued to pull up the drive behind her, dropping even more guests for the ball, Alexa heard, and felt, the tinkling conversations of the crowd inside, and her stomach bubbled with nerves.

'Are you all right, Alexa? Look lively,' teased her father, William, tucking his wallet inside his jet-black dinner jacket having paid the driver. 'You can't be late for your own party.'

Her stepmother, Eleanor, stopped fiddling with her gloves to link her arm with Alexa's. 'We'll see you safely through the door, Alexa,' she said. 'After that, we won't spoil your fun by hanging around you, will we, William? We'll leave you bright young things alone. Oh, my dear, you are shaking.'

'I'm desperately trying not to.'

Alexa took a fortifying breath, lifted the hem of her gown, and set off across the gravel with her father and stepmother either side of her, fighting her rising panic and the strong urge to turn and run.

'You know, it is quicker to walk here from home than motor over,' commented William unnecessarily as they tackled the steps, treating them to another of his musings. 'Down the cliff footpath from Porthdeen, across the quay, back up again. It's simple. And such a fine evening for it. Don't know why I didn't suggest it.'

Alexa glanced at her father and saw his tongue pressed firmly in his cheek. But Eleanor let out an exasperated little snort.

'In these shoes, William? It would be like setting out on one of your hikes over the headland. And, frankly, last time you made me do that, it nearly killed me. *You* can walk home, if you like. Alexa and I will certainly be getting a taxi.'

'He's teasing us, Eleanor,' Alexa said, as the sound of swaying music reached her and her knees wobbled as if she'd just stepped off Harvey's boat onto dry land. 'Dad, please don't. Now is not the time.'

He gave her a crooked, apologetic smile.

Alexa forgave him, took a deep breath and walked under the grand entrance into the wide hall and the chattering crowd.

The scent of flowers and cologne hit the back of her throat, sweet and overwhelming, like a toffee she had once choked on.

'Oh, but how utterly gorgeous,' she sighed.

Even though the sun lingered in the midsummer sky and the evening promised to unfold fair and long, candles burned in every room. They burned at windows, on the candelabra and in fireplaces, competing with the last of the sunlight. Champagne bubbles in crystal glasses sparkled and the diamonds and opals at ladies' throats winked at her. Freesias and pinks, roses and lilies – Harvey knew her favourites – spilled over the edges of urns and trailed around pillars. And there were people, so many people.

Alexa guessed at a hundred heads: hair oiled or marcelled, here and there, a twinkling tiara. The beautiful, not so beautiful, the good and the great of the parish, and indeed the county, were assembled as a joyous mêlée and were, one by one, turning to look at her.

At the bottom of the flight of stairs where the great bannister curved back around itself, Harvey was waiting. She saw him scanning his guests, keeping watch for the door. He spotted her and his face transformed with innocent pleasure as he began to squeeze his eager way towards her.

How the pristine black of evening wear became him. He was dressed identically to every other male guest at the party, but he remained the most attractive man she had ever seen. His wavy tawny hair was slicked back and he looked, Alexa decided, quite divine. Her legs stopped working and she came to a halt, drawing even more attention. Guests parted and began to clap.

Alexa took a step back, flummoxed, only to be caught playfully by Eleanor.

'You can't escape, Alexa,' she whispered in her ear.

And suddenly, reassuringly, Harvey was right there, blocking out the others, taking hold of her hand – how wonderful that felt – and making her welcome and warm and wanted. Her plans for her future, her escape to a new life, withered a little.

'Happy birthday, Alexa. How beautiful you are,' he said. 'I'm so glad you are here.'

'Hello, Harvey,' she said, smiling at her best friend.

He took two champagne coupes from a tray and, with a nod of greeting to William and Eleanor, led Alexa away across the ballroom and out through the French windows onto the terrace where, at last, she could breathe.

They walked through sea-fresh air, down the steps and across the pristine lawn, towards the pines that whispered in the evening breeze, exhaling their sweet, oily aroma. Ranks of rhododendrons created black-green dense hollows. Through gaps in the shrubbery, Alexa saw the yellow of the prickly gorse and, beyond the cliff 's edge, the pure blue horizon, still bright on this, the longest day. Below her, waves roared against the black rocks of Enys Point.

Alexa turned her back on the view.

'The house looks so wonderful, Harvey,' she said. 'Everything is so light, so sparkling. How have you managed it? This is what my mother would have remembered. She once told me what a spectacle the Ferris Midsummer Ball was. She would have loved this.'

'I'm sure she would have done, Alexa,' Harvey said. 'But this is for you, remember. I can't think of a better way to celebrate your eighteenth birthday.'

Harvey's concentrated stare pinned her like a butterfly and she shifted her gaze to the coy statues peeking around ancient yews, the gravel pathways into secret bowers behind box hedges, the sky large, empty and soft over the sea.

'The only thing you haven't thought of, Harvey,' she said, 'is peacocks for your lawn.'

He looked momentarily disappointed, as if caught out. 'Certainly, next time,' he said. 'I will... When I...'

Harvey's parents hailed them from the terrace and began to walk across the lawn towards them, his father stooping a little, peering upwards with a wide grin, while his mother held court with broad-shouldered confidence. Arthur's medals were pinned resplendently on his jacket, and Betty's pearls glowed, suggesting ancient treasure.

She greeted Alexa with a powdery kiss on her cheek.

'My dear girl, you look absolutely divine. You put us all in the shade,' Betty said, self-deprecating even though her precise Scottish accent always made her sound imperious.

Arthur placed an affectionate hand on his son's shoulder, as if to congratulate him, his watery eyes surveying Alexa.

'Good God, when I saw you, Alexandra, across the lawn, I thought that it was Carlotta standing there. I truly did.'

Betty elbowed him. 'Goodness, Alexa, do excuse my husband. He doesn't set out to upset you. He means it as an absolute tribute. Your mother was very special to us all.'

Alexa saw the tell-tale signs of compassion and pity, for her mother had died exactly six years ago, the day before her twelfth birthday.

'I remember visiting you here with her so many times,' Alexa smiled at Harvey's parents, helping them as they stumbled over their kindness. 'And I remember us being served the softest buns for tea. The house seemed enormous to me then, as a little girl. And now,' Alexa glanced at the dazzling windows, feeling the spike of her loss as if it had been yesterday, 'it is just as huge and wonderful.'

'We haven't done this circus for years,' said Arthur, 'but Harvey wanted it this way for you.'

'Come on, enough of this,' cried Betty, grasping her husband's arm, pulling him away, 'we must circulate, attend to our guests.' She threw back over her shoulder. 'Don't hog her, Harvey.'

'I will try not to, Ma,' he called. 'At least,' he said quietly to Alexa, 'I will, if you want me to.'

Alexa laughed brightly. He was teasing her, surely. But his face was serious.

She heard the spicy syncopation of a jazz number starting up, felt the vibrations distract her. 'I want to dance.'

'I wouldn't expect anything else.'

Harvey took her hand and lead her back inside where they merged with a dozen other couples; some older guests marching sedately, the younger ones jigging and dipping, chatting over the music; a warm weight of people. She felt his closeness, his chest so very near her own, with his chin tilted just so and his raised hand delicately balancing her fingers. As he held her, he seemed very grown-up compared to the boy she had known all her life. He guided her, supported her, dipped her joyfully at the appropriate moment. She felt her shoulders drop as she relaxed into the steps; she took in the room, the faces, the smiles and laughter, the last embers of sunlight slanting through the large windows.

Suddenly, the idea of her suitcase packed and ready, hidden beneath her bed back home at Porthdeen, seemed terribly wrong. But she had made the decision. Her train ticket was bought; Lady Meredith's Cadogan Square address branded into her memory for the moment next week when she stepped off the train at Paddington and into her new life. She was leaving home for London to work for a stranger, she just hadn't found the moment to tell her father and stepmother, or Harvey, for that matter.

Tomorrow, she told herself, as Harvey guided her on another circuit of the dancefloor. She'd tell them all tomorrow, during the slow morning of recovery. In any case, she thought, her eyes flicking to Harvey's wonderfully familiar face, his clear eyes watching her, he knew that she longed to leave Porthdeen. He just didn't know how badly.

As the tune came to a halt, she noticed Sarah Carmichael with her punch cup aloft like a barrier, sinking back against the wall, camouflaging herself behind a flower arrangement. Her dress was delicate china-blue, simple but flattering, and her fair hair dressed like a confection on her head. She concentrated on the pieces of fruit in her cup, occasionally dipping the tip of her finger, licking it and glancing shyly up at the room.

'Dance with Sarah,' Alexa said.

Harvey grinned. 'Of course I will. Ma said that I was not to hog you. And one must do what Ma says.'

Alexa gave him a 'thank you' smile and drifted over to the small gathering around the punch bowl where she found her father topping up Eleanor's cup.

'Enjoying it so far?' Alexa's stepmother asked, leaving lipstick on the rim. Her hair shimmered blonde in the light of the candles.

'Of course, it really is so very wonderful...'

'I think we'd better dance,' said her father.

'I'll hold that for you, if you like,' said Alexa, reaching for Eleanor's cup.

'No,' said William, 'I meant with you.'

As he led her onto the floor, he confided, 'Eleanor has been making me practise, but alas, I fear it has been to no avail.'

Alexa laughed with affection, remembering her mother once complaining what a bad dancer her father was and how bruised her toes – in her thin silk dancing shoes – became.

'Here goes,' said William, guiding Alexa backwards into a rather frenzied jazz tune. 'Ferris has really done you proud tonight. He has hired two bands, you know. One specialising in slow, old-time music for us grown-ups, and one for the young folk like you. Must say, I know which one I prefer—'

They bumped straight into Harvey and Sarah dancing in the other direction. 'Please excuse us,' said William. 'My dancing lessons have not paid off.'

But Harvey and Sarah barely noticed. They were talking intently, Sarah blushing and laughing. Alexa saw a veil of ecstasy over her pretty face.

'Are you happy, Alexa?' William asked her.

She tilted her head to look at her father, realising that, just as with Harvey, this was the first time she had ever danced with him.

'I am, Dad. I really am.'

'You're just like your mother,' he blurted. 'And it's almost...' She wondered what he was struggling to say. Uncanny?

Unbearable?

Everyone said how much they looked alike, and, in turn, how Carlotta was the mirror image of her own mother, Beatrice. They shared each other's Venetian heritage: dark hair and trusting blue eyes, such a surprise against the soft-olive tone of their skin. 'That's what Pa Ferris just said.' She saw her father inhale his emotion.

Dad would understand, Alexa ruminated as their dance continued, that it was time for her to leave home. She wanted to step outside of her small, safe world; and she wanted to find her grandmother. She would never be able to do that stuck here at Porthdeen, perched on the furthest point you could get to before toppling into the sea. She had to tell Beatrice to her face how sorry she was. And that six years of silence had been agony.

William slouched with relief as the number ended. 'My, you two looked a picture, cutting up the dance floor,' Eleanor greeted them, handing out punch cups. 'Harvey and Sarah look quite marvellous, too. She was telling me earlier what an honour it was to be invited. Wouldn't have happened in the old days, having the whole village here. But that's Harvey's influence, I suspect. It's almost as if she's a charity case—'

Eleanor looked sharply over Alexa's shoulder. 'Ah, Sarah, did you enjoy your dance?'

Alexa, used to her stepmother's catty edge, turned to see Sarah next to her, flushed and breathing heavily, not sure what to do with her hands.

'I most certainly did,' she said, tucking a damp tendril of hair behind her ear. 'Although, I must have trodden on Harvey's toes a dozen times.'

'What's that you have there?' asked Alexa.

'Harvey's handkerchief,' said Sarah. 'He apologised for the speed of the dance, for making me hot and bothered. He thought I'd better have this.'

She hid her beam of pleasure by dabbing her mouth and her cheeks with it.

Eleanor caught Alexa's eye and excused herself with, 'I wonder where your father has gone?' pulling Alexa behind her.

'Sarah better not be getting any ideas,' said Eleanor.

Alexa wanted to ask her stepmother what on earth she meant, but Harvey caught her by the arm and spun her around.

'I've done my duty,' he said, his hand firmly on her spine, 'now it's time to dance with the birthday girl again.'

'Goodness,' said Alexa, 'now I'm hogging you!'

He gazed down at her, appraisingly, and, in complete seriousness, said, 'Happy birthday, my dear Alexa.'

She forced a laugh. Harvey's devotion, his interest, had baffled her shy young self at first: he was always the bigger boy who came across the headland from Enys Point to Porthdeen to ask her to come out to play. But William and Carlotta had liked him, encouraged her. And she fell easily into step with Harvey in their domain of cliffs and coves and rocks and waves, just as she matched his steps now across the floor.

Dancing with him, she tried to parry his attention, but lost the battle. The intensity in his eyes silenced her. How could she have ignored it? How could she have ignored her oldest, dearest friend? All of this – the music, the light and the laughter – was for her. Always, for her.

The room and its dancing joyous people revolved around her. Harvey's arms supporting her were no longer a comfort and rather his presence shot warning signals up her body. This was not the first time he'd ever touched her, but it felt like it was. Her neck ached with trying to hold herself away from his embrace. He noticed, and stopped her suddenly. He signalled to the band.

The musicians went silent for the briefest spell and then struck up merrily with 'Happy Birthday'.

And as the assembly sang to her, as Harvey sang to her, she forced herself to smile. She made herself think of her plans, of the unknown Lady Meredith, of London, her search for her grandmother, while her heart beat savagely and perspiration flashed over her skin.

The song finished, at last.

'Look at you, just look at you.' Harvey smiled, as if seeing her for the first time. 'Alexa, you really don't know what it is you do...'

He lowered himself and knelt on the floor. The room gasped in collective amazement.

'Alexa,' he said, peacefully, confidently looking up at her. 'I've known you since you were a little girl. All your life, in fact.'

He was speaking as if there was no one else in the room. The air thickened. Dozens of eyes beamed at her. She raised her hands in surrender.

'Please, Harvey, not like this,' she whispered.

But he could not have heard her, for he was speaking, quickly, expectantly.

'Will you, my dearest Alexa, do me the honour of becoming my wife?'

The women surrounding her put their fingertips to their faces, eyes widening; men settled their shoulders in satisfaction. As if frozen mid-tune, the band were poised with their instruments. William looked excited; Eleanor was listening hard. Sarah Carmichael stared in horror, her eyes moving in a slow frenzy.

No one dared say a word, for they were all waiting for Alexa's answer.

Harvey loved her. And she did not realise until that moment, as the look on his face told her over and over again.

A shake of her head brought Harvey back to his feet. Fear darted across his face.

'Don't make me a fool, Alexa,' he whispered, his voice light and coaxing, not understanding.

Behind his shoulder, Alexa glimpsed Betty Ferris, her face fixed with belief, her hands clenched before her. Beside her, Arthur was nodding gently. Neither of them had noticed the shake of her head, or heard what their son had whispered.

This is what they wanted; this is what they all expected. But this was not her.

'I'm so sorry,' she blurted, and turned away.

Bodies parted as she pressed through the slack-jawed crowd towards the French windows, open to the pale evening like the mouth of a dark cave from which she must escape. As she plunged out into the cooler air, it was like stepping into a cold shower of rain. Exclaims of shock and gasps of displeasure followed her. Dipping down, she hauled off her shoes, lifted her skirt and ran.

PART I

1

THE BEGINNING OF SUMMER, 1924

'I'm not allowed to paddle,' Alexa called out, her voice carrying across the cove against the rushing of the waves, 'not today. Mamma said it is far too rough.'

'But I'm here,' insisted Harvey, who had already made a dash towards the sea. 'Should anything happen, I'll pull you out. I'll rescue you. Come on, Alexa.'

'But look at the swell, it is rather choppy.'

'I'm going in.' Harvey perched on a rock and hauled his shoes and socks off in one go, dropping them to the sand. He whipped his cap off, rolled up his trouser legs and gave her a bright, encouraging grin.

'Mamma will be very cross,' said Alexa. 'Come to the edge then.'

Alexa followed him down to the spot where the foaming waves could just reach the tips of her shoes. She darted backward and forward, teased by the water as – in a mild state of envy – she watched Harvey paddle. Just turned sixteen, and a good four years older than her, she could tell he knew he should be sensible and grown-up, but desperately wanted to play. She gave him an amused little wave.

'It is rather fresh,' he laughed as an unexpectedly large breaker soaked his trousers. The pearly blue sea was moving quickly. White crests forming far out suggested a hidden force: a danger that could easily, as Mamma would say, catch you while you weren't looking.

'Why won't she let you go paddling?' hollered Harvey, now up to his knees, his legs pale against the rocking surf.

'You know why. She's afraid of the water,' said Alexa. 'Ever since she was expecting me and she heard my voice inside her telling her not to get on the big ship. So she didn't. And it sunk.'

'It's all so dramatic,' he said. 'It has never made any sense to me.'

'Do you think it does to me?' she called back, laughing, even though here on the sand, watching Harvey splashing through the swell, with the salty wind whipping her hair, and the song of the waves in her ear, her mother's tale of unborn Alexa's warning forced a hard thrill of terror to burrow through her stomach.

'I wanted to take you sailing for your birthday. Indigo Moon is resealed and ready. She even has a new sail,' Harvey said, making his slow way back towards her, his disappointment physical. 'And now you tell me you are going away. Tomorrow!'

'Are you mad, Mamma certainly wouldn't want me to go sailing, unless Dad came with us. Anyway, we are visiting my grandmother,' she said. 'She's Italian, so I'm to call her Nonna.'

'What's she like?'

'I've never met her. Not even seen a photograph.'

'But I won't see much of you when you get back,' he said, 'because you are going straight off to boarding school.'

'So are you, Harvey. And you only have a year left to go. I'm only just starting. And I don't want to. I want to stay here.'

Harvey stood on the sand, shivering, hopping from one bare foot to the other.

'Our parents are mean, aren't they?' he said, 'Making us do things, or making us not do them. Speaking of which...' Harvey looked past Alexa's shoulder and began to wave.

She turned to see the silhouette of her mother at the top of the Porthdeen cliff, calling, beckoning her home.

'Time to go,' said Alexa. 'Mamma wants me to have an early night. Big day tomorrow. It must be two hundred miles to London.'

'Probably even more,' said Harvey, struggling to squeeze his wet feet into his socks.

'All I know is we have to catch the milk train from Penzance at dawn.'

'You'll be up before the seagulls,' said Harvey, settling his cap on his head.

They picked their way back up the beach and began to climb the cliff path. Halfway up, where the track split into two, one way up to Porthdeen, the other along and down to the village, Alexa stopped.

'Goodness me,' she said, 'look at this. I very nearly trod on it.' By her shoe lay half a gull's eggshell, speckled olive-green and dappled with brown, the colours of rock and sand. Gingerly picking it up, she peered inside. A tiny feather was stuck to something runny.

'It's been ambushed,' she said, dismayed. 'Something's stolen this egg, split it and eaten the chick.'

'Oh no, but here's the other half.' Harvey bent down to pluck it from the cushiony grass at the side of the path. 'The chick has pecked his way out. A successful hatching, I'd say. And now he is in a nest somewhere, mouth gaping, being constantly fed by his mother, who is probably by now run ragged.'

He gave it to Alexa and she cradled the two halves of the shell delicately in her palms.

'Is this my birthday present?' she asked, laughing.

'I've not bought you anything else, so I expect it is.'

'Alexa!' Her mother's call reached them again.

'I really must be going,' said Alexa, but instead of making her way up to where Mamma was waiting, she sat down on a tussock of grass.

'Alexa, you will make her cross,' said Harvey, 'and I'm going to go before we both get into trouble.'

Alexa watched as Harvey made his way, following the flank of the cliff all the way down to the village. If Alexa leaned forward, she could just see the slate roofs and the smoking chimneys of Little Porthdeen below and the diminutive quay where two or three fishing luggers jostled for space. Her mother called again, but tucking her hands up inside her sleeves, Alexa decided to wait and watch Harvey walking along the quay. She spotted him as he emerged from behind the Sea Captain's cottage. Head down, cap pulled low, his tiny figure took the steep stone steps in great bounds and quickly reached the path that fed its way up and over the rising headland of Enys Point where the fresh wind combed the grasses, switching them back and forth.

Harvey stopped suddenly, hands deep in pockets. He turned to look behind him. She saw the pale shape of his face as he stared from his clifftop, across the water, to where she was sitting. She had no idea if he had picked her out or not, and wondered if she should stand up, wave and call, give him a proper farewell.

But, clutching her knees close to her chest, blending with the furze behind her, Alexa stayed completely still. Harvey turned, put his face to the wind and strode on his way.

A hand rested on her shoulder and her mother was suddenly

beside her, sitting on the grass. The breeze had teased her dark hair from under her hat. Her face, usually so expressive, was still.

Alexa glanced at her, terrified that she was angry.

'I'm sorry, Mamma, I don't know why but I just had to watch him go.'

Her mother reached out to tuck Alexa's wayward hair firmly behind her ears.

'You should really wear a hat, darling, on a blowy day like today. Don't let Juliet catch you without one.'

'You're not cross with me?'

Mamma shook her head, her eyes clear with understanding. 'I know you'll miss him, Alexa. But we'll only be away a little more than a month. He will miss you too.'

A gust of wind battered Alexa, bringing with it a sudden and magnifying delight.

But she ignored it. 'You don't know that for sure, Mamma.' Her mother stood up and reached down for her.

'Come on home. Juliet is making you supper. And Ovaltine if you ask her nicely.'

Alexa handed Mamma one half of the precious eggshell to carry and, together, they began the long climb back up the cliff.

2

The London cab negotiated a corner, swinging wide and forcing Alexa back hard against the seat. She jolted awake, surfacing from a fleeting but deep sleep into a frightening roar of traffic and a beeping of horns. And electric lights, so many lights, dazzling her. Windows sparkled, strings of street lamps glowed. Row on row of towering buildings closed in on the street, disappearing up into a gloomy ceiling of evening sky. On the pavements, figures switched and huddled and hurried with hats on, heels clipping. The tobacco fumes breathed out by the driver threatened to smother her. She reached for Mamma's hand.

'Where are we?' she asked.

'Just turned onto Piccadilly.'

The word was meaningless for Alexa. All she could think of was the yellow pickle that Juliet might give her with a nice slice of ham for her tea.

'We'll be there in a moment,' said Mamma. 'You fell asleep as soon as the taxi pulled away from the station. It's been such a long day. You must be shattered, darling. Ah, see the Ritz!'

But Alexa, instead, stared at the driver, appalled by the strong smells emanating from him and the thick roll of skin pouring over his dirty collar. Dad's collar and neck were immaculate. He had driven them in the pale early dawn to the station at Penzance what seemed like an age ago, and was now home at Porthdeen with Juliet – in a separate world.

The cab slowed and turned again, this time more decorously. The street was dark, narrow and quiet. Stately front doors were reached by sensible steps, illuminated eerily by the greenish-yellow of gas lamps. Alexa could not quite believe that there were so many front doors in the world, so many houses, one after the other, after the other.

'Half Moon Street,' Mamma leaned forward and called to the driver, 'this is it.'

She paid the man and tipped him. He in turn tipped his cap and the cab rumbled off.

Alexa stood by her mother on the pavement and breathed in city air warm with the mineral scent of soot from a thousand hearth fires.

'Where are we?' she asked again. She glanced up at the white stucco house glowing in the darkness, the number 15 painted precisely in black on the pillar by the door. Her tummy was hollow with fatigue, her mouth sticky inside. She longed for Juliet's soothing words, her milky bedtime drink.

'Oh, Alexa, Alexa.' Mamma bent down so that her face was level with hers, in the shadow of her hat. Her olive skin was perfection; her eyes were wet and yet her smile was wide.

'Mamma, you're trembling.'

'Can you believe that this was once my home?' she asked, glancing up at the tall terraced house. A lamp glowed on the first floor. 'I lived here when I was a girl. It was only for a short time, but long enough for it to stay with me.'

'And my Nonna?'

'Yes, she's here. She's at home. See the light burning. She said she'd leave it on for us,' Carlotta said, urging Alexa towards the steep steps. 'Come on, Alexa. You're going to meet my Mamma.'

'Yes, I know that,' said Alexa, although she did not know nearly enough. 'But why haven't I met her before?'

Mamma stopped halfway up the steps and gripped Alexa by the shoulders. She looked like she was searching for something on her face. Alexa knew that the tightening of Mamma's jaw and stretching of the skin under her eyes meant that she was trying not to cry. A deep line stitched the space between her brows and Alexa felt a tightening knot in her tummy. She could see that being here, outside Nonna's front door, was causing Mamma pain, but she didn't know why.

'Because...' Mamma sighed, 'because there was a time when we weren't speaking to each other. But a little while ago, I wrote to Nonna and, eventually, she wrote back. And so here we are.' Mamma pulled the long bell cord and they waited nervously side by side on the threshold in silence until, trying so very hard to understand, Alexa asked, 'Mamma, does Nonna know that it will soon be my birthday?'

'Oh, Alexa, yes, indeed she does. And that's why we are here!'

Mamma's laughter sounded like the snatch of a happy tune as the front door opened.

* * *

Rooms were stacked one on top of the other and Alexa lost count of how many flights of stairs she climbed and how many lamplit landings she traipsed along on her drowsy way up to bed. Mamma opened the door onto a warm dark room where a gas lamp was popping and the bed covers were being drawn back by a maid.

As she pulled on her pyjamas, Alexa heard a lady by the

bedroom door talking softly in Italian. Getting into bed, she watched Mamma fleetingly embrace her before the lady disappeared along the landing.

'I'll say goodnight, then,' said her mother, beginning to close the bedroom door.

'Is that Nonna?' Alexa called out, not wanting to be left alone. 'Yes,' she whispered back. 'You will meet her properly in the morning.'

'Mamma, I won't be able to sleep now,' Alexa said, sitting up, suddenly wide awake. 'There's too much to think about.'

'There always is with you,' Mamma sighed, coming back into the room and sitting by her bed. 'Here, I forgot, the maid has brought you milk.'

Alexa knew that it wouldn't be like Juliet's.

'Tell me the story again, Mamma,' she said, leaving the cup where it was on the bedside table, 'the one where I warned you from inside your tummy.'

'About the ship?' Mamma said abruptly. 'Oh no. Please don't ask for that. Not here.' Mamma tilted her face away. Even with the light spilling in from the landing, Alexa could not read her expression.

'Please, Mamma, I will never sleep.'

Her mother took in a sharp breath. Alexa waited and when at last she spoke, her words were like shattered glass. 'Look, Alexa, no. I'm telling you no. That's enough. Now drink your milk.'

'I probably won't,' said Alexa, hating how grumpy and tired she felt.

'Then sleep,' said Mamma, planting a kiss on her forehead, closing the door behind her as she left the room.

* * *

The first thing Alexa saw when she woke was a still-full cup of milk, stone cold on the bedside table. In the bed opposite her, Mamma lay snoozing. She turned over and listened to the noises of the house. A man's voice rumbled and a door shut below.

Her dream, of home, still clung to her like gossamer cobwebs. The essence of Porthdeen, the house of silvery granite with its mullioned windows and crooked chimneys, the weight of the sea below and the calls of seagulls above, and Harvey paddling in the sea, seemed to be still part of her as she yawned and stretched her toes in the unfamiliar bed.

Hearing a chink of bottles from outside, Alexa wriggled out from under the covers and padded across to the window in half darkness. She slipped in front of the drawn curtains and peered down to the sunny street. A milkman was unloading his wares from his cart, chattering with someone unseen below, while his horse waited patiently, one hoof lifted off the cobbles. She saw a man in pinstripes, wearing a bowler hat and carrying a briefcase, stride along on the other side of the road and a maid in a cap and apron sweeping the steps of the house opposite. Another man on crutches, his leg strangely truncated, hobbled up the kerb. A car tooted around the corner and in the distance, the faint chatter of traffic.

A knock on the bedroom door roused her mother, who sat up in bed and called groggily, 'Come in...'

The maid who had drawn back the bed covers last night came through with a tray laden with teapot, toast and marmalade and set it on the table by the window. She opened the curtains and sunlight revealed the dark corners of the room.

'*Signora* thought you'd like breakfast up here this morning, madam. She'll be in the morning room when you're ready.'

Mamma thanked her and reached for her hairbrush. She smoothed her hair down, then she gestured for Alexa to tackle hers. She got up, eased her feet into slippers, found both of their dressing gowns and finally, seated at the little table by the window, they were ready for breakfast.

'Did you sleep well, Alexa?'

'I dreamt about home.'

'You are missing it already.' Mamma lifted the lid on the teapot and gave it a stir. 'And how do you like my old bedroom?'

Alexa took a bite of toast and looked around. Her mother's queen-sized bed had a forest-green canopy that matched the shade of the wallpaper. The parquet floor was polished to the colour of honey and laid with a Turkish rug. Watercolours in gilt frames depicted the drowning Italian city with its churches and palaces, shimmering like pewter above the water.

'I like the pictures,' Alexa said. 'That's Venice, isn't it?'

'Yes, yes. Clever girl. Maybe one day we will take you there. Dad and I, and Juliet can come too. You will love it, as much as I miss it.'

Alexa gave her a glance and Mamma elaborated, 'You know when you hear me singing in Italian? That's because I'm thinking about Venice.' Mamma sipped her hot tea and Alexa noticed that the steam was making her eyes water. 'And when you see the city for yourself, you'll know why. You'll want to sing too.'

'And what a lot of dolls, Mamma,' said Alexa, pointing to the cabinet where a delegation of dolls sat with frozen faces and unblinking eyes.

'Oh yes. They all have names. But, you know, the only thing I wanted to bring with me when I left this house to be married to Dad and move to Cornwall was my button box.'

Alexa nibbled her toast in the comforting glow of a happy memory. She loved her Mamma's casket. It was filled with buttons: one for every costume, coat and dress that had ever been made for her since she'd been a baby. Juliet had seen to that, for, before Juliet was Alexa's nanny, she had been Mamma's. It was a treat for Alexa to have Juliet fetch the box from her Mamma's bedroom so that she could explore and count them all. But she hadn't done so for a long while. After all, she was a big girl. She'd be twelve on Midsummer's Eve.

Her mind drifted back to her dream and to home and she wondered what Dad might be doing. He breakfasted early, so he'd be out now walking his land. He often took her with him to visit the cottages and call in on farms, walking up to the blustery top fields, following the tumbledown walls. When she was little she'd scamper off to hunt for pixies under hedgerows, to listen for their singing, hoping to see them dancing around the old stone circle on the top of the hill.

'There's a saying around here,' her father had once said, 'that Porthdeen is the first and last house in England. Certainly feels that way some days, doesn't it, Alexa? When the wind blows in. The ends of the earth.'

She swallowed her last bit of toast and asked her mother, 'Has Dad ever been here?'

'Not here, in this bedroom,' Mamma laughed. 'How unseemly. But he visited the house, of course he did. We met at a ball in Belgrave Square. Such a wonderful time. Summer of 1910.' Alexa listened to the tender drift of her mother's voice. 'Seems so long ago. A great many things have happened since then.'

Alexa wanted to ask what things, precisely, but her imagination was sparking with the notion that this had been Mamma's bedroom, that they were Mamma's dolls. The strangeness of her situation gripped her: being inside a towering house sandwiched between other houses, in a city filled with people. It was all so far from home.

'Is this your Dad's house, Mamma?' she asked.

'No, my darling. This is Grandpa Montgomery's house. Remember, I told you all about it. Oh, perhaps you don't.' Mamma paused, sipped her tea. She watched Alexa warily, softening her voice. 'My father, Pietro, died when I was a little girl. I barely remember him, but I'm told he was a fine gentleman. Just like Dad, actually.'

'Who told you?'

'Juliet.' Mamma smiled on a memory. 'And we came to live here on Half Moon Street when Nonna – my mother – married Grandpa Montgomery. Who, Alexa, you must call Mr Montgomery, not Grandpa, unless he corrects you otherwise.'

Baffled, Alexa grasped at something she knew for sure. 'And, before that, you lived in Venice?'

'I was born in Venice.'

Alexa sat up straight. 'Is he downstairs?'

'Lots of questions,' said Mamma, glancing at her watch. 'If you mean Mr Montgomery, I think he might be. Oh, but perhaps now...' she read the time again, 'he could well be at his office.'

'Does he wear a bowler hat?' asked Alexa, thinking of the man hurrying along the street. 'Does he run along the pavement to work?'

Mamma laughed. 'No, his driver takes him. Now eat your toast.'

'Oh, Mamma—?'

'One more then we must get bathed and dressed and go and see Nonna. We don't want to keep her waiting.'

'Who is that person with you?' Alexa pointed to the silver-framed photograph on the bookcase. 'That's not Dad, is it?'

'That's Luke Montgomery,' she said. 'My stepbrother.'

The photograph was of Mamma in a garden, wearing a pale dress. Rather old-fashioned and rather long, Alexa thought, with too much lace around the shoulders. The toes of her shoes peeped out from below the hem and a large hat shielded her face. Next to her, linking her arm, was a young man in tennis clothes, laughing hard.

'Where is he? Luke? Is he here, too?' she asked, thinking that her mother and the man in the photograph looked so young and playful.

'Oh no, darling, he's dead.'

* * *

Mamma opened the door to the bathroom and emerged barefooted, her hair wrapped in a towel turban, steam cascading around her.

'Such a luxury,' she said, 'to have this adjoining bath. I must ask Dad if we can have one put in at home. En suite, they call it. Aren't you getting ready, Alexa?'

Alexa shook her head and looked down at her dressing gown.

'I think the bottle-green for you. I've hung it up, see?' said Mamma.

Mamma sat in front of her dressing table, unwrapped her hair so that it fell in almost-black locks, soaking the shoulders of her dressing gown. She picked up her hairbrush.

'But I don't like the bottle-green. It's so very old hat,' said Alexa, looking at the shirtwaister dress with the white piping hanging on the wardrobe door. It was meant for a child much younger than her. Not for a girl very nearly twelve. 'I want to wear the indigo-blue.'

Mamma stopped brushing her hair and beckoned Alexa over.

Alexa knew exactly what she had done wrong and knew not to speak until Mamma allowed her. Standing by her side, she watched her mother's reflection in the mirror. Her expressive mouth, that rounded chin, even the curve of her nostril was exactly like her own. And the look in both of their eyes was of disappointment.

'You must do as I ask.'

'But I—'

Mamma lifted a finger.

'I can see it, Alexa,' she sounded weary but proud. 'That little Latin spark on your face. Like a light going on. I know it means trouble. I'm the same. Try to squash it, when you feel it. I do, all the time.'

'A spark?'

'Juliet used to tell me off for it.'

'When I can't bear not to say something?'

'Exactly that. You must wear your bottle-green today and save your indigo-blue.'

Alexa began to tap the dressing table leg with her toe. She tugged at the button on her dressing gown, yanking the thread, punishing it.

'Look what you're doing. Oh, my dear, you've pulled your button off. Don't lose it. We'll take it home and Juliet can sew it back on for you.'

'Can I put it in your button box instead?' she asked.

'Of course you can,' Mamma's anger faded. 'Now get yourself ready, we don't want to keep Nonna waiting.'

* * *

Mamma led the way downstairs, bright and fresh in her crimson dress, with the big rosette on her hip. Alexa followed in her bottle-green, dragging her hands along the bannisters, her tummy fizzing. She must not protest about the dress, for she didn't want to see that look on Mamma's face again. She must be good and keep quiet.

Mamma stopped Alexa on the second landing and drew her mouth close to her ear.

'When we're downstairs, try not to ask too many questions,

Alexa,' she whispered. 'Try to button them up. Remember what I have told you.'

'You mean, squash myself down?'

Mamma's eyes brightened. 'Exactly that. You must let us ladies speak, for we have not seen each other... well, not since you were a scrap of a baby.'

Alexa was prickly with confusion. Sometimes she couldn't speak, couldn't express the words tumbling through her head. Other times, her voice just spurted out of her.

'Say "yes, Mamma",' said her mother.

'Yes, Mamma.'

The maid met them at the bottom of the staircase, led the way along a corridor and opened a door. Alexa followed Mamma into a drawing room, stretching the length of the house, with windows either end, reaching the ceiling. Sunlight beamed under the blinds, glimmering fiercely on glass domes encasing stuffed birds and on the waxy leaves of plants. Pleated lampshades and gilded picture frames peppered the walls. The cloistered air smelt powdery. A vast arrangement of flowers was dropping its petals onto the polished surface of a table. Alexa felt small and younger than she'd ever done before.

A lilting voice said, 'Let me have a proper look at you, child.'

Alexa peered through the maze of dark and monstrous furniture to spot the owner of the command: an older lady, sitting in a high-backed armchair by the fire. Alexa glanced up at her mother in confusion. This was the lady she'd seen in the late haze of last night. And her resemblance to her mother – the way she dipped her head and turned her shoulder, the Italian music in her accent – bewildered her. The lady squinted through a shaft of sunlight and gestured impatiently. Alexa took a tentative step into the room and saw her own clear, questioning eyes peering at her from within an older face.

'Say good morning to Nonna,' said Mamma.

Alexa slipped her hand into her Mamma's and they moved forward together.

'She's just like you, Carlotta,' said the lady.

She gently grasped Alexa's shoulders in the way that Mamma often did when something important was about to happen and moved her gently so that she stood directly in front of her. As Beatrice Montgomery fixed her in her gaze, Alexa saw her brow break into furrows, her eyes grow wet. Her mouth was moving with unexpressed emotion.

'The years have overtaken us, haven't they, Carlotta? I can't believe the child is eleven. We can't let it happen again, for this one's sake.'

Remembering to squash herself down, just as her mother had told her to, Alexa swallowed her urge to remind her grandmother that she was very nearly twelve. Mamma sat down and nodded to Alexa that she should, too.

'Alexa is growing so very fast, Mamma. She is going to boarding school in September,' said her mother. 'A lovely school on Bodmin Moor, not too far away. We've heard it is a very good school. We feel it will be best for her.'

Nonna raised her eyebrows. 'Indeed, it will be.'

Alexa sank beneath her grandmother's stare. She didn't feel it would be best for her. She wanted to stay home with Mamma and read all the books in Dad's library. Surely that could be her education. And when would she ever see Harvey? The dreadful idea of leaving Porthdeen struggled to form in her mind, so she let it go.

'And where is Step-Papa?' Mamma asked.

'In the city, of course,' said Beatrice. 'He leaves stupendously early these days and comes home very late. Works so hard. I take it you slept well?'

While the ladies spoke to each other, Alexa studied her grandmother. The colour of her skin had the same quality as Mamma's – rich and olive – but her face was divided by lines, her features soft, their edges blurred. Her hair could have been Mamma's and yet was flecked with grey, while Mamma's was as rich as a blackbird's wing. And, even though Nonna looked fiercer she, somehow, seemed more fragile.

Realising that she should not stare, Alexa took in the busy trappings of the drawing room and landed on the circular table filled with a battalion of framed pictures. There were no pictures of Mamma, and no pictures of her. Just photographs of a young boy, photographs of a growing boy, a vibrant sketch of a young man; photographs of an older gentleman, with Nonna and the young man. In another, the young man was standing proudly beside a bride, her white dress a waterfall of lace. All the same young man as in the photograph upstairs in her mother's bedroom; all Luke Montgomery.

And Mamma said he died; just like Arnold the gardener. Alexa had sat at the top of the stairs at Porthdeen with Juliet when she was a very little girl, while below in the hallway the servants had gathered around her father reading out a telegram, the flimsy paper trembling in his hand. Women had dabbed their eyes and men had looked at the floor. Juliet had held her tightly, whispering that Arnold had gone. Alexa had not understood, then, when they'd spoken of Flanders and the trenches and the legions of lost men. She had still not understood when later they'd said that Sarah's father, Mr Carmichael, would not be returning home to the village. But she did now.

She must have made a startled noise, for her grandmother and mother stopped talking, turned towards her.

'Did Luke die in the war?' Alexa blurted, unable to squash herself any more.

'Oh, Alexa...' Mamma sighed.

Nonna's eyes were on her like a lightning strike, pinning Alexa into her chair.

'Is that what your Mamma has told you?' she demanded. Alexa wriggled in her chair, struggling to respond.

Eventually, her mother spoke for her, 'No, Mamma. I have not told Alexa anything.'

Her grandmother's eyes flashed back at her daughter and, in terrible silence, Alexa watched the two women stare at each other, linked by vibrating and inexplicable pain.

'May I suggest then,' said her grandmother, her voice small and even, 'that we all go out and get a little fresh air.'

* * *

They left the quiet haven of Half Moon Street, turned a corner or two and soon met with the busy thoroughfare. Alexa felt herself shrink amid the traffic chaos, not daring to breathe the fumes. Beyond the line of iron railings, past the barrier of noise and chaos, on the other side of the road lay the park, a swathe of undulating shimmering green. The grass was sheltered by avenues of trees and dotted with deckchairs, some empty and some filled with snoozing, chatting people resting under the shade of parasols.

Mamma approached a policeman and asked him to help them cross the road. He blew his whistle and, like a miracle, cars and buses slowed their pace. As Alexa stepped bravely down the kerb, Nonna gripped her by the hand. Alexa looked up at her in surprise and chanced a smile, expecting one back. Instead, her grandmother glanced this way and that, as if her stare might stop the traffic altogether.

Once safely through the gates, Alexa shook off her grandmother's hand and hurtled free. Mamma called for her not to go far, but Alexa knew that she need not worry about cliffs and the deep sea and the crashing waves here. The park was safe, the grass soft under her shoes, daisies colonising it like stars. She ran past nannies with perambulators, a gang of young boys chasing a dog. She scooted past gentlemen brandishing canes, walking with ladies who were showing their ankles beneath their swishing skirts. She dodged a man in a wheelchair with medals pinned down his front, being pushed along like a pensioner might be, although he wasn't elderly at all. He was one of the soldiers who had returned, Alexa decided, like the man hopping along Half Moon Street that morning. He gave her a shy smile but her attention was taken by the enormous white house guarded by regal gates just visible through the trees.

With questions bubbling on her lips, Alexa turned around. Her mother and grandmother were a long way back on the path, walking slowly, talking quietly. They were, Alexa concluded, as beautiful as each other: exactly the same height, Mamma in her shorter skirt and Nonna in a longer length, but equally fashionable. With ostrich feathers on their hats and silk stoles lifted by the sunlit breeze, they looked like two fluttering butterflies. Alexa ran towards them. Whatever pain she had caused them by mentioning Luke had vanished and she was bursting to ask them about the large house, the park, everything. But knew she mustn't; she really mustn't.

She stood, her knee jigging with impatience, waiting for them to stop talking.

'... beautiful day, just look at it,' said Nonna. 'It's as if London has breathed a huge sigh of relief. The dark times are over. There's a different atmosphere, Carlotta. You can feel it. There's laughter. And music. People are lifted.'

'Is it hope, do you think, Mamma? Ten years after it all started?' asked Mamma. 'A fresh start after all of the horror, all of the loss?'

'Yes,' said Nonna, and linked her arm through Mamma's. 'It is a new beginning.'

Mamma flinched at her mother's touch and they both remained quite still, as if they'd surprised themselves.

'There was a new jazz band on at the Ritz last week. Your step-papa would not go, but I quite fancied it...'

'Ah, you can see Buckingham Palace... It's been a long while since...'

Spotting Alexa, they took a step back, broke apart.

'We're thinking of some treats for your birthday,' said Mamma.

'How about tea at the Ritz,' said Nonna, bestowing an uncomfortable smile, 'and a trip to the zoo?'

Alexa began to jump up and down. 'Goody, oh yes and—'

'Simmer down, Alexa. Not so lively,' said her grandmother. 'You're going to be twelve, not two.'

Mamma said, 'You'll never guess what else I have planned, Alexa. I'm going to have my hair bobbed. Dad would not let me before. He said he could not trust a hairdresser in little old Truro. But now I'm in London, it's high time. And Nonna knows a salon on Brook Street.'

'Oh, can I come too, please and—'

Her grandmother said, 'I don't think Monsieur Etienne's is the place for a child...'

Alexa's joy drained to her shoes.

'But...' Nonna raised another smile, 'when Mamma has had her hair done, in a few days' time we are going to sit in my drawing room and have our portraits painted in oils. All three of us. Together. To mark your visit and your birthday. Won't that be splendid, Alexa? Won't it be a perfectly grown-up thing to do?'

But Alexa was not listening. The inky mass of Mamma's hair coiling at the nape of her neck fascinated her suddenly, now that she knew it would soon be all gone. It looked heavy, there under the back of her hat, her neck so slender beneath.

'But your hair, Mamma?' she asked, sadness dragging inside her.

Part of her mother would be gone, thrown in a bin.

'I want to wear the new cloche hats,' Mamma said.

'You mean you want to be a flapper,' said Nonna. Mamma laughed, 'I think I'm a bit too old for that.'

Alexa asked, 'When they've cut it off, Mamma, what will they do with all your hair? Can I keep it?'

'I'm never sure if the child is being rude or not,' uttered Nonna. 'But I can see where she gets it from. You were just like that, Carlotta, when you were her age.'

Alexa looked from her mother to her grandmother and back again, realising suddenly where she came from. First one lady, and then the next. And then her. The idea grinded, made her uncomfortably aware of her own skin and she shrank inside it, remembering that she should let the ladies speak and remain quiet.

'Well, Alexa?' demanded her grandmother in the stretching silence. 'Wouldn't a portrait of all three of us be a splendid thing?'

Alexa looked again at her mother, who was nodding furiously at her.

'Yes, Nonna,' Alexa said, at last. 'An absolutely splendid thing.'

'Ah, just like your mother,' Nonna said, 'and that reminds me. After we'd arranged your visit, I had a bit of a clear out. I found this.' She rummaged in her handbag and drew out a photograph.

'Oh my!' cried Mamma, and began to laugh. 'Look at that. That was taken right by your palazzo, Mamma. I haven't seen this for years.'

But all Alexa could see of the photograph was the back. She craned her neck, leaned in and eventually her mother passed it to her.

There was Mamma with Juliet captured in sepia when Mamma was a girl, growing up in Venice. And yet it could have been Alexa posing there on the little bridge over the water with the sun casting hard shadows over their hats and their dresses and Juliet's striped stockings visible at her jauntily posed ankles. Alexa guessed that Mamma was the same age she was now, with her dark hair brushing her waist and her pale eyes laughing. And Juliet, a young woman with hair in a topknot bun and her sun-browned face. Alexa would know her wise and gentle smile anywhere.

'I want to go to Venice,' cried Alexa in a searing rush of passion. 'I want to stand on that bridge with you and Juliet, Mamma.'

Her mother cocked an eyebrow.

'Oh, and you, too, Nonna.'

Her grandmother fixed her once more with her unrelenting gaze.

'Perhaps, then, you'd like this photograph, Alexa?' she asked, her voice surprisingly kind.

'Oh, she will treasure it,' said Mamma, eagerly. 'Won't you, Alexa?'

But Alexa did not answer. She stared into the picture, absorbing every inch of it as it took her dreams around a new and magical corner.

3

The artist set his easel up in front of Beatrice's drawing room windows. He laid out tubes of paint, a pot of brushes and a palette with meticulous care. He had all manner of equipment: rags, pencils, charcoal, a ream of large, robust sheets of paper.

Alexa watched him from the doorway, making herself smaller against the door jamb while the maid offered him tea. He had his back to Alexa, busying himself, accepting the refreshment. As the maid hurried to the door she gave Alexa a little shake of her head.

'Miss Alexa, wait for your mother and *Signora* to come down,' she said as she breezed past. 'Don't disturb the gentleman while he is settling in.'

Alexa eased herself quietly into the room, sidling around the furniture. She was wearing her favourite dress at last: the new indigo silk, embroidered with coils of ribbon.

'Yes, perfect,' Mamma had said, while they were getting ready. 'The blue catches the colour of your eyes. Dad will approve. He will be so happy when he sees the painting.'

But, watching the artist prepare in Nonna's drawing room, Alexa regretted her choice. For it was a winter dress, not a summer one, and the day was becoming very warm. The sky was grey and opaque and the air thickening. She had only had the dress on for half an hour and already the high neck was damp and itchy.

As she crept around one of Nonna's occasional tables, the toe of her patent shoe accidently knocked a leg, making a lamp wobble precariously. The artist turned around and Alexa squeaked in surprise. His eyes were sparkling and friendly, as if he was smiling broadly, but she could not tell for a mask covered the lower part of his face. The curving metal surface concealed his chin and his mouth, and gleamed dully, unnaturally, in the cloudy light through the window.

'Good morning, miss,' he said, his voice rich with kindness. 'I'm Mr Jack Fairling. Are you Miss Rosewarne? It's a pleasure to meet you.'

'And you, too, sir.' She stayed where she was, fixing herself close to Nonna's mahogany sideboard. Mesmerised by the mask and what it might be hiding, she had forgotten how to breathe. No wonder the maid had given her a warning look.

'Shall I tell you what I'm going to do today?' The artist took out a rag and wiped his hands. 'Then you'll know what to expect?'

Alexa nodded. She inched across the room, circumnavigating the jumble of chairs and whatnots. Closer to him, Alexa realised that the parts of his face that she could see – his forehead and across his nose – were wrinkled, resembling delicate parchment. But still his eyes beamed at her.

'Don't mind my face, Miss Rosewarne,' said Mr Fairling. 'The war has a lot to answer for.'

'Like the man with the medals in the wheelchair? The man hopping along the street? Is the war answering for them too?' she asked.

The artist glanced at her, understanding. 'I believe that it is indeed,' he said and asked her if she'd kindly sit in the chair, placed just so in front of her grandmother's curtains.

He picked up a stick of charcoal and told her how he was going to use it to make initial sketches of her mother and grandmother, and of her, of course, if she would be obliged. Clamping a sheet of paper to the easel, he dashed his charcoal over it before Alexa even had time to pose.

'That's perfect, miss. I'm just doing preliminary sketches. We want you to be natural. Look towards the window, please.'

Mr Fairling opened the sash and air rolled lazily through the gap to caress her hands and her face. But Alexa still felt so terribly warm. A film of moisture settled on her top lip and she hoped he would not include the perspiration in her portrait. He sketched some more, focussing on her each time for brief moments before snapping back to his easel.

'Does it hurt, sir?'

A light switched off in Mr Fairling's eyes but, behind the mask, a smile lifted his destroyed cheeks.

'Not any more, miss.'

Mr Fairling took out a handkerchief, lifted his mask a fraction and dabbed his face.

'Is it hot under there?' she asked, and he laughed.

'Ah, Mr Fairling, so glad you've settled in. You've started without us,' called her grandmother, progressing across the drawing room as if in full sail, with Mamma following.

How beautiful they looked. Nonna's gown was a rich midnight-navy; Mamma's a confection of floating panels in light-blue silk. Her newly bobbed hair was bouncing, shinier than ever, her years falling away. She looked as happy and as buoyant as a child.

'Don't you look a picture, Alexa,' said Mamma.

'That's the idea,' said the artist.

As the adults laughed together, Alexa softened beneath her

mother's compliment. She felt, now, that she could look where she liked, instead of trying not to stare at Mr Fairling. She slipped off the chair and went towards Mamma, but Mamma turned her face away quickly to smother a hard cough.

'I heard you upstairs earlier, Carlotta,' said Nonna. 'Are you feeling all right?'

Mamma said, 'Oh, this? Do excuse me. It started this morning. Must have been breathing too much London air. Remember, I'm used to living by the sea.'

'You do look a little flushed,' conceded Nonna.

'We all do,' Mamma laughed. 'The weather is not being kind to us ladies today.'

Nonna settled herself in the spot Alexa had vacated.

'Now, Mr Fairling,' she said, 'you make sure you get my best side.'

'Now that's something I can't ever ask for, for myself,' he said and, above the metal, he winked at Alexa and glanced out of the window.

'There's a storm coming. See how the sky is darkening. But I like this,' the artist said. 'The stormy light is creating a certain magic here. Almost as if we are underwater.'

* * *

After Mr Fairling had sketched Nonna, it was Mamma's turn to sit in the chair. While Mr Fairling outlined her, Nonna poured tea and a quietness settled, broken only by the scratching of the charcoal over paper, the chink of teaspoon against china, and Mamma and Nonna regaling Mr Fairling about the beauty of Venice. Alexa listened and watched, entranced, as the artist swiftly captured the purity of Mamma's eyes, her open and vivid gaze; even the freckle on the side of her throat. Then he turned from his sketches and took up his palette. He dabbled with some oils, squinting at Mamma's dress and selecting a shade of cobalt that he would lighten with titanium white to match. Captivated, Alexa crept to his side and asked what he was doing.

'Trying out my colours, getting as much down in my sketchbook as I can. It's wonderful that you are all in shades of the same colour. The painting will be a study in blue.' He glanced out of the window. 'Blue in a summer storm.'

'But when will it be finished? When will I see it?'

The artist laughed. 'The painting won't be done today.'

From the sofa, Nonna said, 'Alexa, don't bother Mr Fairling while he is working. Come and sit with me. Sometimes I do wonder...'

Stung and embarrassed, Alexa stole over to sit beside her grandmother. But no one noticed her scorching cheeks, for the artist and Nonna, and now Alexa, were all gazing at Mamma.

'Carlotta, your hair,' said Nonna, her voice suddenly sweet with admiration. 'You're like a *Vogue* fashion plate.'

'Is that a good or bad thing?' asked Mamma, trying not to giggle and spoil Mr Fairling's concentration.

'Good, of course. I was worried, but your new hair is surprisingly beautiful.'

'Thank you, Mamma. I was worried, too. It is rather daring, isn't it?' Mamma's eyes went distant, suddenly pensive. 'You know, I didn't realise that Monsieur Etienne's salon is right near the church where Luke and Edith were married.'

The portrait of the luminous bride and handsome groom on Nonna's table caught Alexa's eye.

'What is that you are saying about Luke?'

Alexa recoiled and looked at the door, recognising the voice as the one she'd heard on her first morning and as the sound – the deep rumbling – from the room below while she tried to sleep, all week, so early and so very late at night.

'Oh, my dear Robert,' cried Nonna, getting to her feet, 'I didn't hear you come home.'

Mr Montgomery's long frame slipped into the room and seemed to distort the muggy air. He was dressed for the office in crow-black, his face narrow, his forehead high with strips of grey hair adhering to a pale scalp. The lenses of his circular glasses reflected what little light was coming through the window, shielding his eyes.

'I thought you'd be done by now, Beatrice,' he said.

Mr Montgomery's tone prompted Mr Fairling to excuse himself. He placed his brush down, wiped his fingers, bid them a polite 'good afternoon' and left the room. Alexa heard the first growl of thunder, gentle and almost apologetic, from far away across the city.

'So, this is Alexandra,' said Robert Montgomery, sitting down in a high-backed throne-like leather chair. Nonna, her eyes sharp but her face soft with compliance, was immediately at his side, pouring him tea and offering biscuits. He waved the plate away. 'My God, child, you look just like your mother. Probably a dreamer like her, too. Are you?'

'Remember your manners,' said Mamma, reaching over and giving Alexa a gentle prod. 'Say good afternoon to Grand— Mr Montgomery.'

Alexa slowly approached her mother's step-papa, avoiding his legs that were stretched out on the rug and peering up at his severe, steely face. Closer to him, she sensed something dreadfully still and hidden inside him, a boiling rage that made her want to shrink away.

'Well?' he said.

Fear made her voice escape her, so, wiping her damp palms

over her dress, she summoned her spark and asked brightly, 'Did you know it's my birthday the day after tomorrow? I will be twelve years old.'

'Yes, I had heard.' Robert Montgomery did not look at all interested.

'But did you know, sir, that I very nearly wasn't born?'

Mr Montgomery folded his arms, his eyes flickering behind his glasses. 'How so, young lady?'

'It was all down to me. If it wasn't for me warning Mamma, I wouldn't be here. Neither would she be. Nor Dad.'

Behind her, Mamma made an unhappy noise. 'Now, now, Alexa. None of your stories,' she said.

But Alexa wanted to show Mr Montgomery that she wasn't a dreamer, that what she was saying was real. She turned to her mother. 'But you told me the story, Mamma. How I was in your tummy and you heard me. You listened to me and were so very brave. You told Dad and you refused to get on that ship—'

Her mother's eyes were dark against her paling face. Her voice cracked with disappointment. 'Oh Alexa, what did I tell you the other night, not to talk about that—'

'Such stupid nonsense,' cried Nonna, exasperation tightening her face. 'Does the girl not know what she is saying?'

Mamma glanced at her step-papa, panic trickling over her features. She leaned towards Nonna to say, 'Oh Mamma, be kind to Alexa. She did not mean it. She does not know what she is saying. She's a child.'

But Mr Montgomery's stare cut Alexa in two. 'A child,' he barked, 'who should know better.'

'We're so very sorry—' began Mamma.

'But what is the child jabbering about?' he demanded, his face rigid, deep lines scoring his hollow cheeks. 'I'm hearing this utter poppycock, when my son and his wife and baby were lost in the most appalling circumstances!'

Alexa darted back to her mother, shrank against her. She could feel Mamma's whole body shuddering, her hands gripping Alexa's arms as if to hold her still, stop her saying any more.

Nonna spoke, low and tremulous, 'You do not know, do you Carlotta, that Edith was also expecting? And you see,' she glanced fearfully at her husband, and away again as if she could not bear the expression on his face, 'the first time we saw you afterwards, after that terrible, terrible time, and you had your baby...'

Beatrice's sharp eyes alighted on Alexa.

'Yes,' Mr Montgomery snarled, 'and I had nothing, nothing at all. Just this nightmare. Such appalling pictures in my mind. What the coroner told me should never be repeated.'

Mamma caught her breath and began to cough, doubled over, wincing with pain.

Nonna and Mr Montgomery watched her, silence stretching. Lightning flashed like a beacon, brightening the room. Alexa held her breath, waiting for thunder. The bride and groom gazed happily, innocently, out of the photograph on the table.

'Alexa,' said Mamma, clutching a handkerchief to her mouth. 'Will you please go upstairs to our room. Now.'

Alexa got to her feet, her insides turning over with slow, queasy shame. Under her dress, a trail of cold sweat threaded its way down her spine. This must be her fault. All her fault, because of what she whispered to Mamma, before she was even born.

She walked towards the door, daring to pass Mr Montgomery who stared beyond her at the wedding photograph as if he was looking deep into the past. Something resembling tears moistened his eyes.

As she grasped the door knob she heard her mother pleading, an urgent aching whisper, 'Why can't we let this go, Mamma? Put it behind us? Mamma, you said the other day in the park. We can make a fresh start, after all of the horror.'

'I was talking about the war,' Nonna said curtly, but she sounded weak and unconvincing, barely audible.

Mr Montgomery's terrible voice, however, reached Alexa at the door: 'I think that it's best you both leave this house, don't you, Carlotta?'

Nonna offered a small heartbroken sound. 'Oh, but Robert—' Two wide bursts of lightning bleached the hallway and Alexa began to climb the stairs, counting furiously, expectantly, for the thunder.

* * *

Upstairs, the bedroom window had been left open and Alexa heard the first patters of raindrops on the roof, caught the fresh metallic scent of rain. She wanted comfort, someone to smile at her, so she went over to the cabinet of her mother's dolls, looked at their faces and tried to remember the name of each one: Emily, Charlotte, Anne, Jane and George. Earlier, when Alexa had wondered why a doll should have a boy's name, Mamma had explained that she'd named them after her favourite authors, told her about the Brontës and Miss Austen and that George was, in fact, a lady. Her novel, *Middlemarch*, lay right there on Mamma's bedside table, a postcard of Venice marking the page where she'd got up to.

The door opened and Alexa span around, expecting to see all of them there to shout at her some more. But it was just Mamma, her face struck with sadness, her eyes bright and dismayed.

'We are leaving, Alexa,' she said, hurrying in, breathless from her climb up the stairs, 'straight away.'

'Can I take George?'

Mamma frowned. 'Take what you like.'

She rang for the maid and hauled the suitcases out from under the bed. Struggling with the locks, her fingers trembled, a deep frown dividing her forehead. Behind her, the window was streaked with sheets of silver rain, the skyline ominous.

'Am I not to have my birthday treat?' Alexa asked.

'No, you are not,' Mamma snapped. 'Now help me pack. Fetch my book. It's over there.'

Alexa picked up the novel and, with wicked compulsion to punish her mother, removed the postcard from its place and stuck it near the back of the book.

The maid knocked on the door.

'Madam, would you like to change?' she asked, surveying the stacks of clothes that her mother was scooping out of drawers, her eyes wide with alarm. 'The dress you are wearing is not suitable for travel. And the storm—'

'We really haven't the time,' uttered Mamma.

'Would you like me to hail a cab? With the rain, it might be quite difficult. I can walk down to Piccadilly, to see if I can—?'

Mamma stopped, her hands full of Alexa's underwear. 'You're being very kind, but no. Sorry, I don't know your name.'

'Lily, madam.'

'Lily, do you have a handkerchief?'

The maid nodded, offered it to her. Mamma wiped her eyes, smiling her thanks and shivering as thunder rolled like a lead weight over the chimneypots.

'Button your coat, Alexa. Please hurry. I don't want to spend another moment here.'

'But where are we going? And where did the artist go?'

'He left, Miss Alexa,' said Lily.

'Will I see the painting?'

Mamma snapped, 'I doubt that very much. You must forget about it. Forget everything.'

But Alexa knew she could never forget Mr Montgomery's face, could never erase it from her mind's eye. Nor the way he looked at the photograph of his son and daughter-in-law on their wedding day. If Edith, the glimmering bride, was going to have a baby, and she died alongside Luke – in the most appalling circumstances – that meant the baby died too. Alexa knew that much about babies. And yet still, she did not understand.

'But what does everything have to do with you and Dad, Mamma?'

Her mother groaned, sat on the bed as if her middle had collapsed. Her throat and chest were wet with sweat, two spots of red appeared on her cheeks. She balled Lily's handkerchief over and over in her hands.

'When I refused to sail,' she exhaled the words, a pent-up confession, 'Luke and Edith decided to take our passage. They were newlyweds, like us. They wanted a honeymoon, just like we had planned. They were so happy, so excited. I'm afraid,' Mamma's voice failed her. 'I'm afraid, my darling, that they went down with the ship. And, twelve years on, Robert Montgomery still cannot look me in the eye.'

'Mamma,' Alexa whispered, 'is this my fault?'

But her mother did not hear her, was too busy collecting suitcases, urging her out of the bedroom.

'And now, Alexa, I want to go home.'

'Do you mean to Venice, Mamma?'

'Perhaps I do. But for now, Porthdeen.'

The landing and stairs were dim; the storm had snuffed out the midday light. Their footsteps echoed across the black and white tiles of the hallway.

'Please take an umbrella, madam,' Lily said, following them down.

'No, I wouldn't want to be beholden to anyone here,' replied Mamma, quickly buttoning her thin summer coat.

Alexa heard a step and glanced around. Her grandmother stood in the doorway to the drawing room. Alexa offered her a timid smile but Nonna's face remained still, her mouth a grim straight line. By her side, the wiry figure of Mr Montgomery appeared, his face dark and unreadable. He dismissed Lily with one curt word.

Mamma opened the front door and the hall immediately filled with cool, saturated air. No one spoke and the excruciating silence made Alexa's bones ache. Her mother tapped her on the arm so she picked up her suitcase and walked out into the rain. It drenched her immediately, pummelling her hat and the shoulders of her coat, soaking her legs, soaking her best shoes.

'This was meant to be our reconciliation, Mamma,' her mother said. 'After what happened to Luke and Edith. Don't you think William and I think about it all the time? Every day, we think of it. But, I cannot let it keep on ruining our lives, Mamma.'

Nonna's eyes glistened, she said nothing.

'You haven't seen Alexa since she was first born,' Mamma tried again. 'And this visit was supposed to be a celebration. The portrait, Alexa's birthday...'

Alexa looked down in dismay at her ruined shoes, the soaked hem of her beautiful blue dress. They were all, so absurdly now, still wearing their best gowns.

'Thing is, Carlotta, I simply cannot bear it.' Mr Montgomery's disembodied, hard words echoed along the dim hallway. 'So perhaps this is best all round.'

Nonna instantly glanced up at her husband, opened her mouth

to speak, her eyes boiling, her hands clasped so tightly that the bones of her knuckles were visible.

'Mamma?' Carlotta pressed her.

She waited, the only sound the incessant pouring rain, drumming in Alexa's ears.

'Come on, Alexa,' Mamma sighed, giving a little shake of her shoulders.

She hurried Alexa down the steps and onto the pavement.

Mamma took three strides along the street, stopped abruptly and let out a mew of anguish. She turned back as if she was going to say something else to Nonna, perhaps goodbye, Alexa wasn't sure.

Flooding rain bounced off the ground, ran along the kerbs, gurgled in the drains and Mamma stood staring back up the steps. She dropped her suitcase so that it crashed down and tipped over into a puddle. The front door was already shut.

4

Piccadilly was a confusing torrent of wet cars and buses, the pavements a spikey umbrella forest. Lights had been switched on in shop windows and along the front of the Ritz. People bustled past, heads down. Mamma's light coat soaked up the rain so that it became a sodden weight over her shoulders, and her dress shoes were ruined.

Alexa watched her stoop in distress, hefting her suitcase. Rain trickled through the weave of Mamma's straw hat, so that Alexa did not know if she had tears or water dripping down her face.

'Taxi, we need a taxi,' urged her mother. 'But they're taken; all taken.'

Alexa wanted to hold her arm, to steer her mother, like Juliet would. But they both had their hands full with suitcases and bags. Alexa peered along the street, searching for the kindly policeman. She would ask him to assist them like he did before. But she couldn't see him. And, anyway, why should he come to their aid? Why would anyone when they were just two more people being jostled in the milling, rain-soaked crowd?

Alexa saw a face dip under a huge umbrella, a startling but

familiar flash of metal. He was clutching his leather portfolio, his trilby pulled down low. She heard his voice, muffled by the mask, ask her if she was all right, and where they were going? A stream of raindrops ran off the rim of his hat. Beneath it, peering over the metal edge, his eyes were clear with concern.

'I don't know,' Alexa said, suddenly frightened. She had absolutely no idea what Mamma intended.

'Madam?' the artist asked. 'May I help you?'

Her mother shook her head. 'A taxi, that's all we need.'

Mr Fairling strode into the road with authority as if he was a policeman and performed the miracle of securing a taxi that was in the process of depositing its occupants at the kerb.

Mamma dipped into the back, and Mr Fairling quickly loaded their luggage.

'Thank you, sir,' said Alexa, ducking in beside her mother, 'so very much.'

She saw his eyes soften, as he peered at her through the rain-jewelled taxi window, and she knew he was smiling. His stare was hard, as if he was trying to memorise her. He touched his hat and they left him standing in a puddle as the taxi drove away.

Mamma bent her head to her handbag, scrabbling for Lily's handkerchief.

'Tell the driver, Paddington, Alexa,' she uttered, covering her face and wiping her eyes. 'God, how wretched. How utterly awful.'

'Oh, Mamma,' Alexa put her hand on her mother's arm. 'You mean what happened? With Nonna?'

'Of course I do.' Fresh tears twisted out of her eyes. She took her hat off and dropped it dripping onto the floor of the taxi. 'But also, I didn't thank Mr Fairling.'

'I thanked him, Mamma. Didn't you hear me?'

'I don't know. I don't know anything much at the moment. My head is splitting.' She grimaced and rubbed her hand over her forehead. 'You're a good girl.' She gave her a weak smile. Her face was as pale as the moon. 'I wish Nonna and step-papa had taken the time to see what a good girl you are.'

Mamma broke off in a spasm of coughing. She leant back in the corner of the taxi, folded her arms tightly around herself and closed her eyes. She began to shiver and her trembling did not stop, even after they'd reached Paddington and Alexa had helped her out, paid the driver, tipped the porter, queued at the ticket office, sent a wire to Porthdeen to let her father know they were on their way home – the first time she had ever done that – and found a seat for her mother in the ladies' waiting room. With each task she performed, she felt herself grow a shade taller.

Alexa opened her mother's suitcase and fished out her fox fur, draping it around her quivering shoulders. Mamma thanked her without opening her eyes. Alexa went off in search of sandwiches from the buffet, but her mother could not eat more than a piece of crust.

* * *

At last, settled into their plush-seated carriage – she had, at least, managed to secure first class – Mamma made a cushion of her fur and rested her head against it.

'It's no use, Alexa,' she said, as the train heaved its way out of the station, picking up a head of steam, the rain-drenched suburbs moving past the window. 'I'm so very tired, it's as if I can't stay upright. I can't lift my head. I have to lie down.'

'Oh Mamma, what shall I do?'

'Wake me when the guard comes.'

'Mamma, are you unwell?' asked Alexa.

But her mother did not answer. The train plunged on into the long, wet afternoon that changed so gradually, without Alexa realising, into evening.

Mamma roused herself a little when they pulled into Reading Station.

'I'm so cold,' she said, shivering hard. 'The cold seems to be inside me.'

'Oh Mamma, but it's warm,' said Alexa. 'It's summer.'

She rummaged in the suitcase for her mother's knitted jacket, covered her huddled form with it. As Mamma tried to curl herself further into the seat, something shifted for Alexa. She had to care for her mother; she had to get her home to Porthdeen safely. A large piece of her childhood fell away.

'I'm sorry for what I said, at Nonna's house,' Alexa said. 'I know I must stop myself. I will from now on, I promise. I won't say anything ever again about the ship.'

Silence.

'I started it all, didn't I?'

She wondered if her mother was sleeping, but after some moments, Mamma stirred.

'Alexa... it's not your fault.'

As she spoke, her words grumbled in her throat, her breath jerking sharply. Alexa could hear every shallow inhalation.

'I'm past worrying about it all now,' her mother muttered weakly. 'I just want to be home. Where are we?'

Alexa told her.

'Only Reading? Christ, I don't think I can stand it.'

Alexa recoiled at the naughty word and her mother began to cry, her sobs feeble, gasping. She tried to sit up, swaying against the seat, and pressed her hand to her chest. She coughed, the deepest spasm Alexa had ever heard. She handed her a handkerchief and, as Mamma drew her hand away from her mouth to take it, her palm was full of blood, dripping through her fingers. It splashed down onto her lap, soiling the pearly blue fabric of her favourite gown, the one she'd so carefully picked out from her wardrobe that morning; the one she'd chosen so that she would look her very best, her most fashionable, her most beautiful, to be immortalised in oils.

* * *

The storm dispersed during the night, blew itself out into the east, and as the train drew towards its destination, dawn broke tentatively over the rugged wave-licked coast and wild moorland of Cornwall. In the colourless early light, Alexa saw her father standing on the platform at Penzance in his summer trilby. Before the wheels had ground to a cranking, exhausted halt, she opened the door and leapt from the carriage, running through the steam billowing from the engine.

'Dad, Mamma's here. She's here!' she called.

Her father hurried down the platform towards her. 'Alexa! Good God! Lotte? Whatever is the matter?'

He gave Alexa a sharp look, then stepped up into the carriage where her mother was slumped in the seat, a bloody handkerchief clutched in her hand.

'William, it hurts so dreadfully,' Mamma whispered, reaching up blindly for him. Her breath was jerking. 'My ribs. Feels like they're broken.'

'How can they be? Whatever has happened?' His face was fierce.

He bent over her and helped her stand. As she moved, Mamma screamed out in pain. William commanded the porter to follow with their cases and then embraced his wife, cradled her and struggled with her to the car, half lifting her as her legs gave way.

Over his shoulder, her father spoke to Alexa, whispering harshly.

'I got your telegram. But why did you leave your grandmother's house if your mother was so unwell? And why so soon? You weren't due back for another few weeks. She can barely walk. What happened, Alexa? Has there been an accident?'

Perhaps there had been, but Alexa did not want to tell him what Nonna and Mamma had said to each other at the portrait sitting, what Mr Montgomery had said, for it was, despite Mamma's denial, all her fault.

'I don't understand why you caught the night train,' he pressed on, as he hurried with Mamma to the car. 'Why did you do that? Why not wait for the morning?'

As her father scouted around for the answers, Alexa crept into the back of the car, terrified by his insistent interrogation; questions she had no desire to answer. He fired the engine and pulled away from the station, and her mother's voice rose weakly from the passenger seat in front of her. 'I'm so glad to be here, William. I just want to be home.'

Dad ran a pensive finger over his neat moustache, observed his wife, glancing at her with fear.

'In the past, Lotte, when you've mentioned home, you've meant Venice. Is that what you mean now?'

Mamma let out a long, painful, rattling sigh. 'No, I mean here. I want the sea... to be near the sea. I want to see it.' She rested her head back, panting, fighting for breath.

From the back seat, Alexa watched her father look at her mother in drawn-out, helpless distress.

'We'll telephone the doctor as soon as we get home,' he said, his voice altered.

* * *

Her father drove quickly, taking them west across the countryside, down the peninsula, along tight winding lanes of drystone walls, so close they were in danger of scratching the paintwork. The car climbed higher, strained on the bends and, overhead, the pale sky grew larger and wider. Although Alexa could not see it yet, the sea was there, just over the next rise.

Before they reached Porthdeen, they passed the turning to Enys Point and she wondered what Harvey was doing. Other times, she'd asked her father to drop her here, and she'd scoot over the top fields to find him. But Harvey would have to wait. Her mother's eyes were closed, her head resting on the back of the seat. Alexa reached forward and held her mother's shoulder all the way home. At last, the house appeared against the sea, peaceful in the wild landscape. And there, waiting at the door, Juliet. She darted forward to unlatch the gates.

Dad's greeting through the car window was muted and urgent, and Juliet gave Mamma a fearful, puzzled look as he helped her out of the car and into the house.

'I will call Doctor Paynter,' Juliet exclaimed.

'Please. Straight away,' said her father.

Juliet turned to Alexa and gathered her close.

In the comfort of her nanny's arms and engulfed by her homely familiar smell, the ordeal of leaving London so abruptly and the long journey home burst from Alexa. Tears trickled down her face.

'*Mia cara*, oh look at you,' Juliet whispered, her dark-currant eyes searching her face. 'What on earth has happened? No need to speak. Let's get you inside, too.'

5

Alexa kept watch from the landing window. Beyond the tall rusted gates and the garden wall, the sun was sinking over the headland, changing the colours of the sea. Doctor Paynter had been there all day. The door to her mother's bedroom was shut but she could hear his deep voice inside, and the small answers from the nurse that he had brought with him. Her father, also inside the room, was not saying a word. Alexa was not allowed in.

The sky was an immense sweep of crimson, orange and blue and, far across on the opposite headland, the footpath snaked through glistening grass towards Enys Point. The tide was turning and Alexa knew that, on an evening like this, it would be kind, lapping over the sand in the cove. She also knew that the sea could turn in an instant and swallow people, swallow whole ships.

Juliet appeared beside her, her sharp eyes screwed up in agony inside the wrinkles of her face. Her black hair, streaked with wide stripes of grey, had loosened from its customary tight bun. She was a small woman, the same height as Alexa, and whereas usually she held her short frame so lightly and proudly, now distress made her shrivel. She seemed tiny standing there next to Alexa.

'Come downstairs, *mia cara*,' she coaxed. 'There's no point waiting up here.'

Alexa wordlessly followed Juliet down into the parlour where dollops of the sinking sun flickered over the ceiling in this, her mother's favourite room. The French windows opened to wide steps leading down to the lawn, cushioned by long banks of lavender, planted by Mamma and peppered with the last of the sleepy bees. The stunted ragged hawthorn tree on its little promontory stood out against the sky.

'It's pneumonia,' Juliet said, churning her hands together. Her voice sounded so bewildered that Alexa dare not look at her. 'She is struggling to breathe. She cannot get air. The doctor has given her morphine. She is drowsy now, and sleeping on and off.'

Alexa sat down next to her, 'Will it make her better?'

Juliet grasped her hand, bounced it up and down on her lap. 'It's for the pain, *mia cara*... that's all.'

Alexa focussed on the world through the window, desperately batting away Juliet's dreadful words. The seascape before her was reflected in the colour of the parlour's blue walls, punctuated by the dark Rosewarne oils. The room was quite beautiful despite the blooming damp patches under the windows, which Mamma, with her light pretty laugh, referred to as her 'watercolours'. Everything in here looked the same but was different, shifting, as if even the air could not be relied on. Alexa wondered if the portrait by Mr Fairling would ever grace this room.

Alexa lifted her chin, anger and outrage flexing her voice, 'But why has she got it? How did she get it?'

'We don't know,' Juliet gasped on a sob. 'The doctor explained. It's because of a germ, you see. She could have picked it up anywhere in London. We just don't know. She might even have caught it on the way up there, on the train. Anywhere.'

Alexa had never seen Juliet like this before: her face rigid with panic, her body tensed as if expecting a blow.

'She sat in the taxi; she went to the salon; she went for tea; she went for a walk,' Alexa sprang to her feet, paced the floor, hurried through the past week in her mind, turning corners, trying to remember. 'How can she have it when I don't?'

'*Mia cara*, your questions... Sit down here. I cannot answer them all, I don't know.'

Someone knocked on the door and opened it before Juliet roused herself to say 'come in'. The nurse stood there, hands folded demurely in front of her apron, fair hair under her starched white cap. Her solemn grey eyes would not catch Alexa's.

'Mr Rosewarne has asked that his daughter come upstairs,' she said.

'Why?' Alexa asked, hearing only despair. 'We're losing her.'

Alexa dashed, running past the nurse, nearly slamming her into the door. She must get there quickly, quickly. Mamma must not go.

She found her father leaning against the bedroom doorway, his usually sleek pomaded hair ruffled as if he'd been running his fingers through it. As Alexa hurried towards him, he put his arm across to stop her.

She peered over the top of his sleeve to see Doctor Paynter leaning over the bed, applying a stethoscope to her mother's chest. Mamma lay very still, her arms rigid across the covers, her chin tilted to the ceiling. She looked as if she had been fighting. Her beautiful olive skin was ghostly, covered with a sheen of moisture and her eyes loosely shut, as if she was simply emerging from a dream. Her newly bobbed hair fanned out dark against her white pillow. Outside the window, seagulls wheeled and called in the evening air, oblivious and free.

The nurse slipped past Alexa and her father, through the door and headed for the bed. Behind Alexa, her father whispered, 'I hardly recognise you, Lotte. Your hair. Oh, why did you cut your hair...?'

The doctor looked up suddenly across the room towards them. Alexa saw a terrible compression of his face, a sharp shake of his head. Dad turned violently away towards the landing window, clinging to the curtains, his figure crumbled, a dark convoluted shape against the glass. His hands cradled his face; his head nodding in time with his breathing, a thin howl emitting from his crushed mouth. Alexa looked away and stared back at her mother, just in time to see the nurse tug at the sheet to cover her face.

Something tore inside Alexa, a ripping pain down her middle. She wanted to walk into Mamma's room, to pull back the sheet, to see her face, to wake her, to reverse what had happened, but instead she ran across the landing towards her father to ask him why this was happening. But he put his hand up to ward her off.

'No, Alexa,' he said, turning his back. 'No.'

'But Dad...' she whispered. 'Please, tell me, Dad.'

She heard Juliet speaking Italian in her ear, and felt her warm strong arms around her, leading her away, back down the stairs. The dreadful silence upstairs seeped its poison into her. The French windows were open. Shaking free of Juliet's grasp, she made her way out, haphazardly down the steps and onto the lawn, walking through a nightmare. Surely, if she didn't accept it, didn't believe that Mamma was dead, the terrible dream would end. Dusk had fallen, the day snuffing itself out and, in the twilight, Alexa searched for her familiar surroundings, the headland, the evening star bright on the horizon. She sensed the presence of the sea as it continued to swell and move, the waves whispering their distant balladry. But the primal magic of Porthdeen that had always been with her, always by her side, was gone. However hard she looked, home was not home any more. And her childhood, along with it, had vanished. Tomorrow was her twelfth birthday.

6

'Close the window, Alexa,' said her father at his desk, 'the breeze is ruffling my papers.'

Alexa reached up from the seat in the bay of her father's study and shut the casement, extinguishing the merry sound of the sea, the calling of the gulls who were congregating, as if in celebration, above it. The days were parading past her, each one as bright and as blustery and as glorious as the last. Each morning, presenting itself as bewilderingly normal, as if her mother had not been buried in the churchyard on the cliff the week before.

She took her fill of the view, the sun sparkling on the sea like a thousand diamonds, and then forced herself to look around at her father, a question suddenly tickling the tip of her tongue. A question, from nowhere. The name. She did not know the ship's name.

Her mind suddenly flooded with the memory of Mamma and Nonna facing each other across the drawing room at Half Moon Street, the quarrel flashing dangerously between them, the damage from so long ago, polluting their present.

Without looking up, her father thanked her for closing the window. He was bent to his task, scratching with his pen, answering the dozens of condolence letters. Alexa knew she should not ask any questions, should not break his concentration or his silence. For her father was stumbling from morning to night and night to morning, and she must remain mute and steady for his sake; she must be strong. But simmering there, under the weight of her despair, her need to be outside of the house, away from her father and to run wild like a child was a violent coiling fury.

Alexa tried to busy herself. She drew a chair up on the opposite side of her father's desk and gathered together the sheaf of black-edged letters in his 'out' tray. She took the stamp that bore her father's name in smart capitals and began to ink it. As she pressed it under each of his signatures, she remembered her parents working here contentedly, her mother teasing him about his terrible handwriting and ordering the stamp from a stationer's in Bond Street to solve the problem.

As Alexa progressed through the pile of responses to relatives, friends and acquaintances, inking the stamp every now and then, she kept a look out for his letter to Nonna. She wondered if he knew about the argument, whether Mamma had been able to tell him. He had wanted an explanation, as soon as they had arrived at the train station. Perhaps he had had one, and was willing to let it go.

Alexa glanced up, aware that her father had become very still. He was watching her, scrutinising her, his own task forgotten. A letter drifted from his hand to the desk.

'Miss Graham, housemistress at Trengrouse School, has written to me,' he said, tapping the letter. 'She sincerely hopes that, in the circumstances, you will still be attending in September. She says that the school wholeheartedly welcomes you. That's admirable of her. Of course, you will still be attending. There's no question. It's what we decided, your Mamma and I.'

Alexa jolted in surprise. Surely now, surely he wouldn't make her go.

'Oh, Dad, really—?'

But her thoughts were silenced by the door opening. Juliet eased her way in with a tray of tea, bringing with her the smell of sweet baking. She closed the door with a precise movement of her hip and placed the tray on her father's desk. Set among the cups, pots and plate of Genoise cake was Mamma's button box.

Her father placed his pen in its wooden tray and stared at it. 'What are you doing with that, Juliet?'

'Alexa's request, Mister William,' she replied and began to pour.

He redirected his gaze.

'Aren't you too old to be playing with Mamma's buttons?'

Alexa expected anger, but he looked merely beaten and perplexed.

'I just wanted to see them,' she said. 'Check them. Make sure they're all still there.'

'Careful now,' said Juliet, handing her the box. 'You wouldn't want to lose any, would you?'

'You're not going to count them, Alexa?' demanded her father. 'There must be hundreds.'

'Not count. Just look,' Alexa assured him. The box was rosewood, with a mother-of-pearl lid; a treasure in itself. She ran her finger over the lid.

'Juliet, will you look with me?'

Her nanny quickly shook her head, grief filling her eyes. She rearranged the cups on the tray unnecessarily and left the room.

* * *

Alexa took the box over to the card table and, with her back to her father, lifted the lid. She breathed in the scent it exhaled and knew at once that she, like Juliet, wasn't prepared for this. For the box smelled just like Mamma, just like her clothes – spicy and sweet – and Alexa's mind squeezed tight around confounding, tender memories.

But her fingers could not resist the glittering, shifting buttons that Juliet and Mamma had collected over the years. She caressed and moved them gently, reacquainting herself with the story of her mother's life. There were dozens – pearl, brittle, etched designs in bone, little glass flowers, jet twinkling like night. The metal one with an anchor on it was buried at the bottom – she hadn't seen that in quite a while. She unearthed her mother's sensible navy-blue, school-coat toggle and then chanced upon her favourite: the one from Mamma's wedding dress. Ivory, perfectly round and carved with a bee.

Alexa steadied herself and picked it up, forcing herself to breathe through the arrows of pain ricocheting inside her. She reached into her pocket and pulled out her dressing gown button, the one she had tugged off at Half Moon Street. Making a little well in the buttons, she tucked it in and covered it over with the rest.

'Looks like Ferris can take his own letter home with him,' said her father, suddenly, loudly, making Alexa jump.

She shut the box with a muffled, velvet thud. He was staring past her, out the window.

'He is on his way over. Find the letter I have written to his parents, Alexa. We can give it straight to him. It'll save me postage.' Alexa stood up, went to the window and shielded her eyes.

Harvey was beating a path across the opposite headland from Enys Point, his linen jacket billowing behind him, his cap pulled down hard over his face, a tiny figure way out there in that expansive landscape. An ember of pleasure eased her mind.

They had not spoken to each other at the funeral – not as she would have wished – for there had been too many other faces to acknowledge, too many people not knowing what to say to her, too many baffling conversations for her to have. It was as unnatural for him as it was for her.

'May I be excused, Dad? I need to find my shoes,' she said.

'Well, I hope you know where they are,' said her father. 'He'll be here in no time. You know what a fast walker he is. You'd better scoot.'

* * *

Precisely fifteen minutes later, Juliet opened the front door and Alexa, hurrying along the landing clutching her walking boots, heard his voice, soft and low, as he stepped into the hallway.

'Ah, Alexa,' he said as she thundered down the stairs.

His face melted as he smiled at her, his eyes peering as if to try to read her. He removed his cap and ran his hand back through the dishevelled waves of his floppy fringe, somehow making it stay put across the top of his head. Watching him, a sudden shyness froze Alexa's mouth shut.

Her father came out of his study, calling blusteringly, 'Hello, young man! You've certainly brought the sunshine with you. How do you do?'

'I'm well, thank you, Mr Rosewarne—' Harvey faltered, blushing hard at William's unexpected cheerfulness. 'But I wanted to see how you all are.'

Her father's gesture acknowledged the sentiment and waved it on. 'How are your parents? Oh, I forgot, they've just gone away to the Highlands, haven't they? Marvellous this time of year.'

'Indeed...' Harvey observed, his eyes flicking uncertainly between Juliet and Alexa. 'Ma loves going to visit her sister, Margaret, back to the old country, to the place she was born. Her childhood roots, you know.'

'And so did Carlotta. She longed for Venice. She used to sing in Italian when she was missing home. What was it she sang, Alexa?' Her father sat down on the bottom stair as if suddenly tired and unable to stand a moment longer. 'That's it... "Venice, the moon and you". But I often told her, this is your home now. And when she was ill, you know at the end... Do you remember, Alexa? In the car? She wanted to be here. Porthdeen was her home.' His voice lifted precariously.

Alexa glanced down at her father, half in fear, half in pity.

Harvey twisted at his tie.

'But you haven't told me how you are, Ferris?' her father demanded.

'I am well. Lots of summer school work. They don't let up, do they? And the cricket season is in full swing.'

'We'll have to come over and watch you. Tell us when your next fixture is.'

'I can't quite remember...'

'And didn't you want to borrow a book? You usually do.'

'Yes, on anatomy,' Harvey straightened himself, buoyant and poised, and suddenly, to Alexa, very grown-up. 'I've decided, Mr Rosewarne, that I'm going to become a doctor.'

'Goodness gracious, Ferris. What ambition! And I hear Betty and Arthur cancelled the Enys Point Ball?'

'There was no question, in the circumstances.'

'But Carlotta loved the Enys Point Ball.'

Her father's oddly accusing words halted the conversation.

Alexa caught Harvey's startled eye but dared not look at her father.

In the stunned silence, she watched through the still-open front door as a lone gull soared against the blue. Her urge to be out of the house, away from her father, walking with Harvey in salty sea-fresh air was immense.

Juliet stepped forward from where she had been waiting by the kitchen door, and the atmosphere around them all suddenly sweetened.

'Ah, Alexa, there you go again, I can see it all over your face,' she said, lightly. 'Go off for your walk, then, with Harvey, and pick me up some pilchards from the village while you are at it. Get going. Go.'

Alexa looked questioningly at her father and he dismissed her with a listless wave of his hand.

* * *

Harvey and Alexa reached the steep path that led down to Little Porthdeen moments later.

'Dash it,' said Harvey. 'I forgot to get the book.'

'Good, I hate doctors,' declared Alexa as she began the descent.

'You hate Doctor Paynter now,' Harvey gently reasoned with her. 'Perhaps, in time, your opinion will change.'

Above them, the lone gull had been joined by the rest of the flock and they bantered over the top of the cliff, flinching their wings, their round underbellies the purist of white.

'They are following us,' Harvey teased. 'Keeping an eye on us.'

'My father's spies,' said Alexa. She watched them for some moments, breathing deeply on the fresh air, willing it to clear her head. 'But I do like the baby ones best. Don't you?'

'Indeed, they are the most fascinating. All tawny and soft; brown eyes and big feet. This crew seems to be the grown-ups, though,' said Harvey, scanning the flock. 'But sometimes their feathers are half speckled and half white. Have you ever noticed when it is that their eyes shift from sweet tawny to that steely cruel blue?'

But she was not able to answer. Out of the house, away from

her father and his leaping inconsistency, pain suddenly floored her, twisting inside her, raw and new.

Harvey looked at her sharply, a hundred questions in his eyes.

He said, 'Alexa, you don't have to talk about it. You don't have to even speak to me. Don't even try.' His sudden seriousness struck her, forced her to agree. 'Let's just walk,' he said.

The quayside down in Little Porthdeen was busy when they got there. A fine catch had just been landed and a small crowd was taking its pick of the best. Alexa bought the fish for Juliet, and she and Harvey wandered over to sit on the wall by the Three Pilchards pub. With the chattering villagers bustling around them, they watched as another fishing lugger eased itself into harbour. Alexa's mind meandered amid the pleasant hum of everyday life, but the familiar blue horizon, the protective cliffs and the pure scent of the sea did not ease her sorrow. Something of her world, something she knew so very well had fallen away and was lost to her.

She glanced at Harvey, at his sincere face.

'An awful thing happened in London,' she said. 'A terrible argument. This is what made Mamma want to leave. Nonna was horrible. She hated me. And so did he.'

'Who's he?'

'Mr Montgomery. Mamma's step-papa.'

Alexa squeezed her eyes shut on the image of the last awful look he had given her from the doorway.

'But, Harvey, it's like a nightmare and I can't wake up.'

'That's no surprise, Alexa. You must still be in terrible shock.'

'But it wasn't right. Nonna looked tortured, torn. As much as Mamma was. That's not how it was all supposed to be. We were having a portrait done. We were going to celebrate my birthday. And what must Nonna be thinking now?'

'I cannot imagine,' Harvey said, and Alexa knew that he was desperately trying to, for her sake. 'But, you must remember, it hasn't been long enough for you to understand any of this. Ma told me, it will take you time. Lots of time.'

Alexa could see how hard he was listening to her, paying her heed, trying to understand. But his concern was so overwhelming that she just wanted them to just talk about baby seagulls again. She wanted to remind him of the broken shell she had found, now nestling in a wad of tissue on a shelf in her bedroom. She gave him a smile of gratitude.

'Harvey, do you remember that—'

'Good afternoon!'

Alexa turned around to see Sarah Carmichael, basket full of pilchards, making straight for them. She hadn't seen Sarah in a while and half-welcomed the distraction her interruption might bring.

Sarah's thick blonde hair was coiled sensibly beneath her neat hat, which sported a rather old-fashioned sprig of cherries bouncing gently in the breeze. The end of Sarah's nose appeared a little pink, giving her a peculiar prettiness, but her eyes were her best feature, and sparkled considerably in Harvey's direction. She gave him, and him only, a smooth, wide smile.

When she turned to Alexa, her face fell.

'Hello, Miss Rosewarne. May I say how sorry we, mother and I, are to hear of your sad news.'

Sarah's awkward formality made Alexa's skin prickle. She had never been Alexa's friend, and how could she be? Sarah lived with her mother, the war widow, and her three younger sisters in a small stone cottage crammed into a terrace two streets back from the quay. She had attended the village school and, as Alexa lived on the top of the cliff and her father was, alongside Arthur Ferris, a prominent landlord of the parish, their paths rarely crossed. Sarah was expected to marry a farmer or a fisherman and, at nearly seventeen – and similar in age to Harvey – was probably wondering why she was not at least engaged by now. For, despite being so gauche and brittle, she was a willowy, beautiful girl.

With Alexa only twelve – her birthday all-but forgotten and marked only by the intrusion of the St Just undertaker arriving with her mother's coffin – and being sent away to boarding school in September, the distance between them could only become wider.

'I saw you sitting there, Mr Ferris,' said Sarah, seemingly wishing to avoid any such social gulf with Harvey, 'and wondered where Indigo Moon was.'

'Sulking in our boathouse beneath Enys Point. I haven't taken her out all summer.'

'Then if you are not going sailing may I ask you back to the cottage for some tea? Mother would like to see you.' Sarah's eyes flicked reluctantly to Alexa. 'Both of you.'

'Perhaps another time,' he said. 'Alexa has errands to run for Juliet.'

'Oh, you go, Harvey,' Alexa urged him. 'I'm not fit to be seen in society. I will only make you all miserable.'

'No, not this time,' he said, suggesting that he wouldn't dream of it. 'Thank you, Sarah. Please give our regards to your mother.'

'If you are sure, then I will say goodbye.' Sarah looked hopefully at Harvey, finding for him her best smile.

'Quite sure,' said Harvey.

Alexa watched Sarah walk away across the cobbles with a slight dip to her shoulders. The cherries on her hat, however, still jiggled quite cheerily.

'Why on earth did you refuse tea and buns, Harvey?' Alexa asked. 'That's not like you.'

'You said yourself that you are not up to it,' he said. 'You will be scrutinised by Mrs Carmichael and all and sundry gathering for a gossip there. Let's get this fish back to Juliet and perhaps she will give us tea.'

They stopped halfway up the steep cliff path to rest. Below Alexa, the village seemed so far away and tiny; above her, Porthdeen was out of sight. Even though the punishing climb ruled out conversation, she was pleased that whenever she glanced around in the companionable silence, she saw Harvey's face.

'I've just decided, Alexa,' Harvey said, leaning back against the sloping grassy cliffside. 'One day, I will revive the Enys Point Ball. Not next year, nor the year after that. But one day, when it seems right. And I will hold it in your honour.'

Alexa was still out of breath and could not speak. And if she could, she would not have known what to say. The glittering soirées that her mother had often remembered with such fondness hosted by Arthur and Betty Ferris before the war, when her father trod on Mamma's toes in her silk dancing slippers, had been the stuff of legend. A little light illuminated Alexa's mind and she did not feel quite so lost.

'I think, Alexa, that I might have succeeded in making you smile,' said Harvey, his face animated by a cheerful grin, 'even if just for a little while.'

7

HALFWAY THROUGH SPRING, 1925

Alexa sat alone in a corner of the library of Trengrouse School and opened her writing case. All the girls were obeying the rules, the air was hushed and studious. The supper bell would sound in approximately half an hour, and Alexa had just enough time to do her duty and write a letter home. She carefully loaded her pen with ink but let it hover over the sheet of paper. The idea of composing it, the words she must choose so carefully, exhausted her.

Instead, she glanced around the room. Some of her form were crouched at the bank of desks in the middle, bent over homework; other girls were sitting on the armchairs, flicking languidly through month-old periodicals. Sporadically, one of the prefects would lift their head to check for bookish behaviour and no giggling. Even if talking were allowed, no one would have spoken to Alexa.

A small fire was pulsing in the grate, two or three lamps gave off feeble yellow light in the corners, and the towering bookshelves presented Alexa with tempting secrets and promises, reminding her of her father's study. In this room and in this one period of time

– the quiet, empty space between day and evening – she was able to feel like she used to, to imagine nothing had changed.

The late afternoon sky was still light, the dark moor spreading like an unravelled bolt of coarse fabric. When she glanced back down at her sheet of paper, a huge blot of ink was spreading like an unfurling flower.

She screwed up the notepaper, drawing sharp glances, and selected another. Steadying her pen, she added the date at the top but found that she could not continue, could not write what she knew she must: 'Dear Dad'. She replaced the lid and rested her head in her hands, hoping her tears would disappear before anyone noticed.

Could it be spring already? Last September, when she'd arrived at Trengrouse, a Victorian monstrosity built at the top of a wooded valley on the edge of Bodmin Moor with the heath at its back door, three months had passed since her mother's death. Under the mellowing sun, as the season shifted, she conceded that the moors were indeed as beautiful as everyone – Juliet, Dad and Harvey – told her they would be. Every day, she forced herself to concentrate on the undulating heather, the acid-yellow gorse, the rocky outcrops, stunted trees and the road running across it like a silvery ribbon. Alexa compelled herself to admire the view, the changing light on the wild and alien landscape. She was desperate for something to replace her mother's face in her mind, her mother's voice in her ear, singing 'Venice, the moon and you'.

As different as this place was, the wind blew just like it did at Porthdeen. When Alexa was walking outside from dorm to tennis court, or refectory to assembly hall, on her own at the back of the crocodile of girls, she felt the breeze on her face: fresh and hard on some days, a soft caress on others. But it brought with it only the scent of the earth, trapping her in a fist of claustrophobia. The loamy, soggy woods and peaty moorland, the fields of scruffy sheep, the manicured school grounds crowded around, rising as symbols of grief. And the terrible dreams continued.

Over by the fireside, two of her form were talking in each other's ears, strictly against rules. One of them glanced over at her, her eyes hardening into a stare. No wonder Alexa struggled to make friends, her shell was thick, her pain tucked away. She hardly noticed when a sixth-former commented on the olive shade of her skin and the peculiar colour of her eyes or a water monitor whispered that *her* father did not trust Italians.

Surreptitiously, Alexa wiped the back of her hand over her eyes, picked up her pen again and drew out a fresh sheet of paper. Instead of 'Dear Dad', she wrote:

Dear Juliet

Alexa asked her how she was and she told her a little bit about her lessons in tennis, art and English literature, how many house points she'd won; she asked if Juliet had seen Harvey recently. He was a terrible letter writer. But her father? She skirted around him.

In Juliet's last-but-one letter to her, soon after the beginning of the spring term, she had mentioned that the nurse who Doctor Paynter had employed had dropped in recently at Porthdeen to pay her respects. The nurse had, apparently, an aunt Rose at Little Porthdeen whom she liked to visit. Dad, Juliet wrote, had asked her to stay for tea. In her next letter, the nurse, who, Juliet informed Alexa, was called Eleanor Hammett, had taken him up on his invitation. The next thing Juliet knew, her father had driven to Truro to take Miss Hammett out for luncheon. First of all, Juliet had wondered where they might have gone: the Bull's Head Tavern was passable, or perhaps the Copper Kettle tearooms? Then Juliet had dared to suggest, possibly agonising over the words she wrote, that it must be a good thing that this hard-working young lady could brighten her father's days.

Alexa tried to recall the nurse who had covered her mother's face with the sheet: quite small, slender and energetic. As blonde as Mamma had been dark. Did Juliet believe they should welcome Miss Hammett into their lives, and so soon?

The door to the library opened and the head of Miss Bates, the housemistress's secretary, appeared around it.

'Rosewarne?' she called out, her voice rudely slicing through the silence.

Heads bobbed up; all eyes singled Alexa out. She heard more than one audible tut.

'Ah, there you are. Miss Graham wants to see you before supper.'

Alexa's shoulders sank. She wanted to finish her letter to Juliet, get it ready for the morning post. There were so many questions, so much unspoken, clogging her mind.

'That means now, Rosewarne.' Miss Bates clicked her fingers. A giggle broke in the ranks.

Alexa quickly gathered her things, smudging the wet ink on her letter so that all it was good for was the bin. She rushed out of the room and along the corridor, trying to match the urgent pace of the hurrying secretary. She caught up and perched on a chair in the vestibule where Miss Bates had her own desk outside Miss Graham's office. She waited for Miss Bates to give her the nod, her permission to approach the forbiddingly closed door.

* * *

Alexa was mildly amused that Miss Graham's office, on this chilly spring afternoon, was incredibly warm compared to the rest of the house. Decorated with the trappings of a Victorian parlour, it was reassuringly old-fashioned, as was Miss Graham, with her elaborately coiled hair, as grey as gunmetal. In her high-necked blouse, with pearls, her fashion sense was securely trapped in the time of old King Edward.

'Ah, Alexandra. Do sit,' Miss Graham said, looking up at her over her spectacles under a wrinkled brow. The housemistress's voice was soft and chiding, slipping sometimes into mannish baritone, but never unkind. 'I have something to show you.'

While she rustled with paperwork, Alexa became distracted by the brooch pinned just below Miss Graham's broad and proudly held shoulders. Her jewellery alternated from day to day, from week to week, and Alexa was fascinated to see the brooch she had chosen to highlight the particularly peaty olive-green of her skirt. She peered at it, wondering if she'd ever seen it before as Miss Graham extracted an envelope from under a pile of post.

'I take it, Alexandra,' she said, 'that you wrote a letter to your grandmother a month or so ago?'

Alexa sat up straight and clasped her hands together. In her mind, Nonna was still standing in the hallway of Half Moon Street. She glanced at her housemistress's face with an awakening of hope, a spark of joy.

'Yes, yes, I did.'

Miss Graham leant over the desk, offering her the envelope. 'Well, it seems that your letter has been returned.'

No one had ever told Alexa what Nonna's address was, or written it down for her. But she had pictured the number 15 painted on a white stucco pillar; had remembered Half Moon Street, and had finished off with Piccadilly, London. But, on the envelope, her words had been rudely struck through, with 'return to sender – not known at this address'.

'Not known?' Alexa said, turning the letter over and over. 'How can she not be known?'

'Do you mean Mrs Montgomery, dear?' asked Miss Graham. 'It seems that they may have moved away.' She tilted her head onto one side as if to ask why Alexa didn't already know that.

Alexa stared at the handwriting that abruptly obliterated her own. Was it Nonna's? Might this be the maid, Lily's hand? Had Mr Montgomery returned the letter?

'Are you quite all right, Alexandra?' Miss Graham asked.

'It's just that I so wanted to speak to her...'

Sitting at the top of the stairs at home last summer, sometime between her trip down to the village with Harvey and her packing for school, she'd heard her father on the telephone in his study, his voice squeezed into a tight and bitter tirade as he spoke deeply into the receiver.

'Lily, you say? Well, Lily, what happened, exactly?'

Alexa had waited and listened as the house fell quiet. Through the open landing window came the whispering and chattering of the sea, the noise of the gulls and their constant keening.

'So you're telling me...' her father's voice was strange, as she'd never heard it before, low and measured with rage, '...that your employers turned my wife and daughter out into the street. Into the pouring rain? My wife was dangerously ill.'

Another terrible silence.

'She knows that now, doesn't she?'

The crash of the receiver into its cradle had jolted Alexa. She crept down the stairs and tiptoed across the hall. Just as she reached the study door, it was closed in her face, the key turned in its lock. Behind it, she heard an animal noise, a short, deep moan of anguish. She had dared not mention Nonna to her father again but all the time wanted to speak to her, to ask her a hundred questions, to try to make her nightmare end.

Miss Graham cleared her throat, bringing Alexa back to the stuffy office.

'Would you like to talk this through, Alexandra?'

'No, Miss Graham. No, not at all,' she said, crushing the letter in her hands.

Alexa turned her face towards the windows, the largest in the House, with the best view of the moorland. She pinned her eyes on the far horizon, fighting the sickening revolutions of her stomach.

Miss Graham moved on in her efficiently clipped manner. 'Which brings me to another matter,' she said, checking her diary. 'You are to expect a visitor on Saturday.'

'A visitor? Who?' Alexa struggled to stir herself from despair. All she could think of, all she could hope for, was Juliet or Harvey. 'Your father is paying you a visit. And I've arranged for you to have tea here in my office. I thought you might like some privacy.' Miss Graham nodded towards the comfortable arrangement of brocaded armchairs around her hearth. She waited, no doubt expecting appreciation. 'Won't that be nice, Alexandra?'

* * *

As Alexa walked into the dorm, the talking stopped. The girls were getting ready to play netball and, for once, Alexa wished that she was going too, even though it was a game she hated ever since the goal attack's fingernails had raked her bare arm amid a particularly tight tussle for the ball.

Sunshine was beckoning to her through the window, but as it was Saturday, she was due to take tea with her father.

Kitty, already dressed in her gymslip, extracted herself from the group and sidled up to Alexa.

'Lucky you, Alexa,' she said, perching on the bed while, behind her, the giggling began. 'Having tea in Miss Graham's office while we all have to do games.'

'I don't feel at all lucky,' said Alexa, glancing at her alarm clock.

It was twenty to and her father was expected at three o'clock. A sudden sense of urgency squeezed into a lump of dread in her stomach. She turned her back on the room and fished in her wardrobe for a clean pinafore. When she looked around, she realised that they were all going to watch her get changed.

She peeled off her uniform and blouse all in one go, stuffed them back in the wardrobe and stood there in her liberty bodice. 'Where are you from?' Vivi asked, twirling the ends of her exceptionally long plaits.

'Cornwall,' said Alexa, buttoning up her new pinafore. 'Porthdeen, to be precise. Do you know it?'

'Isn't that in the back of beyond?' someone asked.

'Her mother's Italian,' assured another.

Alexa forced herself to look at them.

'She always preferred Venetian,' Alexa emphasised, 'if you don't mind.'

Vivi made a sarcastic noise. 'Isn't she Lady Muck.'

'Shush, Vivi,' said Kitty. 'Her mother's dead.'

'My parents are in India,' reasoned Vivi, 'so they may as well be dead, too.'

The giggling stopped. Alexa saw Kitty's eyes fill with tears. 'What an absolutely rotten thing to say,' said Kitty.

The girls shifted awkwardly, none of them looking Vivi's way. 'But I never know what to say to her,' Vivi said, tossing her plaits. 'She looks down her nose at us, she never speaks. And we have to pussyfoot around her the whole time.'

'Aren't you all going to be late for netball?' Alexa said, as quickly as she could before Vivi's words sank in enough to hurt. She fixed the girl with an uncompromising stare until she turned her head away.

The group roused themselves and emitted a collective moan as they began to drift out into the corridor.

Kitty hesitated by the door. She whispered, 'I hope you enjoy your tea, Alexa.'

* * *

Left alone in the dorm, she gave the clock another fearful glance. In the old days, she would have enjoyed tea with her father, with Juliet's cake, served in his study. But after Mamma, they had been propelled in entirely different directions. Both of them lost, struggling to find a way home. Perhaps a chat with Dad, she decided, perhaps some quiet advice would set her back on the path she should be taking.

Alexa went to the mirror, picked up her comb and solemnly straightened her fringe, tucking her hair behind her ears. She smiled suddenly at her reflection, thinking how proud Dad would be of the way she dealt with Vivi. But then she saw her mother looking back at her. That was why. She was the image of Mamma, and Dad, too, was constantly reminded of her every time he looked at Alexa. And that was why he had sent her away.

Miss Bates was waiting for her downstairs outside Miss Graham's office.

'Heels with your uniform, Rosewarne?' she said. 'In the afternoon? Oh, I suppose you look quite smart. I've just shown them in, and I'll fetch the tea and cakes. Go on, what's the matter with you? They're waiting. In you go.'

'*They're*?' Alexa asked.

'That's what I said. This is a treat for you, you know. Receiving visitors like this in the housemistress's room. Doesn't happen for all the girls. Don't keep them waiting.'

Alexa's spirits soared: Juliet must have come too. But as Miss Bates opened the door to the office, Alexa's breath caught in her throat. Two people, indeed, were waiting for her, sitting in Miss

Graham's comfy armchairs with the fire crackling in the hearth between them. Her father stood up abruptly, as if he had been caught doing something he shouldn't. He'd shaved off his moustache and looked so much younger.

'Ah, hello, Alexa,' he said and came forward to kiss her forehead, like he always used to. 'You remember Miss Hammett?'

Alexa gaped at the person sitting in the other chair. Eleanor Hammett held herself upright, poised and open-faced in welcome, as if she owned the armchair, the office, the school, everything.

'Miss Hammett?' Alexa's voice squeaked in question.

The woman laughed perkily and said, in mock reproach, 'Miss Hammett? William, you can't have forgotten already...'

Alexa's father cut in, 'Ah, we'll get to that.'

He indicated that Alexa should sit. But Alexa could not move. Eleanor Hammett's cloche hat was quite becoming; it framed her bland but infuriatingly pretty face and allowed for just a wave or two of her fair bobbed hair to show beneath it. She'd kept her hat on, of course, because that's what ladies do when they take tea. But she wasn't a lady; she was a nurse from Truro.

And her dress showed far too much of her knee.

'Isn't this a surprise?' Eleanor said, leaning forwards in her chair towards Alexa as if she was about to clasp both her hands in her own.

Alexa looked sharply at her father, who was busying himself by drawing an upright chair into the group.

'A surprise... yes,' Alexa said weakly, feeling that she had better sit down. 'I thought—'

Miss Bates blundered in with a tray, knocking Miss Graham's paintwork, and lowered it down ceremoniously onto the small table by the fire.

'Tea and cake,' she announced unnecessarily.

Once the door was closed behind her, Alexa's father sat himself on the hard-backed chair. He seemed to be perched far too high above the little party. He cleared his throat.

'How are you, Alexa? How have you settled in to your new term? House all right, is it? Any battleaxes to contend with? Think I've just seen one right there.'

Alexa ignored his joke.

'I hate it here, Dad. You know that,' she said bluntly. 'The girls are catty, and leave me out all the time.'

Despite the force of her words, she fixed an artificial smile to her face. Her father looked at her, mildly baffled.

'I see, well...' he said, adjusting his necktie. 'Needs must, my dear. You have to go to school.'

Alexa thought of Juliet and the education she had imparted to her. She thought of her Mamma and everything she had taught her at her knee. She thought of all the books lining her Dad's study.

'Well, I don't,' she said. 'I can learn everything I need to back at Porthdeen.'

Eleanor let out a tinkling little laugh, reached for the teapot, and began to pour.

'I felt the same way as you did, Alexa, when I was your age,' she said, lowering her voice, trying for intimacy. 'But I wanted to do something with my life, to nurse. It's been my vocation, and I knew I had to have my school certificates.'

Her father took his cup and saucer from Eleanor and immediately put it down on the table with a bit of a crash.

'We can talk about that later, Eleanor,' he said, briskly. 'Let's cut to the chase.'

Alexa heard a note of frightening urgency in her father's voice. In place of the moustache on William's top lip lay an unbecoming layer of sweat and he seemed to be concentrating on everything else in the room but her.

'We have some news, Alexa,' he said.

Icy fear drenched the back of her neck. The tea she was sipping threatened to rise back up her throat.

'News?' she managed.

She tried to sip again but it tasted odd, as if the kettle had not boiled.

'Eleanor and I are married,' her father said.

Alexa flinched, deafened by a clash of voices in her head.

'I know it is rather sudden, and possibly a bit of a shock, but...' Her father was trying to smile at her, 'but Eleanor has made me very happy since your dear mother... She is making me very happy.'

To Alexa's revulsion, he reached over the tea tray and gripped Eleanor's outstretched hand, his eyes glistening.

'It was in the church on the cliff at Porthdeen,' gushed Eleanor. 'We wanted it to be a quiet day. No flowers. No hymns.'

Alexa was no longer listening. Her head filled with pictures of the church, high up above the village, squat and sturdy, patrolled by gulls. There was a crude and mysterious carving of a mermaid etched into the centuries-old oak door and every time she passed it, she'd run her finger along the curving tail. Around the building, the little churchyard was lush with feathery grass and populated with headstones and Celtic crosses – some wonky with age and blooming yellow with lichen, some brand new, the granite sparkling in sunshine. They would have walked right past Mamma on the way to be married.

'We didn't want to drag you away from school,' Eleanor went on. 'Oh, but my aunt Rose was a guest, she lives in the village, as you probably—'

'And Juliet,' her father interjected. 'Juliet was there.'

Alexa gripped the edges of her saucer with both hands, rested it down on her lap, tempted to send it crashing to the floor. 'Juliet didn't tell me,' she said.

'Juliet didn't know until the day,' said her father. 'It happened yesterday, and we came straight here to tell you.'

Alexa was aware of a terrible beating in her ears, the hollow tock-tock of Miss Graham's mantel clock.

'Oh my dear, you look terribly pale.' Eleanor sprang up and wrestled her cup and saucer from her. 'I knew this would be a dreadful shock for you. It is very sudden, we know. A bit of a whirlwind. That's why we wanted to come here and see you. To tell you ourselves. Face to face.' She spoke efficiently, kindly; obviously very good at her vocation.

As Eleanor stood over Alexa, offering her a handkerchief, Alexa looked up at her fresh, bridal face. She deduced that she must be closer in age to her than she was to her father. Eleanor had said: 'when I was your age'. That couldn't have been that long ago, for goodness' sake.

'Are you still a nurse?' Alexa asked, grasping for something, anything, to say.

'Oh no, no,' Eleanor said brightly. 'Not now I am married, and Mrs Rosewarne. Married women don't work.'

Alexa clenched her jaw to stop the roar of indignant words poised to explode from her, even as her mother's sing-song voice gently reminded her of the trouble her Latin spark might bring. She turned instead to her father and instantly pitied him. He looked besieged with worry, hardly able to look at her.

She took a ragged breath.

'Dad, as long as you are happy,' she said, surprising herself at how generous she sounded, over the noise of the screaming inside.

'God knows, I've been so unhappy,' he uttered, shaking his head as if only just realising.

But her father had been happy. When he, Mamma and Alexa took their walks along the stone-fenced lanes; when they all pootled in his car about the top roads on the way to St Just; when he talked quietly with Mamma in the lamplit parlour, their heads close, when Alexa was supposed to be in bed. She remembered them both working in the study; when he laughed, delighted, at something Mamma had said. Their life as a family had been so real, so easy and so natural to Alexa that she had been unaware of it until now; now it was gone.

Alexa watched Eleanor give her a shy, head-dipping smile, and decided that she must sit back and drink her tea. For that was protocol and she must behave as her Mamma had taught her. But as her father accepted a fresh cup from his new wife, fished for a handkerchief, rubbed it over the sweat on his face, he simply didn't seem to be her father any more.

Anger, as hot and as uncontrollable as fire, suddenly surged through Alexa. She sprang to her feet and headed for the door, yanking it open.

'Alexa? Are you all right?' called her father. 'Where are you going?'

'I don't care. Anywhere, but here,' she threw back over her shoulder.

She came face to face with Miss Bates, who had been pottering outside in the vestibule.

'What are you doing, Rosewarne?' she demanded, stepping in front of her. 'That's rather rude when your father has come all this way.'

'I would much rather he hadn't,' she snapped.

Her father followed her to the doorway and stared at her in astonishment. He shook his head. 'I hope you will apologise to Eleanor for your behaviour. Now.'

'Whatever she has done, I'm quite sure that she is very sorry indeed,' said Miss Graham, appearing at the entrance to the corridor, her sudden presence commanding the room.

Miss Bates interjected, 'But Rosewarne here is being quite rude to her father.'

Miss Graham's sharp eyes alighted on Alexa for the briefest of spells, flickering with empathy.

She walked forward quickly to William, extending her hand, shaking his firmly.

'Mr Rosewarne, so lovely to meet you.' She popped her iron-grey head around to where Eleanor was still sitting by the fireside, her eyes wide and her mouth tiny with surprise. 'And Mrs Rosewarne, of course.'

Miss Graham did not draw breath, her low voice equally domineering and delightful. 'Your daughter might appear to you as a little overwrought today, and might have behaved irrationally, Mr Rosewarne, but she has a lot on her mind. A guilty conscience, no less, and it's all my fault, I'm afraid,' Miss Graham flicked her eyes in Alexa's direction. 'She has an important essay she has to complete and time is ticking. Perhaps you will give her leave to do so, or she may be in rather too much trouble with me.'

The housemistress's words entranced Alexa, dripping compassion, easing the chaos in her mind.

'Well, I say, we better be getting along anyway,' her father said, taken aback but accepting of Miss Graham's elucidation. 'Got a long drive home, and El— Mrs Rosewarne is feeling rather weary, as it happens.'

Alexa's goodbye to her father was so relieved, so subdued, that he hesitated before stepping forward to kiss her on the forehead.

'We will see you soon, Alexa, when you've got more time,' he said, his face bright with a smidgeon of guilt.

But Alexa looked past him to Miss Graham. The housemistress glanced up from the stack of letters she had picked up from Miss Bates's desk and gave her the ghost of a wink.

8

MIDSUMMER, 1925

Someone had arranged the candles on the cake into the shape of a thirteen. Alexa suspected – as the gesture was sweet and rather unimaginative – that it had been Kitty.

The girls, some tall, some short, some busty and some sweaty, made a small but energetic gathering in the common room, having evidently been commanded to make an effort by Miss Graham. They all bit enthusiastically into slices of birthday cake while Miss Bates manned the tea urn. Alexa sat at their centre, shying away from their blandly cheerful and self-centred faces, deflecting any under-lash glances in her direction with a fixed smile, feeling secretly pleased that it was such an effort for Vivi to deliberately ignore her.

She allowed the chatter to throb around her while she concentrated on the view through the window. The day was as benign and as bright as any in June and would be, as Midsummer's Eve, the longest. Irritated, Alexa pressed her fingertip into the crumbs on her plate. The length of the day through which she must stumble, pretending to be all right, elongated before her like punishment. For this, her birthday, and all those long into her future, would forever be linked with her mother's death.

Kitty appeared by her side.

'Did you get many presents this year, Alexa?' she asked.

'No, nothing has been sent for me.'

Kitty's face fell. It was not the right answer.

Alexa added quickly, 'But I'm sure there'll be lots waiting for me when I get home.'

'But you've got birthday cards, yes?' asked Kitty.

Alexa nodded, picturing the one that had arrived yesterday, signed with love from Dad and Eleanor. Kitty seemed incredibly relieved, not knowing it lay face down in the bedside table drawer, its cloying poem and painted roses hidden from view along with the handful of short and stilted letters she'd received from her father since his visit in the spring.

Alexa's ears were bubbling with the silly voices of girls. She shut her eyes. But when she opened them again, they and her whole life was still there. The air in the common room was at blood heat, sweet with cake and stifling. The crescendo of competing female babble rose. Alexa felt as if she was being swaddled. She took a breath, but all she could smell was Vivi's sickly parma violet perfume. Had no one thought to let in a little air?

Alexa put down her plate and made her way to the window. The sky was cloudless, the moorland lush with a thousand shades of green. She grasped the latch and pushed the windowas as wide open as she could. Fresh air hurried in, enveloped her face and she breathed it in greedily, thinking that she caught a whiff of the sea, just like she might from Dad's study window. But how could she have done? She was miles and miles from the coast, so far from home. She sat on the windowsill, which was wide enough to be a seat, and glanced behind her at her little birthday party. Miss Bates had her back to her, fussing with the urn tap; the girls were, as was usual, morbidly self-absorbed. She was isolated, quite separate from it all.

Alexa swung her legs up onto the sill, executed a lithe little twist of her body, slipped through the window, and landed lightly on her feet on the patio paving.

And she ran, pelting across the neatly mown lawn, over which it was expressly forbidden for girls to walk, let alone run, a great laugh sprang out even as tears streamed warm and wet from her eyes.

* * *

The scarlet geraniums in Miss Graham's pots outside the windows of her office glowed in the sunshine, bouncing in the breeze. Sitting on the hard-backed chair in front of Miss Graham's desk, Alexa watched them, conscious of a peculiar stiffness in the flesh of her face, as if, like Mr Fairling had, she was wearing a mask.

Miss Graham expressed a little cough. 'Why did you open that window and climb out of it, Alexandra? Why did you run across the lawn which you know full well is out of bounds?' she asked. 'I'll start again. I want you to tell me why *you* think you did it.'

Alexa forced herself to focus on what was being said to her, fought her way up through the agonising reasons.

'I want to leave the school, Miss Graham.'

The housemistress raised an eyebrow at her and paused for a moment in the process of filling her pen. 'You mean you want me to expel you.'

'My father will try to make me stay and his wife will agree with him, of course. But, Miss Graham, I know all I need to know. My nanny, Juliet, taught me for many years at home. My Mamma also... I want to go home.'

'Home, ah...' Miss Graham's eyes tightened. 'Are you sure about that, my dear?'

Alexa straightened her shoulders, understanding what she meant.

'Actually, not home,' she faltered. 'I'll go elsewhere. Home has changed, everything has changed. I don't know where to go.' A sudden sob blossomed in her throat. She swallowed hard, fixing in her mind how she'd felt when she'd escaped across the lawn. That bright starburst of delight. She had not felt anything like that since running through Green Park last year.

'But I will think of something, Miss Graham.'

Her numbness subsided a little now that she had made a resolution. She drew back and waited, expecting a tirade of persuasion and outrage. But Miss Graham merely picked up another pen and began to methodically fill it from her inkwell. 'I'm very sorry, Alexandra,' she said eventually. 'We try to do our best for you here. And there is so much more we can do for you. There's no two ways about it. Trengrouse school – or any other school for that matter – is going to be your home for the next few years.' She glanced at Alexa and seemed to want to mollify her. 'You can leave at fifteen if you like.'

'But I hate it here. The girls are so horrid to me.'

'Envy makes us do ugly things,' Miss Graham said. 'Even the prettiest girls cannot cope with how distinct you are to them. Do you understand what I mean, Alexa? You are noticed. You stand apart. You must relish it, use it.'

Alexa shrugged. She did not want to dwell on how different she was, how detached she had become, when all she wanted was the comfort of friends. 'But fifteen,' she said. 'That's so far away, I can't—'

'Two years, dear. That's nothing in a lifetime.' The housemistress held her gaze, compelling Alexa to understand her.

'Alexandra, you will be safe here. Bored, yes. Rebellious, yes. But safe. And glad of it.'

Disloyal tears leaked from Alexa's eyes.

'Listen, I want to tell you something,' said Miss Graham, ignoring them. 'It's about what I did when I was fifteen, when I left school. Yes, a very long time ago,' she said with a smirk whispering over her lips. She put her pens to one side. 'For I got my real education when I left, and not, in my opinion, while I was at school.'

'That's what I mean. Exactly!' Alexa's outburst was weakened by another round of weeping.

'Ah, yes, Alexandra, but I still studied hard while I was at school,' Miss Graham cautioned. 'What I am saying is that my real education, the real learning came then, after I'd left. Because I became *interested* in life, I became fascinated by people, by different countries, culture, music, art, the whole world. None of this I seemed to get from school. But I still needed my education to set me on my path. Stay with it, Alexandra. Stay with us. You won't regret it. And then, finally, you'll be ready to start your life.'

'But what is it that you did when you were fifteen?' Alexa's tears began to dry, her curiosity expand.

Miss Graham's powdery cheeks reddened and Alexa stifled a cry of pleasant surprise, wondering at some sort of scandal. When her housemistress had been her age, Victoria had been on the throne and the void of time between then and now was, for Alexa, impossible to navigate. She tried to imagine the young Miss Graham in bustle and a perky straw hat but could not see past grey hair, her brooch collection and spectacles. Today she was wearing a particularly exquisite cameo, carved with a bumblebee. Alexa remembered her favourite button, the honeybee one from Mamma's wedding dress, and smiled with secret pleasure.

'I became a lady's companion,' Miss Graham announced with a courageous grumble in her voice. 'And I travelled with that lady, oh, how I travelled. I watched and I learnt, I absorbed. I journeyed in more ways than you can imagine. I, quite simply, saw the world. That was my education.'

'But how did you manage to do this?' Alexa asked. 'How did you ever escape, Miss Graham?'

The housemistress chuckled, animated by her revelation. 'Escape, I like that. Well, I certainly didn't climb out of any windows. It was the simplest thing ever. I happened to see an advert in *The Lady*. In *Situations Vacant*. I answered it, and became an employee and, well... my father, of course, was furious.'

Miss Graham got up from behind the desk, went to her small table by the fireplace to pick something out of a pile of books. She handed Alexa the latest issue of the magazine, saying, 'Of course, in my day it was more like a newspaper...'

On the cover was an illustration of an efficient-looking gentlewoman in sensible tweeds walking a spaniel, with promises of features inside about frocks from France and the Chelsea Flower Show. Even though these did not pique her interest, Alexa's mind was racing headlong. She saw a glorious unchartered avenue, an opportunity, a life. Already, she was making her way out of school, out of Cornwall, leaving Porthdeen behind. She would find something else, somewhere else to be entirely. What and where, she had absolutely no idea. She thought she was smiling, but she wasn't quite sure.

Miss Graham was speaking, '...this has been a very sad time for you, and I'm so very sorry. Even though this is your birthday, I must issue you with two hundred lines for climbing out of the common room window. I can't let you off, or give you special treatment, Alexandra. I have to make an example of you, which I'm sure you will appreciate.'

'That's quite all right, Miss Graham. And thank you,' Alexa said, rolling *The Lady* into a tight tube on her lap.

Miss Graham looked as if she was about to dismiss her, but halted.

'Alexa, do you want to marry?'

'Marry? Miss Graham, I'm only just thirteen!

'Some girls see it as their only choice. I didn't marry for many reasons, one of which was that school governors do not approve of married teachers. I had the chance but chose my profession instead. My contemporaries, and now yours, have been, and will be, lucky in that respect. But there are women perhaps just a decade and a half older than you, born at the turn of the century, who will never marry. Because a lot of that generation of men are dead. Or unable to live as a married man for one reason or another—'

'What do you mean, Miss Graham?'

'You will find this out when you become a wife. But listen, unlike so many of your older sisters, you will have that choice to make. A home, a husband, a family, or not.'

Alexa thought of Harvey, who she decided would do the sensible thing and marry someone his own age. She thought of Mr Fairling, and his poor shattered face, and the men his age with half a leg, or no legs, whom no one seemed to want to be with.

'May I please borrow this magazine, just for tonight? I'll return it tomorrow, I promise,' Alexa said.

'Take it,' said Miss Graham, her face lifting in amusement, her voice rich with admiration. 'Keep it, Alexandra. It's yours.'

Alexa stopped at the door, gratitude swelling her smile as she turned back to her housemistress.

'I love your brooch, Miss Graham,' she said. 'The little bee reminds me of the buttons on my mother's wedding dress. There's only one left now, but I've kept it safe in her button box. It's the simplest, most precious thing.'

9

On the last day of term, the first day of July, Alexa stepped from the train into sunshine. Penzance basked in deep summer. As usual, seagulls wheeled white against a true-blue sky and Alexa still battled a peculiar, futile hope that everything would have returned to normal. Be back as it should be.

She passed through the ticket barrier where families congregated and children were armed with buckets and spades. It was the benign setting for a play against a sunny painted backcloth. But this joyous scenery would soon transform into something far more ominous and untried. For Alexa had not been home since her father had married Eleanor Hammett, and she was struggling to draw for herself the picture of Porthdeen as it would be now.

Dad must be late, for his usual parking spot had been taken by another car, and he would be cross. The porter followed Alexa with her trunk, asking where she was being picked up. And as she turned to tell him she had no idea, she caught sight of Harvey waving at her from the driver's seat of the car that had taken her father's place. He bounced out, taller than she remembered, his limbs liquid with confidence as he dealt with the trunk and tipped the porter.

'Welcome home, Alexa,' he said, lifting his hat vertically from his head, teasing her in an endearing way. 'I'm your chauffer for the day. I do hope you like my new car.'

'Your new car?' she asked, blushing and suddenly shy. She focused on the vehicle, its glossy fenders and smooth bonnet. 'Surely you're too young to drive.'

'I'm seventeen, Alexa. I've had my birthday, remember. Isn't she super?'

He opened the passenger door for her.

'Took delivery of her just after Easter. I spent the morning polishing her. She's just the ticket.'

Harvey's simple delight leaked from him, infecting her, chasing her gloom into a hole.

'Don't you mean...' she said, dipping into the seat, 'your father's car, Harvey?'

He laughed, getting in beside her.

'I suppose I do,' he said. 'If I close my eyes, I can pretend she's all mine.'

Realising how long it had been since she had seen him, Alexa stole a sideways glance at Harvey. Had he grown taller since Christmas? He was a little leaner perhaps, but he looked so wonderfully the same: his face open, peaceful and perfectly happy to see her. Ah, but his hair was longer at the front, flopping, surely maddeningly, into his eyes. And, as he laughed, he brushed it back in a smooth pleasing motion. So much had changed for Alexa, but this simple gesture – and being by Harvey's side – was beautifully familiar.

Harvey pressed the starter button and turned his head to listen to the engine, catching her eye and nodding with satisfaction.

'Make a wish and pretend the car is yours, Harvey?' she

laughed, feeling her confidence rise to meet his. 'Only don't close your eyes while you do so. You're driving me, remember.'

'And I shall drive like a vicar with such precious cargo.'

They motored along the trunk road out of Penzance, deeper into the countryside, turning onto minor byways. Lanes grew narrow, the hills embraced them and the signposts pointed the way to Land's End.

'Well, Miss Alexa. And how was your birthday?' Harvey asked.

A bolt of pain hit her chest.

'As it will always be from now on,' she said.

'Oh, Alexa...'

Harvey pulled the car abruptly to a stop in front of a farmer's gate. A hedge of hawthorn towered before them, the tiny leaves sparkling in sunshine. Through the gap, through the bars of the gate, Alexa saw the familiar quilt of fields, sewn up with pale stone walls, the stretch of land that would take her all the way to the sea, and home.

Beside her, Harvey groaned. 'How utterly stupid of me. To ask you that. What a damned fool.'

Horrified, he cursed himself, running his hand over his hair. She thought he was going to reach for her, so she turned her head away, kept her hands pressed tightly, safely, together on her lap. She couldn't bear it if he tried to comfort her.

When she peeped at him, he was shaking his head, his eyes wide with remorse.

'I suppose... I simply got through it,' she said, wanting to help him. 'Anyway, I received some advice from my housemistress.

'Good advice?' he ventured cautiously.

'Yes, indeed.'

'I'm glad.' Harvey sighed hard. 'I'm sorry, Alexa, for being such an idiot.'

'Don't call yourself that.' She wanted to lift his smile again. 'Anyway, you can't be an idiot. You are going to medical school.'

Harvey chuckled lightly, relieved, but his energy had drained away, disappointing and saddening Alexa. He fired the engine and they set off again, a wounded silence filling the space between them. His courtesy ensured he would wait for her to speak, to start a new conversation.

After the turn of a mile, Alexa began, 'Harvey, why—?'

'I know what you want to ask me,' he said. 'Go on...'

'Why is it you today? And not my father?'

'They—'

'They! They!' she cried, suddenly, her outburst hard against the muffled interior of the car. 'Always *they*!'

'Oh, Alexa...' he turned his head quickly back and forth to look at her and the road ahead in turn. 'Alexa, I can't imagine what it is like for you but I'm here for you.'

She pivoted her head to stare out of the side window, sniffing as tears washed down her face.

'Don't you have a handkerchief?' he asked after another mile. 'I'm afraid I don't have a clean one either. Isn't that awful. Ma would be horrified with me. Whenever I leave the house, she always asks me if I have a clean hankie.'

His chattering brought her back and she smiled weakly. 'Mamma also never seemed to have a hankie. She always had to borrow.'

On the Porthdeen headland, he changed gear, approaching the fork in the narrow lane. One way led down to Little Porthdeen village and the harbour, the other turned sharply, the hand-painted sign pointing along the rising track to Porthdeen. The wheels crunched over broken flints as Harvey steered the car towards the sea, the fields either side of them bare and exposed, the grass parched to ochre. The land rose to meet their ascent and the little car struggled gamely with the gradient. Ahead of them, the sky was the colour of the gown Alexa's mother had worn the day she sat for the painting, the day before she died. Alexa knew that beneath those clouds, way ahead of her, the cliffs fell away to nothing. And the sea was waiting.

* * *

Juliet had judged the timing well. She came out of the front door and across the gravel, even before Harvey had fully stopped on the lane and applied the handbrake. Alexa bolted from the car, opened the gate and found herself in her engulfing embrace, hearing whispered greetings in Italian.

'Come in, *mia cara*,' Juliet urged her when they finally let each other go. 'Come let me make you some tea, or milk, or whatever you want. Goodbye, Harvey! Thank you! He's a good boy.'

Alexa waved at Harvey through the gates as he pulled away, then followed Juliet into the house. She realised her father's car was not outside, sudden relief swamped her; relief that he and, hopefully Eleanor also, was not at home and their awkward welcome for her would be postponed.

She and Juliet went straight through to the kitchen and Alexa sat at the end of the scrubbed pine table, her favourite spot whenever Juliet was bobbing about, busy baking, preparing little delights. Everything seemed the same: the gentle warmth of the stove at her back, a primal pleasure even on summer days, the alcoves towered with gleaming white plates and the kitchen door open to the brick-paved courtyard, a jigsaw of light and shadow. Through the stone archway, Alexa glimpsed a portion of the lawn, the gorse at the end of the garden, the edge of the world. The scents of camomile, lavender and sage in pots around the back door chimed together, buffeting their way into the room; their fragrance the backdrop to happiness, to her childhood.

Cook was evidently on her day off, so Juliet moved with assured territorial ease around the kitchen, found the cake tin, arranged a selection on a plate, set it down in front of Alexa. She'd been turning apricots in honey in a pan on the stove and Alexa could taste their sweetness in the air.

Juliet poured a glass of cool sweet milk from the pantry. She rested it by her elbow. Alexa looked up to thank her. Her nanny was crying.

'I wanted to tell you myself,' she said, subsiding, her face tear-streaked, onto the chair beside her. 'While your father and step-mother were out.'

'Tell me what? Oh, Juliet!' Alexa's sudden fear was like a tiny scream inside her head. Juliet took her hand, and bounced it on her own lap, the way she'd always done since she was a little girl to stop her crying.

'I've been offered a new position. One which I found hard to refuse.' Juliet enunciated slowly, as if to be sure that she was rightly understood. 'You see, Alexa, you're a grown-up girl now. And away at school. Your father has no need—'

Alexa burst out, 'You're leaving me?'

Juliet squeezed her eyes tight as fresh tears erupted. She gave a brief shake of her head as if to reject Alexa's protest.

'But why?'

'I told you why...'

Alexa recoiled, extracting her hand. She stood up and went back to the door. The chickens were scratching at scattered corn, jerking their way around the courtyard. Their low-whirring voices and mildly outraged clucking had entertained Alexa as a little girl; their desire not to be chased had given her hours of stalking fun;

their eggs hunted for in the corners of the yard, under piles of straw. But she was a grown-up girl now.

She turned back into the kitchen, peering into the room which had become a dark, chilly contrast to the sunny brightness of outside. All that was familiar was falling away. Juliet was still sitting, staring at her, her eyes glazed with tears.

'Well, then,' Alexa proclaimed, dredging up a cup of courage, 'Juliet, if you must go, I shall come and visit you as often as I like.'

Juliet lifted her chin. 'That might be more difficult than you think,' she exhaled in exasperation. 'For the position is in Italy. I have decided to go home.' But this was her home. Here, at Porthdeen, at the first and last house in England.

'Oh, Alexa, nothing lasts forever—'

They both turned at the sound of the front door.

'That must be Mr William and Mrs Eleanor,' said Juliet.

Alexa walked unsteadily across the stone-flagged floor, the cool air in the room making her shiver, chilling the ends of her fingers.

'Juliet, you can't go,' she whispered. 'You must help me face her.'

Her nanny linked her arm through hers and together they walked out of the kitchen, along the corridor and into the wide hallway. Voices rose and fell from the parlour and Alexa forced herself to push the door wider, to go in.

'Ah, Alexa, so you are home,' said her father. He'd not had time to take off his linen jacket, crushed a little by his car ride. He threw his hat down onto the sofa and strolled over to greet her with a kiss on the forehead. But his gesture was awkward, as if he'd forgotten how to say hello to her.

'Say good morning to Eleanor,' he said.

'Silly, William. She doesn't need to be told to say hello to someone,' Eleanor hurried over to Alexa, beaming. She'd taken her hat off and her hair was squashed and wonky. In fact, her clothes looked rather odd. And she ought to know that a lady goes upstairs as soon as she comes home to take her hat off. That way, she could sort her hair out and ensure that it was not a mess. Alexa had read about it in Miss Graham's copy of *The Lady*. Eleanor deposited a cute little kiss on Alexa's cheek.

Alexa struggled to return her smile; something distracted her and she looked over Eleanor's shoulder. Her scalp prickled. The walls of the parlour had changed. The periwinkle-blue had disappeared. In its place was beige; dull, ordinary and a little like the colour of undercooked toast.

'Ah, you've noticed, Alexa.' Eleanor seemed to find her expression amusing. 'We had to make the change, my dear. There was the most awful storm earlier in the year, and the French windows leaked dreadfully. So, we fixed the doors and I had the decorators in. And picked out this shade. I think it enhances the paintings, don't you? Well, William thinks so. And, there were the most awful water stains near the windows which we've managed to get rid of. They must have happened some time ago...'

Alexa scanned the walls, wishing to look elsewhere, anywhere but at Eleanor or at her father. Her only respite was that the Rosewarne oils were all back in their places.

'Now, Alexa, have you had tea?' her father asked, but did not wait for an answer. 'Juliet, could you please fetch us a fresh pot. We're gasping.'

Alexa plumped herself down in an armchair, surreptitiously eyeing the rest of the parlour, wondering if anything else had been changed. Eleanor sat, too, and Alexa noticed the strange drape of her dress – it did nothing for her. In fact, it made her look positively matronly, and Alexa remembered Eleanor as being a bit of a stick.

Her father perched close to Eleanor and leant into her ear as they proceeded to talk to each other in muffled tones. Eleanor cast occasional sharp eyes at Alexa who sat, resolutely ignoring them and continuing to glare around at the awful beige walls.

When Juliet came in with the tray, Alexa's father said, 'Now, Alexa, while we have tea, we want to talk to you about something.'

And Juliet asked, quite mysteriously, 'Mr William, do you mind if I stay?'

Her father looked briefly puzzled and then nodded.

Juliet caught Alexa's eye, gave her a warm look and began to pour the tea. Eleanor sat very still.

'You see, Alexa, my dear,' her father leaned forward in his chair, 'you may wish to congratulate your stepmother.'

Alexa glanced at Eleanor. He'd reminded her, suddenly, that this was what this stranger was to her.

Her father cleared his throat. 'We are very pleased to announce that we have started a child.'

'Started a—' Alexa's question dropped away. Eleanor's face broke in two with a rigid grin.

Juliet quickly sat on the arm of Alexa's chair, taking her hand in hers and bounced it on her lap.

'A child?' Alexa coughed the word.

'It's due in the autumn,' Eleanor said brightly. 'So God knows, I've got to get through a hot summer the size of a bus.'

Alexa ignored her and turned to her father.

'But you're letting Juliet go!' she cried. 'Why is Juliet leaving, when there is going to be another baby!'

'Ah, well, that's a different matter. We have plans in place...' her father looked at Eleanor, motioning for her to elaborate.

'Yes, you see, it has worked out quite well,' Eleanor offered. 'With Juliet leaving – oh, it's all so very sad,' she directed a strong look to Alexa's right, to where Juliet was sitting, perched on the arm, 'but, you see, my aunt lives in Little Porthdeen. Oh, you've not met Rose yet, have you, Alexa? She will be the baby's nanny. She's had lots of children. All grown now, flown the nest, of course. She'll be perfect.'

Alexa looked up at Juliet, whose face, in her effort not to cry, had contracted into a web of wrinkles.

She could only manage a whisper, as she squeezed her nanny's hand in her own.

'But it's Juliet, Dad.'

'Life changes, it moves on,' said her father, sounding irritated. 'Alexa, you must learn this. There are choices that grown-ups must make. Some of them beyond our control. The sooner you realise this, the better.'

His brutal words stung Alexa. Sitting next to him, Eleanor gazed artlessly out of the window, casually smoothing down the front of her dress, oblivious to Alexa's horror and Juliet's stifled tears.

10

'Do stay in touch,' Eleanor demanded of Juliet two days later. She stood in the hall by the door to the parlour, itching to get back to her novel or magazine, or whatever it was she had interrupted to say goodbye.

By the front door, Juliet shook Alexa's father's hand and they spoke quietly and privately for a minute. William's voice was rich with sentiment. Juliet, wearing her second-best hat for travelling, nodded hard at him, finishing with her crumpled handkerchief pressed to her mouth. Outside, the taxi driver hooted, conscious of the railway timetable.

Juliet beckoned to Alexa, sitting on the bottom stair, and they walked outside.

Alexa fixed her eyes on the trimmings on Juliet's hat, fascinated as the breeze teased its purple feathers. A memory slipped in sideways: Mamma and Nonna walking in the park, feathers and fringes fluttering. Nonna giving her the photograph taken in Venice. Juliet tried to extract herself, removing her arm from Alexa's tightening grasp, easing herself gently away. Alexa held on.

'I'm sorry. So sorry. I have to go, *mia cara*,' Juliet said, her smile crooked. 'Try not to mind so much. It will pass. You be a good girl for your dad.' Juliet glanced back at the house. 'He is a sad man,' she said. 'He still is a very sad man.'

Alexa did not care that her father was sad; all she was aware of was a sickening, grinding ache, a void opening in the ground before her. The moment of loss returned: the doctor looking across Mamma's bedroom, the grave shake of his head.

Juliet pressed on her a piece of paper. 'My address in Italy. I will write to you. We will write, always, yes?'

'Always,' said Alexa.

The taxi driver honked again and Alexa saw Juliet's face wither.

Juliet went to say something but, instead, clamped her mouth shut, dipped her head and got into the car. The driver shut the door with a conclusive thump. And in the firing up of an engine, a crank of a hand-brake and a rumble of tyres over the ground, Juliet, and the whole of Alexa's childhood, manoeuvred through the gates and left Porthdeen.

* * *

Alexa remained very still, scarcely breathing, trying not to move in case she fell into the hole widening before her. Behind her, her father and Eleanor went inside and shut the door. The sound of the taxi receded, leaving an enormous silence that was soon, and inevitably, broken by a squad of seagulls bickering overhead.

Alexa walked to the gates and proceeded to shut them. She shivered as she grasped the rough surface of the rusted railings, leaning forward to rest her forehead on the back of her hands. The noise of the taxi engine returned, carried as it negotiated the bends and the curves of the lane over the headland, leaving a teasing sound in its wake. It retreated for a moment or two, and then came another burst. And then nothing. Absolutely nothing.

Squeezing her eyes tight, Alexa sucked in the air, tasting the ephemeral flavour of the sea. She heard the chink of a shoe on flint and Harvey appeared at the top of the path from Little Porthdeen. Over his arm lay his broken shotgun, a leather bag bulging with rabbits from the top fields. He stopped on his side of the gate and tilted his face at her in question. She shook her head, and he opened the gate, placing his hand on her arm. His gesture was neither coaxing nor comforting but simply the most natural thing he could have done.

She said, 'Juliet's just gone.'

Harvey's face fell. He shook his head with a spark of anger. 'Oh hell, Alexa.'

'And my stepmother is having a baby.'

He sucked in his breath, his eyes sharpening with surprise.

'Can we go down to the cove?' she said. 'Today, I really want to be by the sea. I'll go in, too, right in, I don't care any more.'

'Alexa, I can do better than that,' Harvey said. 'Come sailing with me.'

She nodded, hurried past him, making a head start to the cliff path; she didn't want him to see her tears of gratitude.

As they descended, the freshening breeze sent white froth over the surface of the sea. Below the swell, churned-up sand clouded the water so that it resembled murky soup, reminding Alexa of the shade Eleanor had painted the parlour walls. Harvey called after her, 'You need to get out on those waves, Alexa, let the wind blow, feel the salt spray.'

She shouted back over her shoulder, 'I think that wind will blow us all the way to America.'

'I expect you imagine that's not such a bad thing,' Harvey said, catching her up.

He noticed the tears drying on her cheeks and offered gently, 'I remember you finding an empty seagull egg along here somewhere.'

'I've still got it.'

'I thought you might.'

Alexa was relieved to reach the shelter of Little Porthdeen harbour, for she had come out without her hat and her hair was being whipped by the breeze.

'Juliet would be so cross with me,' she said with a need to mention her. 'For going about in public without a hat. Can't imagine what my hair looks like.'

She heard Harvey laugh.

'It's all right, Alexa. Always is.'

Little Porthdeen was as busy as ever. Harvey's little skiff, Indigo Moon, with its one blue sail, was moored at the far end of the quay, dwarfed by a fishing lugger unloading its catch. A couple of men supping outside the Three Pilchards greeted Harvey by tipping their caps, and Alexa noticed two women emerge from an alley and head for the baskets of fish arranged on the quayside cobbles.

'It's Sarah and her mother,' said Alexa, a tad unenthusiastically, gritting her teeth. 'We ought to say hello.'

'A brisk morning for July, isn't it?' said Joan Carmichael, greeting them with a sharp glance at Alexa's wayward hair.

Joan, head and shoulders shorter than her daughter, embodied her role as widow and mother in long skirt and drab high-crowned hat, her reddened hands clutching a scarf close to her throat.

'My, may I say, you are growing up so fast, Miss Alexa,' she said. 'It's hard to imagine you are still at school. Back home for the holidays now, are you?'

'Yes, Mrs Carmichael, Porthdeen for the summer,' said Alexa, sounding much brighter than she felt.

'I can't ever have imagined having to go away to school like you do,' Sarah commented. She glanced at Harvey with a shy smile. 'Like you both have done.'

'Well your days at the village school are long past, Sarah,' her mother quickly reminded her.

Sarah recoiled, her face twitching with mortification.

Joan asked, 'And how is everyone up at Porthdeen, Miss Alexa?'

'Ah, now there is a tale,' said Harvey gently. Alexa gave him an appreciative glance.

'I'm afraid Juliet left us today, Mrs Carmichael,' said Alexa, treading over her words carefully. 'And it's quite a blow.'

'My poor *cheel*, after one thing and another,' ventured Joan. 'Rose Hammett mentioned it to me. And I hear there is a new baby on the way.'

Harvey placed his hand on Alexa's shoulder. 'News travels fast,' he said.

'But where is Juliet going?' Sarah asked.

'Back to Italy. She has a job there, and my stepmother wanted to make changes at home. Which I suppose is to be expected... ' Alexa trailed off, not wanting to explain it all.

'Imagine, mother,' said Sarah, leaping in, 'having a nanny like Juliet to look after all the children. That's been my job for the last ten years.'

'And I'm sure you are very good at it, Sarah,' said Harvey.

Sarah seemed to shrivel under his attention. Her cheeks flushed red and she stared down at the cobbles, biting her lip.

'I see you've been busy up on the top fields, Mr Ferris,' Joan Carmichael gestured to Harvey's shotgun and bag of rabbits. 'And your studies?' she pressed on. 'When should I be addressing you as Doctor Ferris?'

'I've still got a while to go, Mrs Carmichael.'

Alexa noticed that Sarah had recovered and was gazing admiringly at Harvey.

'So, where are you two—'

Sarah was cut off by the arrival of her younger sister, Lizzie, trailing the two smaller twin Carmichael girls. They were all of a piece: fair, noisy and rumbustious, and quite in contrast to Sarah's brittle and lanky awkwardness.

'Mother!' cried Lizzie, rosy of face, her eyes gleaming with the importance of her mission. 'You'd better get over there quickly. They are selling out of pilchards.'

'Goodness, you're a proper fishwife, Lizzie,' Joan uttered. 'We must be off, Miss Alexa. Can't stand here talking. We've fish to buy.'

Sarah put her hand on Harvey's sleeve, delaying any departure, spinning out their pleasantries. 'But where are you two going?'

'Out in the skiff,' Alexa answered for him. 'Harvey says it will do me good and cheer me up. But have you seen the swell? I must be mad.'

'How exciting,' Sarah cried. 'I'd love to—'

Her mother nudged her daughter, shook her head.

'I'm afraid, Sarah,' Harvey said cautiously, 'Indigo only has room for two. One crew, one skipper.'

Joan laughed rather too loudly and gave her eldest daughter a hard stare. 'Perhaps another time, then, Mr Ferris.'

Sarah's blush deepened, her disappointment visible as she nervously spun a loose length of her hair around her finger, tucking it back behind her ear.

'It's been lovely talking to you.' Alexa said.

Sarah blanked her, spoke only to Harvey as she said a reluctant goodbye.

And Harvey, ever the gentleman, blustered on with, 'Yes, of course, another time, Sarah, another time.'

* * *

Watching the family drifting off to buy fish, Alexa followed Harvey down the stone steps to where Indigo Moon was moored. She stepped lightly into the little craft, taking her seat at the helm.

'Always a gentle sort of girl, Sarah is, so much more reserved compared to the rest of the tribe,' Harvey said as he stowed his gun and bag below the seat and lifted the oars to manoeuvre the skiff clear of the harbour wall.

'Always seems a little odd to me,' said Alexa. She caught Harvey's critical look, and corrected herself. 'But yes, as you said... a sweet girl. It's just that we've never been friends, real friends. She's a lot closer to you in age. She's always been so much taller than me.'

Harvey chuckled as they moved out of the harbour.

'As for these poor little beggars,' said Alexa, indicating the bagged game under her seat. 'They didn't stand a chance once you got them in your sights.'

'You enjoy rabbit pie, do you not, Alexa?' asked Harvey.

'Yes, I do, very much,' she conceded. 'Can't cook it to save my life, however.'

They were both laughing as they touched open water. Harvey dealt with the ropes, unfurled the sail, secured it, let the blue sheet fill with air, catch the wind and turn the boom. Within moments, Indigo Moon was cutting a diagonal line around the headland, with Alexa keeping a firm grip on the helm, fixing her eye, as Harvey and her father had taught her, on a point at Enys Rocks to set their course.

Unlike the sheltered cove below Alexa's home, Enys Point was vulnerable to everything the sea had in its armoury. And the water today, as they steered around the cliff, was becoming quite frantic, the waves cresting at a foot high.

Alexa thought of how her mother would not have liked her to go paddling on a day like today, let alone out on a boat. But if she could see her now, safe here with Harvey, she'd see what a good sailor he was, and how much she trusted him.

'The wind must be a moderate, stronger than I realised,' Harvey called to her. 'Shall I take it? Is your arm aching?'

'It is indeed, skipper.'

They swapped places. With the ropes secure, the sail taut and without a task to perform until the wind decided to change, Alexa watched the sea, wondering how far into her journey Juliet was now. She listened to the low, monotonous roar of the ocean, the continuous slap of water against the prow, felt occasional spray on her cheeks. Sailing to her was logical, rhythmic and natural. The sea all around her was a wilderness and she welcomed it, as its freshness began to blow away the blackness inside her.

'I know that you are thinking of Juliet,' called Harvey. 'I'm so sorry.'

Alexa was sitting with her back a little towards him, making it difficult to talk properly, but at the same time, somehow easier. For her mind was filled with Juliet, Mamma, everything.

'This is certainly helping,' she threw a smile over her shoulder at him. 'Thank you.'

Harvey was ruminating over something. 'My mother questions the wisdom of your father rushing out of widowhood faster than suits most polite society,' he blurted. 'Not in so many words. She'd never say it like I have just done, blundering on like that, but she says she wonders, sometimes—'

'It's nice of Betty to say,' said Alexa, 'but I don't want to be felt sorry for.' She turned properly to look at Harvey, caught the end of his sorrowful expression. 'I don't want you to feel sorry for me.'

Alexa turned back to her watch, feeling the tug and flow of the tide racing beneath the boat on its way to shore. A sudden switch of the wind caused the sail to snap.

'Best not get too close to Enys Rocks,' Harvey said, leaning hard into the rudder. 'They terrify even me sometimes.'

Alexa looked around sharply. She hadn't realised how close they'd got to the cliff below Ferris House. The rocks at its foot were dark and jagged, a hard buffer for the fractious sea, sending white spray high into the air. At the top of the cliff, she saw the prickly cloud of gorse that sat between the edge of the Ferris property and the sheer drop. Behind it, she could just make out the glossy rhododendron bushes, with the stand of evergreen pines. Beyond were the glorious Ferris lawns, gardens and terraces. The house itself, imposing as it was, was invisible from the sea, but she could picture it so very well; she was always at home there, welcomed by Betty and Arthur. And she realised with a jolt that she hadn't set foot in Ferris House since her mother had died.

* * *

The wind dropped a notch and they settled into smoother waters, the sun daring to peak at them occasionally through sullen cloud. Alexa, sensing the change in the direction of the breeze, unhooked the main rope, loosened the sail, let the boom swing around, pulled the rope tight.

'You're quite the yachtswoman.'

'Hardly!' said Alexa. 'If I am, I don't know where I get it from. You know how my mother had a real fear of the sea.' She leant over the side, let her fingertips break the surface of the water. She licked the saltiness from her skin. 'But I always so desperately wanted to show Mamma that there was nothing to be scared of, not really,' she sighed. 'The sea is beautiful, it is my friend.'

'It is, but there are some days,' said Harvey, 'when it so ferocious, even I wouldn't venture out here. Even on something as sturdy and seaworthy as this beauty.' He tapped the mast with affection.

Alexa said, 'If Mamma could see me now, what would she say? Don't lean over, don't get too close. Don't even get in the boat! She didn't want me to come out with you without Dad until I was much older, but now, she won't even know how—'

Alexa raised her hand to her eyes as a sob burst out of her. 'You must be strong, Alexa,' Harvey ordered her from his spot at the helm. 'Please be strong.'

'I can't be strong,' she uttered. 'For being strong sounds hard and square, with sharp corners. And I'm none of those things. Not really. I'm not a grown-up like Mrs Carmichael thinks. Like everyone seems to expect me to be. They all think I should take this in my stride. But how can I? I'm still a girl.'

Harvey looked poised to leave his post and come to her side, but thought better of it as a strong gust pulled on the sail, jerking the boom in front of Alexa's face.

'Alexa, don't try to hurt yourself even more. Remember that I am right here for you,' he insisted, his words all but taken by the wind.

'Well, that's ridiculous. Soon you won't be.' Alexa disliked the sound of her sarcasm, her wish to test his loyalty, and folded her arms defensively as the ropes in her charge grew slack. 'You're going away to medical school, aren't you? And where did you choose, Harvey? Edinburgh. You couldn't get much further away from Porthdeen if you tried.'

Harvey set his jaw, concentrated for some moments on steering the little skiff as she began to bob off course. A rogue wave breached the boat and splashed him square in the face. He shook his sopping hair out of his eyes.

'Alexa, I've explained that to you,' he said, his voice unusually tight with patience. 'It is because Edinburgh happens to be an excellent school of physicians, and I will be conveniently near my aunt Margaret in Oban. But that aside... Alexa, look at me...'

Alexa turned to face him, struggling as the wind whipped her hair around her face.

'That aside, even if I'm not here physically, I am in every other way. Do you understand what I mean?'

He waited for an answer, which Alexa refused to give.

'Plus,' he said, mollifying her, 'I won't be going away for another year. And I'll be back. We doctors in training get some holidays, you know.'

'I know that!' she cried, suddenly irritated and hating the way she felt bound to Harvey, reliant on him to look after her. 'But despite that, none of this is right. None of it is! Juliet is gone, and there is to be a baby,' she cried. 'And I don't know what to do with it all. How do you think I should behave, Harvey?'

'Alexa, if I knew I would tell you.'

She turned to look at him. The skiff was going her own merry way, the rocks at Enys Point behind them, the waves lively and choppy. She knew she should work the ropes, help bring them back on course, head towards the shore.

Instead, she asked, 'Why do you care so much?'

Harvey's face was pinched with anxiety, his soft, tawny hair lifting off his forehead. He looked like the boy again, the boy he'd been when she'd first noticed him all that time ago. Where or when, she could not say. On the quayside? At a St Just cricket match? Had their families' cars squeezed passed each other on the top lane? Perhaps it was when he'd first come to visit, brought over to Porthdeen by Betty Ferris for tea with Mamma. Harvey Ferris had always been there whenever she turned around. Why did he care?

He looked bewildered and unable to explain himself. And Alexa was suddenly weary, wanting to be home.

'It's all right, Harvey, you don't have to answer.'

'Next time we do this, you will feel better, I promise you will,' he called into the wind.

Alexa knew that he would keep his word, knew he'd take her out again, that they'd cut through the waves together on Indigo Moon. But for a strange reason that was beyond her, she did not want to.

11

Chilled and tired from being out on the water for the whole afternoon, Alexa made herself a hot chocolate and ran a bath. Once the roar of the tank refilling had subsided, to be replaced by the gentle dripping of the tap, Alexa lay back, submerged herself and closed her eyes. But, instantly, the new and unfamiliar pitch of Eleanor's voice reached her as she chattered downstairs, punctuated by the occasional and brief responses of her father.

Alexa took a sip from the hot chocolate cup perched on the edge of the bath and pulled a face. It was nothing like Juliet's. Miss Graham had been right when she suggested that Porthdeen might not necessarily be the place she should escape to. Surely, there was one room left where she'd find a little solace.

Dressed again after her bath, Alexa opened the door to her mother's bedroom. The room was hibernating and dark. Stealing across the rug, she pulled back one curtain so that the summer's evening light eased itself in, brightening the shadows but not quite reaching the furthest corners.

As Alexa opened the wardrobe door, the spice of Mamma's perfume revived itself, pinning her in a thousand memories. But in the half darkness, she could not see how much was left of her mother's things. When Eleanor moved in she'd wasted no time in altering the blue parlour. What else had she done? An appalling memory of the way Eleanor had slipped past her and Dad as they stood in the doorway to Mamma's bedroom, the way she'd so efficiently come in here to cover her face with the sheet, flared in her mind. Alexa reached up into the darkness of the wardrobe and sank her fingers into Mamma's fur coat.

'Thank God,' she whispered, her eyes watering with relief. 'Thank God she has enough sense to leave this alone.'

Her mother's hat boxes, lined the top shelf and were labelled:

Worth

and

Jeanne Lanvin

And below the rail of gowns, coats and two-pieces lay a row of shoe boxes. Alexa knelt and popped one open. Silk dancing slippers, moulded gently to the shape of Mamma's feet, lay wrapped in tissue paper. Alexa smiled at the dirty imprints of her father's shoes on the toes.

As she leant in further, the bottom of a dress brushed her cheek. She teased it out and crushed the fabric in her hands. The last time Mamma had worn it was when she went to have her hair bobbed with Nonna in London. Juliet, desperate for normality, must have unpacked her suitcase as soon as they arrived home.

Alexa took off her dress and slipped her mother's on. It was too long for her, and baggy over the bust, but suited her beautifully, like a light and delicate embrace. And, within its fibres, Mamma's scent intensified. Breathing in greedily, she noticed *Middlemarch* on the dressing table, the bookmark that she had so naughtily moved still between the pages. A prickle of guilt gave her new impulse and she began to methodically open the drawers, looking for Mamma's button box. She found lipstick cases, a dish filled with strings of beads and a brush and comb stowed in a drawstring bag. Alexa pulled out the brush, searched for hair, but Mamma had been meticulous and kept her brushes spotlessly clean.

A bottom drawer was stuffed with paperwork, theatre programmes, postcards and souvenir tickets from long-forgotten train journeys. Alexa ran her fingers over them, wondering where Mamma might keep her most precious thing.

A brochure caught her eye, and she pulled it out, squinting at it in the dim light.

These are the times to travel,

the headline confidently announced,

this is the service to use!

Below it was a flamboyant illustration of a large steamer at sea with the ports of call listed: Southampton, Cherbourg, Queenstown, New York.

Fragments of memory fitted together. School. Sitting at her desk at the back of a history lesson learning about a terrible maritime disaster the year she was born, chilled by the disturbing details, the numbers drowned, the numbers that should have been saved. She had not understood then. But she did now and reality stacked up like blocks of ice inside her.

Alexa heard herself urging her mother: 'The ship, Mamma, tell me about the big ship.'

Her blood stood still.

That's why Mamma had been so terrified of the sea. Mamma had refused to board the Titanic.

Alexa's hands shook as she stuffed the brochure back in its place. She sat down on the bed and rested her head on her knees.

No wonder Mamma had refused to tell her the bedtime story at Half Moon Street. Alexa had begged for it, to help her to get to sleep when, really, all she'd wanted was Mamma's attention. And now the truth of it rang in her face. Her mother's choice meant that she would be born and that Luke, Edith and their unborn child, taking their place, drowned in the icy North Atlantic.

With a whimper of pain, she wrenched open another drawer, pulled out stockings, underwear, cardigans. She plunged her hands deep through layers of folded jerseys, knickers, nightgowns.

'Oh, where is it?' she asked. 'Where on earth is it?'

She heard her father's voice behind her.

He stood in the doorway, a silhouette against the brighter landing.

'Oh good God, Alexa, I thought you were—'

She stuttered, caught in the act, wearing her mother's dress. 'I'm so sorry, Dad, I was just trying it on.'

He nodded vigorously, his face white in the gloom, his eyes wide. She saw no anger, just intense curiosity. Relief made her sway a little.

He took a tentative, shy step as if reacquainting himself with the space.

'It's all been shut up for a while. Is there something you wanted? You can have anything, you know. Anything you like.'

'The button box,' said Alexa. 'Mamma's button box. I can't find it. I'm sorry if I've made a mess. I will clear it up. But, I can't find it. She kept it here. Always here.'

'Ah, yes, the button box.'

Her father came forward and, as if he was helping her look for it, made a cursory glance around the room.

'You loved it, didn't you?'

Alexa bent to the next drawer, finding a pair of elongated evening gloves the colour of ivory and with the finest, most delicate fingers.

'I did, Dad. I do. I just want to find it. Oh, where—'

'I wonder,' he began, scratching his fingers absently through his hair. 'I wonder if Juliet... yes, perhaps she did.'

'What, Dad?' Alexa was exasperated. She sat back down, light-headed from her frantic search, her fingers still moving, feeling for the misplaced and the invisible.

'I think Juliet must have packed it, taken it with her,' said Dad. 'As a memento, perhaps? She loved your mother, Alexa. Pretty much brought her up. All those buttons... perhaps she saw them as her own?'

But they were the story of Mamma's life. Alexa lowered her head against an extraordinary burst of rage. Her anger shocked her, for it was directed at Juliet: for leaving her, so abruptly, alone in all this chaos. And for taking the one treasure that meant the most to her. The idea of it, the full montage of betrayal, left scorch marks in her mind.

She stood up and went to the window. She yanked the curtain across, closing the room to darkness. Her father waited for her on the landing.

'Dad, I did a silly thing,' she said, closing the bedroom door. Her father cocked his head at her.'I wrote to Nonna. You see, there was a terrible argument when Mamma and I left Half Moon Street.'

'I gathered as much.'

'And then I heard you talking angrily on the telephone. To the maid, was it? And I wanted to speak to Nonna. I keep thinking that she must be feeling so awful now. Perhaps worse than we do...'

Her father uttered a feeble and uncomfortable affirmation. 'There has always been such a dreadful animosity from Montgomery,' he said. 'We were hoping the trip for your twelfth birthday, for you and Mamma would set us on the right track. Evidently not.'

'But my letter was returned. It was when I was at school. Miss Graham gave it back to me.'

'Ah, well that makes sense,' her father said. He had reached the stairs and paused, his fingers drumming the top of the bannister. 'I heard, last autumn. I think you had gone to Trengrouse by then. Your grandmother and Mr Montgomery left for Venice. The maid told me. I'd telephoned again and she was packing up the London house. Like you, I desperately wanted to speak to them. I wanted to talk about your mother.' Raw pain contracted his features. 'I'm so very sorry, Alexa, I thought that they would be able to leave the past in the past,' he said, his apology drifting into nothing.

You should be sorry, she screamed inside, *for you have let all of this happen.*

But, seeing the look on his face, she swallowed hard on her anger, 'It's all right, Dad.'

'Come down and have tea with us,' he rallied, his voice lighter, back to normal. 'Eleanor has put the kettle on. But it's the last of Juliet's Genoese sponge, I'm afraid.'

'Then I wonder if Eleanor's Aunt Rose can bake,' Alexa offered, her words false and bright.

'We live in hope, Alexa,' he said, giving her a crooked smile. 'We live in hope.'

* * *

Alexa told her dad that she would be down in a moment, went into her bedroom and sat on the bed. She pulled the slip of paper out of her pocket.

Juliet's handwriting was clear, rounded and beautiful. When she'd taught Alexa to write, all that time ago, Alexa had tried her hardest to emulate it. She got nowhere near.

Alexa read Juliet's new address: a villa, in a village, somewhere in Tuscany.

And so, they had all left her. All of them.

With a groan of despair, Alexa screwed the paper, twisted it, tugged it, ripped it in half. She struck a match, set fire to it, watched it burn in the grate.

PART II

12

MIDDLE OF SPRING, 1930

The view from Alexa's bedroom window changed by the hour. First cloud, streaked and coloured like marble, banked high over the sea. And now sun, glittering on the green rise of the Enys Point headland. The path was empty and it was no use looking out for Harvey yet, she told herself, for he was not due back from Edinburgh until the weekend.

Alexa looked down at the letter she'd started. Her handwriting was not up to scratch, and Juliet would not have approved. Anyway, she'd only got as far as writing the date, her address and the first couple of lines:

Cornish Girl Friday seeks position as companion to Lady in London,

Something held her back. The idea of finishing and sending the letter made her thoughts loop with trepidation. For if it all turned out as she planned, she would leave Porthdeen and not see the scene before her – or see Harvey – for a very long time indeed.

Five whole summers had passed since Juliet left. Time stretched and contracted; time in which Alexa had set herself the challenge, three years ago when she left school, of extending her education by reading every book in her father's library, while successfully side-stepping the most unsavoury nursery duties relating to her new half-sister.

Over these years, Juliet's letters had dwindled to nothing and Alexa's anger about the button box had not faded as such, but now resembled a film of dust over the window pane, half-invisible but still able to obscure her vision.

Alexa shifted in her chair, hearing the old rattan creak comfortably beneath her. She remembered sitting here by the window, in the late September after Juliet's departure, watching the first of the autumn storms roll in from the sea. Her return to school that term had been delayed by a nasty chest cold, caught while out sailing with Harvey. Despite her peculiar reluctance, he'd been typically persuasive and she'd caved in to the solace his company gave her, spending most of the summer of 1925 out on Indigo Moon and had had to suffer the ministrations of Doctor Paynter, whom she still loathed, as a consequence.

And along with the storms, quite early for that time of year, came the midwife for Eleanor. Perched on this very chair to remove her stockings later at bedtime, her school trunk packed and ready, Alexa had heard the baby's first invasive cry. She'd braced herself, tightened her shoulders, wishing to plug her ears, but Melissa's mewling had the propensity to dig its way into the softest part of her.

Alexa could hear her half-sister bawling now down below in the courtyard. But, at nearly five years old, she cried the harder, more considered pitch of a child manipulating her way through her world. Perhaps a hen had pecked her, perhaps she'd fallen over, grazed her knee? Perhaps she simply wanted to cry. Alexa caught Aunt Rose's voice drifting upwards, the reverberation of her thick Cornish accent, appeasing Melissa, pussyfooting around her, telling her that she was a bonny *cheel*, to go and find her favourite toys, of which there were a great many littering the floors of Porthdeen.

As well as the storms arriving prematurely in the autumn of 1925, the baby had done so too. Her father had married Eleanor early in the March – just shy of seven months before Melissa had been born. And Alexa had no doubt that the undue haste of their nuptials, with Mamma not dead a year, was the talk of the village. Alexa imagined Mrs Carmichael spelling it out to Sarah by the fireside of their cramped cottage, counting on her fingers. For surely, they'd whisper, a girl from Truro like Eleanor would have wanted all the trappings associated with marrying Porthdeen parish's most noted landowner, rather than the quiet affair they'd had. What's more, Melissa was such a robust, sturdy baby for one so premature.

Alexa picked up her pen, took a deep breath and willed herself to concentrate on her letter. But straight away, she heard a light tread on the stairs and, seconds later, the slow turning of the doorknob. Melissa crept her way into the bedroom as if Alexa could not see her, the drama from downstairs wiped away by a calculating smile, trailing behind her the unfortunate doll that she was in the process of pulling the hair out of.

Gazing at her half-sister, Alexa knew exactly what Eleanor would have looked like as a child. Melissa had a wiry little frame, tapering limbs and thin fair hair that Eleanor had cut so badly it flicked annoyingly around her temples. Her face, however, was extraordinary, as if it had been plucked from a Botticelli.

'Hello, Lexa,' Melissa chimed, 'What you doing?'

'Writing a letter, Melissa. What are you doing?'

'Nothing,' she said, the word sprawling behind her as she launched herself towards the doll on Alexa's shelf. 'Oh, your dolly! What's it called?'

Alexa stood up and hurried over just as Melissa reached up to the shelf where she kept her treasures: George the doll, her books and trinkets, and the two halves of her seagull eggshell still nestled in a crumpled handkerchief. Melissa began to tug George by her foot and Alexa rescued the doll and cradled it in her hands, at the same time allowing Melissa to clutch at it, to maul the hair, dress and face.

'This is George, and she is very precious to me, so love her carefully. Gently, Melissa.'

The child paused with her fumbling and surprisingly delicately, thoughtfully, rested her cheek against the cold china one.

'George, ahhh.'

Alexa experienced an unusual shot of warmth for the little girl, and believed that, somewhere on earth, it might be called love.

'Now, tell me what you've been up to. Not worrying your auntie Rose, I hope.'

There was no answer.

Melissa let go of the doll and grabbed the small jewellery box that Alexa had found in an antiques shop in Penzance last year.

'What's this, Lexa?'

'It's my new button box, Melissa. I've shown it to you before. Don't you remember? You are to be careful with that, too.'

'Oh, yes. Button box. Mummy says buttons are dangerous. I can choke. If I am a baby, I can choke.'

'What's that, Melissa?'

But the girl ignored her, fingering the little metal latch. Alexa helped her open the lid to reveal the midnight-blue velvet interior, home to just a handful of her own buttons collected since Juliet left.

Alexa said, 'You see, my Mamma once had a beautiful button box. I loved to look at the buttons when I was a little girl, like you. And I was very careful, too. Just like you are being. But this is my own.'

Alexa shook the buttons so Melissa could see the two dozen or so scatter around the dark lining.

'Perhaps, one day, I will give them to my own little girl.'

'No,' said Melissa, suddenly disinterested, peeling herself away. 'No buttons. Mummy says we will choke.'

Alexa felt a sudden cold crescendo of unease.

'Melissa, why did Mummy say that about the buttons?'

But the little girl had moved on, spun around and lunged for Alexa's pen and writing case, scattering a sheet or two to the floor. Alexa squatted and asked her to be more careful as she gathered her papers together.

A car horn tooted and Melissa dived for the window. Eleanor, home from dress shopping in Truro, had pulled up on the lane in the Ford and was waiting patiently, two gloved hands on the steering wheel, for someone to come and open the gates for her. Melissa yelped with pleasure and ran off downstairs.

Alexa watched from the window as her half-sister belted across the gravel and flung herself at the gate, jumping up and down and shouting for her mother. Aunt Rose trotted out, plum-faced and rotund, to deal with the gates and persuade her bonny *cheel* Melissa to get out of the way of the car. Before Eleanor had even closed the driver's door, Melissa threw herself at her, burying her face in the folds of her coat and Alexa's ill-ease stirred into sudden and clear-sighted anger.

If only she'd simply responded to Juliet in the first place, written and asked her outright if she'd taken the button box. Then she would have realised what had really happened. Alexa watched

Eleanor bend to kiss the top of her daughter's head and the scene below blurred with tears.

* * *

Alexa couldn't remember a time she had ever voluntarily gone to her stepmother's bedroom. With lurching stomach and trembling fist, she rapped on the door and a single bright word told her she could come in.

Eleanor was in her slip, the clothes she had been wearing for her shopping trip in a puddle on the floor, her purchases spilling out of tissue paper on the bed. She was furiously brushing her hair in front of the full-length mirror, twisting her head so she could see the back of it.

'Oh, Alexa, come in, sit down, what a nice surprise,' said Eleanor, trying to quell the astonishment in her voice. 'You should have come with me to Truro. We must spend more time together, shopping and having tea and luncheon, you know that sort of thing.'

Alexa gingerly squashed herself in among the open boxes and tissue paper on the bed, equally fascinated and repelled by the knobs of her stepmother's spine visible above the back of the slip, the hipbones moving under the silk, the rather nasty-looking bunion on otherwise dainty stockinged feet.

'I saw a darling dress for you,' Eleanor breezed on, evidently not swayed by Alexa's visit, her mute anger. 'Perfect little tea dress. Little frills here, and here.' She indicated her collarbone and elbow. 'Just your colour, too.'

Alexa glanced at the costumes exploding from their boxes. 'I see you've found plenty in your colour.'

'Help me hide them,' Eleanor urged, leaping on her with unexpected chumminess. 'He won't notice if I bring a new one out once a month. You know, we're about the same size. You can borrow whatever you like.' Eleanor tore at the loose hair in the bristles of her brush and let it drift onto the rug. 'Just ask me first, all right?'

Staring at her stepmother's hair lying on the floor, Alexa pictured Mamma's meticulously clean hairbrushes and despair billowed inside her head.

'Eleanor?' she swallowed hard, her mouth dry. 'Eleanor?'

'What, dear?'

Eleanor at last turned her uninterested face but Alexa could barely look at her. She churned her hands together, blurted, 'Have you seen my mother's button box?'

'Her button... what?'

'Her button box.'

'Not sure if I have—'

'Mamma – actually, Juliet – had collected all the buttons she'd ever had since she was a very little girl in Venice.'

Alexa saw Eleanor flinch when she said Mamma for that word was rarely heard at Porthdeen any more.

'She had them all in a lovely rosewood box. About this big. I haven't seen it for ages. Years, actually.' Alexa spoke quickly. Stopped, took a large breath, watched her stepmother's cheeks redden, her eyes water with embarrassment, and memory. 'Well, I've started my own, as it happens. I'm using that jewellery box I bought a while ago in Penzance. Remember? No, perhaps you don't. I want to gather all the buttons together. And—'

Eleanor's eyes flicked side to side.

'—And you can't find your mother's?' Eleanor finished. Alexa's hopes rose; she desperately wanted to give her a chance.

'Have you ever come across it, Eleanor, in a cupboard or a trunk somewhere?'

Eleanor turned swiftly back to the mirror and continued with her brushing, her voice trailing to nothing. 'No. No, Alexa. Not that. I don't know what you're talking about.'

Alexa watched her stepmother preen for some moments more before excusing herself and leaving the room. As she shut the door, an ancient loss was revived and it was more, so much more than the simple cost of the button box. Something precious had been wasted.

13

Alexa sat on the bench near Mamma's grave. Shadows lengthened among the headstones but the headland rising beyond the graveyard and the church, with its oak door and carved mermaid, still shimmered with light. Over the sea, a milky haze rolled in, blurring the horizon so that she could not tell where the sky and water met.

'I've always hoped that you feel you are not too close to the edge, Mamma,' Alexa whispered, looking to the sky, the ground, wherever her mother may be. 'But the cliff edge is way over there, beyond the wall. You are quite safe.'

Her fresh offering of flowers, foxgloves gathered from the lane on the way up, were a startling pink against the old silver of the granite stone. She knelt to remove the spent flowers from the little urn. They had been the first meadow flowers of the season: wild columbine and cranesbill, now yellowing and way past their best.

'I can't remember if you like foxgloves, Mamma. You see,' Alexa's words clotted on her tongue, 'I won't be able to bring your flowers for much longer. I'm leaving home. And I might not be coming back. I wanted to tell you first.'

The silence was unbroken, absolute. Even the seagulls were

quiet. A tiny blue butterfly wafted up from clouds of cow parsley to rest on top of the gravestone. Alexa put her hand in her coat pocket and ran her finger along the edge of the letter addressed to *Situations Wanted, The Lady.*

'You will be disappointed in me for leaving. I try so very hard, I do. But whenever Eleanor walks into a room, I want to walk out. You won't believe what she did with your button box.' Suddenly, Alexa gave a shout of laughter. 'I really think, Mamma, that I might actually go around the bend if I stay here much longer. But if I could just find Nonna and speak to her, I can mend it for you, for all of us. I'm going to London. I have plans. Have I ever told you about Miss Graham from school, and how she—'

On the far side of the churchyard, a figure slipped into the corner of her eye, squeezing through the narrow gap in the stone stile. But Sarah Carmichael did not look over. Instead, with a concentrated pious look, she picked her way through the gravestones towards Grannie Carmichael's plot.

Alexa watched the young woman bend to place a small posy by the headstone and lift her face as if to sniff the air. She spotted Alexa, and gave her a quick reluctant smile, visibly disappointed at not having the place to herself.

Alexa sat back down on the bench as Sarah began slowly to walk towards her. Her dress was simple, homemade by Aunt Rose, no doubt – the renowned seamstress of Little Porthdeen – and it flattered her slender frame. Her thick blonde hair, usually hidden under a tight hat, was pinned over the top of her head and long strands escaped to trail prettily over her shoulders. On reflex, Alexa touched the ends of her own hair, which straggled limply out from under her hat.

'A lovely afternoon, isn't it?' Sarah said. She sat gingerly down next to Alexa as if any quick movements might disturb her, leaving a politely wide space between them.

'Yes, it is quite lovely,' Alexa agreed, hoping she would not notice the tears burning her eyes.

'Grannie's flowers were a disgrace,' Sarah said. 'She has some fresh ones now.'

'Same here for my mother.'

'Ah, yes. How pretty.' Sarah gave Alexa a nervous glance.

It had been a while since they'd spoken, and sitting close in the spring light, Alexa noticed for the first time that Sarah's youth had faded a notch. She looked a little worn, a little tired. Her cheeks were still smooth, but her complexion was ruddy, made raw by the winter's cold. New, fine lines puckered her forehead.

Realising she was staring, Alexa turned her gaze, struggling to find something else to say. Moments drifted awkwardly by until Sarah suddenly roused herself.

'Oh, you probably haven't heard yet, Alexa. The Ferrises are reviving the Enys Point Ball. And for everyone, this time. Isn't that wonderful.'

'How do you know?'

'I just bumped into Harvey on the quayside. He told me.'

'He's home already?' Alexa fired back, surprised at how cross she felt that she hadn't known.

Sarah twitched her chin, clearly enjoying the superiority of information.

'Mother has told me all about these parties; they're legendary at home. She remembers them from after the war, into the twenties. After she lost father she was in a sorry state, but they lifted her, she said, beautiful dazzling occasions. Of course, she'd only been helping with the silver service. Could watch from the hallway. But now, this time, Harvey says, we will all be dancing.'

Alexa looked down, noticed Sarah was still wearing her winter boots, cracked across the toes.

'I heard all about the Enys Point Balls when I was a child, too.

My mother loved them,' said Alexa. 'They were due to give the last one around the time she died. Mr and Mrs Ferris cancelled it. There hasn't been one since.'

'Ah, yes, I seem to remember...' Sarah rubbed her hands together and screwed up her face, failing to hide her pity. 'It's going to be in several weeks' time. They're extending invitations across the whole parish. But I really can't assume...' she laughed evasively.

'I'm sure Harvey would not miss you out, Sarah.'

Sarah blushed, failing to hide her smile of delight. 'I do hope that I will be on his list.'

Alexa shivered. The mist had crept in silently over the cliff and was enveloping the church, switching the air, making it cold. 'You'll have to excuse me, Sarah,' said Alexa, getting to her feet. 'I've just remembered I have a letter to post.'

'And I must fly, too. Mother's expecting me.'

Sarah said a cheerful goodbye and hurried off towards the stile, wishing to streak ahead, Alexa guessed, so she did not have to walk down the lane with her.

But, Alexa sat straight back down, delight and surprise leaping inside her for Harvey was on the pathway, emerging from the mist.

He stood back to let Sarah pass, lifting his hat and Alexa heard a snatch of a brief exchange of '...keep bumping into each other...'

Sarah laughed shyly and dashed off on her way.

Harvey watched her run down the path for a moment before turning to see Alexa. A warm smile broke over his face and, as Alexa watched him walk towards her, she was captured by a peculiar shyness. The long stretches of time that Harvey was in Edinburgh had not bothered her over the years as much as she had thought they might, for within moments of him coming home, they always fell in together, as if he had never been away. But this time, he seemed different. His long legs carrying his neat tweeds with confidence, the plum-red waistcoat snug under his jacket all worked to attract her, and disturb her. He had become, Alexa realised, a gentleman.

'Hello, stranger,' he said.

He sat down next to her and his presence instantly enriched her, changed the aspect of the day.

'You're back earlier than I expected,' she said.

'And that's a good thing, I take it?'

'It can be.'

'Eleanor said you'd gone for a walk,' Harvey said, smiling at her flippancy. 'And I thought I'd find you up here.'

'You can't always count on that woman to tell the truth.'

Harvey laughed lightly. 'So, what has she done now, Alexa?'

'You don't know the half of it, Harvey. She has thrown away something very precious to me. She has no idea, but she'll regret doing so, I can tell you.'

'What did she throw away?'

'A memento. Oh, you'll think it trivial.' Alexa waved it off, not wanting to explain and take him down that road with her. 'Anyway, I saw you chatting with Sarah. Don't you think her hair is incredibly pretty...?'

'Alexa, look at me.'

But she turned instead to watch the mist feeling its way over the churchyard. The sea had disappeared and the sun was now truly blotted out.

'I asked you to look at me,' said Harvey.

She turned slowly, a shy smile teasing her lips and he returned the joke, appraising her with a mock frown, fighting the deepest of smiles.

'There, now,' he said, 'we've not seen each other since Christmas, Alexa, so let me see... ah, yes. Just as I suspected. Your eyes have certainly changed.'

'What on earth do you mean? Are you studying eyes now, Doctor Ferris?'

'The way you look at me. They are harder, sharper somehow.' He gave in to gentle laughter. 'Remember what we used to say about the seagulls? How we never noticed exactly when their feathers changed from soft-brown to white and grey. The moment their eyes turn that steely blue.'

'But we could never keep track of one bird,' Alexa countered him. 'They are all so alike. It is impossible and, on top of that, tiresome to try. Anyway,' she said. 'I don't know where you've seen herring gulls with blue eyes. They are yellow. An evil spiteful yellow. Is that what you are saying about mine?'

'Oh, Alexa, I'm only teasing. You're taking me seriously. Where has your softness gone?'

'Disappeared, along with my childhood and everything else,' she said sullenly, and their sing-song banter dropped clean away.

'Oh, Alexa, your childhood? But that was inevitable,' he said coaxingly.

'Anyway, it was you who told me to harden up, remember? You were always telling me I must be strong. Well, that's what I'm being right now.'

Harvey shifted closer, his hands, resting on his knees, practically touching hers.

'Alexa, may I tell you something else?'

'No, you may not,' she said and heard an echo of relief in his laugh.

'If you are harder these days,' he said, 'then I only have myself to blame. But I don't think you are. I think you dangerously and beautifully fragile.'

She drew back at the sudden poetry in his words, trying to move out of the shadow of his compliment. Surely, they were simply old friends bickering gently on a bench, both at crossroads in their lives? Harvey, soon to qualify as a doctor and Alexa on the verge of escape to a life yet unimagined. She looked around her. The world beyond the churchyard was blank, white and invisible, blotted out by sea mist. She inhaled a long shuddering draught of the chilled air and stole a glance at Harvey with a flash of joy and a quiet understanding that it might be that he loved her. And still, her old hesitancy crept closer.

He'd sunk back a little, his cheeks flushed, his eyes dampened. He seemed to be waiting for her to speak.

'I remember, Harvey,' she said, her voice thin in the still air, 'years ago when I was in London visiting my grandmother with Mamma...'

Harvey switched his gaze to Carlotta's headstone. 'Oh yes, just before...?'

'There was a moment, in the park. We were walking. They were wearing feathers in their hats and they were so beautiful, so alike. I stood there, all of eleven years old, looking from one to the other and my voice inside said, "that's where I come from".' She caught her breath. 'And I need to find it again, that sense of belonging. And if that means hardening up, growing up and going off in search—'

'You intend to leave Porthdeen?'

'It is certainly on my mind.' As she shifted in her seat, the letter to *The Lady* crackled in her pocket.

Harvey looked winded. He shuffled back on the bench as if to give her more space. He crossed his leg, rested his hand on his chin, considering her. 'You may surprise yourself, Alexa,' his voice lifting with courage, 'and find your happiness right here.'

She didn't believe him and her denial was on the tip of her tongue.

There was not a breath of wind. Alexa existed, suddenly, with

Harvey; just the two of them. Everything else had vanished. She was inside a cage, a loving and peaceful cage.

'I need to pop down to Little Porthdeen,' she said, far too quickly, in case her resolution failed. 'I want to catch the evening post.'

Harvey stood and offered her his arm, but she declined, busying herself by gathering together the spent flowers she'd tidied from her mother's grave. Harvey watched her patiently while she cradled the yellowing petals and dried leaves in her palms, then opened her fingers to allow them to fall through her hands. They scattered the ground around her feet to be taken next time the wind came in off the sea.

14

Alexa picked up the two letters addressed to her from the table in the hall. One was in the looping hand of a stranger, postmarked London, the other local and in writing she knew very well indeed. Sitting at the table that Eleanor had positioned at the far end of the lawn near the lone hawthorn, Alexa took one, then two sips of coffee, not wanting to rush the moment her life might change. Finally, she set her cup down, forced herself to wait another hopeful and quite pleasurable moment before picking up the first envelope and easing her thumbnail under the edge.

Lady Meredith Ainsley's Brompton address was printed across the top of the letter in diminutive type. And in her brief communication below she asked if Alexa would be so kind as to attend an interview at eleven on the morning of the twenty-fourth of June; followed by 'most sincerely'... and signed with a flourish.

Excitement burst with stars in her head. Alexa tried to contain herself, folding the letter discreetly as if it was a piece of precious silk and slotting it safely back inside the envelope. She'd waited four weeks for a response to her advertisement. An interview with Lady Meredith on the twenty-fourth of June? Alexa would have, by then, been eighteen years old for exactly three days. The timing was perfect. This letter was the key to her growing up, her future, it would offer her a world beyond Porthdeen. She turned the thought of London over like a nugget of gold with a curious mixture of elation and fear.

The pure blue of the sky was deceiving, the air cool for early June and Alexa shivered as she opened the second letter. Harvey had addressed the envelope himself, his rounded hand charming and boyish. She tugged the stiff card from the envelope and caught her breath. Puzzled, she read again, turned the card over to look at the back, searching for clues.

Harvey had invited her to a ball at Enys Point. It was to be held on Midsummer's Eve, the day she turned eighteen. And she was the guest of honour. He had kept his promise, made to her on the cliff pathway all that time ago. The ball was for her.

Goosebumps teased her flesh and, in contrast to the curious blossoming she'd felt when she'd read Lady Meredith's letter, Harvey's invitation was like a weight on her back.

'Here you are,' said her father. He was carrying her shawl, bundled up in his hand, his arm a little outstretched from his body as if he did not know what it was, or how to hold it.

Alexa noticed, in the bright morning sun, her father's hair lightened with silver. He had never grown back his moustache, shaved off for his wedding to Eleanor. And, since then, along with his facial hair, he had lost something else. He was still sometimes jovial, sometimes as unaccountably strict as ever, but he was also a curiously lighter man, faded into not a very good copy of himself.

'Eleanor spotted you from her bedroom window,' he explained. 'Told me you might like this if you want to sit out here. It's not the warmest of mornings. Bit of an insipid start to the summer, if you ask me.'

Alexa drew the shawl over her shoulders in silent, uncomfortable wonder at her stepmother's gesture. Perhaps the fate of the button box was pressing on Eleanor. She was trying far too hard to make amends.

'Ah, I see you have your invitation. Ours arrived yesterday,' her father said. 'Isn't this a marvellous idea of Ferris's? A ball at Enys Point. They used to be such marvellous occasions. High time we were jolly again.'

'But, you realise, Dad, that the ball is for me? For my birthday?'

'And why not?'

Alexa pulled her shawl closer to her, not daring to answer.

'Ferris is a fine chap,' said her father, pleased with his summation.

Alexa felt herself smile. 'He is. Always has been,' she offered.

'A gentleman, too. A mean shot when it comes to rabbiting, and I'm sure he'll make a very good doctor,' he said.

'He does have a way, doesn't he?

'Your mother liked him very much. She always had time for him.'

Alexa was astonished. Her father so very rarely mentioned Mamma these days that she struggled to know how to respond.

Watching her, puzzled, he said, 'Alexa, have you changed your hair?'

'Longer hair is back, apparently, so I'm growing it,' she said, surprised that her father had noticed. Eleanor had noticed, of course, and had immediately and gushingly treated her to some curling irons so that she could try for 'a little bit of a wave'. Alexa was hardly going to admit to anyone that the only reason she'd decided to grow it was because of her mild envy of Sarah's hair.

'I wish Lotte had not cut her hair,' her father said abruptly, addressing the horizon, his voice dragging. 'I said she could. I mean, we discussed it, of course, and she was so excited to get it done in London. Simple thing, really. She just wanted to look young again. I said there's no need... I hardly recognised her when she came home, that last, dreadful—'

As Alexa watched the tears in his eyes dry almost as soon as he wept them, an image of Mr Fairling's portrait suddenly came to mind. Had he ever finished it, she wondered. Had he captured Mamma's beautiful hair, the living glow of her eyes? Had he laid the paint down on canvas to preserve her as she – as they all – remembered her? Alexa longed to see the painting, imagined it fiercely in her mind.

'She looked so lovely with it, Dad. Her shorter hair, it really suited her.'

He shook his head; his eyes cold and unreadable.

'As I was saying to you, Alexa,' he said, 'Harvey Ferris has a great deal going for him. His career, his house, the land. And he is a tremendous chap, to start with.'

'He has always been such a great friend.'

'And now?' Her father's face brightened with a worrying eagerness.

'Still, the greatest of friends... but...' She trailed off, lifting her cup to her lips, not noticing that it was empty.

'A shame you should be undecided. For you won't do much better than him in the whole of the county.'

'I beg your pardon, Dad? What do you mean?'

'I think you should marry him.'

Alexa's cup crashed back to its saucer.

'He is perfect for you. We all see it. Eleanor and I were only saying—' he was interrupted by Melissa darting through the French windows, screaming, her plaited hair flying around her head and a look of unexploded rage on her face.

Alexa heard Eleanor calling her daughter's name from deep inside the house, but Melissa's temper appeared to have rendered her deaf. She hesitated on the terrace for the tiniest of breaths, as if wondering which way she should hurl her anger, when she spotted Alexa and William sitting at the table. She scooted across the lawn, her cheeks brick-red, her eyes like pure-blue bullets.

'What's this, Melissa?' her father sighed with inevitability.

'Why can't I go to the ball!' Melissa bawled.

Alexa's skin prickled with urgency. She needed to escape her rising irritation with her half-sister and the danger of her father's conversation. She gathered her correspondence together, tucking the letter from Lady Meredith and Harvey's invitation under her shawl.

Her father looked up at her as Melissa pulled herself up onto his lap, clonking him half intentionally on the side of his head as she did so.

'Alexa, you are going to the ball, aren't you?' he said. 'What are you—'

'I'm going in for another cup of coffee, which I am going to take to my room.'

Her father did not notice her deliberately missing the point and her deflection, for his focus was back on his youngest daughter, fending off the slender fingers that were burrowing into his hair.

In the time it took Alexa to walk back across the lawn, her father had given in to Melissa and had begun to play, like a bear with a cub, releasing her to dash around the table, pretending to pounce. Her shrieks of anger switched to yelps of laughter, running rings around him.

* * *

Up in her bedroom, Alexa sipped her coffee and re-read the brief letter from Lady Meredith, and the briefer correspondence from Harvey. *Marry him? Marry him?* The words turned on a tight circle. Another laughing shriek echoed up from the garden.

When Alexa had been Melissa's age, her time with her father had been a more decorous affair of quiet exchanges and pleasant observations. And now he was steering her into the life that everyone expected of her. He wanted to be free of her, free of his past, so he could continue with a clear conscience with Alexa off his hands. And, as for Harvey: he had said that she might find happiness here at home. Did he really mean with him? Surely, it was too obvious, too easy for her to love Harvey.

Alexa found a blank sheet of writing paper, knowing what she had to do. But her coffee had gone stone cold by the time she could bring herself to pick up the pen, draw up some ink, and begin her reply to Lady Meredith.

15

MIDSUMMER'S EVE, 1930

The sun moved slowly around Porthdeen, lighting each room with an intensifying, honeyed blaze. The air was exquisite, almost too perfect to bear, distracting Alexa, making her want to break out of the house, throw herself headlong into the afternoon. The sea below would be relaxed, slopping lazily, she imagined, against the rocks in the cove. She longed to be down there, alone with Harvey, dangling her ankles into the chill of a rock pool, wriggling her toes among the floating green weed; her submerged feet, truncated and white, looking as if they did not belong to her.

But instead, she stood on a low stool in the middle of her bedroom rug, the promise of the day teasing her through the open window, arms lifted from her sides while Aunt Rose fussed around her, giving her miniature orders through the pins in her mouth, her chubby fingers working over her ribs, her fingertips tickling, prodding gently. Melissa sneaked furtive looks at her, bobbing back and forth behind the door, her disgruntlement at not being able to go to the ball seemingly forgotten. 'You're like a bride, losing so much weight,' tutted Rose, tugging the fabric of Alexa's dress tighter around her waist.

Alexa had hardly eaten for days, could manage just a few morsels of her birthday cake with Melissa's wonky icing that morning. Her appetite had been replaced by constant bubbling nerves, her plans simmering under the surface, anticipation creeping through her.

Under her bed her suitcase was hidden, packed with, first and foremost, the photograph of Mamma and Juliet, followed by other things she would need for the next days, months, years, she was not sure. How long might Lady Meredith Ainsley want her for? She seemed to be an impulsive woman. After inviting her for an interview, Lady Meredith had written again the next day and offered her the job; Alexa's departure from Porthdeen was settled.

Every second that passed, this vast unknown future, and the moment Alexa was to abandon the only world she knew hurtled nearer. She wanted it, and yet it terrified her. If she could just get the ball over with, she'd feel better.

She will tell her father tomorrow in the late morning of the post-party haze. Then she will tell Harvey. And she'll leave Porthdeen on Monday to catch her train, wishing for her father and Eleanor's blessing, a farewell from Harvey at the station. Find a guest house near Paddington for the night. Meet Lady Meredith at her Cadogan Square home on Tuesday. Her secret plans opened like a small flower in her mind.

And yet, as the clocks ticked on and the time for the ball eased closer, Alexa's anxiety approached her in waves, each one more urgent and sickening than the last. How was she going to tell Dad? She glanced at Melissa. The little girl was swinging on her bedroom door now, leaning back, holding onto both handles, singing vague snatches of song. She would go on filling his days, as she did now. Just as Alexa used to. And Eleanor would do the same, just as Mamma had.

Alexa flinched and exclaimed as if in pain. Aunt Rose drew back, her hands raised in apology.

'Sorry, my lovie, did I get you?'

'No, no.' Alexa struggled to remove her mother's face from her mind as she stepped down from the stool. 'No, it's not that...'

'You do look like a bride, Lexa,' Melissa declared, her large eyes glistening with envy.

'Ho, well, you never know, Melissa,' Aunt Rose said, her mouth now free of pins and her voice low and teasing as she rolled up her tape measure, 'this time next year, you might be a bridesmaid...'

Alexa gave the woman a sharp look and turned away to demonstrate her displeasure. Their teasing her about Harvey had become, frankly, preposterous. None of them knew, really. They just saw a match-made girl and young man. Childhood friends destined to be together. But she knew, and surely he did too. Yes, there was a love. How could there not be? But it was not what everyone thought it was, what everyone was expecting: settling down and marriage. For Alexa had moved far beyond it.

She glimpsed herself in the full-length mirror. Beneath the despairing haze in her eyes sparkled joy. The dress was beautiful. Eleanor had sent off for an evening gown pattern way ahead of time and had found a bolt of particularly exquisite silk in Truro, the colour of old gold, layered with delicate lace. And Aunt Rose, a dab hand with the sewing machine, had run up the dress.

'Are you decent?' called Eleanor from the landing, and came straight in, holding a package in one hand and her midnight-blue fur stole in the other. 'Something's arrived in the afternoon post, Alexa, and I have this for you – oh, goodness! Yes.'

Eleanor laid the fur over Alexa's shoulders in a luxurious fashion and turned her to face the mirror again. Alexa's lips broke into a smile. With the inky stole puffing around her arms, the delicate richness of the bias-cut dress sweeping to the floor sending a shimmering halo around her body, and the depths of her dark hair shining in the sunlight, she hardly looked like herself at all. She asked Melissa to pass her the long ivory gloves that she'd found years ago in her mother's dressing table and drew them on.

'I've grown up,' she laughed.

'So you have,' said Eleanor, so honestly that Alexa gave her a glance. 'But still so deliciously young.'

Aunt Rose stepped back to admire her, folded her stocky arms over her apron, nodding with satisfaction. Melissa put her arms lightly around her and rested her cheek quickly against her stole.

'You do look like a bride!' she said. 'Or a mermaid.'

Eleanor and Aunt Rose chuckled appreciatively. Alexa caught sight of the suitcase on the floor peeking from under her bed and the nausea of dread hit her. She would be leaving them, leaving them all, and she could not dismiss the fondness she felt for the child who was, at that moment, on her knees inspecting the case, on the verge of snapping open the catches.

'What are you doing, Melissa!' she cried. 'Looking for the pixies. You won't find them under my bed. They live beneath the hedgerows, in the hawthorn, out on the moors.'

The disappointment on Melissa's face pricked her like a pin. 'Never mind, come here,' Alexa said, and gave her a tight little hug. 'We'll go looking for them together—'

'Melissa, don't muss Alexa's dress. Oh, let me see the back,' said Eleanor, not noticing the suitcase and stalking around Alexa to view her from behind.

She picked up the dressing table mirror and held it up. Alexa peered over her shoulder to glimpse the tiny pearl buttons, like a row of seeds starting at the point of the deep V halfway down her back and ending at the base of her spine.

'How marvellously glamorous, Aunt Rose,' Alexa said, her voice rising with excitement. 'I feel quite the Hollywood starlet!'

'Ah yes, Aunt Rose,' said Eleanor. 'The buttons arrived in time, too. They're perfect.'

'They were fiddly devils,' said Rose, 'but look so elegant.' Thoughtfully lifting a speck of fluff from Alexa's shoulder,

Eleanor said, 'Pity you never found your old button box, Alexa.'

Alexa jolted, swallowed hard. 'What on earth made you think of that?'

Eleanor blushed briefly, violently, concentrating her stare on the dense pelt of the fur stole.

'I was just thinking that I'd expect you would have found something equally beautiful in there.'

Alexa sensed a note of contrition in her stepmother's voice, but saw another story in her eyes and had no sympathy.

Aunt Rose piped up, 'Oh, but Eleanor, hadn't you read a dreadful article in the newspaper about a child dying, her mother finding her on the floor surrounded by buttons? She'd put them in her mouth. And you didn't want your own baby to go the same way.'

Melissa said, 'What baby?'

Aunt Rose scooped her arms around the child and planted a large kiss on the side of her head. 'Why, you of course, Melissa!' Alexa instinctively stepped away, to get out of reach of them.

She wanted to scream: *Stop pretending – I know what you did!* but clamped her lips together, frightened of what might follow. She had blamed Juliet and ignored her letters until she'd given up writing. She clenched her fists deep in the fur of the stole as if to stopper her disgust.

'Ah, before I forget.' Eleanor moved swiftly past remorse, breaking into Alexa's haze of wretchedness and handing her the package.

'Another present?' asked Melissa, her excitement returning with little jigs of her legs.

Alexa sat down on the bed, feeling the unfamiliar drape of the evening gown. She wanted to take it off, get into her pyjamas and curl up in bed. Instead, with them all watching, expecting, Alexa untied the string and pulled off the brown paper. She drew out a note and a puff of tissue paper and dug her fingers in to reveal an exquisite cameo brooch.

Carved at the centre, instead of the usual Georgian lady, was a bee. The short letter on her old school notepaper was signed Deirdre Graham.

For you, Alexandra, on the occasion of your eighteenth birthday and for the start of your own journey.

After all this time, Miss Graham had remembered. Alexa's hands shook hard as she tried to unhook the clasp. Eleanor stepped forward to help pin it to Alexa's dress.

'What a simply lovely thing,' said Eleanor, gazing at the brooch that Alexa's housemistress had been wearing – and which Alexa had so admired – when she told her all about her adventures as a lady's companion.

Alexa wrapped the stole around her shoulders and trembled with a little spurt of joy.

She was ready.

16

She ran. Gravel bit the naked soles of her feet and her gown threatened to trip her. And, still, she ran. Across the terrace, past the ancient yews, around the corner to the front of Ferris House where taxis were waiting.

Some drivers were absent, having supper in the kitchen; some were smoking; one sat in his cab, newspaper over his steering wheel. She rapped on his window.

'Please take me. Take me away.'

Not waiting for his response, she dived into the back seat. The engine fired and she sank back against the cool leather, clutching her shoes on her lap, her stole around her shoulders, her breath scorching her throat.

'Are you all right there, miss?' the driver asked, glancing in the rear-view mirror as he turned out of the drive.

'Quite all right,' she uttered, although she had, after all, just destroyed the man who loved her.

Alexa glanced through the taxi's back window. But no one was running after her, determined to bring her back. She wound down the window and gulped in the fresh air.

'Where to, then?' the driver asked.

She told him to drive straight across the headlands to Porthdeen and to wait for her. For she must leave now. How could she stay? Would they ever forgive her?

The evening was glowing with the colour of translucent honey, and the sea, as she glimpsed different views of it while the taxi drove up and down the rises, looked desolate, beautiful. She caught the woody scent of burning and saw, far off to the south at St Just, that they'd lit the great summer solstice bonfire. The smell of the smoke followed her all the way back to Porthdeen.

As the taxi pulled up outside the gates, her home appeared to be staring straight back at her, startled to see her return so soon. She asked the driver to wait again and, leaving her shoes in the taxi, she crept barefoot up the path and pushed open the front door. Offering a prayer that Aunt Rose was snoozing over her knitting in the parlour, Alexa tiptoed across the hallway. The parlour door was closed, the house quiet, the clocks ticking.

Melissa was surely, dear God, asleep.

* * *

Upstairs, Alexa pulled her suitcase out from under the bed. She had no need to open it and check it, for she had already packed it so well. She grabbed her favourite coat from the wardrobe, plucked her purse from a drawer and stood for a moment at her window.

'I have everything I need,' she said to her view; her familiar cliffs, the shifting tides below, the endless evening horizon.

Just as she was about to turn away, she saw a figure appear on the far headland, a shadow in the golden dusk. Harvey was beating his way towards Porthdeen, along his usual path, casting a long replica of himself over the ground. Of course, as her father always said, it was the shortest route between the two houses, but her taxi had made a good head start. Alexa watched, her breath stuttering. She was not mistaken. His stride was as confident and determined as it ever was.

Raw guilt swept over her. A sob burst from her throat.

'Why did you do that? Why did you ask me when you knew I wanted to leave?' she whispered to the approaching figure, her courage ebbing. 'Why did you make me do that to you?'

But the man on the headland would not be put off. He kept on coming, shimmering and blurred by her tears.

Smothering a cry of despair, Alexa flung on her coat and picked up her suitcase.

She gazed back through the window at Harvey and scolded him. 'You only did it to make me stay.'

Even so, she hesitated, to catch one more look, before creeping down the stairs and out of the house. As she gripped the handle on the car door, she whispered her goodbye.

PART III

17

THE END OF FEBRUARY, 1931

Every time Alexa walked through Cadogan Square its quiet majesty caught her by surprise. It outshone Half Moon Street and possibly all the other streets, squares and avenues in the whole of the clamouring city put together.

Whether skirting the private gardens at the centre to catch a bus on her day off, or taking a morning stroll with Lady Meredith towards Kensington Gardens or Peter Jones on Sloane Square, the huge red-brick mansions, their serene confidence, made her feel small and want to scurry past, while at the same time, swelling her footsteps with pride.

Even today, under a wintry sky, glimpsed through shivering bare trees, the square was forbiddingly beautiful. Each house had an unapologetic, rather masculine, magnificence. From rooftop stonework where pigeons perched, to the dark wells of the kitchen areas and tradesman's entrances, Alexa counted Dutch gables, Parisian façades, English country-house styles. She admired balconies and bays concealing vast ballrooms, drawing rooms, morning rooms and boudoirs. All towering skywards, all adjoining, each one different from the next and yet somehow of a perfectly splendid piece.

Alexa sensed London rain, caught the chill of the damp breeze, and began to hurry, pushing the parcel for Lady Meredith further inside her coat. As her heels rang quickly on the pavement, she berated herself. That morning, as the bus had turned up Park Lane on its way to Oxford Street, she'd known that if she rang the bell right there and then, jumped off and slipped down Piccadilly, along Half Moon Street, she would have been able to steal a glimpse of Nonna's old house.

There had been many such daydreams since she first arrived in London, that grey dawn last summer. And she had faltered every time. For what was the point; what was the use of standing outside an empty house?

But as Alexa approached Lady Meredith's grand railings, opened the gate and walked down the area steps, an idea struck her: what if the business with her returned letter was a mistake? What if her father had made up that her grandmother had moved back to Venice? After all, he'd persuaded her that Juliet had taken Mamma's button box, and that had been a lie. So perhaps... perhaps. She could walk it in half an hour.

* * *

Entering the below-stairs of milady's mansion put paid to her pipe dream: this was the life she'd chosen. The warren of basement rooms was filled with gently clattering industry, a chattering warmth, a subdued bustle. She passed the servants' hall, lamplit to dispel the gloom of the winter's day. The small gaggle of maids gathered there to take quick cups of tea were too busy, heads together giggling, to notice her. The footman did not catch her eye. And when Alexa said hello to Mrs Robinson, the Cook, who was in the middle of preparing fish for lunch and muttering about an unexpected and inconvenient guest, she was ignored. A mortifying prickling of her skin accompanied her as she began the long steep climb up the back stairs to her rooms. Lady Meredith had set aside a small suite on the third floor for her, below the servants' quarters and above the principal bedrooms. Alexa had a bedroom, bathroom and small sitting room. The rooms were simple and cosy, like a comfortable hotel might well be, but they were not homely. She had left Porthdeen with nothing but her suitcase and her coat. And here, in her rooms, she floated between everyone: the maids above and her ladyship in the rooms below. Alexa was neither servant, nor part of the family. She was on her own. And this, she realised, was not much different to life at school or at home after Mamma had died. Except her one solace there had always been Harvey.

Whoever had decorated these rooms twenty years before had had a penchant for wallpaper. A William Morris willow bough pattern lined her bedroom walls, while a pink shell motif adorned the bathroom, suffering the ill effects of steam and splashes. And a fancy trellis had been used to deck out the sitting room. Old unfashionable chinoiserie furniture had been shipped from the main part of the house and arranged up here. She often stubbed her toe on a protruding oriental-style table leg and the photograph frames were made up of what looked like lacquered twigs. She kept her picture of Mamma and Juliet tucked away in a drawer instead. Alexa took off her hat, quickly brushed through her hair, changed her blouse and her shoes, and checked the clock on her bedside table. Her bus back had dawdled along from Hyde Park Corner. She was later than expected and Lady Meredith detested lateness.

* * *

Alexa had lived at the house on Cadogan Square for eight months and it still managed to dazzle her. As she made her way down the main staircase to see Lady Meredith, each new landing, each new space she walked through grew wider and more spectacular than the last. Above her head, a skylight spilled the hazy London light right down to the hallway below, and on its way illuminated gilded picture frames, Flemish tapestries, yawning mirrors, profuse floral displays on mahogany tables, and a scattering of Ming and Meissen.

Clutching her little parcel of embroidery threads that she'd bought for milady from the haberdashery, Alexa crossed the wide first-floor atrium towards the salon. She hesitated in front of the closed door. That morning, milady had wanted her to find a book for her. She was already late but, to pacify her, she'd better get it now. Alexa turned to her right and opened an adjacent door.

The salon, which stretched from the front to the back of the building, was three times the size of the one she remembered from Half Moon Street and the floor-to-ceiling dividing doors were often shut to close off the rear section. Alexa slipped into this portion of the room and hurried over to the shelves by the window overlooking the mews. As she plucked the book from its slot, she noticed that the dividing doors had been left open a touch and she caught an unfamiliar voice drifting through the gap. Meredith Ainsley had company. The unexpected guest that Mrs Robinson had been complaining about. With a spurt of curiosity that displaced her worry about making herself even later, Alexa took a step or two nearer.

'... damn blasted nuisance,' the man was saying. 'They lost the bloody chit. One mislaid bit of paperwork and the whole consignment has gone to my competitor. That fellow, whatshisname, in Pimlico. I wasn't having any of it. These Mediterranean fellows are damned infuriating. They simply shrug, don't they. You know, that irritating thing they do. But I told them so—'

Alexa moved a fraction and saw, above the curved rear top of a brocaded chair, the back of a head: dark and sleekly groomed, a stiff white collar. A fast and agitated hand, finely manicured and deeply tanned, rubbed furiously at a tense and extremely smooth jawline.

'Really, Guy? And what did you say to them? These Mediterranean fellows?' Lady Meredith, sitting sedately in her favourite armchair by the enormous marble fireplace, moved her pocket watch up on its delicate chain and squinted at it.

'That I'd pay them double if they just got their finger out, sorted it and got it to my warehouse at Chambers Wharf by June. That's my deadline.'

Alexa heard the gentleman's hard, angry sigh and the coal fire crackling in the silence that followed.'God, I really could murder a whisky. What have you over there?'

He stood up and, without waiting for an invitation, or offering his hostess anything, approached her drinks table. Alexa saw a broad back in fine tailoring; his wide-cut trousers and turn-ups, the height of fashion. She heard the rattle of a decanter stopper and the chink of glass on crystal.

'It's not the sort of news you need,' he said between two large gulps, 'having chugged back from Rome on what seemed like a slow boat from China. I might need a whole month of showers to get the smell of that cabin out of my nose. As for the Bay of Biscay, I had to invent a brand new religion to get me through the sea sickness I experienced there. It was vile.'

'Why not take the train?'

'Can't afford it, Auntie.'

'And yet you want to pay them double, Guy? How wise is that, I wonder.'

'Ah, yes. I was going to ask you if you could possibly help me out here.'

The gentleman turned towards milady and Alexa instantly saw his suntanned, twinkling and persuasive smile. She drew back, stung by the realisation that she had been eavesdropping, discovery of which would be utterly mortifying.

'No doubt we will discuss this later, Guy, when I've had my before-luncheon sherry. If you will stay for lunch, that is. You are, of course, invited. Now, where is my girl? She was due back half an hour ago...' Lady Meredith weighed her fob watch in her hand, snatching another look at it.

Clutching the book and parcel, Alexa slipped back out into the atrium, stepped a few paces along and tapped on the door.

'Right on cue, Alexa. It's as if you heard me,' Meredith Ainsley greeted her across the expanse of parquet and Aubusson rug. 'I was just wondering where you'd got to. Do you have my embroidery silks? Ah yes, I see you have some sort of parcel there? And my Walter Scott? Good. Now, you've not met my nephew, have you?'

The visitor looked over his shoulder at Alexa. 'How charming.'

He put down his empty whisky glass, came towards her, extending his hand and gripped hers, but didn't shake it. In an instant, she glimpsed entitlement and confidence, sparking like electricity, and was astonished by how attractive she found him.

He held on to her hand until she spoke.

'Good morning, sir,' Alexa said, concentrating on the precise stitching of his lapels, the fine cloth of his suit. His cologne immediately reached her nostrils: thick and earthy, like an exotic oil from the Far East. 'I'm pleased to meet you.' And still, he held on to her hand.

'You must be...?'

'Miss Rosewarne, sir.'

'Guy Moreland,' he smiled, revealing exceptionally straight teeth. 'And not a sir.'

'Although I sometimes think you think you ought to be,' offered his aunt, dismissing Mr Moreland's burst of surprisingly delighted laughter with a wave of her hand. 'Now, come sit, Alexa, put the book on my table and show me what you've brought me.' As Alexa went to draw a slipper chair closer to Lady Meredith's side, Guy Moreland was immediately near her, stopping her, taking charge and manoeuvring the chair into place. He offered her the seat with exaggerated gestures of chivalry, then settled back in his own chair.

'Well, milady,' Alexa began, sensing Mr Moreland's unwarranted observation of proceedings as she opened the brown paper package on her lap, 'we have a jade-green, a sea-blue, a primrose-yellow and a scarlet-ruby colour. There's also a jet-black and this pretty pearl-white shade.'

Lady Meredith's fine finger prodded at the threads as she uttered how pretty they were... pretty enough, at least. Alexa glanced up at the visitor thinking that surely he would be bored by such trivialities, but he responded to her with a fascinated smile.

'Guy,' said milady, 'weren't you going to make a telephone call before luncheon? You better hurry for the gong will sound in' – she checked her watch – 'about ten minutes, and Cook would not want her halibut to spoil. You can use the instrument in the study.'

'Oh, lunch. Ah. Not so keen on halibut. Might skip it. Would you mind if I escape to my club?'

Lady Meredith let out a short, snorting laugh.'I knew you'd do this to me. I'm such a dull old duck, aren't I? Not such a draw these days, am I? Halibut or no halibut.'

Guy Moreland stood up and took time to brush down the suit, which enhanced his broad elegant frame. He sauntered over and stood looking down at them.

'Are you still here?' Meredith asked, raising a pert eyebrow.

'Lovely to meet you, Miss Rosewarne,' he said, his well-ordered features beaming. 'And, Auntie...?' As he bent down to peck Meredith on her cheek, his face fell, losing all expression, his eyes instantly opaque and flat. 'Don't forget the thing I wanted to speak to you about...'

'Go away, boy,' she laughed, dismissing him. 'Be gone, before I make the decision you don't want.'

He left them, shutting the salon door gently behind him. Alexa heard a brief exchange with Simpson the butler, then the main door opening and his footfall down the front steps.

Lady Meredith asked, 'Is that the first time you've seen Moreland?'

A blush burnt Alexa's face. All she could think of was her inadvertent spying through the adjoining doors, and the life in his eyes when he'd turned to greet her.

'Why, yes, it is,' She picked up a skein of embroidery thread, concentrated on it, hoping Lady Meredith would not notice her discomfort.

'Thought so. I have not seen him for pretty much a whole year, and you came to me at the end of last June, didn't you? He only visits his old auntie when he wants something.'

The room, now that Guy Moreland had gone, seemed empty and very ordinary. The air, previously thickened by his presence, now oddly thin. The dinner gong sounded and Alexa gathered the threads together, bundled them back up in the brown paper. 'He's asked for money, of course,' said Meredith Ainsley. 'But that's what he does. What he is. A lazy devil, and a shameless one. Always has been. Come on, Alexa. It's time for Mrs Robinson's halibut.'

* * *

After pudding in the blood-red dining room, a particularly light lemon sponge, Alexa was aware of Lady Meredith's hard appraisal across the polished mahogany of the table.

'I didn't hear you come in, earlier. I didn't hear Simpson, or the front door?'

Alexa put her spoon down.

'Ah, yes, milady. I'm still in the habit, I'm afraid—'

'You are my companion, Alexa. Not a servant. You must not use the servant's entrance. How many times? If I'd had company – well I did, but should I say, company that mattered – then it would not be fitting. It would look like you and I did not know what we were doing. And, that, I cannot bear.'

Alexa apologised. 'I just don't like to bother Simpson all the time. I can just as easily slip down to the basement and make my way—'

'It's not how we do it. You must keep up,' Lady Meredith snipped and put her hand up to cut off the tiresome conversation. 'Now, I've just remembered, you aren't that special at bridge, are you? As you know, I have a little party planned for this afternoon. Lady Lennox is coming with her daughter, but I'm not sure about Mrs Dalrymple. Dare I ask you to make a fourth?'

'I'm quite good at rummy,' offered Alexa.

'Well, we'll have to see.' Milady turned her head of immaculately shingled hair half a degree and hid a wry smile with her napkin. 'Now, where is *The Times*? I thought Simpson was going to bring it in earlier. Must have been distracted by my bothersome nephew. Please fetch it for me, it's probably in the morning room. You can let me know who has been born, who has died and all the rest of it. Ring for coffee to be served in the salon.'

* * *

Lady Meredith Ainsley had the sort of face, Alexa thought, as she returned with a tray of coffee and an immaculate copy of the newspaper, that looked appallingly down-drooping in repose, when she thought no one was looking, but which, on greeting, lifted into a mask of mature beauty.

'Good.' She gifted Alexa with one of those smiles now as Alexa arranged the cups. 'We'll have a nice hour by the fire before our next set of visitors arrive. Pah, I do wonder if I'll hear from Guy again today. It depends how well he dines at his club.'

'Is he in London for long?' asked Alexa, politely.

'Who's to say what he'll do next,' Lady Meredith said. 'You can pour and then you can read to me.'

Alexa offered milady her cup, took a sip of her own coffee, opened *The Times* and turned to the small advertisements. She scanned the pages for names that she knew milady would be interested in; avoiding those that might cause a torrent of scorn; and trying to pick out the ones which might lighten her mood.

'Ah, milady,' Alexa said, 'Here's one. Last Saturday: The Honourable Elizabeth Audrey McKenzie married Brigadier Arnold Hutton at St Bride's, Fleet Street.' She paused, waiting for her employer to absorb and enjoy the information.

'He's far too old for her. Got a wooden leg. Suffered at Ypres. She's his third wife. I give it six months.'

'Oh, and... Lord Somers of Thame, I'm afraid, passed away. Suddenly. Last week... Doesn't say what of, unfortunately.'

Lady Meredith tutted. 'And he was a good one, too. What was it... summer of 1895? He had his great moustache even then. Was a close-run thing. I think I might have very nearly...'

Milady's thoughts had drifted, so Alexa turned to her employer's favourite bit: the engagements column.

'This might interest you, Lady Meredith. Mrs Dalrymple's

daughter. Amelia Mary, engaged to Edward Nicholson of Park Crescent, W1. That sounds like a match...?'

'Yes, very nice. I've been invited to their little celebratory Champagne soirée next week. It's in the diary. I simply can't bear the Nicholsons. You'll like their house. Right by Regent's Park. It's better than this one. Much better outlook—'

Alexa stopped listening. Two or three paragraphs down from the Nicholson announcement were printed the words:

Ferris

and

Enys Point

Her eyes were drawn first in a flash of recognition and then disorientating disbelief. Harvey, according to this edition of *The Times*, 27th February 1931, was engaged to Miss Sarah Carmichael of Little Porthdeen, Cornwall. Dismay, slow and aching, began to grind in her stomach.

'What's that, Alexa? What have you seen? You look like you've had a shock.'

Alexa glanced up at her employer, fixed her face in what she hoped was a neutral expression.

'Oh, nothing. Just when you see someone has died so young.'

'Who?'

Alexa fumbled with the newspaper, landed on the death announcement of an unfortunate school child; read it out.

'Don't know them,' said Lady Meredith.

* * *

It was not until after the bridge scores and finger sandwiches had been dealt with, the afternoon lady visitors had gone and a light supper had been eaten that Alexa could at last leave Lady Meredith to her Ivanhoe in front of her coal fire and make her long way back up the main staircase, as milady would expect her to do, along lamplit landings and up again and again, until finally shutting her bedroom door on the day.

Her rooms were icy, the fire dead in the grate, and she was too cold to get undressed. Instead, she pulled a pair of socks on over her stockings, wrapped herself in her dressing gown and lit the coals in the sitting room. Uncorking the small bottle of ginger wine that Meredith had given her for Christmas, she curled up under a blanket in an armchair that had seen better days, cradling her glass, and stared at the flames catching weakly in the little hearth. A north wind dashed sleet against her windowpane and worked its way through unseen gaps in the woodwork. Alexa shivered and drew her collar tighter around her neck.

She had not written to her father, Eleanor, Harvey, to anyone since she absconded from her own birthday ball. And she'd left no trace of her whereabouts at Porthdeen, having packed her correspondence with Lady Meredith into her suitcase. The cold and the wind may have found her in her lonely rooms in Cadogan Square, she thought, but no one she loved knew where she was.

Alexa closed her eyes and, with a tic of futility, tried to listen for the sea. Oh, the sea. Home, Porthdeen, Enys Point and everything that had happened was like a vivid dream that was impossible for her to remember on waking. Her memory had been stretched by time and distance until it became see-through and insubstantial, impossible for her to grasp. But she remembered something...

Harvey dancing with Sarah. Harvey laughing with Sarah, admiring her long and beautiful hair. And, as she watched, her own calm acceptance. It had been the only thing in the course of that brief, jagged evening that had made any sense, despite it being so surprisingly painful to witness.

As Alexa shivered in her chair, she persuaded herself that Harvey had been taken in by her, Alexa. He'd come home from Edinburgh, on the cusp of qualifying, at the birth of his glittering career. He'd dived into creating a spectacular ball for her birthday and the wild emotion of it all had prompted his proposal. He probably regretted it the moment the words spilled from his lips. And, desperate to take back what he'd said, dashed over the headland to Porthdeen, to apologise no doubt, withdraw his intent and set the record straight. And now, eight months later, the announcement proved this; that he had seen Alexa for who she was. He had chosen Sarah.

Alexa tucked her hands up her sleeves, pushing her chilled fingertips beneath the cuffs of her blouse. Harvey was gone. Tears splashed down onto her hands. The past was behind her. There were just two people from it that she wanted to see again: Nonna and Juliet. And Melissa, of course, but how could she? She can never go home again.

Fumbling for the handkerchief tucked up her sleeve, Alexa became aware of a strong perfume, as if a fragrance had been trapped and was now being released. Earlier, when Guy Moreland had shaken, no, held her hand, his cologne must have transferred itself to the cuff of her blouse and penetrated the fabric. She lifted her wrist and, incredulously, breathed it in. The scent was earthy, savage and quite unforgettable.

18

Alexa's favourite seat on the top deck of the bus was empty. She eased her way down the aisle, not wanting to breathe in the dirty fug of cigarette smoke, and squeezed past the elderly gent who had taken the aisle seat. She tipped down the narrow top window to feel the cold rain-wet air on her face. Her ears drummed with strangers' voices and her bones vibrated along with the rumble of the engine. Among the chattering people, the squashed-in bodies, she was alone, locked in anticipation, for she had dared herself to finally go to Half Moon Street.

The windows were so clouded with dripping condensation that Alexa barely knew where she was. When the conductor called out for Hyde Park Corner, she leapt to her feet, trod on the gentleman's toe, apologised, and scooted down the stairs just in time.

On Piccadilly, the pavements were slippery and crowded, the road choppy with cars and buses. She drew to the side so she could gather herself and keep out of everyone's way. Across the road lay Green Park, saturated, dormant and dead-winter brown. But further along, the solid elegance of the Ritz shone out, sublime even in all this rotten weather. She and Mamma never did get to have tea there, let alone see the jazz band that Nonna had mentioned. Alexa passed the spot where Mr Fairling had so gallantly secured them a taxi in the rain. She often wondered what had happened to the sodden hat that Mamma, in her desperate state, had dropped to the floor of the cab.

As Alexa turned up Half Moon Street her feet grew heavy, her pace slow. She squinted at the parade of buildings, counting down the house numbers. Outside number 15, she stopped. She'd put it off so many times since her arrival in London that the reality of standing there took her breath away.

Now that she was used to Cadogan Square, Nonna's old house looked surprisingly small, cramped and narrow in its terrace. The paintwork was cracked, the windows smeared with dirt. If only she had stayed quiet that terrible morning as Mr Fairling sketched and painted. If only she had not tried to show off and impress Mr Montgomery with Mamma's story. Perhaps, then, she and Mamma would not have left like they did. Her mother may well have fallen ill but she would not have endured an overnight journey on a train. And, surely, Nonna would have called in the best doctors of Harley Street, not a country general practitioner and a two-bit nurse from Truro. Alexa's anger rose like a spurt of venom and she gripped the railing to steady herself.

The front door suddenly opened and a young woman, around her own age, dressed for the office and wearing a jaunty fur hat, dashed down the steps.

'Excuse me. But are you all right?' she asked.

Alexa attempted a smile. 'Yes, yes, I am,' she lied.

'It's just that you looked rather odd standing there.'

'I stayed here once,' Alexa blurted. 'When I was younger. It was my grandmother's house.'

'Oh, it's not a house any more,' said the girl. 'I share the top floor. It's all very modern and communal now. Broken up into flats.'

She checked her watch. 'Were you looking for someone? Because if you are, I'm afraid I can't help you. Said I'd be in by twelve. Must dash.'

'No, no, thank you. Not looking for anyone...'

The girl gave her a quick quizzical shrug and hurried off. 'What a fool I am,' uttered Alexa, as she turned and threw a despairing glance back over her shoulder before trudging her slow way back to Piccadilly. 'Did I really expect Lily to be waiting to open the door for me?'

Anger left her numb. There were no lies, then; this was the truth. Nonna had gone. Alexa was alone once again. She wanted to sit down on the kerb and cry, but instead she kept walking, bumping her way through the busy shoppers, her mind curiously blank, as if cushioning her from the worst, most painful of her thoughts.

'Miss Rosewarne! What are you doing here on this side of the park?'

She had not noticed the taxicab coasting the kerb right next to her or Guy Moreland leaning through the open window, a leather-gloved hand waving, his face beyond it set with amusement.

'I was just... you see...' She glanced back the way she'd come. 'My grandmother, you see—'

'Don't stand there in the cold.' His smile was brief, impatient. 'Get in!'

Alexa did what she was told and climbed into the taxi, which was surprisingly and pleasantly warm, and close with the smell of tobacco and Guy's lingering scent.

'You look frozen,' Guy said and reminded the cab driver to take the next left into Albemarle Street. 'I'm taking you for luncheon. You'll have a Dubonnet and a nice steak and you can tell me all about it. You'll be warm then, and perhaps a little merrier.'

She could not look at him, had no desire to explain. 'And I want to see your smile,' Guy said. 'Do you hear?'

She nodded vigorously, feeling she must please him.

* * *

Within less than a minute, the cab had drawn up outside the discreet narrow awning of a hotel.

'Cosy, isn't it?' Guy led her, and she followed mutely, through a hushed, red-carpeted foyer where the concierge took his trilby, and into the dining room. Guy was greeted by the elderly waiter like a prodigal son and they were shown to a small round table in a velvet booth near the fireplace. Three or four other parties were seated but barely looked up. Flames licked luxuriously over glowing coals.

Alexa sat down and stole a glimpse around the room, knowing that she must speak soon, for she was beginning to appear rude, or stupid.

'This restaurant could fit inside Lady Meredith's drawing room about five times,' she said.

'That's what I like about it,' said Guy. 'It's another world in here. So peaceful. Closeted from the outside.' He shook out her napkin and offered it to her. 'When I'm here, the hands on my watch never seem to move.'

Alexa allowed herself to sit back against the cradling luxury of the seat as the heat from the fire slowly radiated around her legs. She shivered. Reality began to seep back in. She concentrated hard on removing the gloves from her trembling hands and resting them in her lap. If she kept still, perfectly still, Mr Moreland might not notice her misery.

His eyes darted energetically, landing and moving on, absorbing his surroundings, her, at breakneck pace, taking note of everything. When at last he stopped, captured her in his gaze, she expanded as if he'd paid her a wonderful silent compliment. But as the waiter set down two heavy tumblers of drink and handed them both small menu cards, the words instantly blurred with Alexa's tears; Guy's attention was simply too much to bear.

Seeing her struggle, he ordered them both Windsor soup, sirloin and apple crumble and plucked the card out of her hand, his fingertips touching hers briefly. His hands were solid, smooth and exquisitely manicured. They left their mark on her skin.

'God, your hands are like ice,' he said. 'Sip this.' He edged her Dubonnet towards her across the tablecloth and tipped a whisky down his throat. 'What were you doing there, Miss Rosewarne, wandering Piccadilly like a waif and stray? Were you lost?'

Alexa sipped her drink, winced and then gave it a second chance. The twist of sweetness seduced her and she took a huge mouthful.

'Not lost,' she said, feeling braver as the drink toasted her insides. 'Just being a stupid, wretched fool.'

Guy nodded. 'I've been there,' he said. 'And you know what we stupid wretched fools do? We have another drink.'

He motioned to the waiter, who speedily refreshed their glasses.

'When I rescued you from the pavement, you were gabbling something about your grandmother. What was that all about?'

'Yes, I was jabbering a bit, wasn't I?'

Guy's smile had fallen but his eyes blazed with amusement over the top of his whisky glass.

'You looked so lost,' he said, 'So young. It's OK, you don't have to explain.' Guy lowered his voice as the waiter deftly set soup plates before them. 'But I'd rather like it if you did.'

Alexa automatically picked up her spoon, broke her bread.

'That's it,' said Guy. 'You warm yourself with soup, Miss Rosewarne. Thaw out a little. Become yourself again. And while you do that, I'll tell you about me, shall I? Before my aunt gets there first.'

'Lady Meredith has given me a crumb,' Alexa said, as the soup revived her and something resembling courage seeped back. 'That's all.'

'I'm filth,' said Guy, sparking a cigarette.

Alexa sat back in surprise, raising her napkin to her lips as he continued.

'I can see you've not come across the likes of me before.'

'I have barely left Cornwall,' she said. 'My world has been this big.' Alexa held up her forefinger and thumb an inch apart. 'What did you just say you were?'

'Filth,' said Guy. 'It's the acronym. Failed in London, try Hong Kong. My aunt thinks I'm a rogue and a waste of space, but I try my damnedest to prove her wrong. It's hard work, I tell you.'

His father, he told her as the soup was cleared and the steaks arrived, was something huge in the foreign office; his parents lived in India, had been there since he was eleven years old when they packed him off to boarding school.

'Along with my sainted aunt, Father and Mother don't seem to think much of me, either,' he said, his voice distant, the dawn of lonely boyhood sorrow rising over his face.

'Sounds like boarding school was rotten...?' she ventured, realising that, in one way or another, his experience mirrored hers.

Guy nodded viciously, lit another cigarette. He picked up Alexa's empty Dubonnet glass and signalled for the waiter to fill it. Even though she did not want another, she sipped her new drink obediently.

'Mother is Lady Meredith's younger sister,' Guy said. 'And, as you know, she is a spinster, has no children. I am my aunt's sole heir. And they all think I go from one hare-brained scheme to the next, even though I try to make a pretty fair job at everything. The latest project is importing Carrara marble from the port of Rome to the East End docks. So, what with one disaster after another, most of the time, they are damn right.'

Alexa blushed. She already had an inkling of what Guy's occupation might be from her eavesdropping. Her hands twitched at the mention of an Italian city and the vaguest, most tenuous link to the roots of her family. She gripped her knife and fork and cut into her steak, watching the bloody juices run. Her appetite escaped her. She put down her cutlery.

'My grandmother is, and my mother was, Italian,' she said. 'But they were from Venice.'

'Ah, I see it now.' Guy sat back in his chair, sipping his whisky, his pain vanishing as his lips relaxed into a smile, appraising her. '*Una bella ragazza Italiana*. If I may say, your hair, your skin. Yes. And those blue eyes. Yes, Venetian.'

She struggled under his scrutiny and fixed her eyes on the silver pin skewering his collar either side of his tie.

'You speak Italian?' she asked.

'*Naturalmente*,' he said with relish. But his smile instantly dropped away, a light closed off. 'I spend a great deal of my time there, as a matter of fact.'

He requested another drink from the waiter.

'So, Miss Rosewarne. Is there not a jot of Cornish visible in you, then?'

'Oh, there must be.'

Alexa thought of her father, imagined him in his book-lined study. Wondered how he spent his days; how hard he had tried to find her. And Harvey. How much had he missed her after she disappeared? When and where would his wedding take place? At the church on the clifftop, or in the small chapel at Ferris House?

'I'm sorry,' she said. 'We need to change the subject. I think I have just realised how much I have hurt everyone.'

'Not as much, by the look of things, as they have hurt you.' Guy reached across the table with a large pristine handkerchief. She took it, pressed it to her face and was instantly taken, instantly revived, by his delicious perfume.

'I must say,' she said, on the edge of unexpected laughter, 'what a gorgeous scent. That's made me feel a whole lot better.'

Guy screwed up his napkin and dropped it onto his plate. 'Let's get straight to pudding,' he said. 'I knew there was more to you than errands and bridge parties and embroidery silks.'

'Long story,' she said, watching Guy's napkin gradually soaking up the blood from his half-devoured steak. 'You could say that I ran away from home.'

'Ah, I like that story!'

'After my mother died, so many things made me want to... to leave Porthdeen. And I wanted to find my grandmother. I'd decided that that was the one thing I needed to do and London would be the best place to start looking. It's a disaster, really. The whole thing crumbled around my feet this morning.'

'When I found you?'

'You see, I'd been told my grandmother had gone back to Venice years ago. But then, I had been told lots of things.'

Guy tipped his head to one side, waiting for her to go on. 'It's taken me this long to pluck up the courage to go to the house. I thought that maybe, just maybe, my grandmother might be there, or at least someone who knew her.' She broke off, dashed away fresh tears. 'All pretty futile, really.'

'I've only got one handkerchief, by the way.'

Alexa burst into laughter and turned it in her hands, trying to find a dry spot.

'Do you know,' said Guy, 'that, tears aside, this is the nicest lunch I've had here in a good long while.' He glanced at his watch. 'And blow me, usually time stands still. But it's a quarter to three!'

Panic sobered her.

'Goodness, I better get back. I told Lady Meredith I'd only be gone a few hours. She will be checking her watch.'

'Don't you wish you could take that blessed thing and smash it under your heel?'

Guy motioned for the waiter, cancelled the crumble and asked for coffee.

He said, 'I get the feeling you are very disappointed, Miss Rosewarne.'

'Oh no, the lunch was lovely, I'm just not that hungry. I'm so sorry!'

'Not lunch. Sod lunch. I mean with your great big adventure. You've come all this way. Made a great leap of faith. Thought it would be different here in London. Unfortunately, as things in life tend to be, it's all the bloody same. Is that the truth?'

'I certainly feel the same,' she admitted, disillusioned and thinking of Deirdre Graham and her adventure.

'So, your grandmother returned to Venice?'

'She must have done, yes. And I was stupid to think that I could find her here...'

Guy watched her face, dipped his head to speak quietly, 'You were desperate, Miss Rosewarne. When I saw you straggling along Piccadilly, you were lost in one way or another,' he said, pausing. 'We're both as bad as each other.'

'You think so?' Alexa baulked at this intimacy.

'But at least one of us has the advantage of years of experience and a business brain.'

The coffees arrived and Alexa was aware of a creeping disappointment that the lunch was very nearly over.

'You know, my dear old maiden aunt has never seen Venice,' Guy said, adding demerara and stirring his cup, thinking. 'Unbelievable, really. But then she never married, never had a honeymoon, and for whatever reason, never did the grand tour. I think the war must have put paid to all of that.'

'Of course, poor Lady Meredith.'

'There's no poor about it,' he said, grinning.

He watched her, studied her, a peculiar vitality coursing under his skin.

'Aunt Meredith might need some persuading,' he said. 'But leave it with me. Shouldn't take much doing, she's always as bored as hell. Springtime in Venice. What do you think about that, Miss Rosewarne?'

Alexa, unable to express the elation soaring merrily through her, simply sipped her coffee and allowed his words to brighten the air around her.

'Yes!' he said, triumphant, 'There's your smile.'

19

After lunch on the day of the soirée at the Nicholsons', Alexa went upstairs to change. She pulled her gold-lace evening gown from her wardrobe and slipped it on. The seamstress in Soho had done a good job, altering the length and transforming it into a cocktail dress. Climbing up onto the bed, Alexa, at last, could see herself properly in the dressing table mirror. Grabbing Eleanor's indigo fur, she wrapped it around her shoulders, and pinned Deirdre Graham's brooch at her shoulder. Her shoes were at least two seasons old. As a lady's companion attending a genteel champagne party, she would have to do.

Ten minutes later, Alexa stopped with a jolt on the threshold to the salon. Guy Moreland was sitting by the fire talking with Lady Meredith. Alexa hadn't seen him since their lunch at the hotel – surely, a never-to-be-repeated experience – and his unexpected appearance brought shyness down on her with quite a blow. Their shared confidences left a trail of discomfort. And, by keeping their lunch from Lady Meredith surely, somewhere along the line, made it mildly improper.

'I'm sorry to have to say this, Auntie,' Guy declared, 'but Venice is full.' He looked around and his smile flashed with pleasure. 'Why, good afternoon, Miss Rosewarne. I wondered where you were.'

She blushed under his gaze, expanding with joy at the word Venice, but she managed to nod a reserved greeting and quickly found an armchair outside of their circle to sit in.

'Ah, Alexa, you are already dressed,' said Lady Meredith, eyeing her up and down with an expression of vague surprise.

Milady herself was dressed in a cocktail confection, embroidered and pleated, and, as Alexa admired it, compared it to her own second-rate ensemble, she realised she had never seen her employer wear the same thing twice.

'Sorry to ask you when you look so lovely,' Meredith paused with a fortifying smile, 'but would you mind sorting the fire for me; it's so damned cold in here. You've got a much better knack than this one here. My nephew always seems to kill it. I do hope the Nicholsons have considered that we will be in our cocktail dresses this afternoon and it is still freezing outside.'

Burdened by their stares, Alexa knelt on the hearth rug, restacked the coals using the silver tongs and applied bellows to their heart. Watching the infant flames curl, she was relieved to have something to concentrate on, while a tiny decorous voice told her to avoid Guy's eye.

'What was that you were saying?' Meredith asked. 'No room at the inn? Well, I'm certainly not staying at your apartment in Santa Croce. It is distinctly poky.'

'No, no, that won't do at all, Auntie,' Guy assured her. 'You're right, it's not nearly salubrious enough for you. So...' he paused, measuring out his patience, 'I went back to Thomas Cook on Conduit Street and they have booked you in on Lido. Booked you both in, that is, at the Excelsior.'

Alexa's ears tingled as she pretended not to listen.

'The Excelsior?' mused Lady Meredith, 'That, I hear, is where the dreaded Nicholsons camp out for the season. But never mind. If that's the hotel where society goes, then I suppose I must too...'

'And Lido is not as humid as Venice itself, or crowded. Fresh sea air, long gently sloping beaches, cocktails,' said Guy persuasively. 'It's all there in the brochure.'

As Lady Meredith began to turn the pages open on her lap, Alexa got up from her task, wiping her hands on her handkerchief. Guy Moreland had meant everything he'd said, then. And it seemed she would be going to Venice.

'You may as well have a look, Alexa,' said her employer, passing her the brochure. 'See what he has let us in for.'

Alexa gazed at photographs of grand mansions, hotels, what looked like a golden beach with a medley of circus-striped umbrellas, albeit printed in black and white. Excitement beat a little tune around her. Venice, announced the headline, was a mere twenty-minute ride across the lagoon by water taxi. She would be a mere twenty-minute ride from Nonna. Crumpling the handkerchief, she realised it was the one Guy had given her and she dared herself to glance at him as she tucked it up her sleeve.

* * *

'I told you the Nicholsons' house was better than mine,' said Meredith in the back of their taxicab as they turned onto the cobbles of Park Crescent. 'Better aspect but, in my opinion, not a better part of town. New money, you see. And she has more staff. But what she doesn't have, Alexa, is a lady's companion.'

'I think we are becoming a rare breed these days, milady,' said Alexa, peering upwards at the great sweep of effortlessly elegant Regency stucco, her insides flipping like a netted fish, far worse than before her midsummer birthday ball.

She walked into the great upstairs room on milady's tail, her stomach a hefty knot, hearing Meredith sigh with satisfaction as she was offered a glass of Champagne by the footman and even more audibly when she spotted the huge fire crackling in the hearth. The sound of voices in the enormous room was thin, rising and falling through a scattering of stiff black suits, resplendent here and there with Great War medals and mingling with the vibrancy of the ladies' gowns.

'Christ, we're too early!' hissed Meredith, her mouth on the rim of her glass. 'Not nearly enough people yet to swell the party, ah, Clementine...'

Mrs Nicholson, all cropped grey hair and fluttering feather boa, bore down on them with terrifying speed and Meredith greeted her with a warmth that did not match the steel in her eyes.

'This is my companion, Miss Alexa Rosewarne. I don't think you've met.'

The hostess lifted her lorgnette to peer at Alexa and executed a tiny nod of her head, which took her in, from top to toe, and gave her the most lame of handshakes.

'And where is your Edward and his radiant bride-to-be?' Meredith asked Mrs Nicholson, peering around. 'I want to offer the betrothed my hearty congratulations.'

Mrs Nicholson whisked Lady Meredith off, leaving Alexa to take her own glass of Champagne from the tray. She offered a thank you to the silent footman, who appeared to be about her own age, but he kept his eyes fixed firmly on the wall beyond her shoulder.

By the elaborately draped windows overlooking winter-grey Regent's Park, Amelia Dalrymple had gathered her friends around her like the queen with her worker bees. She looked bridal already in an ivory sheath dress, her marcelled hair like rippling butter. The other girls were all in varying shades of pastel, no doubt the new spring season's colour. Alexa glanced miserably down, realising that her own dress looked exactly what it was: out-of-date evening wear altered for cocktail hour. The knot in her stomach tightened but she set her shoulders squarely under her fur stole and proceeded to make her way across the treacherous expanse of parquet, catching up with Lady Meredith just as she finished her round of greetings and was dabbing lipstick marks off her cheek.

'Amelia's just told me. She and Edward will be going to Italy for their honeymoon,' she offered helpfully. 'Fancy that, Alexa.'

'Oh, is that so, Amelia?' Alexa bravely stepped forward, 'You see, my family is Italian, my grandmother—'

But someone giggled into the bride-to-be's ear and she twisted away from Alexa, cutting her off so that her anecdote drifted to nothing and she became, apparently, invisible. Alexa took a fortifying, and far too large, gulp of Champagne and, as the room began to fill up, she kept close to Lady Meredith's elbow – after all, this was what she was employed to do.

* * *

The conversation of the tight little groups raced competitively, but the moment Alexa thought of something interesting to say, the chatter turned to a new subject, about people she knew nothing of, leaving her behind. She soon discovered that her Champagne glass was empty and there was no waiter in sight and that to eat petits fours with gloves on was all but impossible. And when Lady Meredith abandoned Alexa to find the bathroom, Alexa drew closer to the wall, wishing that she could hide herself amid the immense folds of Mrs Nicholson's silken curtains.

Someone chinked loudly with a fork on a glass and Mr Dalrymple, father of the bride-to-be, stood in the middle of the floor and began to drone about next year's nuptials. Waiting alone by the window, Alexa saw the door on the far side of the room open quietly and whoever had walked in began to create a frisson among the ladies. She spotted a ripple of backward glances and suppressed coquettish smiles. Even Amelia, holding her fiancé's hand and standing at her father's side, had become dewy eyed at the arrival of the new guest.

Alexa's scalp prickled in equal delight and astonishment as Guy Moreland, his dark hair gleaming, his tan trumping all the pale winter flesh, emerged around the back of the congregated guests and came straight for her.

'Tiresome, isn't it?' he whispered, standing by her side and facing the throng. 'Don't know what I'm doing here, I wasn't even invited. Plus, I'm hideously late.'

Alexa's relief to see a face she knew, along with the tantalising depth of his confession, was like a glass of cooling water tipped over her.

'So, why come?' she threw back, a little of her spark returning. Guy chuckled. 'You're right, Miss Rosewarne, why put myself through it?' He glanced over at Dalrymple who was still holding court. 'In fact, my aunt had promised to come to the theatre with me. Double-booked herself for this bash. I think she was going to use me as an excuse to get away early but now she is ensconced and won't leave. I just saw her outside in the hallway. She said to take you instead. Wouldn't want to waste the ticket. And I suspect you are in dire need of a little respite, Miss Rosewarne.'

'Take me?' Alexa cried out in surprise and several heads turned her way. She lowered her voice, 'The theatre?' she whispered. 'Now? But isn't that awfully rude?'

'Without meaning to appear ungallant, Miss Rosewarne,' Guy leaned in to speak softly in her ear, his breath warm on her neck, 'just how much do you think they will notice?'

She drew back, startled, ready to be offended but, instead, broke into giggles when she saw the delightful humour in his eyes.

'Go and powder your nose,' he said, nodding towards the door, 'and meet me in the hall before we both die of boredom.'

* * *

Street lamps illuminated the length of Portland Place as the cab bowled them along towards Regents Street. Alexa was buoyant with relief at having escaped the Nicholsons'. She was playing truant and her spirits effervesced like the Champagne she had abandoned. But, instead of turning left into the lights of Theatreland as expected, Guy directed the taxi to head right into the darker, quieter streets of Mayfair. He pulled the tickets out of his pocket and ripped them in two.

'Oh, wasn't that a Noel Coward?' Alexa asked.

'I've seen it,' he said.

'Was it any good?' Mr Coward or not, at that moment she did not give a fig.

'It was indeed. But one cannot talk in the theatre.'

The cab deposited them on a deserted pavement next to railings in a quiet square of white mansions glowing in the darkness.

'Come, Alexa, the Velvet Rose is calling.'

'The what?'

He looked at her. 'It's a club, Alexa. We can eat and we can drink and we can talk all we like in there.'

Trust, simple and surprising, impelled Alexa to follow Guy down dark basement steps and through a dimly lit foyer. She was rewarded by the dark, soft embrace of a hexagonal, plum velvet room. Lamps on circular tables punctuated the space through which waiters flitted, doling drinks to their murmuring clientele from gleaming silver trays and a jazz quartet swung out a smudged rhythm on a small dais.

They were shown courteously and without delay to what she assumed was Guy's usual corner table and, without so much as a prompt, the waiter brought two tumblers of pink-orange liquid, rattling with ice and finished with a twist of lemon.

'Everywhere you go, people seem to know you,' Alexa observed as a couple on another table waved discreetly. She sat back to align herself with the sudden alteration to her evening. For the girl from the first and last house in England, it was difficult to take in her new and exotic surroundings, so, instead, she had a sip of her drink. 'Delicious.'

'Negroni. It's good for you,' said Guy, raising his own glass and saluting her. 'You'll be drinking this in Venice.'

'Ah, yes, of course...' Alexa skirted around thanking Guy for Venice. Otherwise, she'd be presuming that he had arranged it all especially for her. And that would be preposterous. She said, 'I'm not sure if your aunt is completely looking forward to her trip.'

'She doesn't look forward to anything, haven't you noticed? She sleepwalks through life. It's one party, one event after another that she must get through,' he said, laughing, 'This afternoon's caper is a prime example. But how did you find the dreaded Nicholsons'?'

'It was like being back at school, to be honest.' Alexa ran her finger around the rim of her glass, trying to pin the problem down. 'I have always been the round peg or the square one, I can't remember which.'

'You will fit in in Venice, of that you can be sure. With your looks, you'll be mistaken for a native.'

Guy's gaze took in her hair, lingered over her face. He collected himself, his face falling. 'And while you're at it, Miss Rosewarne,' he finished abruptly, 'you will certainly complete your mission.'

'But,' said Alexa, her voice rising, 'it all seems so impossible, so out of reach. I don't know where to start.'

Guy set his drink down and leaned his arms on the table, extending his body towards her, scrutinising. In the light from the lamp on the table, he appeared so much older than her. His eyes in his tanned face were like cut glass and she watched them glitter.

'You want to be loved, don't you, Alexa?'

His words stung her with absolute honesty. And her first name, falling from his lips for the first time, loitered around her. She stared at his hands clasped on the pristine tablecloth and suddenly wanted him to touch her.

Alexa drew back. 'Yes, yes, of course. Don't we all?' The thought of love, of Harvey, of home flashed through her mind. 'I just want to make the past feel right. To mend everything. And just see my grandmother. That's all I want. Nonna I call her,' Alexa twisted out a smile. 'I have this awful vision of her in the hallway of Half Moon Street, furious, just staring at me.'

'And you want to wipe that clean away?'

She sighed. 'It really is all I want.'

Guy sat back, drained his glass and swirled the ice around. 'Pity I won't be there to witness any of it,' he said, his voice switching, business-like. 'I have to get back to Rome tomorrow, Miss Rosewarne. I'm catching the early boat train, for my sins. Lots of business in the world of marble to attend to. You know how it is.'

Alexa had no idea, but kept quiet.

'But I'll ask my aunt,' he said, 'how you got on.'

20

TOWARDS THE END OF SPRING, 1931

Alexa leant out of the carriage window as the train made its final journey along the causeway across the lagoon, trying to spot rooflines, steeples, anything. But Venice remained tantalisingly elusive through the drifting mist. Even so, Alexa smiled secretly. She was almost there.

Lady Meredith Ainsley never stinted on transportation, and so the brown and cream liveried Orient Express had been Alexa's bed and board the past two nights. But, for all its bijou salons, feather beds, crystal glassware and attentive stewards, the train was rocky and bumpy and spent an awful lot of time waiting in sidings.

'Thank goodness that's over with,' said Meredith as they stepped down onto the busy platform of Ferrovia Station.

Milady's face, despite being shielded by a wide-rim hat and large dark glasses, revealed the tell-tale droop of irritability. So Alexa jumped immediately to her job: securing a porter, finding the water taxi dock and ensuring smooth passage. And her grateful smiles and the nuggets of Italian learnt at her mother's knee seemed to work.

It wasn't until the little boat, stacked with the vast set of Louis

Vuitton cases, eased itself out onto the water and chugged in an arc into the lagoon and around the island that Venice began to peek through the haze. Alexa spotted spires, brickwork rosy in the grey light, the domes of a basilica. She saw the façades of pale stone from her mother's paintings. Between sublime buildings, the enticing dark canals, flickering in and out of her vision like a dream. The water hypnotised her, flooding to the invisible horizon. It was quiet, less frantic than the sea at Porthdeen and it seemed to want to welcome her. But she had to watch Venice fade back into its misted shroud as the boat left the city behind and headed to the island of Lido.

'Unpack, please, Alexa,' commanded a weary Lady Meredith the moment they had been shown up to their rooms at the Excelsior. 'I'm going for a nap'. And she shut their adjoining door.

Alone at last, Alexa stood in the centre of her bedroom, savouring the quietness and the space, such a relief after the long hours confined on the train. The sun had broken the mist and blazed through the slats in the shutters, glimmering on walls painted the colour of ancient plaster. She threw the double doors to her balcony open and stepped out to take in the whole of the long stretch of sand and sea below. Boats criss-crossed the water, children and grown-ups splashed and played in the lapping shallows of the Adriatic and beach balls sailed overhead. But the Lido playground, she decided, could only delight her for so long.

She unlatched her suitcase and rummaged for the photograph of Mamma and Juliet. Squinting as she'd done so many times before at the blur of the wall behind them, she wondered if she'd ever be able to make out where the picture had been taken: no street sign, no clue, just a little stone bridge and deep shadows sharpened by the sun.

Alexa propped Mamma and Juliet up on the dressing table. 'I've come this far,' she told them, 'but it isn't nearly far enough.'

* * *

The hours on Lido, dictated by Lady Meredith, drifted languidly, transforming themselves, almost without Alexa realising, into days, stretching into weeks. She breakfasted late most mornings with milady on a marble terrace under the shade of an awning, listening for the gradual build-up of voices from the beach, of laughter as the day expanded. Before she knew it, it was time for an aperitif before tucking into a lunch of seafood and a dish of pistachio ice cream. Come the afternoon, when the sun grew too full and fiery, Lady Meredith invariably retreated for a snooze. And, pocket watch in hand, milady knocked on Alexa's door at five sharp for cocktails.

Alexa quickly realised that it was too far to make it across the water to Venice and back again while milady had her siesta, so during the burning afternoons, she wandered along the deserted Gran Viale to the quay and watched, instead, the flotilla of *traghetti* course back and forth between the islands. Venice, a pale-gold mirage in the heat haze where Nonna, perhaps, was also snoozing, seemed as remote to Alexa as it had ever been.

And, as she sipped yet another Negroni with Meredith, once the sun had gone over the yardarm on another meaninglessly lethargic day, her frustration peaked.

'I was wondering, milady,' she began tentatively, sitting on the veranda outside the bar, 'would you like to take an excursion across to Venice tomorrow? Or sometime soon? Please?'

Meredith sniffed and dunked her olive-on-a-stick back into her martini.

'Oh no, Alexa. Clementine Nicholson tells me it smells dreadfully bad. This is possibly the worse time to come to Venice. It's stinking hot, busy, full of tourists. I don't know why I was persuaded by Guy. He should have known better that I'd hate it.

Ah, but I can see by the look on your face that you are longing to go.'

'As you may know, milady, my family were from here and I was hoping—'

'Yes, I believe my nephew mentioned something about that.' Lady Meredith lifted her dark glasses to get a better look at Alexa. 'And his continuing interest in you does not surprise me. But I think we need to do something about your clothes first, Alexa. That's the fifth time I've seen you wearing that since we've been here. I take it you have nothing else?'

'No, milady,' Alexa twitched at her dress. 'What you have seen so far is the extent of my wardrobe, I'm afraid.'

'You really should have told me. This is the Excelsior, for goodness' sake.'

Meredith opened her handbag, fished inside and drew out a neat wad of *lire.*

'I should have thought of this before. Here's your clothing allowance. Go shopping, and impress me,' she said. 'And then I may consider a trip across the water.'

* * *

In the coolness of the late afternoon, when the sun was more friend than enemy, Alexa tripped her way along Gran Viale to the row of boutiques tucked under candy-striped canopies that she'd discovered on her wanderings. Able to make herself understood to the proprietress with a little Italian and delighted with what she found, she came away laden with parcels and with just a few *centesimi* of milady's change chinking in her purse.

The next day, while Meredith took morning coffee with the newly arrived Nicholsons, Alexa wriggled into her new black and white spotted bathing costume and lay on the sun lounger on her balcony. She picked up her book and put her dark glasses on. For years, she had put it off, but now it seemed entirely appropriate to at last start reading her mother's copy of *Middlemarch*, the bookmark still in place.

The light was intense, bleaching the pink of the hotel walls to the colour of English flesh and the bougainvillea scrambling around the doors to her room wilted with thirst. Drowsy in the heat, Alexa could not concentrate as old hibernating sorrows began to reawaken and tap on her shoulder. She squinted at the pages through tear-misted eyes, gave up reading and instead stared at the blue haze of the Adriatic. Gradually, the shadow of her parasol moved on its way across the balcony. She slipped off her sunglasses, placed the novel over her face and fell in and out of a snooze as Mamma and Juliet crept from the photograph on her dressing table and chattered in her mind.

Half-waking, Alexa was conscious of the echoing music of people at play on the beach below and then, suddenly, so much closer, a footstep on the balcony next to her own.

'Miss Rosewarne, what a sight for sore eyes.'

Alexa sat up with a yelp of surprise, her book falling to the floor.

Guy Moreland leant on the balustrade separating Alexa's balcony from Lady Meredith's, sunglasses on, smoking a cigarette, his hair glossy under the noon sun, his smile fixed and dazzling. Alexa scrambled for her silk shawl, draped it modestly around her shoulders, snatched up her sunglasses and snapped them on.

'I've come to rescue you,' he said.

'I thought you were in Rome,' she countered, pulling the shawl closer around her arms.

'What kind of welcome is that? I wrote to my aunt last week, told her I'd be dropping in. I hadn't heard from her at all. Not even a postcard.'

'Well, I don't need rescuing,' Alexa tried to sound cross, even though her blood was fizzing with wild delight. 'This is my job, Mr Moreland. I'm paid to do this.' She'd been disappointed when he inferred in the Velvet Rose that he wouldn't be coming to Venice. And, looking at him now, she realised exactly how much. Amid the monotony of the holiday, the sight of him, burnished by the pitiless sun and smoking on the terrace, was worryingly attractive.

'Auntie says it's fine,' said Guy. 'Now she has the Nicholsons to play with. Literally. She is planning to succumb to bridge with them in the salon this afternoon. I was accosted just now as I tried to sneak in through the foyer. I had to get away before Clementine Nicholson's stare turned me to stone.' He flicked his ash over onto her side of the balcony. 'Thought I'd come and find you. And I'm to take you across to Venetia.'

Alexa sat up straight and her voice leapt with pleasure. 'But doesn't Lady Meredith want to come too?'

'Doesn't look like it. She's such a stick-in-the-mud. She may as well be in Bognor Regis and not two miles from the most sublime city on earth. Anyway, Alexa, we can set off today, after lunch if you like. Ah, I like the look on your face. Even with those glasses on I can sense your utter joy.'

'You know, it's what I came here for.'

Guy appraised her, he seemed amused. 'I ought to be more of a gentleman really, and not creep up on you like this. I'll leave you now so you have time to get ready.' He turned to excuse himself. 'Oh, I've managed to get hold of *The Times*. Do you want to read it?' He brandished the rolled-up newspaper like a baton. 'It's the day before yesterday's, but late news is better than no news, don't you think?'

She eyed the newspaper, half curious, but did not want to be tempted into reading the small-print announcements. For they were now in June, and that was the month, wasn't it, that brides usually chose for their wedding day.

'No, thank you,' Alexa said, pushing Harvey and Sarah out of her mind, while trembling far too much at the delicious idea of being taken to Venice at last.

21

The midnight-blue dress with white collar and clinching red belt was perfect and the hat with its gorgeous sweeping brim presented her face with all manner of flattering shadows. Alexa pulled on her neat white gloves, looked at her reflection and stifled a giggle of excitement.

She rapped gently on the adjoining door and popped her head around. In the darkened room, Lady Meredith was lying on her bed, an elegant figure in unnecessary frills, a mask over her eyes. 'Excuse me, milady, I'm so sorry to disturb you,' said Alexa. 'We are leaving very soon. Enjoy your bridge with the Nicholsons.'

'I shall see you later.' Meredith lifted the mask.

'Let me look at you,' she said, peering at Alexa and taking her in from hat to shoes. 'You'll do.'

'Oh, thank you—'

'Wait. Lipstick,' Meredith said and pointed to her dressing table. 'Take the Elizabeth Arden. It's in the... yes, that's it.'

Alexa obeyed, picked up a smooth gilded cylinder, opened it. The paste had softened in the heat but the ruby shade, even in the dim light of the bedroom, was stunning.

A question fluttered in Meredith's eyes.

Alexa waited, her hand poised on the doorknob, anxious to get going.

'You'd tell me if my nephew behaved in a less than gentle... manly way, wouldn't you?'

Alexa was about to ask why on earth he would, but the mask was back over Lady Meredith's eyes, her hand waving her away.

* * *

Today, the city had nowhere to hide. Under the blue sky, reflected in shimmering water, Venice rose at the edge of the world, a mirage toasted by the sun in colours of sand, of rose, of stone punctuated by the spires and great demi-spheres of churches. Within it, around it, the water was populated by little boats with russet-red sails cutting briskly over the languid surface, and the curving gondolas paddling smoothly through the throng.

Alexa, sitting low on a hot, white leather seat, clutched her handbag with one hand and the side of the teak-decked speedboat with the other. Beside her, Guy was calling out directions to the driver. He turned to her to explain where they were going but she could barely hear him above the roar of the engine. He smiled his dazzling smile, realising – his dark glasses hiding his eyes, as hers did – that their means of communication was diminished to grins and nods. Inside her tumbled a kaleidoscope of guesses and doubts, of wondering and sparks of glee. What a turnaround for a girl from Porthdeen.

The boat swung around a promontory, passing the mighty pale-stone basilica that Alexa had spotted on her way over to Lido and plunging, as Guy imparted to her, his mouth close to her ear, into the Grand Canal. He gestured to his right towards St Mark's Square and the Doge's Palace and she spotted some landmarks she'd seen in Lady Meredith's brochure: lions atop pillars, the red-brick bell tower.

The driver slowed his pace, easing into the flow of the water traffic, which came at them, avoided them, passed them by from every direction. All was bright and busy on the canal, watched over by palazzos – great palaces of the sea – their façades in yellow, in white, in pink and in terracotta, so dominant, each one more stupendous, more glorious than the last. But every so often she glimpsed a quieter world, a darker, sleepy channel leading into the heart, shaded and traversed by delicate bridges, the odd gondola dipping and bumping along.

Guy pointed out the Rialto as they slipped under the sublimely famous bridge and the canal turned a great corner, settled, grew quieter, wider but no less incredible to each one of Alexa's senses. They docked in front of the church of San Stae, a great fascia of white stone, and Alexa got to her feet, her knees unsteady, reaching her hand shakily for Guy to lift her up and onto the jetty. He hauled her with a grip so firm and strong, and yes, gentlemanly that she felt the resonance of him through the fabric of her glove. Her first step on Venice.

* * *

They sat outside a café in a square canopied by trees, having found it, quite by chance after squeezing through a quiet and perplexing labyrinth. A dozen corners had been turned, empty courtyards and blind alleys contemplated. They had crossed miniature bridges spanning narrow backwaters which appeared as refreshing gifts around unexpected turnings. The oblong chink of blue sky above seemed so very far away.

Alexa sipped her coffee. Sunlight stippled mellow walls with dollops of gold, and she experienced an extraordinary peace, a settling of excitement, a cooling of fear. The streets of Venice, this kingdom of stone, offered her their immense age, their deep shade, their wisdom and their silence. Here, she would find Nonna, and all would be well.

People sat at other tables or strolled across the cobbles where sparrows skittered among fallen tree flowers. She heard Italian voices, a steady murmuring in the Venetian dialect. In a repressed part of her memory, she understood every word.

Guy watched her as she listened. 'You speak Italian?' he asked.

'It's an odd thing. I understand it,' she said, 'but I can't always express myself properly. My mother often spoke in Italian. She sang in Italian when she was sad and, I suspect, missing this place. She sang the same song, always the same: "Venice, the moon and you".' Alexa paused, stirred the froth on her coffee. 'I must have absorbed much more than I realised.'

She opened her handbag, drew out her photograph.

'There's my mother,' she handed it to Guy, 'with her nanny Juliet.'

'*Bella*,' he smiled on instinct.

'I need to find that bridge they're standing on. It is outside the palazzo where Mamma was born. The palazzo where my grandmother, apparently, returned after Mamma died.'

Guy did exactly what Alexa had done many times, and peered closely at the wall behind the girls in the photograph.

'I can't see a street sign,' he said. 'It will be like trying to find a needle in a haystack. This city—'

'Do you have a map?'

Guy laughed. 'Yes, I do, here, folded in my pocket, for what it's worth. But, Alexa, this city is unmappable. More than once I have found myself somewhere, in a dead end, in an unnamed *campo* or *calle* that's uncharted, simply not there. And I'm never where I expect to be. There's not just the streets, you see. There's the water to consider. That's the mystery of this place. The mystery you will fall in love with.'

Alexa took the photograph from him. 'I think I already have.' Her skin prickled, hoping Guy would not misread her, imagine her meaning something else. She studied the picture again.

'There's some sort of niche on the wall behind them, halfway up, with a little statue. I've been looking out for it ever since we got off the boat. Can you make it out?'

'Ah, yes, a shrine to the Virgin. There's hundreds of them, too.'

Alexa laughed. 'This impossible place.'

'Yes, but even more perfect for it.'

The bells of a nearby, but invisible, church began to ring out. 'Ah, *la marangona*,' said Guy. 'The bell for the end of the working day. It's a summons.'

'A sacred chime to mark the hours,' said Alexa, enjoying the peaceful sound.

The sun had shifted and corners of the square held new, violet shadows. Guy asked for the bill, offered her his elbow again, and they strolled across the square, choosing a new and particularly enticing street.

'So why did you decide to come to Venice?' she asked, adding swiftly, 'to see your aunt?'

'I found that I suddenly had a spare few weeks,' he said. 'My latest consignment of marble is well on its way to London. I was in Rome and I thought...' he glanced at Alexa, 'that I'd see for myself how you were getting on.'

'As you now know,' she gazed at the impenetrable streets, the mystifying, limited view, and felt an equal measure of rapture and defeat, 'I've rather been stranded on Lido. But tell me,' she brightened, 'where do you stay in Rome? Your hotel bills must be very expensive?'

'Oh, no, I have a villa just outside the city. Rome, as you can guess, is a fascinating place, but not, in my opinion, as divine as Venice.'

'You seem to know Venice very well.'

'I don't think anyone can know it, not really.'

He stopped her and their toes clashed on the cobbles. 'Would you like an ice cream?'

She giggled. 'I'm not twelve any longer.'

'That you are not,' he said, in all seriousness.

She looked up at his suddenly solemn face. His eyes had lost their usual glitter and seemed to be glowing with a much fiercer, deeper fire.

Guy took off his hat and tugged her gently towards him. His kiss was dry, brief and oddly demanding, as if he was making his mark on her. Alexa pulled away, dazed by an unexpected memory of Harvey and the moment in the middle of the ball when he'd asked her to marry him. Had Guy's kiss and Harvey's proposal really been that unexpected?

Alexa touched her hand to her lips, as if to remove the kiss. But Guy didn't give her a moment. He urged her to walk on, pressing her hand, which she rested on his arm, harder into his sleeve. He continued to chat, as if the kiss had simply not happened. Alexa matched his stride as best she could, her mind reeling and switching from home and Harvey to the enigma of Venice and Guy with every new corner they turned.

* * *

Doorways darkened, the water became black, the sections of sky over Alexa's head turned a voluminous deep navy-blue. Lamps began to flicker in windows and in the niches dedicated to Mary. Nocturnal Venice closed in around them. Footsteps belonging to unseen walkers receded, voices echoed over stone, water slapped under bridges, a gondola glided by into darkness.

They dined at a circular table, covered with a pristine cloth outside a tiny restaurant by a little bridge where two slender waterways met. The candle's flame illuminated her fried fish, delectable and as light as air, and brightened the bubbles in her fresh almost-green Frascati.

'Tell me about your family,' said Guy, twirling spaghetti with his fork.

Alexa resisted ordering pasta because she had made such a mess of it the first time she'd eaten it one evening at the Excelsior under milady's unnerving stare.

'Tell me more about yourself first?' she said, boosted already by half a glass of wine.

'There's not much more to know, except I'm part of the lucky generation. Although father thought I should have lied about my age. I wasn't eighteen until October 1918 and he thinks I should have been in the thick of it long before. Useless, you see.' Sorrow turned over in Guy's eyes. 'I could not even die for my country.'

Alexa said, 'Surely not useless, think of your successes, your business, your villa in Rome—'

'I know you're from Cornwall,' he interrupted her, 'the ends of the earth, you said. And you told me that your mother was – and your grandmother is – Venetian. Brothers or sisters? What about your father?'

Alexa took a long slow breath. Guy brought her back to her reality. He cocked his head, giving her a serious but encouraging smile. In the half-light, he looked like the boy that Lady Meredith still thought he was. But in the hard Italian sun of earlier, it was easy for Alexa to see the years of seniority he had over her. Years of travelling, of business, of drinking whisky. Years of living, and maybe of loving. And yet, here he was, helping her, patiently teasing out her story.

'I have a little half-sister, Melissa,' said Alexa, 'And our neighbour at Porthdeen was, is, like a brother to me.' She sipped her wine, studied its flavour, feeling uncomfortable disloyalty to Harvey. 'And I have a confession to make.'

Guy raised one eyebrow, his eyes sparkling in the half darkness. 'Oh good. I like a confession.'

'No one has any idea where I am.'

Guy exclaimed, took a large sip from his glass.

'I told you I was a runaway,' said Alexa. 'And not at all proud of myself. But I have a suspicion that I'm not really that missed.'

'Rubbish,' blurted Guy.

'No, really. My father has a new life. A new wife, and a new daughter. He was trying to get me off his hands, anyway, marry me off to our neighbour, the man I just mentioned. And so, I applied to become a lady's companion. They didn't even know I was in London, let alone in Venice.'

'I see,' said Guy. He reached over the tablecloth and linked his warm heavily tanned fingers around hers. Encircled by his, her hands looked surprisingly white. 'And are you the marrying kind?' He studied her face in the candlelight. 'Of course you are.'

Alexa stiffened at his presumption.

Guy said, 'But I think that, really, you love him, this neighbour fellow. Am I right?'

'He's chosen someone else now,' she said.

'Well, that settles it then.'

She made a protesting noise that was less than a word, more of a sigh. 'Yes,' she said, 'I suppose that it does.'

***

The speedboat was waiting where they'd left it at the jetty near San Stae. Stepping down into it, Alexa was overcome by immense tiredness in her limbs, and crushing defeat in her head. As she slumped into the seat and Guy woke the driver from his snooze, a sense of failure overwhelmed her. Despite all of the bridges they'd crossed and tight corners they'd turned, they had barely scratched the surface of Venice and were no closer to finding the elusive spot where Mamma and Juliet had been photographed. Alexa's sigh dragged with disappointment as the engine fired, broke the silence of the night and they moved off.

Infrequent lanterns on landing stages and at dark water doors threw fragmented beams over the surface of the canal. And inside her, her own light had gone out. Talk of home, of her family, of Harvey deflated her. The dreamy golden glow of the Grand Canal slipped by and, sooner than she expected, they plunged into the inky black of the lagoon. Out here, in the middle of the water, Alexa realised how alone she was. Ahead, the lights of Lido were brighter, brasher, like a slice of cut diamond on the night horizon.

In the dark, Guy found her hand and cradled it in his fingers, his touch branding her with a rush of desire, a suggestion that he had sought her out; that he needed her. But his kiss earlier had been so very gentlemanly, almost chaste. She suddenly felt protected, no longer alone. And that there was no need to tell Lady Meredith a thing.

Guy led her up the steps into the hotel foyer. While he collected their room keys from the concierge, she leant against the reception desk and, through a mute and exhausted haze, spotted Mr and Mrs Nicholson coming out of the bar. They paused, noticing her and Guy, and Alexa thought for a moment that they were coming over to say goodnight. But instead, she watched as

Clementine Nicholson leant in to her husband to whisper something, and then turned to walk away.

* * *

The next afternoon, Lady Meredith finally made her first trip across the water to Venice, for dinner and theatre with the Nicholsons. Alexa longed to go back and, for a moment was poised to grasp at the chance but, instead, feigned a headache. With milady, her time would not be her own, she'd not be the focus she'd been with Guy. And the frustration would be unbearable. But milady was resigned to going on her own anyway, for the dreadful Nicholsons had decided to snubAlexa and had only bought one extra ticket.

In her room, Alexa drew down her blinds against the afternoon sun and eased the cords so that the slats threw soothing shadows over the walls. Relishing the unexpected gift of solitude, she bathed and washed her hair and ordered peppermint tea, all the while, thinking of her conversation with Guy at dinner the night before: about Porthdeen, her family, those she'd left behind. Guy's company and his kindness had piqued her confidence.

Sitting at the desk, Alexa opened a window in her mind that she'd kept firmly shut for a year. She selected sheets of letter-headed notepaper, the name Excelsior resplendent in gold, and filled her pen with ink. The joyful sounds of the beach outside faded as she bent her head and wrote to her father. She told him where she was – in case he didn't readily connect the hotel's address on the notepaper – and how she was employed. Alexa was sure that he would approve of her ambition, approve of Lady Meredith, be glad she was making her way in the world.

As she sealed the envelope, the wave of noise from the beach increased and, above it, seagulls cried sporadically, like emissaries from Cornwall sent to find her. A bolt of homesickness ran through her like a sword. They are Italian sea birds, she told herself, nothing like the gulls that colonised the cliffs of Porthdeen, nothing like the gulls she and Harvey used to watch and wonder about. Nothing like home at all.

22

THE HEIGHT OF SUMMER, 1931

'My aunt has no scruples,' said Guy, a fortnight later, lifting his cup for Alexa to drop a slice of lemon into it. 'She hates the Nicholsons as much as I do, and yet she now is constantly in their pockets, accepting their invitations to speed across the lagoon. I knew once she set foot on Venice, she'd fall in love with it. And I know you have too.'

They were taking tea in the shade of the veranda, waiting for Lady Meredith to join them. Two weeks had passed since Alexa sent her letter; fourteen days in which milady had decided to tick off as much of Venice as she possibly could, with excursions, guided walks and tours organised by her social adversaries.

And, because Guy had become too busy to take her across to Venice himself, Alexa had trailed along with milady, all the time sensing snobbish hostility from the Nicholsons. She'd kept her distance as they stepped inside the rosy pink colonnade of the Doge's Palace and marvelled at the expanse of St Mark's Square. She had stood apart from them among the hushed crowds giving off a collective sigh at the first sight of heavenly mosaics vaulting overhead, tripping with angels and saints and with cherubs peeking around corners. She had basked alone in the glow of demure Madonnas that lit up the room, and portraits of illustrious noblemen and women so vividly alive that they seemed to be winking at her, knowing all the time that she'd never find Nonna here tussling with hordes of tourists.

'Of course, I have,' said Alexa, 'who wouldn't. It's just...'

'It's just...?' Guy tipped his head to one side, waiting for Alexa to continue. He unsettled her. His eyes were glazed, his expression blank. Perhaps other preoccupations – business, money, Carrara marble – were filling his mind.

'Since I first met them, at the soirée in February, the Nicholsons have not taken to me at all. There was a way Mrs Nicholson looked at me, when she saw us together, that evening we returned from Venice—'

She stopped and blushed hard. She thought of Guy's kiss, firm and hard, laying claim to her in the street; of Guy holding her hand in the dark of the speedboat.

'Clementine Nicholson is a silly snob,' Guy said, 'she looks at everyone like that. Perhaps she is still miffed you bailed out from her son's awful party. She's impressed by my aunt's title and can't see beyond it. Ignore her. I do.'

He returned to his day-old *The Times*, cutting conversation.

Since the kiss, Alexa had noticed a polite distancing, Guy's attentions – sporadic, sparse, like the cooling splash of rain at the beginning of a summer storm. Perhaps he was so distracted by his latest shipment of marble to London that he had forgotten all about the kiss. Perhaps it had not meant to him what it did to her. And yet she could not stop thinking about it.

'If milady gives me leave, we could go back across together,' she said, hopefully, catching his eye. 'I'd like to see if we can find that little bridge in the photograph.'

Guy looked as if his chair had suddenly become very uncomfortable.

'I'll see if I have the time,' he said, folding his arms. 'Remember what I said. It's a needle in a haystack—'

'There you two are.'

As Meredith approached the table she paused, standing quite still for a moment, looking first from her nephew to Alexa and back again, perception circling her eyes.

'You two. Taking tea, I see,' said milady, and accepted the chair that Guy drew out for her.

Alexa offered her a cup, tea and lemon while Guy picked up his newspaper, opting out again.

'Isn't this heat extraordinary?' commented Meredith, sighing and flicking her fan around her face. 'And it's going to get worse, I'm assured by all and sundry. The Nicholsons are talking about decamping to Lake Garda in August. And I'm hatching a plan.'

'Really, Auntie,' said Guy, crunching down a corner of his newspaper. 'You're thinking of following them?'

'Think how beautifully fresh and cool it will be there by the lake, beneath the mountains, compared to this cauldron. I've heard the lakes are absolutely splendid, Alexa.'

'Of course,' Alexa said, and panic began to sniff around her. Of course. Her adventure in Venice would have to end at some point, but with milady voicing her plan with such precision, it was an inevitability that Alexa would have to accept. Defeat hit her. She had absolutely no control over where her life would take her next. Her one chance to find her grandmother was slipping at speed through her foolish fingers.

'*Scusi, signora.*'

The waiter stood by their table holding a silver salver on which lay a letter.

Lady Meredith picked it up without looking at it and waved him away.

'Oh,' she said, in complete surprise, and handed the envelope across the table to Alexa. 'It's for you.'

Alexa glanced at the handwriting and gasped. She snatched up her handbag, excused herself and hurried out into the foyer, her parasol tucked under her arm, the letter from Eleanor clutched in her fist.

* * *

Under the burning sun, the promenade was a long stretch of infernal white heat at the end of which Alexa spotted a cluster of trees with a bench, an oasis of shade and solitude. She fixed her parasol in front of her face and headed for it. On the beach, mad Englishmen were still frolicking in the waves, while sensible Venetians were snoozing behind shuttered windows.

She sat, panting from the heat, perspiration soaking the back of her dress, and ripped the letter from its envelope. Eleanor's breathless words flew off the page and Alexa battled to rein them in, to slow herself down, to understand, to soak up the news:

> *please, please come home. We received your letter... such a surprise. Dad misses you... doctor says he is depressed. He's very weak. Oh, Alexa. Help us. He calls me Lotte by mistake. He is confused... so sad... it has been far too long... Melissa keeps asking for her sister. We are all still in terrible shock from what happened at the ball, desperate to understand... we need you here. Harvey will marry Sarah in August.*

Alexa crushed the letter down on to her lap and pressed her hands over her eyes. In an instant, tears soaked the cotton lace of her gloves. She wanted to cry out and her mouth twisted with a ferocious effort to contain herself. Her limbs were light as dust, as if she would be just blown away by the breeze off the sea. Her blood throbbed through a hollow space in her chest. Harvey will marry Sarah. Her father ill. A violent sob erupted.

A shadow fell over her.

'What's this?' Guy Moreland said.

He sat beside her, the weight of his body like a prop, suddenly bolstering her, keeping her from falling over.

She struggled to speak, did not, for a moment, know how to. She could not look at him. Instead, she scrabbled in her handbag, realising she'd forgotten her handkerchief as panic burst through her.

'A letter... my stepmother.'

'Bad news? Oh no, look at you.' He put his arm around her, pulled her close to his chest. 'Take a deep breath,' he said, his mouth on her hair. 'Only tell me if you want to.'

She did as he asked, screwed her eyes tight, her cheek against the smooth fabric of his shirt. The deep musk of his cologne hit her, awakened her like smelling salts.

'My father is unwell,' she said, at last. 'They all miss me. They want me home.'

'Of course they do,' said Guy. 'I would want you home.'

His words sobered her. She straightened up, smoothed her dress down, carefully secreted the letter into her bag. People were still splashing in the waves, the gulls still wheeling. She must gather her wits, not show Guy that she was a foolish girl, responding to him, naïvely devoted to him. She tried to breathe, gather her strength to stand up and walk away. It was no use. Another, harder cry erupted from her chest.

'Come, come,' he said, his arm around her waist, helping her up.

As she swayed on her feet, her insides seemed to drain away, leaving her empty and cold.

Guy looked at her with a quick, almost photographic, glance and slipped his own sunglasses onto her face.

'We'll go this way.'

* * *

Through the shaded lenses and a haze of fresh tears, Alexa allowed herself to be led along a deserted side street, around the back of the Excelsior and through the quiet rear entrance. They took an unfamiliar staircase and entered a corridor she did not recognise, crossing a wide upper floor lobby, replete with floral displays and gilded mirrors. Guy opened the door to his suite.

'Sit yourself down. Something strong, I think, is what is needed here. You've had a shock. A terrible shock.'

Alexa stumbled to an armchair in the bay window, her heartbeat kicking hard. The slats of the blinds were closed to the glare of the day, but slithers of sun beamed through at intervals, scattering her dress and her arms with chinks of light. His room was larger, more well-appointed than hers – of course – but was furnished with similar finery. She quietly opened her bag to peer at the crumpled letter again and filled her lungs with air, trying to make sense of her despair.

Apart from her father being unwell, which was appalling to learn when she was a thousand miles away, why had the other news made her cry so? Her family was missing her. Why did she feel so surprised? And she had known since February that Harvey and Sarah were engaged to be married. Yet, reading about Harvey's impending wedding, there in Eleanor's looping hand, separated her, once and for all, from the life she had known before. And she had made it happen.

Hearing a chink of decanter and glass, she glanced over to where Guy was busy fixing drinks. The image of her spotting him through the half-open doorway in Cadogan Square, helping himself to Lady Meredith's whisky, cut through her. Guy, equally then as he was now, an enigmatic and thrilling force.

'It's Scotch, I'm afraid. I have a feeling you won't like it.'

His fine and handsome face filled her vision, his tanned hand holding a cut-glass tumbler for her, his eyes searching hers, engaging her, not letting her get away.

'Try it.'

She did as she was told. The liquor flared down her middle like flames licking at kindling and she grimaced, rested, and took another sip.

Guy laughed lightly. 'That's my girl.'

He sat on the chair opposite her, and waited. She sipped again, wanting to please him.

Here in Guy's suite she was out of the punishing glare of the sun but the heat had adhered to her, was radiating from her. The ceiling fan flicked and turned overhead, hardly breaking the thick, warm air. She glanced at Guy. His features had fallen again into his vacant, bland expression. A band snapped in her head.

'You're not really interested in me at all, are you?' she said.

'Alexa?' He was aghast, then laughter brightened his face. 'I have been fascinated by you since I first saw you; since you first stepped into my aunt's salon, with your dark hair, your beautiful skin, your eyes... clutching those stupid sewing threads. How could I not be?'

'Why on earth should you be?' she responded, sulkily, looking away.

Sighing exaggeratedly, he knelt on the floor by her side and slipped his arms under hers, around her waist. His lips rested lightly against the side of her neck, his presence hot and powerful.

'If you're not going to talk to me about it,' he said, his voice muffled, 'then I can show you.'

'Show me what...?' she faltered. A pulse was tapping hard at the base of her throat, her thoughts tumbling. Scent became touch, sight became sound. He had told her months ago in the Velvet Rose that she wanted to be loved. And she did, so very much.

She looked down at her hands; the ink from Eleanor's letter had stained her gloves.

'I think I need to go home.'

'Oh no, that's not the answer. You know it.'

Guy drew back, held her face in his hands and covered her mouth with a slow kiss. Desire, breathless and darting, coursed through her. She drew away from him, new tears soaking her eyes.

'Then what is?' she asked.

She sincerely had no idea. Home and everyone there were so very far away from this insistent, whirling, glamorous paradise. She had chosen not to be at home, among her family who loved her. She had chosen not to be with Harvey who had, now, most certainly and, quite rightly, discarded her. And her quest to find her grandmother was melting away under the blistering Mediterranean sun.

'Then what is, Guy?' she repeated.

He carefully lifted each of her hands in turn and stripped off her gloves, dropping them to the floor.

'This is.' He pulled her up, his arms cradling her, supporting her. 'This is the answer, Alexa. Come.'

He coaxed her, guided her across the room. Alexa's frame was fluid, weak and flowing. Half of her mind realised where she was being taken, the other half did not care. She had no control of her smile, which stretched across her face luxuriously, her chin tilting languidly as she rested her head on his shoulder. 'You were right, Guy,' she whispered, 'I do want to be loved.'

He lifted her up, and she laughed like a child as he carried her into his bedroom.

23

Through the cracks of fractured sleep, Alexa heard the breakfast trolley creaking along the corridor and, through the window, the first bathers taking their early dip. These noises reached her, as they had done every morning since her arrival at the Excelsior, hurrying in yet another day on Lido, much like the one before. But, waking in the bed in the unfamiliar bedroom, she landed, with a thump, in an entirely unknown place. Yesterday, the path of her life had divided and the terrifying direction that she had chosen rose up before her.

The sound of Guy breathing beside her spiralled through her, the weight of his body strange and imposing. She kept her eyes tightly shut as she felt him stir and slip out of the bed. Within a moment, she heard water splashing and running in the bathroom. Only then did she dare open her eyes.

Alexa leapt up from the bed and tussled with her clothes that were strewn over the chair in the corner, a twisted record of what had happened the day before. As she dressed, questions split her mind. Was this, then, the solution to her troubles – here in this situation, which felt neither wrong, nor right? In the small hours, when they had left the bed, opened the shutters and looked out together at the moon, luminous and ripe over the inky sea, she'd dared to ask him if he, too, wanted to be loved, just as he'd asked her an age ago during that stolen evening at the Velvet Rose.

'What a question,' he'd uttered, his face crumbling briefly as she glimpsed the man Guy would have been had he been shown love as a child.

But his weakness was temporary, for his face realigned to its unfathomable best when he wordlessly took her hand and drew her back to bed. His pain vanished and he once again became the person Alexa was in awe of, the person in charge.

Buttoning her dress, Alexa walked over to the windows and teased open the shutters again to stare at the empty spot in the sky where the moon had hung. In daylight, Lido was the same, Venice, the same. Everything, in fact, was the same, except Alexa. She turned at the sound of the bathroom door opening and Guy emerged, in vest and trousers, his hair still damp, his dishevelled appearance chopping away his years. He greeted her brightly, cheerily, as if she was an old friend.

'Ah, you're up and dressed. Good, we can get a head start on the day,' he said. 'I expect, in the circumstances, you will be resigning. My aunt won't be particularly pleased, but you can't stay shackled to her forever. In any case, she will be leaving soon for Lake Garda with the infernal Nicholsons.'

Alexa watched him run a comb through his slick hair in front of the mirror and wipe on his pomade. In an instant, his maturity returned and he was the man that she realised she barely knew.

'But, Guy...' she ventured, feeling a sickening pulse of nerves in her stomach. Her world, overnight, had turned inside out, '... what are the circumstances?'

He came to her, and pulled her into his arms, and her relief at the comfort of his touch made her gasp.

'You can't go with her,' he said. 'You have too much to do here.'

'Yes of course, I must find my grandmother.'

'And you'll stay with me, of course,' he said into her hair.

Alexa found herself smiling as the day brightened a shade and gently fell back into place.

He released her and strode over to the table to pick up a set of keys, jingling them.

'These are for my apartment in Santa Croce. My aunt will hate me for stealing you. But I assure you, she won't give you the satisfaction of any sort of reaction. She will lose her little runaround and she must endure the Nicholsons on her own. But no matter.' He playfully tossed Alexa the keys. She sat down on the bed amid the rumpled sheets, exhausted by life's sudden revolution, turning the keys over in her hands.

Ripping the paper covering of a fresh new shirt, Guy gave her a puzzled look.

'You're very quiet, Alexa. Oh God, I know this is so very unconventional for a girl like you. But these are modern times. It is what you want, surely? I can't see you trailing after my auntie until you are both old, and very old, ladies.'

Alexa watched his eyes soaking her up and she breathed hard with a sudden courage.

'Yes, Guy,' she said and she laughed, teetering on the edge of tears as she dared herself to set off along the path that he was taking her. 'This is most definitely what I want.'

* * *

Alexa found Lady Meredith breakfasting on the terrace. She said good morning, gave her half a smile, slipped into her usual chair and picked up the teapot.

'Milady, I wish to give you notice,' she said before she'd

finished pouring her cup. 'I'm going to stay here with Guy.'

Meredith narrowed her eyes, replaced her own cup with precision onto the saucer. 'So, you are to leave me and run off with my nephew, Alexa,' she said, her face widening with sudden understanding, and odd amusement, 'now that he has stopped behaving like a gentleman.'

'Oh, but he is a—'

Meredith shut her off. 'And pray, what am I to do in the meantime?'

'I wouldn't call it running off, as such. We're not going far,' Alexa faltered in the headlights of her employer's unruffled glare. 'We are going to his apartment in Santa Croce. It will do for now, until such time...'

Alexa trailed off. She had no idea what such time she was referring to. The way ahead was dark. There was nothing else but Guy beyond today.

'I know all about his apartment,' clipped Lady Meredith. 'Funny little place. You couldn't swing a cat in there. And, you say it'll do for now? Now that you are his *mistress*?'

Alexa's skin tightened like a shroud being stitched around her; the first real sweat of the day began to ooze down her back. She sank beneath the surface of embarrassment, grappling for the correct response.

Watching her flounder, Lady Meredith said, 'He's a rum one, that fellow. I must say, Alexa, he never surprises me.' She pulled out her pocket watch, glanced at it and called for a waiter. 'I won't keep you. I'm sure you have packing to do. Good morning to you.'

She stood so quickly that the waiter failed to secure her chair and it fell with a clatter onto the terracotta floor. But Lady Meredith's breeding ensured she did not bat an eyelid as she walked imperiously away, leaving the waiter to right the chair and push it neatly in place and for Alexa to finish her tea alone.

24

THE DOG DAYS, 1931

One of the first things Guy did for her, after they moved into the Santa Croce apartment, was to have Alexa's photograph framed, for it was becoming rather tatty. He gave it to her on her nineteenth birthday, along with a bracelet of peridot, the stones suspended from a white-gold chain like green glass, the colour of the Venetian lagoon.

The frame was in rosewood, like her Mamma's button box, beautifully polished, with delicate silver edges. Alexa set it on the shelf beneath the huge mirror which reflected the waters in the canal beneath the window. And from there, Mamma and Juliet beamed out of the hazy captured sunshine. It was small enough to slip into her handbag and, every day, Alexa took it with her as she set out in search of the spot where the two girls had stood at the turn of the century.

As the morning bells rang out above the rooftops, Alexa eased herself from Guy's embrace under the sheet and opened the shutters slowly, carefully, to allow him to wake gently.

'Where to today, Alexa?' he asked.

'I go wherever my feet take me,' she said. 'Always a new direction, a new bridge, an unfamiliar alley.'

Guy laughed. 'They are all unfamiliar.'

She brewed coffee while he dressed in his cool linen suit to counter the burgeoning heat of the day.

'But there is no question, Alexa,' he said, coming through to the kitchen, 'that the bridge or the *calle* where your mother was standing will not have been altered since the photograph was taken. This city is timeless. Will never change.'

'And yet,' she said, her resolve draining, 'remains inscrutable. It's impossible.'

'You'll find her,' he said, his thoughts trailing off to another place.

He set his panama on his head, kissed her and went off to pursue his business of the day at his rented office near St Mark's Square.

* * *

As soon as Guy had gone, Alexa's determination fired again and she slipped his map – for what is was worth – along with her photograph, into her handbag. Leaving the apartment, she fastened the door behind her, throwing the communal corridor into darkness. She gingerly took the shallow, slippery marble stairs down through what would have once been the palazzo's grand entrance hall, and slipped out into the narrow street.

She chose the shaded side, kept close to the walls. The houses appeared delicate, almost weightless, towering above the drowsy water that lapped below her feet. Today, Alexa sensed salt in the air, blown in from the encircling lagoon, and saw the melting silvery traces of it on the crumbling walls. She was fascinated by the buildings and the gaps inbetween them, wondering which way they would lead her. She might, she decided, make it through Ghetto to the edge where the sea was the horizon, as it had always been at Porthdeen. But, as she passed the parish well in the square, where the women gathered and greeted her with a sunny *buongiorno*, they reminded her that Santa Croce, that Venice, was now her home.

And here, cloistered from the outside world, she was tripping through a fantasy, her old life behind her. Eleanor's letter had settled it: with her father so unstable, word of her new situation might prove to be too much for him. And with Harvey to marry Sarah... she could not possibly go back to Porthdeen. For how could she when she had chosen Venice, chosen Guy?

* * *

Two hours later, having taken a *traghetto* across the Grand Canal, Alexa found herself in a blind alley, somewhere in the ancient streets of Ghetto. The noon sun was blazing and she was exhausted. Life in Venice, she discovered, was conducted out of doors: in the squares, in the markets, on the canals, in the cafés and restaurants. But now, the streets were emptying, shops shutting, Venetians drifting indoors for private, daytime rest, leaving her to make her solitary way home through hot, empty streets.

And once Alexa closed the heavy front door behind her, she had not a soul to speak to; only the bells of the churches marking the hours to keep her company. The daily maid, Nerina, had come in while she was out to tidy up and prepare some food, revealing her visit by the orderliness of the rooms, the swept floor, and the fresh fruit arranged under a cloth on the table.

Alexa's view through the narrow windows was limited: a small slither of green water below and the patched wall of the next building across the canal, so close she could almost touch it. As she stood and listened to the sleeping afternoon, her fatigue translated gradually into hollow, aching loneliness; another day's failure. She pulled the shutters closed and lay down on the bed. As she drifted off to sleep, she decided that tomorrow, just for one day, she would abandon her search and go with Nerina to Rialto Market to pick out vegetables, fish and fruit, to select the bread and the wine. She would relish Nerina's easy, chattering company; it would be a nice change, and the idea of it gave her a glimmer of delight. Except that afterwards she would be home again, alone, as she was now, no closer to finding Nonna and waiting for Guy to return when the sun went down.

* * *

His key in the lock woke her in half darkness and she struggled to rouse herself. He stood in the doorway of the bedroom, his pale suit luminous in the gloom.

'Why aren't the lamps lit, Alexa?'

'I'm sorry, I've been sleeping.' She stretched, hitched herself up against the pillows. She'd been sleeping for far too long.

'I can see that. What is for supper?'

'I'm not sure... what has Nerina left?'

He shrugged. In his hands was a bundle wrapped in fancy paper. He threw it onto the bed.

'Put this on.'

He shut the door.

Alexa dragged herself from the remains of her sleep, wondering why he might be so short with her, and opened the shutters to let in the last of the evening light. She picked up the parcel and weighed it in her hands before ripping it open. A beautiful silk dressing gown, patterned in colours of sand and terracotta and red and black, lay folded within the paper. She lifted it up and it shimmered and flowed through her hands like water. As she slipped it on, easily, like a delicious luxury, she decided he must have had a bad day, rotten news about his latest shipment.

Guy had lit the lamps, had found wine, was breaking bread and slicing cheese. Alexa came through from the bedroom, barefoot. The gown floated around her, belted at the middle. He glanced up.

'You like it?'

'It's beautiful,' she said. 'What a lovely surprise. Thank you.'

'Come here then.' He held out his arm.

She walked over, stood beside his chair and tucked herself into the crook of his elbow. The scent of his hair oil and earthy cologne, after a day's work, intensified and permeated the air. His presence salved her loneliness temporarily and yet she fizzed with nerves, unsure of his next move.

He poured a glass of wine for her and held it up to her lips, delicately feeding her, while, with a sense of satisfaction, he caressed her body through the draping silk. Instantly, like a reflex, his passion warmed her. Something tightened inside, her body responding, but her mind seemed to stand still. Despite his attention, his desire, she remained alone.

Alexa had lied to Guy, for the dressing gown was not a surprise. Every other day he came home with a gift for her. And now, as his hands teased and stroked, she realised that she was always disappointed. Yes, the dressing gown was beautiful, but there was a gap, a pause, between what he gave her and the reason behind it. Even as she thanked him, she could not cross that breach.

Alexa responded to his touch, searched his eyes as if the answer lay with him. But he didn't look at her, instead concentrated on his wine. His face was passive, verging on angry, just like the first time she'd seen him through the gap in the doors to Lady Meredith's salon.

Holding off her panic, Alexa concentrated on pushing her fingers into his hair, caressing his neck.

'Guy, how was business today?' she whispered. 'Did everything go well?'

'Nothing I cannot handle. Nothing for you to worry about.'

He set down the wine, stood up suddenly, his chair loudly scraping the floor. Gripping her by her shoulders, he pulled the silk down, pressing his lips into her throat.

Suddenly he was different, terrifyingly so.

'Guy, I'm so very tired,' she uttered, her back arching painfully. 'It was so hot today, I walked miles. I don't know... so very...'

He stoppered her mouth with his own, tore at the belt of the dressing gown, the air around them snapping with fear and anger.

'You think you've had a bad day,' he muttered indifferently as he pushed her down. 'You know nothing about it.'

Trying not to cry, she heard the silk rip tenderly as the hard floor pressed into her back.

'This won't take long,' he whispered in her ear, 'then you can sleep all you want to.'

Outside the window, a deep-black Venetian night snuffed out the sky.

25

Bells, chiming sedately to announce the new day, woke her. Alexa stirred and winced, her neck and shoulders sore. Guy had been holding her closely all night, tight in an unconscious grip, and she'd slept awkwardly, a painful, unnatural position. She extracted herself, quietly opened the shutters and padded through to the kitchen to make coffee. The dressing gown lay in a crumpled heap on the floor. Alexa stepped over it, and began her morning routine.

Everything went on as it usually did: the opening of the windows, the letting in of the new light, the pouring of water, the chink of china cups as she tried not to make any noise that might wake him. Even his keeping hold of her through each of the watches of the night was normal. But last night, something terrible had happened between them, as if they had had some sort of accident. And this morning, she wanted to keep quiet and still, to see how far she had travelled from what she thought of as acceptable, and how she could possibly make her way back. She gingerly rubbed at her stiff neck; the rest of her body, deep inside, was numb.

Guy stirred in the bedroom, and she turned quickly to attend to the coffee.

He was suddenly behind her, his arms around her; his kiss firm on her neck.

'Good morning, Alexa.'

She didn't want to look at him, but knew she must, to assess him, discover what he might be thinking. And then, as she watched him calmly sit at the table and reach for the jug of milk, the sugar bowl, she realised, in a sudden squeeze of panic, that she never knew what he was thinking.

'I'm sorry I ripped the dressing gown. You had rather a... wonderful effect on me,' he said. 'Alexa, you are just damned beautiful. Do you think you can mend it?'

'I'm not sure. I'll see if Nerina can do it.' The coffee pot vibrated in her hand.

'I was rather distracted by you last night...' he began, glancing up at her. She saw a look in his eyes that veered towards sadness. 'I was going to tell you something, and I didn't get the chance. I must tell you now.'

She set the cup before him, liquid slopped into the saucer. 'Oh?' she uttered, trying to gather her wits to engage with the man she'd – terribly, dangerously – fallen for.

'I have to leave today for Rome,' Guy said. 'I have an important negotiation to do, with the supplier from Carrara. It's for a very important client. I can't mess this one up. Lots of business to attend to. I may be away some time.

'Some time?' Her mouth was dry. 'How long?'

He looked up at her, his eyes a now-familiar void. 'Weeks, a month. Two. I have absolutely no idea.' She winced in surprise.

'Who is this client?' she asked, knowing that she sounded as if she didn't believe a word.

'*Signor* Mussolini, no less.'

She immediately pictured the terrifying profile, the ridiculous uniforms, believing Guy even less.

'My father says he is a tyrant,' she said.

'A tyrant who is having his villa done up and I'm supplying half a quarry load of the best marble in Italy. I don't deal with him personally, of course. I speak only to his lackey. And I know he's not popular with the English chattering classes, but I have a business to run. This could lead on to even bigger and better things, although you can't get much bigger, better, or uglier than this. But I no longer want to be a failure.'

'Well, I could come with you, surely,' she pressed him, treading carefully. 'I could stay at your villa – your place just outside the city.'

'That won't be possible.' He sipped his coffee, his expression opaque. She detected the ghost of a shrug.

'But what about me?' she asked, hearing the pathetic edge to her voice.

'You are searching for your grandmother, Alexa. I can't drag you away from that.' He lowered his voice and a shadow of regret flickered over his face. 'I'm only sorry I have to go. I wish I could be more help. But then... ' he shifted in his seat, his eyes bright with reproach, '... if it wasn't for me, you would not be here at all.' Alexa's debt to him, her obligation, nudged her. His smile softened her momentarily. He held out his open arm to her, and she walked over to him, allowed herself to be held.

'You know I think the world of you?' he asked, touching her briefly at the base of her throat.

Her instinct was to say no, no I don't. But, instead, she smiled and reached for his hand.

'Yes,' she said. 'Yes, I do.'

Guy, warmed by her admission, held her fast, kissing her, his hands travelling over her spine as if imprinting her body onto his memory. She glanced over his shoulder, through the window where the sun shone on the crumbling wall of the building opposite, fearing, suddenly, the empty days stretching before her.

He paused in the middle of his kiss, looking down on her face.

'Don't look so worried, Alexa,' he said, laughingly, gesturing to the window. 'You will not be alone. You have all of this. You have, quite simply, Venice.'

She nodded. She had to pretend that their clash last night was a one-off, a mistake, for she had no alternative. She must step carefully over it and keep on walking. This was her path; this was her adventure. She thought of Deirdre Graham and how her well-meaning words of encouragement had brought her to this.

Guy barely smiled. He was no longer in the room with her. He was on his way, already, heading for Rome.

'Now, tell me you love me,' he said. 'Quickly, for I have to go.'

* * *

Nerina arrived at her usual time when the bells chimed for noon. Diminutive and head to toe in black, her sweet singing carried up the stairs towards the apartment. Her customary bright smile fell when she greeted Alexa.

'*Signora?*' Her dark little eyes questioned her. 'Are you feeling unwell?'

'No, I'm fine,' Alexa assured her, 'just feeling a little...' She tripped over the Italian, searching for words that might be close to the truth, '... under the weather, that's all. Can I make you a cup of coffee?'

Alexa busied herself with another pot while Nerina bent to the sweeping of the floor, the washing of the dishes. With the coffee made, Alexa decided to keep out of her way and went into the bedroom. All plans to follow Nerina to the market forgotten.

'Scusi, signora.' Nerina tapped on the door. In her hand was the dressing gown, 'This was on the floor. It's ripped. Would you like me to mend it?'

'No, thank you,' said Alexa and took it from her, stuffing it into the drawer. 'I'll probably just throw it away.'

'Such a shame, it is very beautiful,' said the older woman. 'Always, the beautiful gifts...'

Alexa glanced at her.

'Is *Signor* busy? At his office?' Nerina went on conversationally, turning to attend to the shutters with her duster.

'He's gone to Rome.' Alexa replied.

'Ah, of course.'

Nerina subtly rearranged her expression of comprehension into one of sympathy.

'You take care, *signora*, until he returns,' she said. 'And if you don't, then I will get cross, as I must take care of you myself, *mia cara*.'

A slap of grief, like a gust of wind around her head, forced Alexa to open the wardrobe door and busy herself with rearranging her clothes so that Nerina would not see the tears running down her face. *Mia cara:* she sounded just like Juliet. Alexa fingered the lace of her dress, suddenly, violently, longing for Porthdeen and everything she'd left behind. Now so different from the original sweeping elegance of the gown she'd worn for the Midsummer Ball, the dress still managed to conjure for her the music and the candlelight and the look on Harvey's face when he took her into the centre of the floor for their first dance. She clutched the fabric in her fists as the force of homesickness threatened to pull her under and drown her. Alexa quickly shut the wardrobe door.

An hour later, her chores complete, Nerina, whispering endearments, squeezed Alexa's hand to say goodbye.

* * *

Alexa lay on the bed trying to gather her strength, to face the rest of the day. Perhaps later, when the sun was lower, she'd venture west in the direction of Dorsoduro to explore, ask a gondolier to take her through the shady backwaters there. But the mere thought of it exhausted her. She had not slept well in the prison of Guy's embrace. She closed her eyes. Two sets of bells chimed the quarters as she drifted in and out of sleep.

Someone knocked on the door, startling her awake.

No one, apart from Nerina, ever came to the apartment; she must have left something behind. Alexa got up and hurried through the kitchen and into the vestibule.

'What have you forgotten?' she asked, pulling on the latch.

Beyond the doorway, the communal hallway was dim. He stood in the shadows, a tall figure in pale shirt and trousers. He lifted his panama above his head.

'Good morning, Alexa,' said Harvey.

She shrank, every part of her body contracting, squeezing tight like a startled animal. Reaching out for the wall, she turned as if blinded and felt her way back along the short corridor and into the kitchen. She found the table, sat down and cradled her head in her hand, watching the doorway in bewildered expectation of the apparition reappearing.

After a short pause, she heard the front door shut and Harvey's steps coming towards her across the kitchen flagstones.

'Dad? Is it Dad? Is he—?' she uttered.

'No, no, not that,' he said quickly.

Alexa forced herself to look up at him. Harvey was trying to smile through the wary closed-in stiffness of his face. He placed his hat on the kitchen table and Alexa kept her eyes fixed on it. She recognised it from two summers before, and its familiarity made her want to touch it.

He said, 'Alexa, I'm sorry to turn up like this, out of the blue.'

How could she mind? He was the person she most wanted to see in the world. The only person who could comfort her. Even so, she had to force herself to look at him. 'I should be the one saying sorry... to you, for what happened at the ball, for everything.'

'There's no need for that.' He went to the stove, gestured to the coffee pot. 'Do you mind if I...?'

Alexa shook her head, unable to say any more as she watched him fill the kettle, set it to boil, so confident, so comfortable in his own skin.

In the long, perplexed silence, broken by the increasing sound of simmering water, Harvey glanced over his shoulder.

'Is Mr Moreland at home?' he asked.

'No!' she jerked, almost shouted, wondering how on earth Harvey knew about Guy, finding it hard to hear him speak his name. And to see him standing at her stove, measuring coffee, clattering cups into saucers was astonishing, his presence in the kitchen so very different to Guy's.

'Why, Harvey...?' she asked. 'Why are you here?'

He set two steaming cups before them and added the milk. The sun was heating the tiles of the roof, seeping down into the apartment. She couldn't face another cup of coffee, even one made by Harvey. He took out his handkerchief, wiped his forehead, undid his cuffs and rolled up his sleeves.

'Alexa, when you wrote home from Lido, your stepmother came straight to see me. You know how upset she is, and that your father had been very depressed, confused. But, Alexa, your letter must have been more of a shock than we realised. For, a week ago, he had a stroke.'

'Oh my goodness,' Alexa moaned, pressed her hand over her

mouth as guilt contracted into agony. Tears leaked unchecked from her eyes.

'And, because you had not responded to her letter, Eleanor asked me if I would write to you,' Harvey said, politely ignoring her tears. 'She thought that maybe I could relay your father's illness better. Persuade you, as she couldn't, to think about coming home, for a visit at least. I decided to go one better.'

He stopped, tilted his chin to appraise Alexa. She watched as questions paraded over his wonderfully comforting face. She wanted to look at him forever.

'No one knows that I'm here,' he continued. 'God knows, it's been a bit of a rushed affair, trying to secure passage. But I had to come, to see for myself. See that you are all right. And that being here in Venice is what you want. What you really want.'

Alexa bristled, gathering her wits, 'Of course it is. Well, it was before you told me about Dad. But why ever would it not be?'

Harvey calmly sipped his coffee, glancing at her naked wedding ring finger.

'I arrived last night, went to the hotel on Lido, which is where I imagined you'd be. Asked for you. Then I asked for Lady Meredith Ainsley, as you had mentioned her as your employer.' He paused. 'She came down to the bar, and I bought her a cocktail. She quite happily informed me of the address of her nephew's apartment. Told me that you were... staying here.' Harvey's eyes sharpened. 'She's quite a character, quite the grande dame, isn't she? Not sure if I took to her or not.'

'Not, probably,' said Alexa, wondering just how much milady had told him about her and Guy.

'Alexa, you don't look yourself.'

'Are you surprised?' she said. 'You've just appeared on my doorstep, and last time I saw you, I humiliated you in the middle of the ballroom, in your own home, surrounded by a hundred people.' She broke off, her words catching. 'And you tell me that my father, a thousand miles away, is ill. And it appears that I cannot cope and don't look myself.'

Harvey drained his coffee, noticing her cup was still full. 'Perhaps coffee is not the right beverage to be drinking on a day like today. Is it always this hot?'

'We should be having tea, like mad English people do,' said Alexa. Tea was Dad's answer to everything. 'And I have none.'

Harvey's eyes glistened wet. 'Are we mad, Alexa?'

She looked beyond him, not wishing to answer.

'Come on, I think we both need some air,' he said. 'What were your plans for today?'

Alexa tried to remember, when her only thought was of her father, struggling, confused, bedridden.

'I was going to walk to Dorsoduro, a parish in that direction,' she took a large breath, gathered her wits, pointed back over her shoulder. 'But, it's getting too hot now, and I'm really quite tired.'

'Eat something, drink a good glass of water. Freshen yourself up. I have an idea.'

Alexa watched him slice some bread, dab it with butter, find the fresh grapes that Nerina had brought.

'Eat,' he said, as he set it all before her, his pleasant authority lifting her spirits. 'Drink.'

'Yes, doctor,' she said, chewing and sipping, wiping at fresh tears as she thanked him.

She caught his old smile.

'You know, Eleanor wanted me to persuade you to come home,' Harvey said, gazing at her with a tender, watchful expression. 'But I have come to realise, Alexa, that making you do what you don't want to do is never a good idea.'

* * *

At the jetty at San Stae, Harvey engaged a gondolier and Alexa sat in the boat in the little cabin comfortably alongside him, his proximity a physical message from home.

Here – in the shade, low and close to the water – she was cooled by breezes, sheltered from the sun. She was happy to let Venice drift by, to hear the pull and dip of the gondolier's oar, the gentle dripping of water behind her the only sound that she was aware of, apart from, next to her, Harvey's gentle voice. And together, they were steeped in tranquil shadows and shielded from the outside world as the gondolier propelled them down deserted channels, under crumbling bridges draped with trailing vines, walls rising either side, dappled with reflections of water.

When they paused a moment at a crossing of waterways, the gondolier calling to his friend – his voice hollow and echoing across the water – Alexa noticed Harvey steal another glance at her ring finger.

'In case you are wondering,' she said, self-consciously rubbing her knuckle, 'my wedding ring is at the jewellers. It had to be altered.'

'Ah, I see.'

Alexa knew what Harvey had been thinking; what, no doubt, Lady Meredith had imparted to him. She offered a prayer that he would not see her lie; could not bear that he would think badly of her.

'How things can change in a year,' he said as the gondola moved off, bumping brickwork stained green with lichen. 'It all has happened rather quickly – for both of us. And it will be my turn in under four weeks.'

Alexa was instantly cross with herself for minding. She had known for months that Harvey was to marry Sarah. And she had chosen this life with Guy, as unsettling and as grubby as it was; a life separated from Harvey and from home.

When she left Porthdeen, her desire to escape, to keep running, was perpetuated by her need to find Nonna. But even now, cruising through the canals of Venice and as close to finding her as she'd ever be, stealing a glance at Harvey, at his face, kind and simply lovely in the flickering shade of the gondola cabin, she thought perhaps she had come too far. And now, it was an awfully long way to get home.

'Where on earth does Sarah think you are?' she asked, bravely, experiencing a slap of resentment and an unravelling of her dignity. 'A month before your wedding?'

'Visiting my aunt Margaret, Ma's sister, in Oban. But I must be on the train home tonight. I know I have only just got here, but it took long enough in London to arrange the passage, and the only return ticket I could secure was the twenty hundred hours tonight from Ferrovia. I must be back in time for the preparations.'

'Of course you must,' said Alexa, even though her shoulders drooped with disappointment at his imminent departure. But she mustn't mind, she told herself, she simply mustn't.

'I'm certainly glad of this shade,' Harvey laughed, 'for what would it look like if I got home with a Venetian tan. How would I explain that away?'

'Why is it a secret – your visit to find me?'

'I have to think of Sarah.' Harvey's cheeks coloured and he looked away.

The gondola swung around a corner through deep shadow, an ancient smell emitting from the water. Alexa shivered, suddenly chilled. She found that she could not speak, did not want to say Sarah's name again.

Into the silence, Harvey said, 'Alexa, may I explain?'

She nodded reluctantly.

'After you left, your birthday ball melted away into nothing and Sarah stayed on with her mother to help tidy up. In the past, we'd have stragglers for breakfast but most were gone by midnight. You did rather spoil the party, Alexa.'

Harvey tried to laugh but they both struggled to find it funny. 'In the weeks that followed, I suddenly became aware of Sarah,' he said, as if he was making an apology. 'Of course, I knew her. But after that, I noticed her. Do you know what I mean? She was kind to me. And peaceful. I needed peace. She left me alone. She did not challenge me. She's a good girl.' He paused, as if to let this notion sink in. 'The gossip died down and I proposed in January. Quietly, in private, without half of the parish looking on. I had learnt my lesson.'

Alexa tried to keep her regret in check, wound it around her finger.

'I get the feeling that she is most probably ecstatic,' she said, generously. 'I'm not going to come home to ruin it.'

At that, Harvey sat up and seemed to focus on the task he had set himself.

'But Alexa, we need you home. Your family want you home. Just for a visit, of course, Mr Moreland's business allowing. I'm sure everyone would love to meet your husband. Everyone at Porthdeen and Enys Point would want to see you happy.'

Alexa could not respond to Harvey's suddenly enthusiastic mood. The idea of her two worlds meeting was beyond her.

'What is he like, your Mr Moreland? I don't know anything about him.'

And neither do I, not really, Alexa decided. 'He's something in marble,' she said out loud.

Harvey laughed.

'You make him sound like a classical statue! Something we'd see on display in the Doge's Palace.'

She thought he may as well be.

'You know,' said Harvey, considering her, 'I'd forgotten how dark your hair is. You fit in so well here. You belong here. I shouldn't be trying to drag you home.'

Alexa wanted so much for him to drag her home but was too frightened and too proud to say so. Guy, she realised then, was so very far from the centre of everything.

'And I'd forgotten how fair you are, Harvey,' she said eventually. 'Are you suffering in the heat?'

Harvey fanned himself with his hat and gave her his knowing smile.

'A little.'

They passed a cobbled square under the shadow of a church. At tables in the shade, people were chatting, drinking and eating. Violin music seeped from the open doors of the church, the notes carrying over the water towards them. Harvey asked the gondolier to stop for a moment. He stepped out and went across to a café, coming back with paninis stuffed with pancetta and cheese.

'I still think you are not yourself, Alexa, but this should perk you up,' he said. 'Perk us both up.'

As she unwrapped the paper and bit into the delicacies, she realised how ravenous she was. They ate as the gondola eased under low bridges, Alexa catching brief, fascinating glimpses of strangers passing overhead.

'That's better, you were looking a bit peaky,' he said.

'Is that your best diagnosis, doctor?' she laughed lightly. Harvey studied her, his face quite grim.

'There was a moment, Alexa, when I thought you might be dead.'

'I'm so sorry, Harvey.' She kept her eyes ahead, fixed on the sharp beak of the gondola prow.

'Why did you go!' he cried, suddenly, passionately. 'I was left standing there, drowning in my guests' sympathy, hating every minute. As soon as I could shake them off, which didn't take me long, I assure you, I headed over to Porthdeen, pretty much doing myself in on that cliff path, those bloody steps. I was furious with you. I wanted to speak to you. Make you listen to me. I didn't want to let you go.'

Alexa opened her mouth to say yes, I saw you through my bedroom window, coming for me, but knew this would injure him, more, perhaps, than her rejection had done. For she had seen him, and she had still run.

'Your father called the police before dawn when he realised you had not come home,' he said. 'We eventually tracked down the taxi driver, so we knew you'd got the train from Penzance. But you could have been anywhere, Alexa. You were missing. For all we knew, you were in danger. You were dead. It was, quite simply, dreadful.'

Alexa lowered her head, shut her eyes, realising that, in her rebellion, she had succeeded in punishing them all.

'I'm so sorry,' she managed to whisper. 'I didn't plan to do that. To behave like that. But I was going to go anyway, you knew that.' Harvey glanced at her and she saw his wound open again. 'I had my employment settled, my appointment with Lady Meredith. I was going to tell Dad the day after the ball. I wanted to make a new life for myself. To mend the past. I wanted to find my grandmother, Harvey, and it has brought me this far,' she said. 'I needed to find what was missing.'

'I wish I could stay here and help you,' he said, his voice breaking with pain. 'Stay here with you, Alexa. But I have a pressing engagement.'

He took her hand and held it in both of his. Alexa could scarcely breathe, understanding the permanence and the enormity of his feeling for her, despite everything Alexa had put him through, despite his promise to his bride-to-be back home. They sat like that for some time in compassionate but terrified silence, watching Venice drift by and the day turn from gold to honey and into a soft velvety dusk.

* * *

'Think about visiting Porthdeen, please, Alexa – both of you – when Mr Moreland has more time,' Harvey said, leaning out of the train window.

Alexa looked up at him from the platform. He seemed so far away already.

'Good luck with your wedding day,' she said, generously. 'I hope the Cornish sun shines.'

'Thank you, Alexa. I've done what I set out to do,' he spoke quickly, suddenly sounding horribly matter-of-fact, so not like himself at all. 'And now I can report back to your father and step-mother, in confidence of course. Knowing that I've seen you well will, at least, be a comfort to your father.'

Aching thoughts of home ground slowly through her head. Remorse found her and wrapped its bitter arms around her. But it had to be like this.

'Send them my love, Harvey,' she said, and the whistle blew hard and long. 'Tell them I am sorry. So very sorry.'

'Take a gondola back to your apartment, you look done in,' he raised his voice over the huge surge of mechanical noise as the wheels began to turn and the steam began to billow.

'No, I will walk, Harvey. I know Venice better than I realised.'

He remained at the window, staring back at her, uttering a hundred goodbyes.

She lifted her hand so that he could see her, a vanishing figure on the dark platform, and she did not turn to leave until she could no longer hear the train or see its lights.

* * *

Alexa had never walked alone through Venice at night. Making her way back across the Ponte degli Scalzi, the nocturnal streets enticed her with new, profound mystery. Between the occasional lamp high up on a wall, or burning in niches to the Virgin, the darkness was complete, the air haunted by its own magic. She did not have to consider the way home. The map of Venice was deep inside her, as if she had inherited it.

She passed a darkened church, its great doors barred for the night, and yet inside, the sound of an organ playing rose eerily. The shape of a rat, its belly low to the stone, slithered around a corner and a pungent smell, the type Lady Meredith feared, drifted from the black water.

Alexa strode on, turning the corners left, then right, by instinct, feeling her way amid the reality that Guy had deserted her and she didn't care much that he had. Surely, he was lying about his famous client, fibbing about the reason he had to be away so long. But then, she pondered, why make up something so preposterous.

Music funnelled along the passageways, reaching her and drawing her on with its muffled, swaying sound. And in the square at Santa Croce, just paces from the apartment, she discovered its source. Venetians, twenty or more and dressed to the nines, were gathered around the well and beneath the trees strung with lanterns. A gramophone, its large horn visible in the golden lamp-light sweetened the hot night with popular tunes.

Alexa lingered unnoticed, leant against a wall to watch. Gentlemen chose their partners, or ladies danced with each other, their faces serious as they paced out a slow waltz, a rhumba, a sedate tango. Their couplings astonished her. Each was natural and respectful, their joy visible on their faces, but silent, not proclaimed. Alexa gazed, mesmerised by the music, the moving shadows, the dancing that reflected straight back to her that she was utterly alone.

Dragging herself away, she turned the last corner to the apartment and the music faded. All she had left was the memory of her first dance with Harvey; Harvey leading her around the ballroom, holding her as if he would never let go.

26

On the front of the postcard was a grainy photograph of the Roman Forum; on the back, a succinct message from Guy:

Wish you were here x

Alexa shuffled it like playing cards with the other two postcards that had arrived over the weeks that he'd been away. One was of the Colosseum and one of Vatican City, each an equally concise missive about the weather and the tourists, and each securing her fascination, offering a crumb of affection with a kiss or two.

During her days of solitude, Alexa had read them again and again, brooding on the reality of her relationship with Guy. He had made her feel small and squalid on their last evening together and, the next morning, affectionately blamed her. She pondered on how she had tried to blot the wretched episode out of her mind and how Harvey's arrival, a wonderful distraction as it was, had muddled her even further. Because now, after her visit to the doctor in Ghetto yesterday, and his confirmation, her despair over Guy had eased into small chimes of hope that, now, he'd be delighted with her, that he'd do the right thing. Alexa propped Guy's latest postcard next to the card from Lady Meredith inviting her to take tea with her at the Excelsior and went through to the bedroom to get ready. She put on her blue dress with the white collar and scarlet belt, securing it two notches looser, the glamorous hat and the borrowed ruby lipstick. She left the apartment and took a *vaporetto* bus across the sparkling lagoon to Lido, wondering what had prompted Meredith to invite her, for she'd had no word, nothing, since the day she left her employ.

As the strip of land drew nearer, Alexa remembered what day it was. Harvey was marrying Sarah in the little church with the mermaid on the door, on the cliff at Porthdeen. Her life had changed beyond measure, and so must Harvey's. It struck her like a punch, but as she disembarked on quay at Lido she did everything in her power to hold her head up, walk at a brisk and positive pace.

* * *

Alexa waited for Lady Meredith on a chaise in the quiet foyer of the hotel, not appreciating how far her nerves had stretched until her former employer glided down the stairs and indicated imperiously that she should rise and walk with her into the salon.

'Good morning, milady,' she said, conscious of Meredith's damning summation of her the last time she saw her. But things had changed and milady would have to get used to it. 'Thank you for inviting me.'

'Oh please, enough of all that,' she snapped. 'You must call me Meredith now, surely.'

As they were shown to their table and had ordered tea, Meredith regaled her with the difficulties she was having packing, now that she did not have anyone to do it for her.

'What a fix you left me in, Alexa. I'm to leave for Lake Garda tomorrow. The Nicholsons are already there. I'm staying in a different hotel, thank goodness, but will no doubt see them from time to time. The lakes and the mountains will be bliss. I can't wait to leave all this blessed heat behind. So...' Meredith slipped a lemon into her cup, and glanced saucily at Alexa. 'I had the pleasure of meeting the delightful Mr Ferris a few weeks ago and, it seems, he's a little piece of your past, Alexa dear.'

'Yes, indeed.' Alexa's fingers quivered as she placed her cup into its saucer. Tears moistened her eyes. She did not wish to talk about Harvey, today of all days. 'He is my neighbour back in Cornwall. In fact, a so very dear friend. I've known him all my life.'

As Meredith gave her a hard look and Alexa asked, 'Have you heard from Guy at all? It's just that—'

'—That boy loves you, you know.' Meredith interjected.

A bubble of bliss exploded in Alexa's head. 'I must admit,' she said, a smile of joy, of relief splitting her face, 'your nephew is sometimes very difficult to work out, to live with. Actually, he is quite a challenge, but—'

'No, no. Not Guy, Alexa,' Lady Meredith corrected her. 'I said boy, not lazy, self-centred good-for-nothing man. Oh dear, you are an intelligent girl, Alexa! But rather dim, it seems, when it comes to matters of the heart.'

'You mean Harvey? He can't love me,' said Alexa, even though, at that moment, she knew that he must, that he did, had always done. 'Harvey is engaged to be married. In fact, today is his wedding day.'

Lady Meredith raised her eyebrows, shook her head slowly in wonder.

'Pray, what's that got to do with it? Of course he loves you. He didn't need to come all the way here, to seek you out. When he could have so easily written,' she lowered her voice conspiratorially. 'I must say, Alexa, I thought what a splendid chap he was.

Such a kind face. So very polite and grateful to me for any information I could give him. Didn't flinch when I told him of your living arrangements over at Santa Croce.'

'That is as maybe,' Alexa quickly interrupted. 'But I am with Guy. And I'm expecting his child.'

Lady Meredith's eyes grew enormously and her mouth slackened into an ugly shape before twisting into a sardonic smile. Her teacup remained poised between saucer and lips.

'My, my...'

Alexa hurried on, 'And I know this is all very unconventional, but I want to make Guy happy. Yes, he is self-centred but there are reasons behind that. There are always reasons. He struggles with things in his past. I'm sure, in no time at all, we will be married and I will be making him happy. Very happy indeed.'

'Unconventional, you say? No, no Alexa. This is usual.'

'Not for me, milady... Meredith... not usual at all. Maybe in some societies, in some circles, but I come from an entirely different world. That's why I'm uncomfortable with my, as you say, living arrangements. This is not how I have been brought up, I can assure you. I want things to change and when Guy returns—'

Meredith let out a wide and exasperated sigh.

'My goodness, Miss Rosewarne, you are just like all of Guy's other girls.'

A cold fist thumped Alexa in the centre of her chest, her breath knocked out of her.

'Other...?' She swallowed hard and it felt like razorblades.

Her tongue lay dry and heavy against her lips. 'Other...?'

'Oh, how can I tell you all of this when you have that tragically innocent look on your face?'

Alexa squeezed the words out. 'Tell me all of what?'

Meredith leant towards her, the spidery red veins on her cheeks starkly visible, the chain of her fob watch knocking against the china cups.

'Guy is married. He has a wife and children in Rome. Marietta is due to give birth any day now. Their third. Where do you think he is now?'

Alexa watched Meredith's mouth move, heard words spilling out, felt their waves reaching her, although their meaning seemed to pass straight through her.

Cold sweat soaked her neck, her collar, her feet. 'Married?'

'Oh my silly little girl. You had no idea, did you?'

Lady Meredith stood up, and motioned for her to do the same. 'Come upstairs to my suite. Quickly now. Don't make a scene.' As Alexa walked mutely behind her former employer, following her impeccably dressed figure up the stairs and along a corridor, a flame of despair repeatedly flared inside her head. Its brightness blinded her, snuffed out her senses.

'I think you'd better sit down,' the woman urged her, her hard face melting with a smidgeon of compassion as she opened the door and watched Alexa walk past her into the room.

In a daze, Alexa stepped around the stack of luggage ready to be collected by the bellboy, perched herself on a slipper chair, aware that she should try to breathe and, at the same time, not expose her private agony.

'I blame myself, of course,' Meredith clattered around and found a cigarette. She placed it in Alexa's trembling mouth. The dry end stuck to her lip. 'I should have chosen an ugly matron to be my companion. But I liked your style, Alexa. Your advertisement had a perky edge to it. "Cornish Girl Friday." I liked that. You seeking adventure, I suppose, attracted me. And that's why I engaged you before we even met. But when I saw you and realised how young and beautiful you were...' she struck a match and held it to the end of the cigarette. 'Inhale, dear, inhale, that's it... it was too late, of course. I'd made my mind up. Took the risk.'

Alexa breathed in and, in an instant, the smoke scorched her throat, expanded in her lungs. She coughed, plucked the cigarette from her mouth, focused on its glowing end, the steady plume rising to the ceiling while she fought with waves of nausea. She offered the cigarette to Lady Meredith.

'Please put this out, it's horrible.' Alexa said and she took a long, ragged breath and dared herself to look up. 'This... he has done *this* before?' she asked, her voice thick with misery.

'He has I'm afraid, my dear.' Meredith placed the cigarette at the corner of her own mouth, fishing in her handbag. 'And I have done this before.'

She gestured at Alexa. In her hand were three folded fifty pound notes.

'Take this. I will give you the address, the woman in London. She's just off the Fulham Road. It will be about a hundred pounds. See the rest of it as your travelling expenses. It's impossible to have one here, of course, being a Catholic country.'

'Have one?'

'You need to get rid of it.' Meredith scribbled something on a piece of paper, thrust it at Alexa. 'Guy has his family, his children. He will not abandon them. He will not support you. You can't go on living in that apartment, you realise that, surely. You will be ruined if you don't do this. Cast out, alone and absolutely ruined. You will not be able to function.' She looked at her, hard sparks of pity in her eyes. 'You understand that, don't you, Alexa?'

'There were others?' she asked, her words clotting on her tongue.

'One poor girl tried to do herself in.'

On reflex, Alexa took the money, a groan rising from her throat. Who was this man who she had become involved with? A string of memories paraded before her: climbing from the freezing February pavement into his taxicab on Piccadilly and her first glorious steps onto the island of Venice; his encouragement, his postcards and gifts. She heard Nerina saying: 'Always, the beautiful gifts.' Their last night together. Everything was empty. Everything in disguise. Alexa squeezed her eyes shut, pressed her fingertips into their sockets. Her future unrolled before her, swaying like a capsizing boat in a desolate sea. Beyond this present sheer moment of pain, there was nothing. Absolutely nothing but the bleak truth.

'You'll get it done, then?' Meredith pressed her. 'You can't wait around.'

A scream pierced Alexa's mind, sliced through her, turned numbing shock into something physical. Automatically, she placed her hands over her stomach as if to feel for the baby inside.

Her own foetal self, cradled inside her mother, had whispered, had foretold death, had warned of the drowning, of the great surge of seawater, of the mighty ship floundering, sinking with human cargo into unimaginable cold. Alexa, the blind, sleeping baby, had convinced her mother not to board the ship. Had changed the course of lives. What was her own unborn scrap whispering to her now?

Alexa looked up at Meredith.

'You're quite the expert aren't you?' she said bitterly.

'Unfortunately, my nephew has become a dab hand at messing up young women's lives. He has, it seems, a talent for flattering and attracting girls such as yourself. He's a personable man, is he not? Quite good company. A handsome devil. I thought you'd be all right, though, would resist him, as you seemed to have a suggestion of hardness inside you. I see it in your eyes sometimes. That steely look you're giving me now. That must have been what drew him to you. He really is the end.'

Alexa grasped at her courage, floating past her like wreckage.

'What makes you think I am like all the other girls, that I will do what you want me to do?'

Lady Meredith, still holding the burning cigarette, began to smoke it furiously.

'Look, I know, it's a terrible, ghastly business,' she lowered her voice an octave to conjure an intimacy that made Alexa feel queasy. 'And, of course illegal. But this Fulham woman specialises in early procedures. I'm told she's very good. Quick, and over in the blink of an eye.' Meredith's sharp gaze travelled the length of Alexa's torso. 'I take it we're still nice and early. Imagine, Alexa, afterwards, a particularly heavy episode that's over in a day. A couple of analgesics, which she provides, of course. And then it's all over, and this can be forgotten.' She sucked on her cigarette and shuddered delicately. 'This woman is nice, I hear. She's a mother herself.'

Alexa jolted at the word as the truth of her situation rose before her. The transient pleasure she'd felt when, earlier, she had mistakenly thought Lady Meredith was telling her that Guy loved her returned like a narcissistic reflection to show her what an utter fool she was. Guy had never loved her. To him, she was sport. He had owned her, used her. And finally, he had defeated her.

'I am to congratulate you, Mrs Moreland,' the doctor in Ghetto had said, confirming her pregnancy, his dark eyes kind behind circular spectacles.

And she had smiled back, ignoring the doubts about Guy spinning in her head, wanting her life to be as the doctor, as the others, saw it.

But it was not. And Alexa was not like her Mamma, a bride on her honeymoon, safe in the arms of her husband, listening to the whisperings of her unborn child. She was a mistress, a married man's floozy. Not like her Mamma at all.

Alexa bent her head as everything pitched sideways, as hot tears washed out of her eyes. She felt Lady Meredith's bony hand press her shoulder and cringed away from her touch, but the fingers remained there, impelling Alexa to give her attention.

'Shall I ask the concierge downstairs to arrange your train back to London? It will take several days. And, in these circumstances, time is of an essence, don't you agree?'

Alexa fought her way out of her anguish, as if gasping for air.

'And, let's be clear,' said Meredith. 'After it's all over, I suggest you go home to Cornwall, my dear, to your family.'

'You want me to disappear.'

'I suppose I do. That's best all round, don't you think?'

Alexa slowly crushed the money and Meredith's note in her hand, secreting them in her handbag. Could she go back to Porthdeen, explain everything to her father and Eleanor, and watch Harvey and Sarah live out their happy, normal lives at Enys Point, while hers lay in humiliating, shameful ruins?

'I really thought he'd stop,' Lady Meredith uttered between puffs. Cigarette smoke drifted across the room, curling in the sunlight, the heat of the afternoon intensifying. 'With a third child on the way, I had hoped he'd not do it again. He won't ever leave Marietta, you know.'

A hot spurt of anger cracked Alexa's despair. Something snapped inside, her voice exploded from her mouth like a roar. 'I don't want him to!' she cried. 'I don't want him to come anywhere near me, ever again!'

Alexa stood up abruptly, riding over the sudden spinning in her head, the plunging of her stomach. She gathered her handbag and hat, clutching everything in hands slick with sweat.

She faced Lady Meredith, saw that, in the heat, her make-up was melting. Her cheeks, rugged with wrinkles, were damp with sweat; her neatly shingled hair loosened by her present difficulties. And yet, milady remained charged with power, in imperious control of this, and of any, situation. Alexa wanted to break the façade.

'Forget the concierge, forget the train. I don't want you, or Guy, to do anything else for me, ever again,' she said, her voice tight with fury. 'You are both despicable people.'

Meredith nodded appreciatively, lifting her chin to exhale a sharp plume of smoke.

'Of course we are, my dear. We've never pretended otherwise.'

27

Lido quay shimmered in a haze of heat, bustling with straggling tourists and busy Venetians. How Alexa got herself there, along the scorching grid of streets, she did not know. Relief swamped her as she caught sight of the *vaporetto* bus stop, but she did not want to sit with strangers, have them witness her pain and perhaps guess its source.

She kept walking, holding her handbag in front of her stomach as if to hide her unborn child from the world, peering through tears, towards a small flotilla of *traghetto* bobbing next to a jetty further along. In her daze, the boatmen, standing up and balancing inside their craft, looked like saints, as if they were walking on the water.

'*Scusi, signora,*' one or two called out to her. 'Do you want to go to Venice?'

Alexa nodded, even though she had no idea what she wanted to do, and took the first hand that was offered up to her. Within moments the clamour of the quay and the hubbub of Lido slipped away, and Alexa was sitting in the flat-bottomed *traghetto*, alone on the lagoon, inside a peculiar silence. The boatman laboured with an ancient rhythm and, with every other stroke of his oars, over the music of the water, he uttered the tiny snatch of a song. The tune spoke to her and she latched onto it, realising suddenly that it was 'Venice, the moon and you'. She let it sink in like a balm. A slight breeze licked at her face, drying her tears and, for a second or two, Alexa smiled.

The boatman noticed. 'Are you on holiday, *signora*?' he asked.

She glanced up and saw under the shadow of his hat that his pale Venetian eyes were cool and uncomplicated.

'Not as such,' she said. She tipped her own hat down further over her nose, conscious of her red, tear-filled eyes.

'Ah,' he said. 'I thought you might be a local, and I am right. Am I?'

'I'm half-Venetian,' she offered with a sudden and profound sense of self. 'I'm here to find my grandmother.'

He absorbed this information and, in courtesy, did not ask any more. The *traghetto* continued its cruise across the luminous flat water. Orientating herself, Alexa shifted in her seat and looked ahead to the golden streak of Venice, and then to the west. Here, a line seemed to have been drawn across the surface of the water, beyond which the lagoon was grey and dark and distinctly choppy. Above it, half of the sky was taken by a deep, wide and threatening cloud, swollen and portentous, casting its shadow over the water, heading their way. Little gusts of scorching air began a barrage over the water, and the boatman, sniffing the air, uttered something and turned his back on the stiffening breeze.

'Storm's coming,' he said, 'yes, you've seen it. I planned to drop you at St Mark's, *signora*, but I'm going to take us in that direction, towards Dogana, that promontory there, instead. We'll be more sheltered that way.'

Alexa peered to where he was pointing and saw that the great silvery domed basilica on that finger of land at the opening of the

Grand Canal was already in shadow. The rest of Venice shimmered and twinkled, russet and gold, under the fast-fading sun. Beneath her, the water began to rock and eddies of air coursing over the waves created little swells and dips. She watched, amazed, as dimples appeared and disappeared from the surface, as if an invisible cat was scooting across it. The wind turned cooler, suddenly, like a fire switching off. She shivered and glanced at the boatman, but he looked unalarmed, his swarthy face tranquil, almost relishing the anticipation of the incoming storm.

'I take it you have not found her yet,' he said, when he noticed her looking at him.

'Oh, my grandmother? Not yet, you see, I—' After the distraction of the quay, the boats and the water, her grim reality suddenly caught up with her and she could not continue.

'Excuse me for mentioning, *signora*, but you look familiar,' the boatman ventured. 'Have I carried you before?'

Alexa shook her head. 'I don't think so.'

'Ah, I know what it is...' he bent to his work, fighting the current, the surging tide.

The cloud was looming, travelling as fast as the wind, Alexa guardedly watched its vast body churning with black and grey and green, rolling to cover the sky, to cover the whole of Venice, to smother it and blot it out. She held on to the boat with both hands, telling herself she was safe, for the boatman was strong and capable. Had seen this sort of storm before.

'You remind me of a lady,' he went on, unperturbed. '*Signora* Montgomery. She uses my boat a great deal to take her to and from her palazzo. She is Venetian, but she has an English husband. God, look at that sky.'

The *traghetto* lurched violently and the boatman braced himself against sudden, violent force.

'Hold on, *signora*.'

The whole sky was suddenly dark venomous green, like a shutter closing on the sun. The wind lifted. Cold rain fell in huge splashes from all sides. Alexa gave a little squeal and ducked down, her hands instinctively around her stomach as the boatman steered precariously around the headland.

'*Signora* Montgomery?' Alexa gasped, looking up at the boatman, half blinded by the hard rain washing her face. Huge drops of water found their way into her mouth. 'You know my grandmother?'

He struggled to hear, to answer her. The storm hit them, tumbling along the Grand Canal. The air span, full of liquid, droplets sparkling and blotting out the buildings, the bridges, the other vessels rolling on the muddied swell. The palazzos were immersed, their colours leaking and melting into a uniform and diluted leaden green.

The little boat slid precariously around a set of mooring posts and into a small channel. And yet, still they found no shelter. The saturated air funnelled down the narrow passageway, washed over them, the turbulence concentrated in the confined space. Alexa cried out in terror as the towering walls closed in on her and the *traghetto* slammed against a great water door set deep in a stone arch, its threshold submerged by churning water. She watched, incredulous, as the boatman stood up, surely taking both their lives in his hands, lifted his oar and used it to hammer on the door while the vessel rocked and lurched beneath him.

'Montgomery!' he called through the thick, soaking air. Alexa saw the door open a fraction.

In an instant, the boatman pulled Alexa to her feet and the boat listed, her balance in jeopardy. He grabbed her by her elbows and lifted her up and over the step, her feet pummelling air for several treacherous seconds before she felt solid stone beneath them. An arm circled her, a soft, welcoming embrace, and she heard the words: '*mia cara?*' uttered questioningly near her ear.

The boatman cried a farewell and slammed the water door shut, silencing the maelstrom. Alexa leant back against the wall of the small vestibule, her clothes saturated, dripping and heavy, her hair streaming over her eyes. She'd lost a shoe, and her hat was a wreck. Her cold hands held fast to her handbag.

Gentle fingers teased her sodden locks apart and she saw Juliet's face – replete with wrinkles and yet so beautifully the same – cracking with a wide disbelieving smile.

'Alexa,' she cried. 'You're here! You've come to us. Born from the water, like Venus. Oh, *mia cara!*'

Alexa was scorched with joy, and dumb with wonder. Soaked and still terrified, she dropped her handbag onto the stone flags and felt her hands being clasped tightly in her nanny's tender fists. She fought to recover her breath, to find the words that cluttered her head.

'Oh, Juliet,' she said at last, inhaling on a shuddering breath. 'It's been such a long, long time. Such a long time since I've heard you call me that.'

Juliet kept on staring, almost laughing, drinking her up with her eyes, until she reluctantly dragged her gaze away.

'*Signora, Signor*!' she called up the staircase, her words echoing on marble and stone. 'Please come down here. The water door. Quickly!'

Alexa heard footsteps above and a questioning exclamation resounding down the stairwell. At the top of the stairs stood a pair of figures; the man in casual linens and the lady with a slender scarf tied around her grey hair.

The woman's hand flew to her mouth as she cried, 'My God, Alexa, what are you doing here?'

Alexa flinched at the angry sound of Beatrice Montgomery's

voice. She could not speak, but Nonna did not wait for an answer and started her eager but cautious way down the stairs, holding on to the rail, assisted by an open-mouthed Robert Montgomery, who stepped before her, glancing at Alexa, and back at his wife.

As her grandmother drew nearer, Alexa realised that the question had not been a scold, nor a reproach, but a cry of shock.

Nonna's tears started. Seeing his wife's distress, Robert steered her towards Alexa, his presence authoritative.

'What has happened? Oh, Alexa.' Her grandmother pulled her towards her into a firm and emphatic embrace, her chin pressing into her shoulder. 'Why are you here? In Venice?'

And the heart of Alexa's answer was filled with the truth. 'I came to find you, Nonna.'

28

Alexa was guided by Nonna up two flights of stairs and into the *salotto* lined with chartreuse silk and a collection of Venetian mirrors that appeared to give birth to light. Juliet led her to a sumptuously comfortable chair, while her grandmother dipped down to help her remove her remaining shoe.

A gramophone record – the cheerful and so very English 'Down Sunnyside Lane' – came to an end and the needle stuck, crackling in its groove until Robert lifted it and switched the instrument off. In the sudden quiet, Alexa grasped the years that had passed since she'd last seen them; how her grandmother and step-grandfather were both not as tall, and no longer intimidating, were somehow lighter, more delicate.

'I'm soaked,' Alexa protested. 'I'm going to leave damp patches all over your lovely furniture.'

'No need to worry about that,' said Robert, somewhere behind her. His voice still boomed as it had done through the rooms of Half Moon Street and yet now it had a kinder ring to it. 'You look like you need a drink, my dear.'

Alexa heard the clatter of a crystal decanter and was taken straight back to Guy, his treachery and his fondness for whisky.

'May I just have a cup of tea?' she asked.

Juliet hurried off to organise it, scooting back almost immediately to take her place by Alexa's side and joining her grandmother and step-grandfather as they all threw animated questions at her. She attempted to sip her tea, to try to haul up some answers, their voices bouncing around her.

'I'm sorry,' she said, shaking her head. 'I'm struggling here—'

'And we're overexcited, and rather in a state of shock. We're so sorry. Hush, now Robert,' Nonna said. 'One thing at a time. Alexa, let's get you warm and dry. Come, I'll show you upstairs.' Alexa walked with her grandmother up an exquisite staircase shaped like the inside of a shell, within curving walls the colour of almonds. She passed tall, narrow Arabic-arched windows, catching glimpses of water and of rooftops; she passed niches that were home to terracotta angels and a profusion of lilies in ceramic urns, absorbing it all in astonished silence.

Nonna opened the door to a bedroom and hesitated on the threshold. 'Take a bath... no need to rush... I'll find you a new dress... I think we're the same size... some shoes...' she paused and gestured into the room. 'Alexa, this was Mamma's bedroom, when she was a little girl. See, her dolls are there. We brought them home from London.'

She pushed the door further ajar. The dolls – minus George who remained at Porthdeen – were safely stowed in a delicate cabinet. Alexa took a tentative step into the undisturbed sanctuary. Her mother's room was sublime, panelled in sea-green, with emerald curtains trailing to the floor and a white-glass Murano chandelier sending weak glimmers over the ceiling.

'Oh, Nonna,' Alexa uttered through a burden of emotion. 'I simply can't believe that I'm here.'

Her grandmother reached across and held Alexa's cheek delicately, as if her face were a piece of porcelain, her eyes searching her face, tracking each one of her ever-changing expressions.

'Neither can I, Alexa. The last time I saw you, I'm ashamed to say, I did not behave as a grandmother or as a mother should.'

She turned sharply, tears filling her eyes. I'm so very sorry,' she uttered, hurrying back down the staircase.

'Nonna, wait—'

But hearing her grandmother's footsteps continue to fade, Alexa walked across Mamma's bedroom floor and pushed open the window.

* * *

The storm had passed, leaving in its wake a faint-blue sky, streaked and saturated stone, cooler, more temperate air and a sense of exhaustion. Below her mother's window lay a small terraced garden leading down to the Grand Canal, with fragrant box hedges, a scattering of terracotta pots and a committee of statues. Beyond the ironwork gates, Alexa could see that her grandmother, as well as having the water door at the side of the palazzo, had her own landing stage on the canal front where, now in calm water, boats and gondolas had taken up with their merry dance again.

Alexa had noticed this very garden, the topiary against the pink façade, had admired it on the dozen occasions she'd cruised along the Grand Canal – that first time with Guy and then on her excursions with Lady Meredith. To think Nonna may have been sitting here in her *salotto* all along, may have caught a glimpse of her passing *traghetto*. The thought of their proximity made her shiver in her wet clothes. She bathed, dried her hair and changed into the linen dress that Nonna had left for her, slipping into the room and hanging it on the wardrobe door while she was in the bath. At the end of the bed were a pair of her grandmother's pretty Mary-Jane shoes. They fitted her perfectly.

Juliet tapped on her door and asked to come in.

'I've been sent to find you. Your grandmother is becoming impatient downstairs. There, that's better,' she said as she drew closer to Alexa, her eyes bright and adoring. 'Oh my goodness, what a beautiful young woman you've become. I knew you would be, we all did.'

Alexa opened her arms to Juliet, just as she always had done as a child and, as they embraced, Alexa felt the vibrations of Juliet's sobs.

'How tall you are,' said Juliet, breaking free, laughing and brushing at her eyes. 'You used to only come up to my shoulder.'

'I'm simply amazed that I've found you all,' said Alexa. 'That I'm here, suddenly here in the house where my Mamma grew up. It's such a shock. Only this morning, I—'

She stopped, not wishing to think of her traumatic encounter, just an hour or so ago, with Lady Meredith and the revelation of the enormity of Guy's foul behaviour. But finding Nonna would not change the terrible situation Alexa was in; its urgency tapped her on the shoulder, dirtying her joy.

'I've been in Venice for months. Had given up hope of finding Nonna,' she said, 'but, Juliet, I had no idea that you would be here, too.'

'When I left Porthdeen, as you know, I went to work for a family in Tuscany,' Juliet said, busying herself, sorting Alexa's wet clothing as if they had never been apart. 'I wrote to your grandmother, as I had written to you...' She paused and gave her a look. Alexa bowed her head, avoiding her gaze. 'Beatrice and I reacquainted and I eventually came to live here as a sort of housekeeper. But really, I feel like part of the family.'

'You always were, Juliet,' said Alexa.

'Your grandmother and I have become a solace for each other. We'd lost you both. She needed me, someone from her past, someone who remembered Lotte.'

Juliet's face froze with sudden pain.

Alexa took a step towards her, pressed her hand onto her arm. Juliet forced a smile. 'And I hear you have a new little sister.'

'Melissa. Yes.' Alexa's guilt scratched at her, for she had left Melissa without a goodbye. 'Not so little now,' she tried to smile. 'And not so new.'

'Oh, Alexa, you didn't write. I still wonder why. Was it Eleanor?'

Alexa nodded, incapable of relaying her helpless sense of rejection, her anger when Juliet left Porthdeen. How this had coloured her behaviour, had forced her mistake in believing Juliet had taken the button box, her petulant ignoring of Juliet's letters. How she had let Juliet slip out of her life.

'It was Eleanor's influence,' she offered, which she believed to be half the truth. 'And I'll regret it until I die.'

Juliet sighed, her sharp eyes reading her.

'Please don't, Alexa. Have no regrets. For they eat into your life. When I left, I told you not to mind too much, but I'm sorry I did. It seems that it was the wrong thing to say to a grieving twelve-year-old girl. For you did mind, so very much. How sad you must have been to come all this way. You've come on your own? How brave, how modern! Nonna will be so proud of you. How did your father take to that? Where have you been staying?'

Alexa had no urge to correct her. Her scalp crawled as she embroidered her explanation.

'Up until this summer I was employed as a lady's companion. And, more recently, staying in a *pensione* in Santa Croce, but oh, Juliet!' Alexa involuntarily touched her tummy as her mind spun wildly with the need to resolve her problem. 'I have to go back to London tomorrow. I must. My father is ill, you see. He has had a stroke.' Tears leaked from her eyes at the realisation that she should have left with Harvey, gone straight to see her. Now she must go, instead, to the woman in Fulham. 'Eleanor says he is asking for me. I cannot stay. I have to get back to England. And I have only just found you!'

'Come,' said Juliet, taking her hand. 'That is for tomorrow. For now, come downstairs and tell us about your Mr William.'

'Wait a moment,' said Alexa, opening her handbag and handing Juliet the little framed photograph. 'Remember this? I have a habit of carrying it with me, always. Where was this taken?'

'Dear Lotte...' Juliet sighed, gazing at the picture, her face brightening with joy and pain. 'Alexa, I'll show you.'

Alexa followed Juliet down the staircase to the ground floor and through the great front door that creaked open onto a shadowy *calle*. They walked just a few paces around the corner and into a slice of sunlight where a pretty bridge arched over a narrow channel, small, silent and insignificant amid the rest of the crumbling splendour of Venice.

'So this is it,' Alexa could hardly breathe. 'This is what has brought me here.'

Juliet quietly took her hand and bounced it up and down in hers. They stood, side by side, in the watery reflected light as a symphony of bells began to chime, ornamenting the air, and Alexa was a child again.

'The six o'clock *campane*,' said Juliet. 'Come on, *mia cara*, Nonna will be waiting.'

* * *

Beatrice and Robert were sitting by the windows of the *salotto*, the life and business of the Grand Canal a backcloth behind them. Alexa took her seat next to her grandmother. Fresh tea was poured and Juliet's famous Genoese cakes served. Her hunger suddenly brutal, Alexa ate one piece in an instant. As she swallowed, she feared she may have appeared rather rude, but the cake settled her stomach and eased persisting vibrations of shock. Her grandmother watched her in satisfied silence, understanding her.

'I trust you feel refreshed, Alexa?' Robert asked, his face altered by compassion. 'We can't tell you how wonderful it is to have you here.'

She thanked him. There was a pause in which she sipped tea and gathered her thoughts, her truths and her lies; to begin the tentative task of explaining herself. The fact Alexa had been living in Santa Croce during her search for Beatrice raised eyebrows and expressions about the proximity of their palazzo to that parish. Alexa had, she said, been going on a trip over to Lido when she'd been caught in the storm. By chance – 'actually, by some miracle,' Juliet interjected – the boatman had known Beatrice and Robert and had brought her right to their door. But she must leave tomorrow, must get home to her father.

'Oh, I'm so very sorry to hear he is unwell. Please do send our regards to him and Eleanor,' said her grandmother expansively, 'and our love, of course.'

'The boatman!' Alexa suddenly cried. 'I didn't pay him!'

'No need to worry,' Nonna laughed gently, 'Silvanio won't mind. We'll pay him tomorrow, or next week. Next time we see him.'

Alexa relaxed under their laughter, took in the beautiful room. She thought she recognised some of the furniture from London and the solid English pieces sat surprisingly easily with the rest of the Italian finery. She stole a glance at her step-grandfather. He seemed lighter, looser, dressed in a white shirt, sleeves rolled up, a proper Englishman abroad. His smile, a welcoming surprise, softened his hard, grey eyes and made them twinkle.

Behind him was the table, laid out with the framed

photographs from Half Moon Street, a gallery of Robert's loss, of his grief.

'May I?' she indicated the display and strolled over to it. Among the many images of Luke, from baby to young man, from school uniform to wedding suit, was the one from her Mamma's room at Half Moon Street. Carlotta and Luke on an Edwardian summer lawn, before the war, before either of their weddings, before everything. As Alexa picked it up for a closer look, tears streamed from her eyes.

'I remember this one,' she whispered.

She felt her grandmother's hand on her shoulder.

'They were such friends,' her grandmother said. 'Stepbrother and stepsister. That was taken just before they each met Edith and William. Luke was home at Half Moon Street that summer –1908, I think. They both married their sweethearts within months of each other. Your parents, autumn 1911. Luke and Edith, New Year, 1912. A busy time for weddings.'

Nonna plucked a delicate handkerchief from her sleeve and pressed it into Alexa's hand.

'I have something to show you, Alexa. Dry your eyes,' she said, 'and I will dry mine, too.'

Her grandmother opened double doors onto a dim space, a dining room decorated in deep-red with blinds drawn down to protect its contents against sunlight. She asked Alexa to stand in a spot on the far side of the long polished table, on a Turkish rug in front of the fireplace. She went to the windows, gradually opening each set of blinds so that the sun rose gently into the room.

'We only usually see this in lamplight when we dine,' she said. 'But I think it looks glorious, perhaps somehow happier, in daylight.'

Alexa turned to where her grandmother was pointing. Sunlight, reflected over water, illuminated the painting above the mantelpiece. Three women shone down on her out of the lightening gloom, each dressed in a different shade of blue, each looking a little to the left, as if watching over the one beside her. They were almost identical, their brush-stroked eyes a clear Venetian azure, complexions creamy olive, but each representing a different age: the young daughter, the mother, the grandmother.

'Our portrait,' Alexa breathed out, trembling. 'It's us.' Nonna stood beside her and clutched her hand in hers.

'I think Mr Fairling created a wonderful thing here,' she said. The artist had applied his paint in confident, generous daubs, the touches of his brush visible, capturing Alexa's own inquisitive expression, the fire in Mamma's eyes, the wisdom in Nonna's face. Behind them were the drapes of the drawing room in Half Moon Street: golden flowers on russet cloth. Alexa remembered how much she had disliked those curtains, but here, as a steady backdrop to the divine, almost religious aura of the grouping, she thought them wonderful. Jack Fairling had depicted the window, too, behind young Alexa's shoulder. In the painting, Beatrice looked over Carlotta, Carlotta watched over Alexa and Alexa gazed through the window at a deep and glowering, thunderous sky.

Nonna spoke quietly, her voice low in reverence, 'Mr Fairling entitled it: *A storm in summer – three generations.* See his signature here? He was a fine man. Soon after he heard that Carlotta had died, he presented me with the painting, would not accept payment. Do you remember him, Alexa? Do you remember the storm? Oh, of course you do.'

Alexa nodded, powerless to speak. She remembered the rain-soaked streets, and Jack Fairling peering at them through the taxicab window, almost as if he was taking a photograph, memorising Mamma's face, studying Alexa's for the briefest of moments, before they sped off into the mêlée. She replayed their sudden departure, felt again the ripping apart of the generations, experienced, in a bright flash of pain, the grief that followed.

'Nonna, I thought you hated us,' Alexa said, unable to tear her gaze away from the three captured faces. Hate sounded childish, but she could not explain herself any other way. 'But now I've learnt. Now I know how it must have been: you simply hated the situation.'

'We both did; Robert and I. And we did not deal with it thoughtfully, or properly. Robert admits he was out of his mind with anger, with grief.'

Alexa heard the break in her grandmother's voice.

'We have had many years now to contemplate the fact, to try to come to terms with what we did, how we behaved. How we were. I was ashamed. Losing Carlotta was my punishment for being so mulish, for being wrapped up in how Robert was feeling and not thinking beyond that. When Luke and Edith died... oh my goodness, Alexa, I get the feeling you have no idea what happened. You were just a baby—'

'I do know,' said Alexa, a newer, braver skin forming around her. 'Mamma and Dad handed their passage for the Titanic on to Luke and Edith. And Luke and Edith were lost.'

Nonna wiped her fingers over her face to extinguish her tears. 'Do you remember what you said to Robert?' she asked, something ominous littering her voice. 'That you had warned your Mamma? Whispered from inside her?'

Alexa nodded and looked up at her mother's painted face, at the luminous light captured on the canvas, at the shifting layers of joy and sorrow.

Nonna said, 'Carlotta told me soon after the Titanic went down, that she'd had a premonition, that something had spoken to her.' She squeezed Alexa's hand. 'You must know, Alexa, that Luke and Edith boarded that ship perfectly happily. In the joy and expectation of a wonderful trip to America. None of it is your fault. None of it.'

* * *

Dinner was served by the light of a dozen lamps, with the shutters and windows open to the night. Alexa was soothed by the murmur of the evening traffic on the water, the shouts from gondoliers, such a contrast to the well of silence in Guy's apartment.

As she sipped her lobster bisque and broke her bread, she listened to Robert reminiscing about his retirement from the City – 'that nightmare job of yours,' remarked her grandmother – and how Venice, the music, the art, the food and the sunshine had transformed him. He'd begun to play popular tunes on his gramophone, he added, something he'd never have dreamed of enjoying back in London.

'You are quite the jazz fiend now,' laughed Nonna. 'We take in classical concerts, of course, and go to the opera, but Robert is especially animated when we hear that a band from New York or Chicago has arrived in the city. We're quite bohemian these days. You know, Alexa, I've done away with corsets, have encouraged Juliet to do so too!'

Juliet, sitting next to Alexa, blushed in the soft light and refused to be drawn on the subject. Alexa glanced fearfully at Robert, expecting fury at the mention of lady's undergarments, but he laughed lightly and filled their wine glasses.

'I wonder if you realise, Alexa, that this palazzo,' said Nonna, 'belonged to your grandfather Pietro's family, was passed to me on his death. We believe its foundations to be Renaissance, the rest of it baroque.'

'I sense its age. I can feel it. The beauty is in the stone, this ancient stone,' said Alexa, 'Now I know just what Mamma was thinking about when she was singing, missing her home.'

Juliet said, 'She was born in the room you are staying in. I helped deliver her.'

Beneath the fold of the tablecloth, under her napkin, Alexa pressed her hand to her stomach and listened. She glanced up at the portrait, alive in the lamplight, and saw herself, her family, the three generations. Inside her was a nugget of new life, the fourth link in the chain. The idea stung her, dragged her heart sideways. It became hateful. She would be outcast; the child wretched. Alexa would be responsible for creating misery, for giving birth to suffering. Would she be a monster if she ended it, or a monster if she took the risk and carried on? She thought of her home, of Porthdeen, isolated on the tip of the peninsula. Would it be possible to take the child there? To let it live? There? Alexa concentrated and pressed her hand down more firmly, squeezed her eyes shut and listened again. She heard nothing.

'Are you all right, Alexa?' asked Juliet.

'Just a little tired, but I am fine,' she said as brightly as she could. 'I was just thinking... of home.'

'Of course you are. It must be such a worry with William so ill,' said Nonna. 'But you will come here again? For this, Alexa, is also your home.'

Robert said, 'Juliet, would you fill our glasses? We will drink to our absent friends, like we do most nights. But this time, one of them is here, right here with us.'

Alexa put down her cutlery, dipped her head and wept.

'I'm so sorry that I have to go, I'm so sorry,' she said, her sobs shuddering. 'I really cannot delay. It's vital, that I... you see, I must...'

Robert got up from his place at the table and came around to her chair. He knelt beside her and waited while she dried her eyes and finally lifted her head to look at him.

'You're torn in two, aren't you, my dear,' he said, his hard stare punishing her with unexpected tenderness, with love. 'We are all so sorry that this is the case, but we're also so very happy that you are here, that you found us. As Juliet said, it was a miracle. We are so happy that you were blown in with that storm.'

* * *

The bell in a nearby *campanile* rang for midnight as Alexa climbed the curling staircase with Juliet leading the way with a lamp. As tired as she was, she tried hard to absorb the happenstance of her situation, on a day of surprises and catastrophe that seemed to have dawned so very long ago. Guy's offhand dishonesty and the flippancy of Lady Meredith still hovered around her, threatening her. For she, too, was responsible. She willed herself to shake it off, to remove the degradation that clung to her, despite the luck and joy that had followed so swiftly on its tail. But how far should she go to rid herself of this terrible feeling?

'As loath as I am to say this, *mia cara...*' Juliet stifled a yawn and handed her the lamp. 'I have to say goodnight.'

'And I wish I did not have to sleep,' replied Alexa. 'I wish we could sit and talk all night. All of us. For already, it is tomorrow. And today, I must leave.'

Juliet gripped her arm. 'But come back soon. Please. Mr Montgomery will insist. And we must do what he says.'

They laughed gently together but Alexa stopped abruptly as fatigue overtook her; her limbs turned to lead. She thought of the long journey ahead of her, all the way to London, and then, finally, she supposed, to Porthdeen, to the ends of the earth.

Suddenly, she asked, 'Do you remember Harvey Ferris?' Juliet's face curved with a fascinated smile.

'Of course. I remember him, oh so very fondly. Such a wonderful boy. A gentleman now, I can imagine. A fine gentleman.'

'He has married Sarah Carmichael from the village. Today – well, yesterday now – was his wedding day.'

'Goodness! I must say, yes, what a surprise. I remember Sarah. Yes, I do...' Juliet peered at Alexa's face and Alexa was glad of the haphazard lamplight, for the shadows it cast over her. 'I always thought that you two... oh, not to worry. Please give him, them both, my best regards then, when you get home. I always thought he was an exceptional man.'

'Harvey came here to see me,' Alexa blurted, fixing on this one point of pleasure in a stream of desperate days. 'He came here to Venice, to persuade me to go home.'

'But why would he need to persuade you?' Juliet asked. 'If your father is ill?'

'I had fallen out with Dad,' Alexa admitted. 'But I was hell-bent on finding Nonna. And I suppose I didn't realise how bad things were at home... I was in a bit of a mess...'

'Oh, Alexa. And so Harvey came all this way, just before his wedding? He came here, for you? Alexa—'

Juliet broke off and gripped Alexa's hand, ignoring the tears that were spilling down Alexa's cheeks. Juliet read her face like she had always done, seeking the truth among the broken, scattered lies.

* * *

They couldn't spot Silvanio and his *traghetto* from the landing stage, so Robert commandeered a passing gondolier to take Alexa back to her *pensione*. She told them she must collect her suitcase and go on to the station. Between tears and promises to write and the sending of love, there were many enquiries about tickets and timetables, which Alexa managed to sidestep. For her suitcase was yet to be packed and she had no idea what train she would be catching. But catch one she must.

She watched the waving figures of her grandmother, Robert and Juliet for as long as she could, straining her eyes to absorb them, imprint them on her mind, until her gondola slipped around the bend and merged with the flotilla under Rialto Bridge.

At San Stae, she asked to stop, told the gondolier that she would be ten minutes. As she dashed down the narrow passageway to the apartment, she recognised her recurring behaviour: escaping once again like she had done from Enys Point and Porthdeen, except that this time, instead of leaving the man she loved, she was fleeing the man she loathed.

Before she allowed this notion to sink in, perhaps to try to laugh about the odd symmetry of her situation, she was struck by a devastating thought. What if Guy had returned to the apartment? What if he was waiting for her there?

Alexa slowed her pace around the last corner. If he was inside, she decided, her hands shaking as she unlocked the door, her stomach lapping with dread, she would not speak to him. She would simply leave, leave everything behind.

She held her breath as she pushed the door open slowly, and eased herself in. A tap was dripping, a tinny echo in the silence. She walked into the kitchen and peered around, trying to find clues in the familiar objects: the bowl of fruit, the pile of linens, the cups on the draining board. In the centre of the table was a new postcard from Rome. Glancing with a flash of terror towards the open bedroom door, she braced herself to run, but there was only silence. She breathed again. Nerina must have been in to do her chores, must have taken delivery of the postcard, and had left it out for her to see.

Alexa hurried into the bedroom for her suitcase. The bed was made, the sheets tight and fresh. She thought of her nights with Guy, of the passion, once seeming so vital to her happiness and now sordid and superficial. She thought of the depth of her gratitude towards him and what it had led her to.

She turned her back on the bed, opened the cupboard, grabbed her clothing, filled the case and took a handful of lira from the drawer. Back in the kitchen she wrote a swift note for Nerina, thanking her over and over, and folded it around the money. She paused, gathering her thoughts, letting her breathing settle until her eyes flicked involuntarily to the new postcard.

On the front was a photograph of the Trevi Fountain, with two lovers perched on its edge, holding hands and kissing. On the reverse Guy had simply, manipulatively, written her name.

She turned in an instant and threw up into the sink, each wrenching spasm forcing a sob of disgust and of terror to break from her. When at last she stopped, drank handfuls of water from the tap, she sprang back to the table, snatched up the postcard and ripped it in half. She seized the others he'd sent her and did the same, leaving them all in a neat pile. Finally, she unhooked the peridot bracelet from her wrist and lay it on top. This must stop now. He could not reach her any more with his empty gifts, his worthless postcards, his trifling sentiments.

She left the apartment, closed the door and slipped the key under the mat, wishing that her terrible present was already her past.

PART IV

29

THE END OF THE SUMMER, 1931

Waiting on the step for her knock on the door to be answered, Alexa stared down the street of terraced Victorian houses towards where the children were playing. Three grubby kneed boys, one of them barefoot, were sitting on the kerb, tossing stones across the road and shouting if they managed to skid their missiles all the way to the other side. Two girls, a few years older and distinctly taller than the boys, were pushing a huge pram up and down, rocking it and singing idly, their attention on each other and their gossipy exchange. They remained separate from the others, but Alexa had the feeling that the boys were under their guardianship, along with the unseen baby in the pram. A young boy scooted from the door of a house further down the terrace and let out a battle cry as he ambushed the group and was welcomed into their posse. There were no cars, either parked or moving past, to interrupt play, and no trees either, despite the road being called an avenue.

A woman in an apron and turban-style headscarf opened the front door. She was possibly under thirty but her face was carved by deep lines and wore a dull veil of fatigue. Her smile was brief as she wordlessly beckoned Alexa inside the small, dark house, gesturing that Alexa should leave her suitcase in the hall. Weak daylight found its way through the fanlight over the front door, and Alexa blinked in the gloom. A short distance along the passage a door was open onto a room, from which the grizzling and fretful sounds of another child reached her – boy or girl, Alexa could not tell. She sniffed at the scent of yesterday's cooked cabbage and heard a murmuring tune from a wireless.

The woman led her up the dim staircase, chattering about the weather, which Alexa had barely noticed: dull, grey and still, as if the day was dead. The bannisters were painted an oily green and the wallpaper, she saw, had a raised pattern, the whole thing covered with thick and glossy varnish, the colour of milk that was on the turn. A different, more personal smell greeted her at the top of the stairs: airless bedrooms and unwashed laundry. Alexa followed the woman into a tiny room at the back of the house. There was space for a narrow bed with a candlewick cover and a cabinet, and that was all. A tatty rug had been laid over the strip of linoleum between these two pieces of furniture and at the small window hung limp curtains depicting the ever-repeating pattern of a ship in full sail. Alexa supposed it was a boy's bedroom, when it was not being used for its other purpose. The woman, whose name she did not know – she was neither offered it or asked her own when she telephoned from the Paddington boarding house when she'd arrived in London the day before – opened a door in the cabinet and began to remove objects and place them on the top.

'Sit down then, dear,' the woman said over her shoulder, incongruously cheerfully, and Alexa gingerly perched on the edge of the bed. The woman turned from her task and with a little tip of her head said, 'Cash?'

Alexa opened her handbag and extracted two of Lady Meredith's fifty-pound notes. She squinted into the dark interior of her purse to calculate how many pennies, shillings and pounds she had left.

The woman thanked her and studied the notes for longer than Alexa thought necessary, then folded them away into the deep pocket of her apron. She touched the scarf covering her head, adjusting it like one would a hat, and said, 'Now, dear, remove your shoes, stockings and underthings. That's all.'

Alexa did as she was asked, fumbling with the buttons on her grandmother's shoes, sensing the woman's impatience at this part of proceedings.

'Now lay back, dear, that's right,' she spoke encouragingly, as if to a child taking its first steps. 'That's it and we will get on with it.'

Alexa duly placed her head on the hard pillow but was not sure what to do with her hands, or her feet. She stared at the ceiling, at the trail of dusty cobwebs, and heard the clatter of something hard, caught the vague smell of rubber.

'Now, dear.' The face was above her but she felt the touch of a hand further down, somewhere near her knees. Alexa was aware of the muffled sobs of the infant downstairs and listened in wonder as the sounds of children playing in the street reached her, here, at the back of the house.

The woman paused, seemed to look at her properly for the first time.

'Oh, you have a lovely colour, dear,' she said, 'have you been somewhere nice for your holidays?'

* * *

Alexa was sure that it was the same seagull that had been following the taxi ever since it turned off the road from St Just and journeyed towards Land's End. The bird dipped and hovered, cruising on currents of warm air rising from the gorse and the emerald stone-fenced fields, turning its yellow beak to the sea that Alexa glimpsed every now and then as little sections of blue, sparkling like fish scales.

Her spirits rose marginally on seeing the peninsula, on seeing Porthdeen for the first time in well over a year. They would have soared if she had not taken the two large tablets that the woman in Fulham had pressed on her.

'Now, you will go and lie down, rest for a day, dear,' she'd said around her front door as she pushed it closed. 'That's what is recommended.'

Alexa had nodded and thanked her, then made her way straight to Paddington Station to catch whatever train to the West Country was leaving first. Sitting in her third-class carriage on the overnight service, the medication began to seep through her, forming a rather pleasant cloud of numbness through which she peered at the world, surprisingly without pain. She paid the taxi driver with equal detachment, and stood in front of the iron gates to her home. Melissa, absorbed in her game in the front garden, did not notice her. The gull, her guide for the last stretch of her journey, had disappeared, but the sea, the blissful, blue sea, greeted her with its enduring presence. She breathed in greedily the moist, sweet air, willing it to cleanse her body, to eliminate yesterday.

Melissa spotted her suddenly, her head jerking with surprise.

She slung her doll aside. 'Lexa! Lexa!'

Her footsteps slapped over the gravel, her blonde hair untamed and streaming behind her. She hauled the gate open and grasped Alexa's hand, tugging her through.

'Lexa, you're home!' The little girl's eyes were bright spheres of astonishment. 'And Mummy said you got married and I wasn't your bridesmaid, even though I was promised. I was promised! Aunt Rose had said I would be one day. And I wasn't!'

Melissa had gained inches but no maturity in the time Alexa

had been away. Alexa found herself laughing and wanting to cuddle her. How quickly she stepped from one world to another. 'How are you, Melissa?' she asked as her half-sister wrestled her suitcase from her.

'Do you have a present in here for me?' she asked.

Alexa stopped halfway across the gravel, guilt snaking around her head. She'd left home without a goodbye, leaving everyone bereft. She'd sent no word for nearly a year. Her family, and Harvey, had considered, quite rightly, the fact that she might be dead. The least she could have done was buy Melissa a present.

'Oh hell. I'm sorry.' Melissa's face crumpled.

'Typical,' she said, dropping the suitcase and running ahead, around the corner of the house.

With absolutely no desire to pick the case back up, Alexa followed her slowly, treading carefully through the remains of the hefty painkillers, her mind swaying with a sluice of wooziness.

Her father and Eleanor were sitting in the garden at their table by the lone hawthorn. At least, she thought it was her father. The figure with Eleanor was hunched in his chair, a rug over his legs, dark glasses on and a cap pulled low. Her stepmother was engaging him in her usual streamlined and elegant manner.

Eleanor saw her and stood up. Her father stirred, jerked in shock and tossed aside his blanket. As Alexa approached, tentatively, shyly, Eleanor was torn between greeting her and ensuring that her father stayed safely in his seat.

'Oh my goodness, my goodness. I thought I heard Melissa shouting. Oh, Alexa, Alexa,' Eleanor ran headlong at her and wrapped her in a fierce grasp. 'We've missed you so much,' she breathed into her ear. 'Harvey told us that he found you, safe and well. But he wasn't holding out any hope that you'd actually come to visit.' As she pulled back, Alexa saw her face streaming with tears.

They both turned to see her father ease himself out of his chair and slip off his sunshades.

Eleanor began to gesture.

'Don't you say a word, woman!' he cried. 'It's high time I got off my backside. I can stand up and say hello to my own daughter, can't I?'

'Oh, William, you must be careful. Oh God, another shock for him, oh my goodness...' Eleanor hurried back to his side and seized his arm, supported him like any good nurse would. She held her husband as if she was presenting him to Alexa.

Alexa's sorrow reared up through her analgesia, as her father reached out shakily for her and gripped her head in both of his hands, tears squeezing from his eyes in drawn-out, distressing silence.

Eleanor broke in, fussing around them both and insisting that William sit back down. She pulled up a chair for Alexa.

Her father said, 'Welcome back, my dear Alexa. My, my, it's been such a long time.'

'Dad, I can explain. I'm so very sorry.'

'Eleanor did not want to try to convince you, to force you. We just wanted you to visit of your own accord. Sounds like Ferris did a good job, in any event.'

'If I could tell you why I left Porthdeen, perhaps you will understand.'

'No need to explain.'

Alexa looked at her father, at the sorrow trailing through his eyes and knew he understood her. This sudden, unspoken recognition from him was like a soft light, warming her face.

As her father peered back at her, she flinched, noticing him properly. His skin had a grey, dusty pallor; the wrinkles had deepened, charting his troubles. He had grown back his moustache and it was full of silver. And yet his eyes were as alive as ever, sparkling as he searched her face, incredulous that she was sitting there, on his lawn, at his table, in front of him.

'Dad,' she said, 'I found Nonna.'

Her father reared back in his chair, his eyes broadening with delighted surprise.

'She is well, she sends her love, her love to you all,' Alexa looked at Eleanor, whose smile of gratitude worked to put to rest their one-time discord. 'And Mr Montgomery, too. And Juliet.'

She saw her father's pale cheeks redden.

'Juliet, too, oh thank goodness. Such an awful business,' he uttered, shaking his head, astonished, deliberating over memories. 'Well, you have Beatrice's address?' he asked finally. 'I will write to her immediately. Where I will start, I do not know, but start I will.'

Her father shifted in his seat as if trying to get comfortable with his own conscience. Eleanor reached for his hand, but he kept it clasped with his other, tightly together on his lap.

'But Alexa?' he asked, clearing his throat. He glanced past her, as if expecting someone else to be there. 'Where is your husband?' Alexa pressed her hand to her forehead, her consciousness stretching and awakening inside her blank and exhausted mind. Guy and everything to do with Guy had been blocked off and sedated, by distance and by her decision to visit the woman in Fulham. But now the effect of the tablets was easing off, the medication ceasing to work. She was emerging from a frozen fog and the dragging sourness began to roam again.

Alexa looked at her father.

'Dad, I'm not married to Mr Moreland.'

Alexa heard Eleanor beside her gasp and then collect herself to speak. Alexa ignored her, kept her gaze on her father. The light in his eyes intensified briefly.

He calmly commanded, 'No hysterics, please, Eleanor.' Eleanor yelped, 'But Harvey Ferris told us—'

'Quiet, Eleanor.'

Alexa waited, her breath shortening and her body fizzing in expectation of her father's fury.

He rubbed a hand over his mouth, let out a long sigh.

'You can tell me all about it one day, Alexa. Tell me all about Venice and Lady Meredith. I expect you have quite a tale,' he said. 'But for now, you look done in. Doesn't she, Eleanor?'

'Yes, yes, she does,' said Eleanor in a surprisingly calm voice, patting Alexa's hand, a sudden, intense look of perception on her face. 'She looks like she has had a lucky escape.'

Alexa glanced up as Aunt Rose cheerfully pottered across the lawn carrying a tray of tea, trailed by an energetically bouncing Melissa.

'Good old Aunt Rose,' said Alexa, trying to laugh. 'What a welcome.'

Rose greeted her dramatically and Melissa joyfully circled her chair, trying to sneak onto her lap, while Eleanor sat quietly observing her, biting her mouth and bursting to speak to her. Amid the commotion of Rose's and Melissa's excitement, her father leaned forward to say to her, ardently under his breath, 'I'm over the moon that you're here, safe and sound, Alexa. You must stay if you want to.'

Alexa accepted a cup of tea from Rose and the briefest of cuddles that Melissa would bestow before she scooted off across the lawn.

She said, 'Dad, this is not just a visit. I have come home.'

* * *

After Alexa had stifled a fifth yawn, Eleanor insisted she go indoors and rest. It was very nearly lunchtime. Eleanor urged her to have a bite to eat, and then sleep.

'Sleep, yes,' said Alexa. She longed for it, wasn't sure how she had managed to get through the last few days.

Her father eased himself gingerly from his chair, and offered her his arm.

'Come on then,' he said. 'Escort your old Dad into the house.'

They walked slowly across the lawn, her father leaning into her more than she expected. Guilt found her again and fell into step with her. Her father's anxiety of the past year and his stroke were all her fault. But she was home now, and Porthdeen was all around her: the sky, the sea, the gulls, her family. The sense of being in the right place infiltrated her bones. She tried to capture that feeling and pin it down at the centre of the woolly mess inside her head. 'I'm so sorry you have been so unwell, Dad,' Alexa ventured cautiously. 'I really feel that it has been my fault—'

'Doctor Ferris has been very strict with me, as has our very own Nurse Rosewarne,' Her father interrupted her, saved her from her confession.

'Oh, yes, of course. So, Harvey—?' She could barely speak his name. 'Harvey has been checking up on you?'

'Only on a friendly, non-professional basis. Of course, he is still in training, attached to a general practitioner over at St Just. But he visited me, gave me lots of advice, was duly concerned, as he was about you, Alexa.'

Her father glanced sideways at her, his eyes penetrating hers. 'We have lots of things to be grateful to him for. I trust you were able to make amends with each other, when he tracked you down in Venice?'

'Indeed, yes, he was most kind, most forgiving...' Her words sounded limp and transparent, mere phantoms of her feelings for him; imposters to the emotions that had formed when she was a very young girl. 'But Dad, were you well enough to attend the wedding?'

'Take it carefully now, William. These steps are your nemeses,' Eleanor cried, catching up with them and grasping her husband's other arm, just as they reached the terrace.

Alexa's question was lost amid the fuss and commotion as William hesitated at the bottom of the steps, thoughtfully lifting first one foot and then the other.

'Well done, William,' Eleanor beamed as he steadily conquered the climb. 'That's the best you've been in ages.'

'Is it any wonder?' he asked, gripping Alexa's arm even tighter.

* * *

Melissa was charged with fetching Alexa's suitcase from the drive while Rose hurried ahead to find fresh sheets and make up the bed in what had been Alexa's room.

Sitting in her wicker chair by the bedroom window to take off her shoes, while Rose busied herself, Alexa let her gaze wander over the unchanging seascape. The headland was peaceful, not giving anything away. Beyond it, always invisible from Porthdeen, but lying in her imagination, was the house at Enys Point.

Alexa tried to picture Sarah there with Harvey, sitting in the glorious drawing room with the doors open to the terrace and the gardens, flitting around the vast hallway, gliding down the great staircase to greet Harvey when he came home, eating at his table alongside Ma and Pa Ferris. Alexa began to think of what an elevation for Sarah her marriage to Harvey was, what an accomplishment, but, curiously, her mind fell blank. A picture of Sarah living at Ferris House escaped her.

'Miss your old view, did you, lovie?' asked Rose eagerly. 'And missed Mr Ferris, too, no doubt?'

Before Alexa could answer, Eleanor came in, asked her aunt to leave and flicked the curtains halfway across to dim the room.

'Rest for a few hours,' she said, 'you'll feel better then. I must say, Alexa, you do look a little beaten.'

Alexa set her grandmother's Mary Jane shoes neatly together on the floor and looked up at her stepmother.

'I suppose they aren't there, then?'

Eleanor cocked her head, frowning. 'Who do you mean?'

Melissa bumped in with the suitcase and plonked it on the floor.

'There, done that, Mummy,' she declared, immensely pleased with herself. 'Mummy, Aunt Rose says that the weather report for tomorrow is nice and sunny. Shall we all go to the cove? Can Lexa come too? Can we take a picnic?'

'Ah, but look, Alexa is tired. She has had a long journey.'

'I'm sure I'll perk up tomorrow, Melissa,' Alexa assured her sister. 'Some sea air, a little bathing will do me good.'

Melissa gave a whoop, bestowed on Alexa a sweet kiss on the cheek and scarpered off to tell Aunt Rose.

Eleanor followed her to the door, but instead of walking out, she closed it, came back and sat on the end of Alexa's bed.

'Who did you mean, Alexa?' she asked. 'When you said they weren't there?'

'Harvey and Sarah, of course. They won't be there, at Ferris House. They must be on honeymoon still.'

'Oh. No. No...'

Eleanor's succinct words were left drifting in the room, but Alexa was so weary she hadn't enough strength to ask what on earth she meant by them. Eleanor grew impatient, drew back her shoulders.

'You're not married, Alexa,' she said, her face brightening. 'And the news here is that Harvey and Sarah aren't either.'

Alexa kept perfectly still. 'But, it was all arranged,' she said, incredulous. 'Harvey had to leave straight away from Venice. He had to get home in time.'

Eleanor warmed to her subject and moved closer down the bed, brimming with gossip.

'He called it off. The day before. Went down to the cottage at Little Porthdeen to see her. Aunt Rose told me all about it. You know how friendly she is with Joan Carmichael. Gosh, such a terrible business.'

'He jilted her...?' she said, her surprise tinted by a chime of hope.

'Sarah was hysterical as soon as he knocked on the door because it is bad luck for the groom to see the bride, etcetera, etcetera. Very bad luck in her case.'

'Oh, poor girl...' Alexa dare not imagine Sarah's pain.

'We don't know all the details, because they upped and left. We think Harvey paid for Sarah and her mother to go on an extended trip somewhere in the North – the Lakes, I think – until it blows over. If it ever does. These things tend to never be forgotten. Instead they stay with people. They had to drag her away, Rose told me. Force her into a taxi. She didn't give up easily.'

'And what about Harvey?'

'Lying low, I should suppose,' said Eleanor. 'Must be a week and a half ago now. We haven't seen or heard of him since it happened. Haven't seen his parents either. But they will rise above it, as the Ferrises are wont to.'

Alexa shuddered under the rolling wave of shock.

'And yet,' her stepmother went on, 'this whole awful business puzzles me. Harvey came home from Venice, believing that you were Mr Moreland's wife. You were taken, married to someone else, and so why would he call it off?'

Alexa jolted, caught the suggestion in Eleanor's tone.

'Really, that's no puzzle at all, Eleanor,' Alexa's voice was bright and hard. 'Whatever has happened between Harvey and Sarah obviously has absolutely nothing to do with me.'

Eleanor lifted an eyebrow. 'There's nothing obvious about it at all,' she said.

Pressing her hand to her forehead, Alexa shook her head. 'Sarah must be devastated,' she whispered.

Her stepmother shifted closer, wanting to draw out the conversation, her gestures excited and encouraging.

'Alexa, what do you think is going on?'

'I don't know, Eleanor, but I must rest,' she said.

Eleanor patted her hand and left, shutting the door behind her.

* * *

Alexa lay down and closed her eyes, tried to blot out the shocking news of Harvey and Sarah. The sound of the latch on her bedroom door clicking into place echoed the rhythmic clacking of the train from Venice. Throughout her journey, she'd been desperate for sleep but kept awake by the punishing thought of her unformed child. Now, in the half darkness of her bedroom, so secluded and familiar, at last, the sickening constant movement of the carriage faded. Her journey was over and she was no longer so far from Harvey. For the first time in years, she belonged at Porthdeen.

Tears washed her eyes as she listened to the sounds from outside. The hundred voices of the sea against rocks far below singing her a lullaby. As sleep came for her, she opened her eyes briefly and saw, through the gloom, on her shelf, the two halves of the broken seagull egg nestled in its handkerchief.

30

FIRST DAY OF SEPTEMBER, 1931

The weather report was spot on. By the time Rose had packed the picnic, Melissa had found the blankets and Eleanor her old sunhat, the day was bright and beaming, calling Alexa to come out and greet it.

They picked their way down the pathway to Porthdeen cove, Melissa leading the way, glancing cheekily back at Alexa to make sure that she was still there. As soon as they reached the beach, they all took their shoes off. Alexa and Melissa ran down to the water's edge, letting the foam of the spent waves fizz around their bare toes. The day was glorious; the air full of sunlight, of moving water and the hiss and draw of the waves, the gentle sloshing eddies around the rocks.

Back up at Porthdeen, her father was having a good day, according to Eleanor, and was happy to sit and read in the parlour. Alexa looked back to where her stepmother and Rose were laying out the blankets on the soft sand in a sheltered spot under the cliff and, lifted by a surge of joy, waved enthusiastically at them. The two women responded with equal vigour.

'Come on, Lexa, we must go in for a bathe,' cried Melissa. 'Let's get our costumes on.'

'Mine's already on,' said Alexa, the sun and the sea making her feel young again. 'I just have to peel off this dress.'

'Me too!' cried the little girl.

They scarpered up to the little encampment where Rose was decanting steaming tea from a flask and quickly stripped off.

'Bathing cap on, Melissa,' urged Eleanor, accepting a cup from Rose. 'My, Alexa, what a wonderful costume.'

'It looks very continental, dear,' observed Rose. 'Very fetching.'

'A find in Venice?' asked Eleanor. 'Must have cost thousands of lira.'

'Yes,' said Alexa. 'I bought it on Lido. I can't remember how much it was...'

Her mind drifted to the last time she'd worn it – the first and only occasion – on the balcony of her room at the Excelsior when Guy had admired her from behind his dark shades, like a searchlight, seeking her out, his seduction well under way.

'Are you all right, Alexa?' asked Rose. 'Perhaps it is too chilly to bathe?'

'Not at all!' Alexa cried, banishing Guy. 'Come on, Melissa.'

She grabbed her sister's hand and they hurtled down the beach, skipping over shells and pebbles embedded in the hard, wet sand at the water's edge, and splashing into the shallows.

'Let's go further, deeper,' cried Melissa.

The sea was colder than expected and Alexa began to laugh in surprise. She dipped down until her shoulders went under and emerged, water streaming off her. Melissa was already doing the doggy paddle, her yellow bathing hat bobbing away, matching the ball of the sun overhead.

'Not too far, Melissa.'

Alexa lay on her back, relishing the weight and the pull of the waves. Fronds of seaweed trailed gently around her toes, occasional splashes hit her mouth and she licked off the salt. She took one deep breath, and then another, letting the pure air cleanse her.

Melissa splashed close by.

'Lexa, I don't believe in pixies any more,' said the little girl. 'Oh why? That's such a shame,' said Alexa, disappointed.

'When you went away, I decided there was no magic any more.' Melissa trod water next to her, occasionally taking sips of seawater and dribbling it out.

'But there can be magic, there will be,' urged Alexa, desperate suddenly for the little girl's innocence to return. 'Just don't look for it too hard. Who do you think puts the tangles in the moorland ponies' manes? Who do you think does the housework when we're sleeping? Who do you think steals naughty children away?'

Melissa laughed, her face wide and trusting.

She said, 'Perhaps I will believe again. Now that you are back.'

'Do you know, that makes me feel a whole lot better,' Alexa said, even though she felt suddenly very tired.

She put her feet down, stood up out of the waves, surprised that the water only came up to her waist and glanced back to the beach. Eleanor was standing at the water's edge, sunglasses and hat on, shielding her eyes and staring intently at the horizon.

'Have you seen what I've seen?' she called.

Alexa turned. Dipping around the Enys Point headland was a small craft with a blue sail. Alexa's heart began to tap, warmly and insistently, as if to get her attention.

'Melissa,' she called, tearing her eyes away, 'let's get out now. You must be ravenous. Shall we see what Aunt Rose has packed for us?'

The little girl emerged with a cry of joy and splashed past her. But Alexa walked towards the shore, not brave enough to look back at the boat, her knees pushing wearily through the heavy water. Perhaps she had not been as rested from her journey as she thought she was and swimming had done her in. As she reached the beach, she stopped dead, a pulsing ache gripped her deep in her stomach.

'Gosh, this is hard work,' she called out to Eleanor, fighting the pain. 'Perhaps I've overdone it.'

Eleanor nodded distractedly. 'I thought that he'd gone away to St Just, thought he'd be settled in at the practice with Doctor Paynter. Perhaps he's heard that you are back.'

'Really, Eleanor. He's allowed to have a holiday from work. He's allowed to sail his own boat around his own... Goodness... ouch—' Alexa pressed her hand over her stomach.

'Cramp is it, dear? You haven't swum in the sea for ages. You need to take it slowly.'

Eleanor fell into step beside her.

'You know, Alexa, if you take a walk up to the churchyard, you'll see that every grave has a fresh bouquet. The flowers for the wedding, removed from the church. Still going strong. They were beautiful, a whole florist's shop.'

'Is that so,' said Alexa, refusing to be drawn, refusing to look again out to sea. The pain in her stomach had disappeared as sharply as it had gripped her.

'All I know is that when Harvey came to see me in Venice, it seemed so right for him, and Sarah. He told me how much she suited him,' she said, perching on the edge of the rug between Melissa biting into a Scotch egg and Rose unwrapping sandwiches. 'I'm staggered that this has happened.'

'None of us are, dear,' said Rose, and sank her teeth into a crust.

'Anyway,' piped up Melissa, her mouth full of egg, 'I thought Lexa was going to marry Harvey.'

Alexa blushed, her eyes smarting.

Eleanor gave her aunt a hard look that suggested they ought to change the subject.

As Alexa accepted the ham sandwich Rose offered her, she shivered. She was cold, now, out of the sun. The tranquillity of floating in the sea had disappeared and, in its place, came a creeping, nagging sense of ill-ease.

'Oh, look, Alexa, you're all goosebumps,' said Rose. 'Borrow this.'

As Alexa slipped Aunt Rose's beautifully knitted cardigan on, Eleanor eyed her once more.

'Now tell me, Alexa, how it is that you could afford such things as this Italian bathing costume, and the pretty blue dress and the dear hat that I found crushed at the bottom of your suitcase? Did Lady Meredith pay you well? We're all dying to know.'

Alexa glanced at Melissa, who was expertly peeling a banana with her delicate fingers, entranced by her own skill.

'It's all right, Melissa can hear this,' said Eleanor. 'She will have forgotten it in five minutes when Aunt Rose brings out the chocolate cake.'

* * *

Not feeling at all hungry, Alexa nibbled a corner of the sandwich and told Eleanor and Rose how she had already been engaged by Lady Meredith when she left Porthdeen after the ball; had been completely undone by Harvey's proposal and had bolted.

'At least you've made your peace with Harvey now,' chipped in Eleanor, glancing towards the horizon.

Alexa followed her gaze and saw, with a smudge of disappointment, that the boat had gone.

While Rose poured more tea, Alexa told them how generous her clothes allowance from Lady Meredith had been.

'That explains the lovely things, Eleanor,' advised Rose.

'But it doesn't explain Mr Moreland,' added Eleanor.

The two women stared at her, expectantly, ready for her answer.

Alexa trembled. How could she possibly explain?

'We can't talk about that in front of—' Alexa breathed out. A throb of pain crushed the pit of her stomach and she leant forward into it, trying to disguise her agonised cry.

'Goodness, Alexa, are you all right? You look ghastly,' cried Eleanor.

She placed her cool hand on Alexa's forehead. 'You're soaking. You have a fever,' she said.

'I must say, I thought you were looking peaky,' said Aunt Rose.

'I'm not feeling particularly well—' Alexa began.

'Particularly well?' said Eleanor quickly, 'Your skin is on fire. You should not have gone in the sea.'

In an instant, Eleanor was helping Alexa to her feet. Alexa swayed as she tried to stand. A strange sloshing began inside her head and she was grateful for Eleanor's firm arm around her waist.

'I am rather dizzy,' she confessed.

Eleanor handed out efficient instructions to her aunt and daughter for them to stay put while she took Alexa back up the path.

'Sorry to break up the party,' Alexa uttered.

She heard Rose's sympathetic answer, Melissa's startled questions and Eleanor's calm words deep in her ear, but could not see any of them. Black curtains pressed in from the sides of her skull, across her eyes, blinding her. The final glare of the sun at the centre of her vision became a sheer flash of agony through her head. Weightless, her body plummeted through the briefest amount of space and thumped onto the ground. She felt the sharp prickle of sand beneath her cheek and her hands, the grains stinging her, like the little bites of insects. And the cove, the cliffs, the sea went black.

31

Alexa heard a rabble of voices in the darkness, but it was her father's that seemed to make the most sense to her, that made her want to open her eyes. At least try to.

She glimpsed the outline of his face, as if peering through a fissure in her mind. Behind him the glow of a lamp was like a yellow cloud of dust, expanding and moving towards her across the room. The window was a block of deep inky blue. Night had fallen, but which night? How long had she been lying here? She tried to move her hands but they were huge cumbersome lumps. Her whole body was expanding, enormous, filling her bed. She was a giant; she could walk around the entire world in three mighty steps.

Heat rose from her drenched skin. She was lying in a furnace. She scrabbled at the sheets, tearing them off her. There was not enough oxygen to breathe; not enough sea air. She couldn't speak – her mouth felt like it was full of stuffing.

'Open the window wider, Eleanor,' she heard her father say. 'Let in the breeze.'

The cool hand on her forehead again, followed by a cloth

dipped in icy water. The shock of it made her suck air in through her teeth. Eleanor's voice this time, gentle but persistent: 'Is there anything we need to know, Alexa. Anything we need to tell the doctor?'

In a far corner of her mind, she saw the little back bedroom of a house in Fulham. She twitched her hands, tried to shake her head, to convey a negative to the fading outline of her stepmother.

'... shouldn't have gone swimming... more ice, Rose... thought she looked unwell when she arrived... assumed she was tired out from her journey... no, Melissa, not now. Lexa's poorly...'

A methodical clacking sound as a number was dialled on the telephone, registering in her muddled mind, all the way up from her father's study. She was sitting on the stairs, a twelve-year-old in a summer dress on a summer's day not long after the solstice, cringing at the sound of her father's voice. Another urgent conversation but, this time, her father was not angrily criticising whoever was on the other end, but politely entreating this person to come, yes, please come at once.

The burning pain in her belly seemed to have become part of her, snaking up her middle, clamping tight. She was being punished, and she knew why. She'd warned her Mamma from her floating cushioned safety. She'd whispered to her Mamma and had let the other people die.

'They all drowned.'

Her father's face, blurred with concern into something almost unrecognisable, floated over hers.

'What's that, Alexa? What did you say?'

A sudden lucidity washed through her brain. She said, 'All my fault.'

'I think I know whose fault this is,' Eleanor corrected her. She towered over Alexa, a slender, fair-haired angel. 'I think we can blame Mr Moreland.'

Alexa twitched at the name. Guy and his aunt in a photograph standing on a Venetian bridge in sunlight outside Nonna's palazzo. Guy's face a blur. Lady Meredith wearing old-fashioned stripy stockings, hitching her skirt jauntily to show them off. A burst of laughter spluttered from Alexa and she tried to turn from the image, to roll away.

Two hands pressed her shoulders firmly back, easing her down onto the pillow which had become little more than a hard rock under her neck.

'Does your stomach hurt, Alexa? Tell me where it hurts?' She didn't have to open her eyes to know that he was there.

She knew the voice, just as well as she knew her own.

The shape of Harvey, the movements of his hands, the familiar tilt of his head flickered around her like projections on a screen. She heard his firm instruction, his reassurance. But how could everything be all right, for surely, she was about to die.

He lifted her arm and his touch cleared the pain and the revolting fever long enough for her to see him clearly. His tawny hair was ruffled, his face pinched with concentration, his eyes dark as he focused on the syringe in his hand. His smile was trying, not very successfully, to hide his fear.

'Just a scratch, Alexa,' he said. She didn't feel a thing.

Harvey, her bedroom, everything faded. But she fought lurching waves of oblivion ferociously for seconds, seconds which ticked like hours. She wanted to talk to him, so desperately wanted to hear him speak to her. She wanted to explain, to tell him everything.

32

'Have you looked inside your button box yet, Lexa?' said Melissa, steadying the breakfast tray as she came through the door. 'Oh, did you know your face is the same colour as the sheet? You look like a spook.'

She placed the tray carefully onto Alexa's lap.

'That's not a very cheering thing to say to your sister,' chided Eleanor, following in with a pot of tea.

'I think it has to be the nicest greeting I've ever had,' murmured Alexa – it was all she had the strength to say.

Melissa's observation was entirely accurate. Alexa's body felt light and transparent, hardly there at all, as if her blood had been drained; the pain had gone and her head was an empty space. She barely mustered the energy to smile when Melissa laughed triumphantly and planted a kiss on her cheek.

She was, however, ravenous. Melissa had made her two slices of burnt toast, with marmalade. Eleanor poured her a weak cup of tea.

'Now you've given Lexa her breakfast, you must go, Melissa, as we discussed.'

Melissa loitered around the bedroom door, peering hard at Alexa, before closing it.

'She was desperate to see you, to make sure you were all right,' said Eleanor, sitting in the wicker chair by the window.

'Am I all right?' Alexa asked, taking a tiny nibble of toast and immediately setting it back down.

'I must say, you do look so much better this morning,' said Eleanor. 'A vast improvement on the last few days.'

'Even though I look like a fright.'

'You certainly gave us all one. You have been, Alexa, desperately ill. As I nurse, I...'

Alexa looked at her stepmother, saw her face move with uncomfortable doubt. '... I wasn't that confident of being able to make you better, to be honest.'

The teacup rattled on the tray as Eleanor knocked it, reaching for Alexa's hand, squeezing it tight.

'Your skin feels better,' she said, her eyes bright with tears. 'Feels dry. The right temperature, yes. It will take you a long while to convalesce, so you must, I'm afraid, stay where you are and do as I say.'

'I feel as weak as a kitten,' Alexa said, trying to match Eleanor's smile. 'I don't think I can manage Melissa's breakfast.'

'And that's why you must follow nurse's orders.'

Alexa gingerly sipped the tea, took a few more bites of toast, barely tasting it. But as she swallowed the morsel of food, it comforted her and a small part of her returned, as if she had put a section of jigsaw in place. There were a great many more pieces to go.

'Where is Dad?' she asked, licking marmalade off her fingers.

'He's in his study, writing to Beatrice, as it happens. He wants to offer the olive branch. You being so ill scared him, Alexa. Has brought back terrible memories from the past. He wants to make amends to everyone as best he can.'

When Alexa had eaten all she could manage, Eleanor removed the tray and set a bowl of steaming water on the bedside table, dipping in a soft flannel, squeezing it out. As her stepmother tenderly dabbed Alexa's face, affection for her rose quickly, taking her by surprise.

'This is supposed to make you feel better,' Eleanor said, smoothly, 'Not make you cry.'

She continued to dab until Alexa's tears stopped.

As Alexa leant forward so that Eleanor could plump her pillows, she noticed her jewellery box on the shelf, the one she'd found in the antiques shop. The replacement for her mother's.

'What was it Melissa said about my button box?' she asked. Eleanor went over and picked it up from its spot next to George the doll and the two halves of seagull egg. She placed it on Alexa's lap.

'Look,' said Eleanor.

Before Alexa left Porthdeen, her new box had contained a woeful collection; just a handful that barely covered the blue velvet bottom. Alexa lifted the lid. It was full of buttons: carved, glittery, delicate, fancy little flower shapes and jet-black beauties. She dipped her finger in, stirring, hearing the faint clicking as they moved, just as the buttons used to in her mother's casket.

Astounded, she looked up at her stepmother.

'After you went away, Melissa was distraught,' said Eleanor. 'We all were, but it took all of our strength to console her. She could not understand how you could just disappear. None of us could, really. This was her idea. She decided that if she collected as many buttons as she could, and kept them for you, then, you'd come back for them. And you did.'

The buttons swam, and melted together. Alexa shut the lid quickly. 'How can I make it up to her, to all of you?' she whispered.

'You don't have to. Just get yourself better.' Elenor said gently.

Alexa brushed the back of her hand over her eyes. 'I'm trying my hardest,' she said.

Her stepmother set the button box aside, and began to gather the contents of the tray together. Alexa watched her, her strength, momentarily boosted by her mouse-size breakfast, was waning. A cloud of sleep billowed through her but she resisted it, wanted to fight it, to see the hours of daylight through, to be normal again.

'Eleanor,' said Alexa. 'What happened to me?'

Her stepmother sat back down. 'Alexa, you nearly died. Your poor father was beside himself, was reminded of Carlotta.' Eleanor gripped her hand. 'This time, I could be of better assistance. But if Harvey hadn't come over when he did—'

'What was wrong with me?' Alexa interrupted her. She could spare no strength to contemplate Harvey being at her bedside. 'I have a good idea, Eleanor, but I need to hear you tell me.'

'Infection due to abortion,' said Eleanor, her voice clipped and professional. 'That is what Harvey told us.'

Alexa lowered her head, could not look at her stepmother as her naïvity became a cleaner, sharper reality.

'I was lost, Eleanor,' she uttered. 'I could see no other way. I had been living as Guy's mistress but he was married. He had children. I had no idea. His wife was in Rome giving birth, probably at the same time I was destroying his child. I was ruined.'

Eleanor tugged on Alexa's hand, forced her to look at her. 'What possessed you to go to that butcher? If you had just come straight home, I would have helped you, found a solution one way or another,' she said, her voice rising persistently.

'I could never have come back home, back here pregnant,' said Alexa. 'I did not want Dad and you, or Harvey, to see me in such disgrace. I lied to Harvey about Mr Moreland being my husband. I didn't want him to know how low I had sunk...' Alexa faltered.

Harvey, as the doctor by her bedside in her moment of extremity, knew all too well now the depth of her degradation. 'I had to finish it, be done with it. Leave it all behind.'

Eleanor persevered, 'I would have come up to London, to meet you. Brought you back to Porthdeen.' She stopped abruptly. 'But it's done. What use is it, me saying all of that? You're home now. We're so very glad that you are here...The sun is shining, it's a lovely day...' She stood up, and went to the window to open it.

Alexa lay back drowsily on her pillows as the room filled with the robust force of Porthdeen; the salt air healing her, the sky pierced by seagulls calling and responding to each other; the sound and scent of home.

'Alexa,' Eleanor said, 'looks like you have a visitor. He will be pleased with your progress. He's not yet seen you awake.'

Alexa sat up abruptly and was instantly dizzy. She braced herself and began to ease out of bed.

'I didn't mean for you to get up. Oh, do you want to? Take it carefully, then. Slowly...'

Eleanor helped Alexa set her feet firmly on the floor, drew her upright and supported her over to the window.

Alexa pushed it wider, leant on the windowsill to prop herself up. On the far headland, on the snaking path from Enys Point, striding through golden end-of-summer grass, the sky a painted arc of blue behind him, was Harvey. His cap pulled low on his head, as it always was, his pace determined.

Tentative hope found her. Perhaps Harvey was able to look past what she'd done, and they could start again. Eleanor's hold grew tighter as she leant against her, her bones trembling. She had dodged the grip of death, had stepped over the chasm between her past and her future. She was alive. And Harvey was on his way to Porthdeen.

* * *

Eleanor found a fresh nightgown and a decent dressing gown. 'I can't believe I'm not strong enough to wield a hairbrush,' said Alexa, as her stepmother tenderly brushed her hair before rushing off to her own bedroom to fetch a bottle of cologne.

'Really, Eleanor?'

'It's only toilet water. Just a little splash, Alexa. Now, get back in under the covers. Like any good doctor, Harvey will be furious if he finds you out of bed.'

Eleanor slipped away, her excitement tangible. Not long afterwards, Alexa could hear Aunt Rose showing Harvey up the stairs, his voice reaching Alexa before she saw him, the notes of it rising and falling like a song that was always on her mind.

'Alexa, may I come in?' Harvey stood in her doorway.

'That's very formal of you,' she said, cheerfully.

Her smile was not reciprocated. 'You still sound very weak,' he said.

He drew the wicker chair nearer the bed, sat down and picked up her wrist, his movements swift and professional.

'Melissa said I'm as white as this sheet,' Alexa said. 'But I haven't had a chance to look in the mirror yet. Perhaps it's best I don't.'

'Pulse is good.' Harvey dropped her hand, moved the chair away and sat back down on it. 'I'm satisfied that you are on the mend, but Doctor Paynter will continue with your care from now on.'

'I suppose that is more appropriate,' offered Alexa, unable to understand why she felt so incredibly disappointed.

Harvey caught her eye, but not at all like he used to: with amused fascination. He regarded her only as he might a patient.

'I don't wish to tire you out, Alexa, so I will say goodbye.'

'Perhaps I will see you in a few days,' she ventured, wondering at his sharpness. 'when I'm up and about?'

'That won't be possible. First of all, you will not be strong enough in a few days for anything like what I know your "up and about" means. Alexa, you have had a very serious infection and you must rest. Secondly, I've asked for a transfer to a practice in Truro to continue my training, so even if you disobey my orders, you will not see me.'

Alexa peered at him. There seemed to be far too much space between them and she was not used to it. She swallowed hard, tried to collect her strength and compose herself.

'You're going to Truro? How long for?'

'Permanently. It is best all round, don't you think?'

'Of course, for Sarah...' Alexa sank with disappointment.

'Yes,' he said. 'For Sarah.'

'But you see, Harvey,' Alexa tried to keep calm, despite sudden, sickening fear, 'it seems that I'm always running away from something. From you, from here, from myself, some would say. But now I'm home and I've found the place where I want to be, you are leaving. And, I'm not sure I like the idea.'

He gave her a hard look.

'Do you think that is a reason for me to stay?' he uttered, and the suppressed fire in his words was brutal. 'I have to do this. I can't just breeze along as if nothing has happened. My behaviour over Sarah makes me hang my head in shame. At the moment, she is away with her mother, and I vowed that I would be gone when she returned. I have made a pure and utter mess of it all.'

'Then why did you let it go so far in the first place?' Alexa snapped, her fury biting into her words.

Harvey looked at her, aghast.

'Alexa, you and I have both been incredibly selfish in all of this. But I could not marry Sarah,' he pushed on. 'I did not love her and it was better for me to walk away before it was too late, feeling as diabolical and as heinous as any man could do. She doesn't believe that it was the better thing to do now. But perhaps in a year, in two, she will. Perhaps then I will be able to look her – and her mother – in the eye again.'

'Can you look me in the eye again...?' Alexa mumbled, chastised.

'Alexa, you left Porthdeen. You disappeared. I can understand why you did that. But getting yourself into that terrible situation. Taking that risk with your life.' He waited. 'For that, I cannot forgive you.'

Alexa reeled as his words hit her like arrowheads. Terrible images tumbled through her mind, as if she was plummeting backwards through time to the moment Eleanor covered her mother's face with the sheet. She had lost something so very precious. And she was losing it again. Harvey was unrecognisable and she had no hope, no strength left to do anything about it.

She whispered, 'I only did what I did because I was lost, so lost.'

'You had your family. You had me, Alexa.' Harvey's eyes were bright with tears.

'But I was desperate to find my own way in the world, desperate to heal the rift in my family. And I did, eventually. I found my grandmother. She is the only way back to my mother.'

'But did you have to let yourself be seduced like that?' Harvey's words seethed. He did not elaborate.

'Is all of this because I became a man's mistress?' she asked.

Harvey flinched, he said nothing.

'I did what I did,' Alexa cried, 'because I was dreadfully sad. And frightened. You were going to marry Sarah. I saw the notice in *The Times.* In Venice, all you could talk about was how you had to run home to Sarah. I thought you had married Sarah!'

'And you told me you were Mr Moreland's wife,' he countered.

'Even so, I broke it off with Sarah, without knowing the truth of your situation, because I knew that mine wasn't right. But that doesn't mend this. Doesn't change anything.'

'But it does, Harvey, it does. It changes everything.'

'I must leave, Alexa.' He stood abruptly, headed for the door. Alexa let out a tiny wounded cry.

He paused and glanced back at her. She saw the old essence of him in that look, when he'd cared so much for her. But that was also when she'd thought she'd be able to walk away from him, and that he'd still be there when she came back.

Harvey lingered for a moment, took in the view from her window and then spotted the two halves of seagull eggshell nestled on her shelf. His face eased with a suggestion of memory, of affection, and Alexa thought, for a second, that perhaps he would stay.

'I had a dream for both of us, Alexa,' he said, his words fractured, 'but the dream is now a nightmare. Somewhere along the line your goodness was taken and broken, and mine too. For look what I have done. To Sarah, and to you.'

He gave her one single, trembling look and left.

Alexa tried to get out of bed, pull back the covers, plant her feet on the floor, run after him, make him stay, but her body was weak and useless. Her flesh had melted and there was nothing left of her. Harvey might as well have ripped her in two.

33

WINTER SOLSTICE, 1931

Aunt Rose knitted Alexa and Melissa matching berets, from a pattern in her weekly magazine, for Christmas. They were the latest fashion, jaunty and with a little rosette to the side. Alexa's was in a shade of raspberry; Melissa's in sky-blue. They were lovely and warm, perfect for their walk down the steep steps to Little Porthdeen on Boxing Day, two sisters together, their breath forming in white clouds before them as they chattered.

Melissa was eager to see the mummers, for it would be her first time.

'I want to see the poor dead hobbyhorse,' she insisted. 'And the knight kill the dragon.'

Alexa wasn't sure if she was ready for anything as ghoul-like as a horse skull being paraded around on a stick but admitted that she was a little excited too. She had missed the celebrations last year, having spent a formal, deathly quiet Christmas in Cadogan Square with Lady Meredith.

She heard the drumming while they were still only halfway down the cliff side and, when they turned a corner, Melissa cried out with glee when she spotted the raw flames of the bonfire on the quay, pagan heat in the depths of midwinter. The boom of the drums carried in the still, cold air as sound and vibration, hitting Alexa at the centre of her chest, its primal urgency enticing her, waking her at last from her deep sleep.

* * *

Alexa had taken a lot longer to recover than Eleanor or Doctor Paynter had anticipated; she had retreated, shut herself away, had sunk into a stupor as the minutes, hours and days after Harvey had left lengthened and spun themselves out to become her appalling reality. And her family – Dad, Eleanor, Melissa and Aunt Rose – had each ventured into her room, ignored her protests and broken through with books, food, story-telling, knitting patterns and an endless supply of new buttons for her button box. She rose, finally, on the day before Christmas Eve, humbled and grateful, and determined to be better.

'Let's hurry, Lexa,' Melissa cried back over her shoulder, 'Mummy said we must be home before it gets dark. And we don't have that long.'

The early afternoon was already shrugging off daylight. The sky was overcast and dusky, making the torches and lanterns of Little Porthdeen down below glow like beacons. From the path, she could see the dark mass of a bustling crowd on the quay, hear laughter, the cadences of the fiddle and accordion, snatches of sea shanty reaching her in the shape of little refreshing chants.

'We'll have time for at least one pasty each,' Alexa assured her sister. 'And maybe a little jig or two?'

'Yes, let's,' Melissa giggled and picked up her pace; Alexa gamely kept up with her, reaching the quay in no time.

Coal-fire smoke from cottage chimneys unfurled over frosted roofs and every cobblestone was lined with puddles of ice. The sea was grey and heavy like molten lead, the tide high, the harbour full, and the fishing luggers rested quietly at their moorings. Indigo Moon was nowhere to be seen.

'Come, Lexa,' urged Melissa, pulling her by the hand towards a pasty stall. 'I'm so very hungry.'

Alexa laughed, 'Why is it you're always just on the brink of starvation!'

They handed over their pennies for their pasties and pressed through the buoyant crowds of villagers and parishioners, the fishermen, the farmhands from the Rosewarne and Ferris estates, their wives and children, all out in their finery, drinking from tankards of beer or mulled cider. Women were wearing old-fashioned corsets streaming with ribbons, men in Victorian tailcoats with sprigs of wintergreen pinned to lapels. Top hats were sported with flourish by both men and women. Some wore masks, some had blackened faces, laughing, dancing, immersed in primitive ritual. The bonfire at the far end of the quay created a glowing backdrop to the gaiety, bringing warmth and light back to the world, to Alexa's corner of Cornwall, to the ends of the earth.

Melissa drew herself close, went up on her tiptoes and hissed into Alexa's ear.

'We don't have masks. Why do they have black faces?'

'It's the tradition,' Alexa whispered back, 'so their landlord won't recognise them if they get too merry in their cups.'

'Landlord? Do you mean Dad?'

'Yes, but we won't tell him if we see anyone stumbling about or singing too raucously.'

'Aunt Rose should have made us masks,' said Melissa, biting eagerly into her pasty, steam escaping from her mouth.

Alexa laughed, 'I think people might guess who we were even if we were wearing them.'

The drumming was relentless, tribal, and Alexa found herself walking to its beat, losing herself in it. She paid for a cup of warm cider and sipped it, enjoyed its fire oozing inside her, rousing her. Villagers nodded at her, acknowledging her as they squeezed past. She wondered how many were still talking about the night of the Enys Point Ball, how much of her shaming of Harvey had filtered down to the cobbles, the hearths and the snugs of Little Porthdeen.

Outside the Three Pilchards, a little troupe in steeple-crowned hats were strumming and singing, one calling, the others responding, stamping and keeping time. 'Oo-ray and up she rises, oo-ray and up she rises.' Melissa gave a squeak of excitement, loosened her hand from Alexa's and eased herself into the dancing throng, endeavouring to match her steps to the jig.

Alexa stood for a moment, relishing the warmth of the bonfire at her back, its simple and fierce primordial heat. It could do nothing else but revive her, remind her that the darkest day was over, the dead winter was turning its face towards spring. In a week, no longer, the calendar would shift, a new year arrive. A new life, a new beginning, surely. Then why, Alexa wondered, did she peer at every man who passed her by, trying to see beneath the mask or the blackened face, hoping, longing for it to be Harvey. But he hadn't been home since September. He was a man of his word; it could no longer be.

* * *

A great cheer burst from the people, startling her. On the far side of the quay the mummers' play had started and through the mêlée, Alexa saw St George wield his sword in the direction of a dancing figure with a gigantic green dragon head. Prancing around them was a man holding a grinning horse's skull on a pole, collecting coins in his upturned cocked hat. Her sister was missing her poor dead hobbyhorse.

She heard a sharp scream and instinctively knew it was Melissa's, even though she had lost sight of her amid the throng. 'She's fallen,' someone, a young woman, cried. 'Careful! The little girl's fallen!'

Alexa dropped her cup, pushed through, blazing with intuitive terror.

Melissa was on the cobbles, clutching her knee and bawling. The musicians stopped mid-bar, the crowd parted, except for the girl in the purple mask who'd shouted and was now stooping to Melissa, her arm around her, soothing her.

Alexa knelt and saw blood seeping through Melissa's stocking below her knee.

'Ah, Miss Rosewarne,' said the masked woman, 'so this must be Melissa. So much rough and tumble here, too much for a young *cheel*. Looks nasty. My mother can help. We're only through there.'

Melissa's face was ghostly, her eyes wide and frightened, seeping tears.

Alexa mutely let them both be led by the girl, supporting Melissa between them, coaxing her to walk, to limp towards an alleyway, away from the quay. Behind them, the mummers' play continued, the music struck up again, the singing resumed as they made their way along the crooked passageway. It was only when they'd walked two streets back and the young woman stopped outside a small whitewashed cottage and lifted her mask that Alexa realised that it was Lizzie, Sarah's sister, and that she was opening the front door to the Carmichael home.

Inside was swept, bare and dim, the lamps extinguished to save on oil. An old-fashioned range glowed with pinpricks of red from dampened-down coals, before it a single rocking chair. The table was scrubbed, small and square, laid with a lace cloth, a simple, fetching display of pride. Around the walls, three or four hard upright chairs stood to attention; on the stone floor, a rag rug.

'Mother!' called Lizzie up the dark tunnel of the spiral staircase. 'Are you there?'

Alexa heard Joan Carmichael's response and her step on the floorboards. She hesitated, curiosity outdoing her desire to flee.

'Mother, Miss Rosewarne has hurt herself. Can you help?'

Mrs Carmichael stopped on the bottom step and her face hardened when she saw Alexa, then softened, noticing Melissa.

'Good afternoon,' she said, looking puzzled.

'We don't want to interrupt you, Mrs Carmichael—' Alexa began, but her words were dismissed by the woman's quick gesture.

Following down the stairs behind her, to peer solemnly at the unexpected guests were the two younger Carmichael girls, almost identical and neither so little any more.

Lizzie bustled the still whimpering Melissa into the rocking chair and spoke to her gently, telling her that it wouldn't hurt for much longer. The girls took instant interest in her and hovered around, staring at her pretty beret, her tears.

Joan, at last, looked away from Alexa and knelt by Melissa, batting the twins out of the way.

'Ah, so you are Rose Hammett's great-niece,' said the older woman, peering at Melissa's bloodied knee. 'And so we must make you welcome, young lady.'

'Am I, Lexa?' Melissa, between sobs of pain, looked up at Alexa to ask. 'A great-niece?'

'You are,' said Alexa, keeping very still by the doorway, creeping discomfort unnerving her, 'now sit still and let the lady see to you.'

Joan Carmichael acknowledged her with another stilted gesture, increasing Alexa's ill-ease. But she told herself that, even though it was so very odd for her to be standing there in the small, dark Carmichael kitchen, Harvey's traumatic jilting of Sarah had nothing to do with her. Because at the time everyone, including Harvey, believed she was married to Guy.

'You're going to have to come further into the room, Miss Alexa,' said Mrs Carmichael, mildly chiding her, 'for you are blocking what little light we have, standing there.'

The girls giggled, Alexa apologised and Lizzie pulled up a chair for her at the table.

'Marianne and Julie, scoot will you, go somewhere else,' said Lizzie, and the girls slipped away. 'The water's just off the boil. I'll make Miss Rosewarne some tea.'

Joan threw Lizzie a warning look and glanced up at the ceiling before turning her silent concentration onto her task, dipping a clean rag into the bowl of steaming water that Lizzie offered her and carefully dabbing around Melissa's wound. The little girl winced.

'You're being very brave,' Joan said kindly. 'And what a lovely beret you have.'

'Aunt Rose knitted them,' offered Melissa, as Lizzie leant over her and dried her eyes with a handkerchief.

Joan glanced at Alexa again and Alexa, on reflex, touched her hand to her own hat.

'She's a clever woman, that Rose Hammett. She is making my wedding dress,' Lizzie told Alexa. 'Did you know, I'm marrying my Jimmy in the spring? I've picked out a beautiful fabric, although Mother wanted me to economise, perhaps have a hand-me-down.'

'Aunt Rose is very skilled at many things,' agreed Alexa, thinking of her dress for the Enys Point Ball.

'I was supposed to be a bridesmaid for Alexa,' Melissa said, taking the handkerchief from Lizzie and completing the job of drying her eyes. 'But I wasn't. Can I be yours, Lizzie?'

'Oh, Melissa, shush,' cried Alexa, trying to laugh.

Joan stood up, left Lizzie to finish off bandaging Melissa's knee, and sat at the table opposite Alexa.

'Yes, we heard that you got married in Venice, Miss Alexa,' she said, pointedly.

Alexa pressed her hands together to stop them trembling. 'You were misinformed, I'm afraid, Mrs Carmichael,' she said, her mouth dry and sticky. 'There has been some confusion—'

'Rose made my dress, too,' came a voice from the staircase. 'Would you like to see it, Alexa? It's never been worn.'

Sarah stood on the stairs, dipping her head down; the ceiling was too low at that point for her willowy frame.

'I'm sure Miss Rosewarne hasn't the time, Sarah—' began Lizzie.

Sarah captured Alexa with a reproachful look, peering at her expectantly. Alexa's memory flashed with the ball and the last time she'd seen Sarah, gaping with horror as Harvey got down on his knee and proposed.

'We ought to be getting back, I'm afraid, so Lizzie is right, we haven't the time. It's lovely to see you, Sarah...' Alexa offered cautiously. 'We promised my stepmother we'd be back before it got dark.'

As if to prove it, she looked out of the small window at the front of the cottage. The day was still lighter outside than it was inside the house, but night was closing in like soft creeping sleep. The faint sound of music and the smell of the bonfire reached her through the Carmichaels' closed front door.

'Oh, it won't take a moment,' said Sarah, overly brightly.

Even in the gloom of the kitchen, Alexa saw that her pretty face had lost its plumpness; her eyes were flat, as if she had no soul. Her spirit preserved only in the peppy sound of her voice.

Sarah insisted, 'And I'm sure, Alexa, that you have a moment.' She disappeared back up the stairs.

Lizzie leaned across to her mother and whispered, 'Now can you see why I insisted on Rose making me my own wedding dress?

It just wouldn't be fair for me to have that hand-me-down. It would bring me such bad luck.'

Joan Carmichael bristled, but her silence suggested acquiescence.

'It has hit Sarah hard that Lizzie is getting married to Jimmy,' she told Alexa in a whisper. 'You'd expect sisters to marry in order of age, but...'

Melissa picked up Lizzie's mummer mask that she'd left on the table and excitedly tried it on, her painful knee forgotten. Alexa got up from the table and hurried over to her.

'Come on, Melissa, leave that now, it belongs to Miss Carmichael. I'm sorry,' she said to Lizzie, 'we've not time for tea, after all. But thank you so very much for everything.'

'And I'm sorry if I've caused you any embarrassment, Miss Rosewarne. I realise now that it might not have been appropriate to come back here...' Lizzie tilted her head in apology. 'I thought Sarah was out for the day...'

Before Alexa could answer, Sarah was walking back down the stairs tenderly carrying a white dress over her arm. She stood in the centre of the room and held it up against her, pressing it under her bust and around her waist, holding out the empty sleeves, turning on her heel so that the lacy panels of the skirt flared out.

'I've lost lots of weight, like a bride should,' she said, her voice singing with pleasure as she began to tiptoe around the table, dancing to an invisible tune. 'I expect it will hang off me now.'

'And Rose did a wonderful job, Sarah,' said her mother, her voice low and persuasive. 'Miss Alexa already knows what a good seamstress she is.'

Lizzie put her arm around Melissa, who was playing happily with the mask. 'It's all right, you can keep it, Melissa,' she said, smiling at the little girl while guardedly watching her sister. 'I wonder, did they have masks like this in Venice, Miss Rosewarne?

We've read about the Mardi Gras in the newspaper, haven't we, Mother, and all the glamour and spectacle there. I don't suppose the Venetian masks would be as rudimentary as mine. Imagine the Mardi Gras, Mother. And Venice!'

'I wasn't there for the Mardi Gras,' Alexa hurriedly corrected her, wishing to truncate the conversation so that they could leave. Sarah waltzed behind her, swishing the back of her head with a pretty white cuff. 'But I did see the most beautiful masks for sale—'

She stopped speaking when Sarah stood beside her, so close that she could hear her breathing.

'Feel the softness of the lace, Alexa,' she said, offering the dress to her.

'Yes, Sarah, yes, how lovely,' Alexa hurriedly agreed, as Sarah twirled away. 'Come on, Melissa, I really think we'd better go.'

But Melissa placed Lizzie's mask back over her face, jerking her head from side to side, grasping for more attention.

'Harvey should have bought you one when he visited you in the summer, Lexa,' Melissa proclaimed. 'Don't you think that would have been a nice thing for him to do?'

Alexa lifted her hand as if she could stop the name Harvey being spoken. She opened her mouth but her voice was missing.

Sarah froze, mid-whirl, beside Melissa. The little girl proceeded to advise her, quite proudly, that her dad had told her all about Mr Harvey going to Venice for them to find Lexa and bring her home.

'And Lexa did come home, soon after. So, we like Harvey, don't we?' Melissa said looking intently at Alexa.

Sarah shook her head slowly at the child, an eerie smile stretching her mouth. She began to stroke the lace on the dress in her hands, her eyes fixed on the movement of her fingers as they caressed it. 'No, you're wrong, Miss Melissa,' Sarah said, her voice small and trapped in her throat. 'Mr Ferris visited his aunt

Margaret in Scotland in the summer before… before the… our… wedding.'

Joan Carmichael got to her feet, approached her daughter, uttering, 'Sarah, don't mind that now. Mr Ferris is long gone, and good riddance to him.'

'That's not what you said, Mother, when he asked me to marry him. You said it was the most glorious thing. Love, real love. The most beautiful journey two people can make,' Sarah accused her. 'What did you really mean? How glorious it would be for your eldest daughter to marry a Ferris. With their house, Enys Point and their money and all of it.'

A chill crept over Alexa's scalp; she glanced at the door, longed to be away.

'I think you'd better put your gown away now, Sarah,' said Joan. 'We don't want to upset our visitors.'

She touched the dress, but her daughter flinched it out of her hands.

'So Harvey was lying to me,' pondered Sarah quietly, her fingers kneading the folds of lace. 'Right up until the wedding. Even then.' The deadness of her eyes had vanished, replaced by a dark spark of pain.

Joan's voice was gentle, 'Please don't dwell on it, Sarah.' Her daughter blanked her, turned to Alexa.

'He put you above me, before me,' she said. Sarcasm dirtied her face. 'Of course he did. Whatever was I thinking. Me, a poor chit from a low fisherman's cottage. Marry Mr Harvey Ferris? Have you ever thought of such a ridiculous idea!'

Alexa watched agony alter Sarah's face and wanted to look away.

'But like your mother has said,' Alexa offered carefully. 'Harvey has gone. He lives elsewhere. I doubt he'll be coming back.'

'And this is why, Sarah…' said her mother, stepping around her daughter gingerly as one might a wild animal. 'This is why we cannot lay this at Miss Rosewarne's feet.'

'But Harvey still loves her, I know he does,' sneered Sarah. 'I asked him outright, that morning he came here. The morning before what should have been my happiest day. I asked him and he denied it. Said he didn't love her. Of course he did. But he does. He still loves you, Alexa. Always has done. That will never change.' She screwed the dress up, clutching it in her fists, crushing it to her chest. Her face was the same pale shade as the fabric, her eyes black with unspent tears.

'Sarah, I'm sorry,' Alexa said, unable to elaborate.

'Don't be,' Sarah replied, 'you leave sorry to me.'

She closed her eyes as if to shut Alexa from her mind, turned and began to walk up the stairs, holding her crumpled wedding dress before her like an offering. As she disappeared into the darkness, she began to sing, her intonation small and light like a child's. Alexa knew the tune, an old sea-song. 'Rocked to sleep, rocked to sleep, I was rocked to sleep in my salty seabed cradle.'

Lizzie sighed hard, as if she had been holding her breath the whole time.

'Mother, is she quite well?'

Mrs Carmichael twitched her head in a startled gesture of ignorance.

'I used to sing that song to Sarah in her cradle. My firstborn, she never slept,' Joan whispered in astonishment. 'I'm surprised she remembers it.'

Alexa retreated to the door, dragging Melissa with her, to leave the Carmichaels to mull over their woes and their memories in private. She said quick and thankful goodbyes and they stepped out into the darkened street where the midwinter night had fallen black and heavy. Their feet rang on the cobbles, Melissa clutching Lizzie's mask and limping a little but not complaining, hurrying along the alleyways and snickets running down towards the sea.

* * *

'Oh thank goodness,' Alexa sighed when she felt the warmth of the bonfire and saw the flare of the torchlight, the peculiarly reassuring heathen ritual.

They stopped to catch their breath in the yellow lamplight cast through the windows of the Three Pilchards. The merry-makers were drifting, their number thinning out on the cobbles and squeezing into the pub or gathering around the bonfire which had shrunk into a smouldering pyre, sparks darting to the black heavens.

'I couldn't wait to get out of there, even though the nice lady mended my knee,' Melissa confessed, panting to keep up with Alexa. 'It was very peculiar in there. Did I say something wrong?'

'Ha, Melissa, you're a little like me,' said Alexa.

'How am I like you, Lexa?'

'You think everything is your fault when it really isn't. Everything that seemed strange and horrible just then in Mrs Carmichael's kitchen was down to me, one way or another. Me and Harvey.'

Melissa slipped her hand into Alexa's and they began to weave their way across the quay.

'I thought that you were going to marry Harvey, I really did. I love Harvey.'

Alexa ignored the grinding stab of regret and urged her sister on. 'Come on, missy, we have a cliff to climb and it's pitch-black. Eleanor will kill me.'

'She won't, really. She won't because we will tell her what

happened to my knee. And I'll show her Lizzie's mask. She'll like that.'

They borrowed a lantern from a friendly fisherman who was sitting out on the harbourside, mending his nets, and were halfway up the steep stone steps before Melissa asked to sit down to rest. The lights of Little Porthdeen had disappeared behind the corner in the cliff face. The drums had stopped; the night was huge and silent. The air frozen and still. Below lay the inky, unfathomable sea and above, in a deep-black endless sky, a universe of starlight. Alexa gazed into primordial darkness.

'But that lady, Lexa...?' Melissa mused, her face a funny pensive puzzle in the glow of the lamp.

'Do you mean Sarah?' Alexa shivered. Although there was not a breath of wind, the cold was stronger, fiercer up on the cliff. Alexa longed for the animal warmth of home.

'Yes, that bride lady, with her dress and her so-sad eyes. When she sang my salty seabed cradle. She looked like she was dying.'

'Dying? Oh, Melissa,' said Alexa, and wrapped her arms around her little sister and they shivered together. 'I know exactly what you mean.'

34

VERNAL EQUINOX, 1932

One by one, baby seagulls hatched and Alexa heard their insistent piping and whistling from the nests in the cliffs and on the chimneys of Porthdeen. Parent birds swooped and hollered protectively, a rapid rush over her head. Days were filled with their noise and began to glow with expectation. The air softened, the sky was milky and kind, the sea sparkling in bursts of sunlight.

Coming downstairs one morning, the letter propped up against a vase on the hallway table caught Alexa's eye. Nonna wrote once a month, but this was not her usual stationery. And Aunt Rose, with her customary inquisitiveness, must have left it like that so that Alexa wouldn't miss it.

The envelope was typed, seemingly official, and as Alexa turned it over in her hands, Rose appeared, brandishing a steaming cup of tea as a small bribe to learn its contents. Alexa accepted the cup, thanked her. She took the tea along with the letter into the beige parlour, giving Rose a humorous glance that told her that she needn't bother following her. Through the French windows Alexa saw her father digging a new flower bed. Quite an early start for him for the dew was still on the ground. He was supervised, as always, by Eleanor, who was wrapped up against the strong breeze coming off the sea.

In the past few weeks, under Eleanor's encouragement and direction, Alexa had noticed her father's return to fitness, as if, with the spring, he'd made the decision to shake off his frailty. Watching him work, a stranger would not be able to tell what had happened to him. And, if Alexa looked in the mirror, she could not tell what had happened to herself either, apart from a trace of pain in her eyes and a new, deep line between her brows.

Aunt Rose had lit a small fire in the parlour grate, for there was still a chill in the air. Despite this, Alexa popped a small window open, for she wanted to hear the gulls and the gentle thump of her father's spade against the earth. She heard, also, Rose's step as she hovered outside the door.

Alexa sighed, sat down, rested her cup and saucer on the arm of the chair and slit open the envelope. A formal printed letterhead greeted her, causing her to blink rapidly: a solicitor's office in Mayfair. She began to read, halted, took a sharp breath and went back to the beginning.

Dear Miss Rosewarne,

My client, Mr G Moreland, has requested that I enquire of you, in reference to an impending inheritance, whether you carried out the advice given to you by the late Lady Meredith Ainsley, of Cadogan Square, SW1, in August 1931.

Propriety and decency dictates that I am not at liberty to have any further discourse about the details and the nature of the aforementioned advice given, but you are required to inform this office of the outcome of your decision at your earliest possible convenience.

Yours, etc.

Alexa dropped the piece of paper as if it was in flames and got to her feet so quickly that she knocked her cup, breaking it, spilling her tea all over Eleanor's rug.

Aunt Rose was immediately by her side, stooping to the rescue, plucking the letter from the mess.

'I'm very sorry,' uttered Alexa, 'I'll mop up.'

As Rose's eyes dipped to the letter in her hand they grew wide and luminous. She thrust it back to Alexa.

'Don't worry about the cup, lovie,' she said, 'are you all right? You look like you've had a bit of bad news.'

Stepping over the puddle and broken china, Alexa went to the mantelpiece and threw the letter into the fire.

'I don't wish to have anything to do with any of those people,' she uttered, 'alive or dead.'

'Which people?' Rose asked, blushing all the way to her ears.

Alexa knew full well Rose realised who and what the letter was all about and not wishing to add more fuel to her instinct for gossip, Alexa ignored her and walked to the French windows, her body loose and juddering. The news of Lady Meredith's demise was a shock but was snuffed out by rage rearing hot inside her. How dare a solicitor, a stranger, ask in such a way about the baby she would have been preparing to give birth to any day; the child she had, instead, chosen to destroy.

'Anyway, Alexa, I came to tell you...' Rose persisted, following her to the window, the ruddiness lingering on her heavy cheeks, 'Eleanor sent me to find you. Not sure if you're prepared to hear this or not. But she's just spotted Mr Harvey walking over the Enys Point headland.'

'That doesn't mean he is coming here!' Alexa cried angrily, startling Rose so much she took a step back. 'He could be going anywhere. He might be going down to see Sarah Carmichael for all you know. And why would I want to know anything about Harvey

Ferris's whereabouts? Anyway, Aunt Rose,' she folded her arms tightly, struggling to sound normal, challenging her, 'I certainly don't want to see him.'

She left her lie floating, turned from Rose's disbelieving and, frankly, excited face, opened the French doors and burst out into the fresh morning. Eleanor spotted her immediately, left her father in mid-conversation and hurried over, her face switching between concern and barely veiled delight.

Alexa raised her hand to stop her speaking. 'Eleanor, don't say a word,' she warned her. 'I don't believe for one minute he is coming here. Why would he? He is simply taking a morning stroll like any man should do on a pleasant morning.'

Even so, she dared herself to peer beyond the garden, squinting against the sunshine to the footpath on the far headland. It was empty.

'You're wrong, anyway! There's no one there!' she cried out knowing full well that Harvey had probably already reached the quayside. Her cry shook her father from his meditative labour. He buried the blade of his spade in the soil, rubbed his back with both his hands and beckoned them both over.

'Eleanor,' he said, 'would you mind leaving us. You are being rather skittish around Alexa and I think this situation calls for a little more calm.'

'What situation is that, Dad?' Alexa asked.

He stopped her with a look. Eleanor gave her an apologetic smile and went back into the house.

'Let's sit,' said her father, walking Alexa over to the table and chairs by the hawthorn. 'Perhaps if we stay here long enough one of those kind souls will bring us both tea.'

'I'll probably only spill it if they do,' uttered Alexa.

Her father raised his eyebrows, deciding not to question why. 'Now let's get this straight, Alexa,' he said, his voice rich, drawing her closer. 'Harvey finished his relationship with Sarah while he thought that you were married to another man. This, in my eyes, makes him a good man, for he did the right thing, no matter how bad it appeared at the time. His reputation, his honour has gone. Even in this day and age, it is a highly prized attribute for a man.'

'As much as a woman's virtue?' asked Alexa, bravely.

Her father paused, contemplating her. His face softened with compassion. 'That is a subject for another day, Alexa. For now, we'll move on. It was a terrible thing that Harvey did to that girl, there's no getting away from it. And believe me, I have heard, through Aunt Rose – you know she is at the forefront of village communication – how the Carmichael household pretty much collapsed under the dreadful blow Harvey Ferris visited upon them. Think about it: a family without a father, stalwarts of Little Porthdeen for centuries, part of the cobbles and the stone, the fibre of the community. And Sarah, due to marry into the richest family in the parish. Poor, yes. Dirt poor. But proud. And what a come-down for them. What a humiliation. But Joan Carmichael lifted her head, set back her shoulders. Her other daughters rallied. These folk always do.'

He was trying to make her feel less uncomfortable by telling her how strong the Carmichaels were. She pictured stoic Mrs Carmichael, breezy and cheerful Lizzie, the giggling twins. And Sarah's haunted face. The seabed cradle lullaby she sang to herself, grasping for comfort.

Alexa looked up to see Eleanor and Rose at the French windows gesturing wildly.

'Dad, I think he is here…' Alexa breathed out shakily in submission.

'My God, that man can walk fast,' her father uttered. 'Alexa, just remember that even though Harvey thought you were lost to him, he didn't want anyone else.'

'And neither did I, Dad. Oh God, help me.'

'Just be honest, Alexa. With him, with yourself. That's all you can be.'

Eleanor opened the French doors and Harvey slipped out into the garden. He gave Alexa a cautious glance, clutched his cap in his hand, descended the terrace steps and slowly walked across the lawn towards her and her father, his expression fixed and anxious.

'I'm surprised you want to show your face in these parts,' her father said, his smile broad as he stood to shake Harvey's tentatively offered hand.

'Well, sir, I don't suppose I'll ever drink in the Three Pilchards again.'

Her father said nothing more, and walked away. Alexa fixed her eyes on his departing back, suddenly longing for him to stay with her, to give her support, to give her his lopsided smile.

'May I?' Harvey asked with unusual shyness, indicating the chair next to Alexa.

She tilted her head in the affirmative, unable to speak as she contemplated him, saw the look in his eyes for the first time in months. Saw contrition, and hope.

'I've come to ask you a question,' he said.

'You've come all the way from Truro for that?' she asked, her voice returning. 'What's wrong with putting it in a letter?'

Harvey's grin broke his face.

'I'm glad to see you have not lost your little spark,' he said.

'It's all I have,' she retorted.

Harvey took a deep breath. 'I know it's a bit blowy, and rather fresh—'

'You want to talk about the weather?' Her lips twitched into the briefest of smiles.

He laughed. 'Alexa, will you come sailing with me today?'

Her mouth fell open. 'I haven't seen Indigo Moon in the harbour for months,' she said, contrarily.

'Yes, she's tucked away in our boathouse the other side of Enys Rocks. I couldn't very well have her over winter at Little Porthdeen. She may well have been scuppered. And I wouldn't have blamed anyone if they had.'

Alexa watched his face colour, watched regret darken his eyes, felt herself soften.

'I know you like your walks, Harvey,' she said, 'but all the way down the path and back up again, then beyond Enys Rocks to go to collect your boat will be too tiring for me, on top of sailing.'

'I haven't thought this through at all, have I? Story of my life,' he said, grimacing sadly. He pulled out his watch. 'The tide needs considering too. I didn't check. That's what happens when you wake up late one morning and set out of the house with just one thing in mind.'

Harvey's solemn, open gaze fell on her, and Alexa saw in it the length of the years they'd shared: she a girl, he a boy, Christmas, Michaelmas, summers home from school, paddling in the shallows, messing about on the boat. And he had become this man. This, her dearest friend.

Alexa stood up, her decision made.

'Dad will run us over to Enys Point in his car. He has just started driving again, he'll be glad to. He likes you.'

Harvey half-laughed. 'At least I know for sure that he does.'

'I think that Melissa might have a soft spot for you, too.' Alexa said.

* * *

Wearing her warm jacket and trousers, and her perky pink beret, Alexa sat in the back of her father's car, with Harvey in the passenger seat. As the car drew away, she turned to see Eleanor and Rose waving enthusiastically, joined at the last moment by an ecstatic Melissa leaping up and down, both hands fluttering madly in the air.

The greeting at Enys Point was more subdued but brimming with affection. Betty Ferris held Alexa tightly to her large perfumed bosom for some time, while Arthur, with watery eyes, sedately shook her hand.

'What took you so long, son?' Harvey's father asked him.

'What do you mean, Pa?'

'You know full well what I'm talking about,' said Arthur, and let his gaze slip to Alexa.

'Ah, I see, Pa, I see,' said Harvey, with a delighted wink and a smile at Alexa.

Betty plonked a hamper and flask into Harvey's hands. 'Hush, Arthur, enough of that,' she glared at her husband.

'I've done you both a picnic, Harvey. And if you don't like the sandwiches, Alexa, give them to the seagulls.'

While Harvey thanked his mother, Alexa kept very still, unable to believe that she was standing again in the glorious hallway of Harvey's home, being welcomed by his parents, immersed in their easy warmth.

'Now, William, would you care for a coffee, or perhaps a sherry? Is it too early for sherry?' Betty Ferris's strong Scottish inflection boomed, leading William away to their drawing room. 'And why didn't you bring the lovely Eleanor over?'

'Thank you, I will. Never too early for sherry,' William assured them. 'And I thought the occasion called for a little more tact and restraint than my dear wife might be able to offer...' he cast a quick look at Alexa and Harvey, 'so I left her at home.'

'You did right, old chap,' said Arthur, patting him on the shoulder and the seniors drifted off through the doorway.

* * *

'God, the rhododendrons look spectacular this morning,' said Harvey as Alexa walked with him out of the front door, around the corner of the house and across the sweeping lawn. 'It must be something to do with the light.'

Alexa could certainly smell the heady fragrance of the purple flowers, but the beauty of the show-off blooms in the hedge did nothing to ease her mind. Half an hour before, she'd been quietly sipping a cup of tea, her life continuing as it had done for months. She had been gradually putting her past behind her, gathering her strength, getting herself well again. But a terribly cold, brutally formal letter had dredged up her guilt, trivialised her pain; and now Harvey was walking jauntily beside her, making small conversation, as if nothing had happened.

'You're quiet,' said Harvey.

She said, feeling prickly, 'I didn't much like that wink you gave me.'

He looked amused. 'I couldn't help it, Alexa, I feel like winking. I can't get over the fact that you are here, walking by my side, that you actually want to talk to me. To come sailing with me. I don't deserve any of it.'

At the far end of the lawn, near the cliff's edge, he opened the little wicket gate.

'Neither of us do,' she answered as she passed through, reaching the path which led down to the boathouse.

He offered her his hand, as the way was steep, but she stubbornly refused it, carefully picking her way, following him Indian file.

'You haven't really explained yourself,' she called down after him. 'Are you on leave from the practice in Truro? Why are you home?'

He turned to look at her, incredulously. 'I'm here for you, Alexa.'

Not willing to contemplate the solemn depths of his eyes, she gestured that he should keep walking.

'So tell me,' she said, lightly, 'how is it all going up there?'

'Going well from a medicine-learning point of view,' he said. 'Spectacularly dreary from any other.'

'That's the second time you've said something is spectacular in the last few minutes.'

Harvey laughed. 'Even though Truro is busy and full of people, I was cut off. Isolated. Not lonely, just not at home. I wasn't myself. You know, last September, I had to get away from here...' Harvey spoke carefully. Alexa watched him struggle, her heart flipping over. 'I had to put time and space between myself and everything that I did, everything that went on, God knows I did... but...'

'Are you home for good?' Alexa asked, catching up with him. She needed to know that one thing, that he was not going to leave her again.

He turned to look at her. 'If you'll let me be.'

Alexa switched her head to one side, pretending to think about it and struggled to keep her face straight. She burst with a giggle.

'You know...' mused Harvey, joining in with her, 'your eyes no longer have that steely look I used to complain about. Makes that spark of yours seem even brighter.'

'But something has changed, and might never go back,' she spoke suddenly soberly, carefully, to warn him, thinking of the unformed life she had extinguished. 'I'm not the girl I was.'

'You are still you though, Alexa. You are that girl.'

She saw Harvey turn and continue his way down the path with a peculiar feeling that he was not quite real. She had stepped back and was watching him like she would in a dream. But, as she picked up her pace and fell in behind him, a surge of joy hit her and it felt odd, as if she had forgotten how to be happy.

'But anyway,' she said, a little breathless when they reached the narrow pebble beach. 'Spring is here. I feel like I'm emerging from a deep sleep.'

'You and me both,' Harvey said. 'As much as it can be, the damage has been mended.'

As their footsteps crunched noisily, skirting the base of the cliff, she said, 'It feels like we need to have gone through this.'

His silence was normal to her; he didn't have to say anything for her to know that he agreed. Her pain at his leaving Porthdeen and leaving her – his privilege in the circumstances – faded into a ghost of itself. Harvey unlocked the boathouse where Indigo Moon had been sleeping in darkness all winter. Alexa helped him push her on her trolley down the little sloping causeway and, with some difficultly, over the shingle.

'I've misread the tide,' he said. 'I thought the waterline would be further up the shore, and we'd be able to launch straight from the causeway.'

'And you a sailor,' Alexa laughed.

They worked together to lift the little skiff off the wheels, pushing her to the edge of the water, unhitching the rolled-up sail, hauling on the main rope to raise the sheet so that it fluttered blue against blue.

'First time this year she has seen the light of day,' Harvey said, as the boat settled into the shallow waves, lifting on the swell once or twice before they could both hop in.

'Same here, skipper,' said Alexa.

She stowed Betty's hamper and flask under her seat at the helm as Harvey secured the ropes. The sail snapped taut against the wind, and together they launched onto the surf, just as they'd done so many times before.

Immediately, Alexa had to work hard at the tiller.

'Current's racing today, isn't it?' said Harvey from his post by the boom.

'I'm surprised I can do this at all,' Alexa said. 'Ferrises have always been such fine sailors, whereas us Rosewarnes, with our feet planted in the earth, will never be. And with Mamma so fearful of the sea—' Alexa stopped. Her mother's premonition, Alexa's own whispered warning, was on the tip of her tongue, but she did not want to burden Harvey with it again. Instead, she laughed, 'You were probably born with webbed feet.'

'I'm not going to prove that to you now,' Harvey chuckled. 'Anyway,' he nodded towards her, her firm grip on the helm, 'you seem to be doing all right.'

Harvey watched her face for a moment. 'Last time I saw you, you told me you'd found your grandmother?'

'Yes, and I stayed there, just one night. In the room where Mamma was born. She would have loved to have been there, reunited with Nonna,' she said, smiling, thinking of her grandmother in her palazzo, perched by the water. 'When I was a child, I wanted to tell Mamma everything that happened to me; each thought I had, each thing I saw. I wanted to fill my mother's world with my own. And I would have told her about today, sailing like this, with you.'

'I remember so clearly her kind and beautiful face,' said Harvey. 'Everyone loved her.'

Harvey's words vibrated inside her. For a moment, Alexa lost sight of him behind the sail as he switched seats and began to loosen the rope and she allowed herself to weep, privately, as she leant on the helm, focusing on a point along the coastline, steering towards it, the sail above her billowing, until the wind dried her tears.

'It wasn't so much the water Mamma taught me to be afraid of, but something deeper,' pondered Alexa, as the little boat leaned hard onto her side, riding the waves under an exhilarating stream of air. 'A fear of fate, I think. Terrified of making choices. Of reaching a fork and taking the wrong one. And I've certainly done that.'

'I don't believe, Alexa Rosewarne, that you are actually afraid of anything.'

The wind dropped suddenly to little puffs, buoying them cheerfully along the choppy swell. Harvey took the helm and Alexa began to unwrap their sandwiches, pouring tea from the flask, passing the cup between them. They had come around in a circle. In the distance, rose the sheer cliff of Enys Point, the black rocks below.

'I tried to cheat fate, in a way,' Harvey said. 'I came to Venice to see if you were all right. I promised your stepmother that I would find you, bring you home. On the surface, I was being all very noble but, deep down, I was selfish. There I was, about to be married, and I wanted to know if you still wanted me, like an old dog that you can keep kicking. It was a rash and very stupid thing to do. But then again, I worship you.'

'And, as it turned out,' she said, quietly absorbing his momentous words. 'I wasn't all right.'

'When I saw you, I knew I couldn't be without you. I wanted to give us both another chance of happiness,' Harvey spoke urgently, as if appealing for her to understand. 'But then you told me, as a passing matter of fact, that you were married, and that was that. I left. It was nearly time for my own wedding. I didn't plan the breakup. But I had a strong feeling that, whatever happened, Sarah would be destroyed. Either then, when I walked into her cottage, or later – a year, two, or ten years down the line when it eventually fell apart. I'm not proud of myself. Of that you can be totally assured.'

'I know you're not, Harvey.'

They were silent for some time, finishing their picnic as they cut nimbly through the water. Alexa gazed around her at the cliffs rising, topped with new green, the waves foaming, dipping, the surface of the water a hundred shades of blue.

She said, 'You know, Venice was astonishingly beautiful and I loved it so very much, but I missed Porthdeen. It is my home. And I missed the sea, this sea. It is never the same, whenever you look at it.'

'And you aren't either, Alexa,' said Harvey with a smile. 'Always so wonderfully mercurial.'

'You're making me sound simply stroppy.'

He laughed briefly and his face fell. 'Listen to me, Alexa. I should never have let you go. Should never have let you run off from the ball. From your own birthday party, for goodness' sake. I should have insisted you stay. Insisted you saw sense. Locked you away if I had to. God, that sounds so arrogant, but still...'

'I wish you had, then we could have been happier sooner.'

'But then you would not have found your grandmother.' Harvey reminded her.

'We could have searched for her together. Two heads are better than one. We are better together.'

She rose from her post at the sail, stepped the two paces along the deck and squeezed up against him in the seat at the helm.

'She's going to be drifting all over the place in a minute,' said Harvey as the little boat pitched gently.

'Do you care?'

Harvey put his arm around her, drew her close, pressed his lips to her forehead. 'Not one bit.'

She sank into his embrace, falling sweetly, blissfully, into a sensation that was at once so fascinating. The wind teased her hair and fine sea spray sprinkled her hands and her face as she pressed her body to his and discovered him, discovered Harvey, her wonderful Harvey, kissing his eyes, lips, nose and cheeks. He responded, his kisses both deep and gloriously light, while Indigo Moon bobbed across the waves.

'Do you know how long I have loved you, Alexa?' he asked, his words low and intense as he ran his fingertips through her hair. 'I can't remember a time when I didn't.'

Alexa drew back, desperate to read his face, not quite believing the happiness coursing through her. Not quite believing that her life was meant to be this way, if only she had trusted fate, and let it happen.

He said, 'I wanted to tell you the time you found that broken seagull egg. I wanted to tell you that time I picked you up from the station when you came home from school. All the times we've sailed, and talked, and when we danced our first dance at your ball. I wanted to tell you the moment I saw you in Venice.' His words were as profound as a promise made and a promise kept. 'But something in your face always stopped me. As if you would not be able to love me. As if you have never been ready, until now.'

'I am, I am ready,' she whispered.

This was nothing like before. Nothing like the false, duplicitous and sad world that Guy lived in. Harvey's world was clean and true and real. This world was full; the other was empty. She had fallen in love with Harvey as a child, and it had taken her until this moment to look it in the face and to go with the consequences. 'Harvey,' she said, tripping and stumbling as she prepared to set their fate in motion, 'you came to my house this morning with a question to ask me. Well, I now have a question for you.'

He placed his fingers gently on her lips, his eyes bright with joy and surprise.

'You don't have to ask,' he said, gently. 'Because you know the answer. Yes, Alexa. Yes, I will marry you.'

'You will!'

'Of course, what did you think? The sooner the better, don't you agree?'

He held her, as the sea rocked beneath them. The ropes and pulleys clanged against the mast, tapping a haphazardly restful tune as they overshot Enys Point and faced endless open sea.

'But in the meantime,' Harvey said, 'I think we'd better get back on course again, or Indigo Moon may well end up in America.'

Alexa quickly took the helm and Harvey trimmed the sail and the little boat turned around, finding the wind, and set forth back into sheltered waters. Ahead of her, Alexa could make out the narrow beach in front of the boathouse and, past it, Enys Rocks tumbled at the base of the cliff, as dark and as jagged as newly mined coal.

'Set your sights on the rocks, Alexa, that outcrop there,' said Harvey, pointing, 'and the current will take us to the boathouse.'

Alexa said, 'Aye, skipper.'

As they drew closer to Enys Rocks the wind got up. Indigo Moon made good headway and the boathouse appeared suddenly much clearer and nearer, as a welcoming sign post. But Alexa's eye was drawn constantly by the dark mass of granite at the bottom of the cliff, pummelled by a heavy sea the colour of deep-jade, tipped with white foam. The waves smashed into the rocks in a constant, repeating motion. Fountains of spray lifted gracefully and regularly as if dancing a ballet, their elegance belying the deadliness of their force. Seawater rained down on crevices, soaking the sharp stacks of granite, before running back down to the sea.

The woman stood amid all this turbulence, tall and straight, far too close to the violence at the edge. She was as still and as frozen as a ship's figurehead inside the mist of sea spray, the wind lifting and whipping her loose hair around her head.

Even though she could only see a blurry suggestion of a face, Alexa knew that it was Sarah Carmichael. Knew the constant twisting of her hair behind her ear, her arm protective over her chest. Knew by the way she was shivering.

Since they'd been out, the tide had come in, the water was high. Sarah must have climbed some distance up and down over rocks to reach the spot she'd chosen. And she stood, staring towards the boat, oblivious to the danger, her face locked with despair, frozen into madness of the cruellest kind. For she was wearing her wedding dress and it was billowing and pulled taut by the wind across her frail and bony frame. As the boat drew closer, on its inevitable course, Alexa knew the moment Harvey saw Sarah too. He flinched, his hands loosening from his work at the ropes. And she knew that he also heard what she heard, carried like a siren's wail by the wind over the waves. Sarah, narrow and white against the rocks, singing, tunelessly, child-like and to herself: 'Rocked to sleep, Rocked to sleep, I was rocked to sleep in my salty seabed cradle.'

Sarah saw them, recognised them. She took a precarious step. And before Alexa could blink, she jumped and the sea swallowed her.

35

SUMMER SOLSTICE, 1932

Aunt Margaret's crofter's cottage, whitewashed and snug under its thatched roof, overlooked the loch beneath an endless pale northern sky. The waters here were motionless, and the constant, utter silence of the wide-open spaces crept through Alexa's bones. Inside the thick stone walls, inside the little rooms, the peace was so profound, and so hard to adjust to, it unsettled her.

They were so far north that throughout their midsummer honeymoon weeks, night-time never fell completely and Alexa could see Harvey, so beautifully clearly, the whole time that they made love in the big pine bed upstairs. His adoration of her elevated her and moved her momentarily into a bright future. But in the tender twilight nights, she wished, instead, that she had complete darkness so that she could hide her face, for the reality of Harvey, of their love, the path they had to follow to get here, made her weep.

As she woke on Midsummer Eve's morning to the blissful scent of mountain air through the open window, Harvey was standing by the bed, grinning at her over the top of a raggedy bunch of flowers.

'Happy birthday, my love,' he said, resting the posy of heather, harebells and plume thistle into her hands. 'It's OK, I've taken off all the thorns, see. I let you sleep in, crept out at dawn in my slippers and pyjamas for these. Went halfway down the lane. Got funny looks from some sheep over the way.'

'I'm not surprised,' Alexa laughed as she took her fill of the wildflowers' simplicity, their delicacy, and gazed out the window to the mirrored surface of the loch, the backdrop of mysterious hills and glens beyond.

In offering them her cottage, perched here at the extremities of her estate, Aunt Margaret had given them a lifeline. It was incredibly remote; miles from the main house, miles from anywhere. It was, they all agreed, the perfect place for newlyweds. But, even more so, an opportunity for Alexa and Harvey to put a great deal of distance between themselves and Porthdeen. Straight after their quick and quiet wedding at Truro Town Hall, they said goodbye to their families and set off on the long journey to Oban so that they could try to begin to forget the past and the frightening spectacle of Sarah on Enys Rocks.

But Sarah remained an unspoken subject: an odd vacant silence, a third party in the crofter's cottage. Harvey did not mention her name, but Alexa knew when she walked into the room and his book lay face down unread on his lap, or she saw him troop out to the woodpile and heard his whistling stop halfway down the path, that he was thinking of her. And every day that she woke, in the clear Highland dawn, Sarah tapped her on the shoulder.

Alexa cradled the flowers in her hands. Already, on her birthday, Sarah encroached into their bolthole like mist rolling in over the loch, as if they had no right to all this serenity, had no right to love. And Alexa longed to be free of her, to be out of the cottage, out in the wilds from where the flowers came.

'How about hiring a boat today for a little birthday outing?' she asked. 'I have a real urge to get out on the water.'

Harvey cocked an eyebrow. Sitting down on the bed, he asked, 'Really?'

'Yes, Harvey, really. Perhaps you don't think we deserve our happiness, after everything... but I want to make the best of our time here. And we promised ourselves that we would not dwell on it. We love boating, we love the water. Let's get back to it.'

He ran his finger gently around her chin. 'I know full well that we deserve to be happy, Alexa. I just thought that you might not want to go on the sea or the loch. But, if you are sure...'

'Let's find out if we both still have our sea legs.'

Harvey's relief was physical, enthusiasm brightening his face. 'We have Champagne, and we have the crab that the fellow sold us yesterday from the back of his little van. How about I make our sandwiches. A perfect birthday hamper for you.'

'You are going to make the sandwiches?' she laughed.

'Yes, Mrs Ferris, and I will make you sandwiches every day for the rest of your life. If only you'd let me.'

'That's probably a good idea. You know what a terrible cook I am.'

'Alexa, you don't cook sandwiches...'

'As I said, terrible...'

* * *

They spent the morning drifting around Loch Linnhe, with a lazy line for fishing over the side of the little rowing boat, sipping Champagne naughtily before lunch. After their delicious crab sandwiches, Harvey took the oars and Alexa sat back as the afternoon unfolded, spotting seabirds she'd never seen before, listening for the rhythmic piping of the storm petrel and the plaintive call of the eider, waiting for Harvey to land a rainbow trout or two for their dinner. She willed herself to relax, for her mind to empty, but the watchful presence of the purple mountains unnerved her and the steep dark woods reaching the scree edges of the loch held on to shadows so deep that they seemed to draw out her fear. Each time the oars knocked the boat in the wide, empty silence, she sensed the enormity of the depths of the black water below them, expected to see a figure in a wedding dress standing on the shore.

She sat up, rocking the little boat, a sudden blast of dread whistling through her mind. A window banged open onto their future and she tried to peer through it but could not see and she was frightened suddenly, so dreadfully frightened. She gripped the sides of the boat, expecting, any moment, for them to pitch into the bottomless water.

'Are you all right, Alexa?' Harvey cried.

'Harvey, I'm so afraid.' Alexa said desperately.

'Stop struggling, stop fighting fate, Alexa,' he said earnestly. 'You are with me now.'

He rested the oars and leant forward to hold her fast, his arms around her. But the fear lingered, a cold cloak around her shoulders, so heavy she could hardly lift her head.

'Harvey,' she murmered, 'there's something terrible here, something terrible on our tail. I cannot see what it is.' She pressed her cheek into his shoulder and stared with tearless eyes across the grey water to the edge of the loch. There was nothing there, except her own quiet, dark desolation, whispering to her. 'I can't explain.'

Harvey dipped his lips to her cheek. 'You've been through so much, it's no wonder you're unnerved. But, Alexa, we are on this journey together. We know the way.'

Harvey immediately began to row back. Alexa gave him a tight little smile, not daring to tell him that, despite his assurances, the fear had lodged inside her – that tiny voice, warning her. It came to shore with her, evolving into a peculiar strained emptiness, a reality she must step into, if only she could see it, could place her finger on it. If only she could follow it as it burrowed its way inside her mind's eye.

* * *

Above the chimneys of Ferris House, Alexa watched the sickle moon peer through dark drifting cloud. Below, the sea was invisible, as black as pitch. Even though she couldn't see it, she could taste it, smell it, feel it. She was glad to be here; for Harvey's home was her home. Harvey paid the taxi driver and the headlights and the slamming of car doors drew Ma and Pa Ferris through the porch and into the night, both in their dressing gowns and backlit by lamplight, offering cheerful cries of welcome.

'We'd almost given up on you for tonight, son,' said Arthur. 'It's nearly midnight. Difficult journey?'

'Arduous. I think it's taken us as long to get from Scotland as it does to travel from Venice,' said Harvey, setting their suitcases down at the bottom of the great sweeping staircase in the hallway. 'Train from Oban broke down and, knock-on effect, we missed our connection yesterday at Crewe.'

'Oh, but you're here at last!' cried Betty, ushering them across the chequerboard floor. 'Margaret sent a telegram to tell us you'd set off and we've been on the edge of our seats ever since. Welcome, dear, oh, you looked shattered.' Betty embraced Alexa, rubbing her gently on the back. 'Don't worry. You're home now.' She led Alexa through to the softly lit drawing room and made her sit on one of the vast armchairs, guiding Harvey towards the one next to her. Alexa sat back, reacquainting herself with her mother-in-law's exquisite but comfortable room and accepting the cup of hot chocolate that Pa had conjured up from the kitchen with a smile of gratitude.

'Betty's had the milk on the simmer for the last hour,' he said. 'Sweet enough?'

'And how did you like my sister's little cottage?' asked Betty, her eyes bright, eager to talk. 'There is something so special in the air up there, isn't there? We're so looking forward to getting on our way tomorrow. Our annual pilgrimage to Margaret's. She's a great hostess, isn't she? We'll be staying with her in her house, of course. But we do love that sweet croft of hers.'

Harvey sat in the armchair next to Alexa in front of his mother's hearth and, while he listened to his mother, he unconsciously reached for Alexa's hand, holding it across the gap between the two chairs. Alexa didn't have to look at him to guess at the expression on his face. She squeezed his hand, hoping it would convey to him her relief to be home. He caught her eye, gave her a little companionable wink.

'Betty,' said Arthur, 'leave the children be with all your chatter. Let them get up to their quarters and fall into bed. They must be dog-tired.'

'Pa, you're making it sound like you've put us in some army barracks,' laughed Harvey.

'Well the decorators have worked several miracles,' said Betty, warming to more conversation. 'In the time you've been away, they created quite a little palace for you. Shall I lead the way?'

'Betty,' admonished Arthur. 'Harvey knows how to get to the Mizzen wing.'

'After all, Ma,' laughed Harvey, 'it was my nursery. Or have you forgotten, it was so long ago.'

'Let's go to bed,' Arthur hooked his arm through his wife's and encouraged her towards the door. 'We won't wake you in the morning, children. Early start for us. Taxi at six.'

'Should have asked your driver to stay the night,' Betty mused and, with a little wave, said, 'Goodnight, my dears. Lovely to have you back. Short but sweet. We'll see you in another month's time.'

They trailed upstairs and Alexa went through the door that led onto the Mizzen wing, while Harvey lingered to have a quiet word with his mother. As she walked through a short vestibule into their own first-floor sitting room, she was greeted by a faint and pleasing smell of newness. There was a modern three-piece suite in peacock-blue – a wedding present from Ma and Pa – and a very glamorous sideboard. A door led through to a bedroom, with a marble bathroom off that. The curtains in the sitting room were drawn against the night and Alexa immediately pulled them back, searching for the moon.

Harvey opened the door and she heard more drifting good-nights and promises of a postcard from Oban.

'What do you think of your new quarters, Mrs Ferris?' he asked, taking her in his arms, ready to dance her around the room.

'I'm a little overwhelmed to be honest; I can't take it all in. But it all looks so marvellous.' She realised suddenly how very tired she was, but still, she wanted to know: 'What was your mother saying, just now?'

Harvey drew back, tilted his chin, appraised her expression, before he said, 'Only that she wanted to tell me that Sarah is still under Doctor Paynter, is on some sort of medication. And I have a good idea which. There is talk of sending her away to an institution. But, of course, there is no money.'

'But you'll want to help Mrs Carmichael, financially?'

'Of course, but Paynter advised that I don't get involved in any other matter. Totally understandable.'

Alexa watched his face carefully.

'Do you realise, Harvey,' she said, 'that this is the first time we are properly talking about it. In a practical, rational way.'

Harvey nodded his affirmation.

'Come on, let's have a nightcap. Aunt Margaret packed us a single malt.'

'I won't have any,' said Alexa, thinking of Guy and his greed for whisky. 'Can't stomach the stuff. You go ahead.'

Harvey returned from the sideboard with a tumbler and they sat on their smart new chairs, the moon sailing high through the window.

Alexa reached for his hand.

'But I must know, Harvey,' she said warily. 'That day. On Indigo Moon. How did you feel, when you saw her? Just standing there? And when she jumped—'

He let out a ragged sigh, his eyes moistening.

'Helpless,' he said, sipping. 'For it would have been madness for us to try to sail close to the rocks, to try to help her. I still can't believe how we managed to get into shore so quickly to raise the alarm. The worst bit was when the coastguard said they'd called off the search. Were going to start looking for her body.'

'But she wasn't lost. She's alive and being cared for.'

'What sort of life, though...'

'Harvey, come on, you mustn't—'

'I often wonder... how she managed to haul herself out of the sea somewhere, where she went, those two dreadful days she was missing, until she walked back into the cottage kitchen. Barefoot, her wedding dress in tatters, according to Rose Hammett. And Joan hysterical, running down the street one way for help, Lizzie the other. The young Carmichael girls weeping... I can't bear to think of it.'

'Harvey, we have to be able to live with this,' Alexa said, trying to sound strong, trying to be brave, although she couldn't stop picturing Sarah. 'There is nothing else we can do.'

He caressed her fingers one by one. 'And you didn't have your wedding at Porthdeen Church.'

Alexa's laugh was gentle with acceptance. 'Ha, that was the least of our worries, Harvey. That doesn't bother me. The town hall and leaving straight for Scotland was the right thing to do, no question.'

She turned her ring slowly on her finger, still not used to wearing it.

'I feel so very sorry for Sarah,' she said. It sounded weak and trite but there was no way else to say it. 'It's been so utterly bloody for everyone. But let's not have her with us all the time.'

Harvey's sigh was weary, but his eyes sparkled. He drained his glass, set his tumbler down.

'Yes, Mrs Ferris, you are right,' he said.

He switched the lamps off in the sitting room and led her through to the bedroom.

Eleanor had evidently been over and filled one of the wardrobes with Alexa's clothes. Her books, writing case, George the doll and her new button box still sat in their packing cases, waiting for Alexa to place them where she wished.

Alexa told Harvey not to bother with the lamp in the bedroom. She opened the curtains and stood in front of the window, looking out. In the midsummer twilight, she saw the lawn, like a still deep pool, and the dark mass of rhododendrons at the cliff 's edge; behind them, the void of the sea.

'You like to watch the night, don't you?' Harvey said.

He stood behind her, his arms around her, his lips finding the nooks and dips of her shoulder bone. The press of his hands on her waist intensified her desire for him; she no longer felt tired. 'The sun has only just gone,' she said, turning to Harvey and kissing him. 'But in a few short hours, it will be back with us. Let's make the most of what little night we have.'

36

Alexa woke late, stretched out in delicious comfort, rested by a deep and wonderful sleep. Harvey turned and kept on snoozing, so she crept from the bed, slipped on her dressing gown – new, a present from Eleanor – and padded downstairs. Betty had given the daily Cook the week off, so that the newlyweds could trip around the place in privacy. But Cook had been in, first thing as arranged, and left fresh milk, eggs and bread.

As Alexa brewed tea, made toast and scrambled the eggs, she noticed she'd already marked the cuff of her new dressing gown. The Venetian one, torn and screwed up in the drawer in the apartment where she'd left it, sprung into her mind and her heart gave a sudden knock. She shuddered, thinking of the letter she had burnt in the fireplace at Porthdeen, how her shame had followed her home.

A seagull swooped low outside the window as if checking up on her. She laughed with sudden pleasure. She was on her journey with Harvey now and the past, she told herself, was behind her. She was standing in her slippers, in the Ferris House kitchen, burning toast and overdoing the eggs, stewing the tea, with her husband sleeping upstairs. How could she have wanted it to be any other way?

On her way across the hallway, carrying the laden tray, she noticed a stack of post on the console table. Resting the tray down for a moment, she scanned through the letters. Lots for Harvey; a whole month's worth. She left them to one side for him to look at later. A great many wedding cards for them to open together, perhaps with their morning coffee. At the bottom of the stack, two letters addressed to:

Miss A. Rosewarne

postmarked Mayfair two weeks apart, forwarded a week or so ago from Porthdeen, with Aunt Rose's redirection instructions on the front.

Alexa recognised the formal weight of the paper. The sealed edges looked bumpy, as if the envelopes had been caught in a shower of rain when the postman delivered them. She shrugged, had no desire to read anything more of what Guy's solicitor had to say about the thing she'd allowed to happen in that back bedroom in Fulham. Because if she hadn't gone to visit that woman in her mean little house, she told herself, she would not have this life, this future. Without bothering to open them, she ripped the envelopes in half and stuffed them in her dressing gown pocket. Alexa turned to pick up the breakfast tray and stopped in surprise. A large crate sat near the front door, rather battered at the corners and covered with various customs stamps and tickets. She must have been more tired than she realised last night not to have noticed it when she arrived. It was enormous, and addressed to:

Mrs Harvey Ferris

She dashed over and peered on all sides of the crate, searching for the sender's name, and gave a delighted squeal when she discovered the return label:

Signora R. Montgomery, San Polo, Venetia

Alexa picked up Betty's iron doorstep – the one in the shape of a fish – and began to knock at the edges of the nailed-down lid. The wood splintered and she eased the top off. Resting on packing straw and balled-up newspaper inside was a folded letter. She snatched it up just as Harvey appeared, hurrying down the stairs, tying the cord of his dressing gown.

'To dearest Alexa,' she read out loud to him, her voice lifting in amazement, 'Please accept this, our gift, on the wonderful occasion of your wedding to Harvey. You must promise to come and see us, both of you, if not this year, then the next. With felicitations and *amore*, Nonna, Robert and Juliet.'

She plunged her hands in and pulled away the packing material.

'What a lot of noise you made and what a lot of mess, Alexa,' laughed Harvey, stepping through a pile of scattered straw. 'What have you there?'

Alexa saw, in the crate, the elaborately carved top of a picture frame. Speechless, she pulled back slightly, as if she did not want to touch it, as if her intervention might damage or spoil it, change it forever.

'Whatever it is, you look overwhelmed,' said Harvey. 'Stand there. Over there, at the bottom of the stairs.'

She mutely and happily did as he asked, a tingling of expectation in her limbs, joyful anticipation buzzing in her ears.

Harvey stood behind the crate and reached in with both hands. He grappled a little, braced himself and lifted Jack Fairling's portrait out, holding it high. Alexa gasped, her hand to her mouth, spontaneous tears wetting her eyes. Three faces, three figures dressed in shades of divine blue. The three generations: Beatrice, Carlotta, herself. She sat down with a thump onto the bottom stair.

'Ah, Nonna,' she whispered, her eyes swimming.

She had sent a letter to her grandmother just before the wedding, telling her their news, pressing her to ask Juliet all about Harvey. She'd written that she did not know how anyone could be happier than she was at that moment. But she had been wrong. For she was, now, so gloriously, unbelievably happy.

Alexa stared at the luminous oh-so similar and familiar faces, at their steady and knowing gazes, at the light that emanated from within the painting, as the painted storm through the window approached the young girl, brooding over her shoulder. She began to laugh with happiness, the blissful sound of it bubbling out.

Harvey carefully propped *A storm in summer* against the wall and joined her at the bottom of the stairs. He wrapped his arms around her and they looked at the portrait together, while their breakfast on its tray grew thoroughly cold.

37

Time moved at a dreamlike pace, slowing down and speeding up so that Alexa lost track of the days they spent together, alone. A week or two after the portrait arrived – Alexa could never quite remember, but they were still in the midst of their extended honeymoon – Harvey appeared just after lunch in his oldest shirt, sleeves rolled up, tweed trousers and braces.

'I feel like going for a tramp over the top fields,' he said, as Alexa poured the coffee. 'Would you like to come with me?'

They were sitting, for a change, in Ma's drawing room and Alexa glanced out of the window, at the enticing peace of the garden, at the delicious portion of shade at the side of the lawn.

'I think I'll stay here and read for a while,' she said, 'I'm feeling rather bushed, as if I'm coming down with something. A little queasy, a bit off colour. Oh, nothing to worry about. It's probably the heat, I'm sure, but perhaps a little doze, a lazy afternoon, won't go amiss.'

Harvey leant forward and kissed Alexa on the nose.

'Sounds like you've been overdoing all of this relaxation, my dear,' he said. 'But you do exactly what you like. If you are feeling under the weather, lolloping over the headland in the sun is certainly not what the doctor ordered.'

'I'll make us a nice tea for when you get back, how's that?'

Harvey laughed, 'I shall be very much looking forward to it.' He drained his coffee cup and went out to the gunroom, tucked away around the back and under the stairs. Alexa heard him rummaging.

'Now where is that old fellow...?'

'Where are you planning on going?' she asked, following him out to the hall and leaning in the doorway. The Ferris gun collection was modest and the small dark room that housed it emanated an old metallic smell, deepened by leather and oil and gunpowder.

'Up on the headland, the bit before you get to Porthdeen Church,' Harvey said, scanning the regimented racks of glossy air rifles. 'Where Ferris land meets Rosewarne. There's a little warren tucked under that thicket of gorse there. Worth investigating.'

'Pity those poor rabbits!' she said. 'Mind you don't shoot any of Dad's. He'll have you for poaching. Oh, remember they have invited us for dinner, in a day or two. I can't think when it is: Friday or Saturday...'

'Should take them over a brace, then. I hear Melissa loves rabbit pie.'

'Yes, when it's not been made by me,' Alexa laughed.

'Here he is!' Harvey exclaimed, reaching up. 'Pa's ancient wildfowler. What a handsome old gentleman.'

Harvey lifted the shotgun down from its bracket and broke it to squint down its barrel, blowing at a speck of dust.

'Looks like an antique, so well cared for,' said Alexa, peering at the polished stock, the metal plate etched with pheasants. 'Not your usual one.'

'I like this old fellow. See if I can't give it one last hurrah before it gets displayed for all eternity inside a glass case.' He slipped a box of cartridges into his pocket. 'I won't be long, Alexa. I'll be back in time for your delicious tea. You know what a fast walker I am.'

'If you get as far as the church,' she said, 'say hello to Mamma and the mermaid.'

Alexa stood and waved to Harvey from the front door, watched him troop off with his long determined stride, gun broken at his elbow, cap pulled down low against the sun, turning to wave as he neared the last corner of the drive.

* * *

When Harvey had disappeared, she shut the door, took a deep breath and listened to the silence. She had not been outside of Harvey's company or his care since the terrifying episode when they'd been sailing on Indigo Moon, and yet she was looking forward to a few hours on her own: they would make his return all the more sweeter.

Suddenly longing for sunlight and air, she slipped outside into the garden. She found the parasol in the shed and set it up on the lawn, laying a rug half in, half out of the shade. Collecting cushions from Betty's drawing room, she scattered them over the rug, fetched her mother's copy of *Middlemarch* and a jug of Cook's lemonade from the cold box in the kitchen. As she lay down to rest, her queasiness returned, bubbling softly in her stomach. She poured a glass of lemonade, hoping it would ease her unsettled tummy. She sipped and made a face. It wasn't up to Cook's usual standard. Perhaps the batch of lemons had been particularly sour.

The gulls were quiet, for once, and the air was still. Beyond the glossy barricade of rhododendrons, the sea was flat and sparkling. The little wicket gate that led down to the boathouse and gave the best view of the water caught her eye, but she resisted it.

Alexa picked up the book, read the flyleaf again, reacquainting herself with it. She had not opened it since that morning on the Lido hotel balcony before Guy whisked her across to Venice. Her mother's old postcard bookmark was still in its place, near the back of the book, but Mamma would never know the ending. Tears burned Alexa's eyes. The lemonade fizzed in her gullet. Swallowing hard to beat waves of nausea, she breathed steadily, waiting for them to fade. This sick feeling had been coming and going since halfway through their time in the Highlands and she could hardly dare to think that, perhaps, it was a symptom of another new life inside her, just starting to stir.

'Well, Mamma, what do you think of that,' whispered Alexa, as sweet realisation flowered in her mind. 'You would have been a nonna. And what a simply delightful one too.'

As her plans began to form, she brushed her tears away, imagining the look on Harvey's face when she told him. The afternoon snoozed dreamily on. Alexa watched the shadows of the statues and the box hedges move across the lawn; heard the rustle of the lofty pines, caught their scent as they were warmed by the sun. She glanced up, smiling, at the tranquil façade. The once-forbidding Ferris House had truly welcomed her home. She slipped off her shoes, wriggled her toes in the sunlight, rested her head on a cushion and, feeling bone-tired, closed her eyes.

* * *

Something was tickling Alexa around her hairline. She woke, forgetting for a moment where she was, lifting her hand on reflex. She brushed the hem of a ragged, dirty dress.

'This was meant to be my home,' said Sarah.

Alexa sat up quickly, cringing with untapped fear, and shifted backwards across the rug. Sarah's pale and malnourished face stared down at her, her thin shadow extending towards her. Alexa uttered a cry of shock. Sarah's eyes, darting from Alexa to the ground, to the sky and back again, were vacant. Her once-beautiful hair was an unloved mess and her fingertips jerked at the fabric of her wedding dress, spoiled and stained, the pearly sheen of it turned to grey. Looming over Alexa, the real Sarah was terrifying, worse than the suggestion of her, the ghost that had stalked her since the episode on Enys Rocks.

'It's beautiful here, isn't it,' Sarah declared.

'Why, yes, Sarah, it certainly is...' Alexa said tentatively.

Rocking gently at the knees, Sarah began to hum her sea song, about her salty seabed cradle, lilting and off-key like a child, and Alexa glanced desperately around, hoping to see Joan Carmichael, Lizzie, anyone.

'Have you walked up here alone, Sarah?' Alexa said cautiously. 'Is anyone with you?'

Sarah stopped singing, gave her a hard look.

'Where is Harvey?' she said, staring at the house, the terrace, the French windows. 'Where is he? I've come to see him. We were going to be married.'

'Oh, Sarah, I am so very sorry...'

In one sudden movement, Sarah sat down, cross-legged in front of Alexa. She was close, so very close, and Alexa could hear and feel her breath. Sarah's face beamed with a ghostly light, her mouth wide in a grimace. Her empty eyes, once so pretty, lacked any hope and were bulging and luminous, as if her tears had frozen permanently to her lashes. Alexa caught her briny personal scent, saw the dirt under her broken fingernails.

'How could you do that to my poor man?' Sarah hissed, far too near Alexa's face. 'Shaming him in public, in front of his family, his friends, in front of everyone. There! Right there.'

She pointed behind Alexa towards the French windows, and the ballroom inside.

'You broke him, Alexa. And he is such a good man. A wonderful man.' Sarah's voice lifted and she offered a wistful smile which hardened immediately into a snarl. 'You don't deserve to be here, living at his house. He was meant to be mine.'

Alexa, back suddenly in the evening of her eighteenth birthday, realised that she'd been able to make Enys Point her home without brooding over her treatment of Harvey that night. Until now.

'Sarah, I did not accept Harvey's proposal at the ball because, you see...' Alexa struggled under the pressure to explain, her words feeble and empty, clogged with regret. 'Because I was so desperately confused. I needed to get away... to leave home...' She stumbled beneath Sarah's terrible gaze. 'There were so many reasons why...'

But Sarah wasn't listening, her face was fixed and placid and her eyes, dead.

'He turned to me.' Sarah gave a minute, proud flick of her shoulders. 'I picked him up after his dreadful humiliation. I saved him from *you*. Made him happy again. He wanted to marry me. Me! We prepared for our wedding. My dress, look at it, sewn so beautifully by Rose Hammett.' Sarah ran her hands down the fabric over her knees, lifting it at the sides, letting it fall. The lace bore a traumatic legacy of stains, dirt and grime, utterly ruined, but had somehow survived its encounter with the sea. 'We filled the church with flowers. So many flowers. You should have seen it. We were going to be so happy.' She lifted her hands in front of her face, palms facing each other. Her rigid fingers began to shake. 'I was *this close*. This close.'

'Sarah,' Alexa spoke low, coaxingly, 'won't you come and sit in our drawing room? You seem so very tired. Can I offer you tea, perhaps? Or we have lemonade, look here—'

Sarah snapped from her daze and shook her head in a violent blast of rage.'I don't want to take tea with you! I want nothing from a floozy such as you,' she seethed and leapt to her feet.

Alexa reared back, expecting attack, a blow, a slap around her face. But Sarah stumbled away, turning her ankle as she ran across the lawn, the dress billowing behind her. She stopped by the gravel, turned and fixed Alexa with her eyes.

'You see,' she said, muttering to herself, so quietly that Alexa strained to hear, 'I know exactly what you did, Alexa Rosewarne.'

* * *

Alexa left her rug, her book and parasol, her quiet oasis ruined, and sat at the kitchen table, seeking the warmth of the vast range cooker, the summer day chilled and spoiled. Two hours after Sarah's departure, Alexa had drunk five cups of tea, her core still shaking.

When she finally heard Harvey's step in the hall, his cheerful call, her relief surged, like being at the helm of Indigo Moon and dropping off the top of a huge wave. She ran out to the hallway and fell into his arms, pressing her face into his shirt, smelling the heath and the gorse and the fragrant earth on him, feeling the warmth of the sun still in his hair. Happiness soared around her like a seaborne breeze and she vowed not to spoil it by telling him about Sarah's visit. Maybe tomorrow she would; perhaps she never would.

'Have you had a lovely afternoon?' she asked, drawing back to gaze up at his face.

'Yes, yes, have you? Are you feeling better? Alexa, you look incredibly excited! Rosy cheeked and dewy eyed!'

'You're back, that's why. Oh, where is your gun and your booty?'

'I left it all outside on the porch. I'll clean it, deal with it later. First I want to kiss my wife and tell her I love her.'

'How many did you bag?' she asked, seeking solace in his kisses, hoping they'd remove Sarah from her mind. 'Enough for a pie or two for Dad and Eleanor and Melissa?'

'None. I got none. I saw a little gang of conies up near the church. Little baby ones snuffling around the gorse, put my gun away and I left well alone. Let them enjoy nibbling the grass. I'll take you up there tomorrow if you like, and show you, if you're feeling better. See if we can find them again.'

'I'd love that,' she said, not wanting him to ever leave her on her own again.

'Now, give me a few minutes to wash and brush up. And you, put on your gold lace dress, the one you wore for your birthday ball. Meet me down here. No peeking. I have something to show you.'

Intrigued, Alexa watched him wink at her and cross the hall towards the ballroom. She went upstairs to do as he asked and decided to take her time, to allow even more moments to elapse after her encounter with Sarah. To get the day back to normal. Her unsettled feeling followed her upstairs, but, as soon as she slipped into her dress and she realised it felt tight, she held onto her secret with a smile; her excitement growing.

* * *

Half an hour or so later, Harvey was waiting for her outside the closed door to the ballroom, wearing his smartest shirt and trousers, his smile bright.

'Perfect,' he said as she walked towards him. 'You are so utterly beautiful. I know you have done something to that dress, and I must say I like it a whole lot better.'

'You're pretty spruced up yourself,' she said, remembering how lovely he'd looked on the night of the ball. But almost at once

Sarah's words burned in her ears: 'You broke him, Alexa. You don't deserve to be here.'

She wanted to tell Harvey about Sarah, and that along with Sarah's visit, her fear had returned, but he was smiling at her and opening the ballroom door. She gasped. A hundred candles burned steadily all around, mixing with the low sunlight slanting through the windows, conjuring a magic so tangible she could grasp it in her hands. He had opened the French windows wide and the scents from the garden flowers drifted into the large room, the early evening sky beyond pale-blue and rosy, the sea a gentle rhythm in the distance.

'Oh, Harvey, it is wonderful.'

'But Alexa,' he pointed to the fireplace, 'you have not noticed...'

The portrait, sitting on the marble mantelpiece, glimmered in the candlelight, the expressions on each of the three faces blessed, lively, benevolent.

She tried to thank him, but her words were melted by joy. 'Wait there, darling,' he said, 'exactly where you are.'

Harvey walked across the empty parquet to the gramophone on its little stand by the wall. He lifted the lid, set the stylus down. Immediately 'Venice, the moon and you' drifted from the speaker, easing its way around the ballroom, loosening tears in Alexa's eyes.

'You found a recording? How did you get it?'

'Made a few telephone calls, wrote a few letters. It's quite the rarity, I can assure you. Now, Alexa,' he stood to attention and offered her his hand, 'will you dance with me?'

Shaking and giggling with joy, Alexa found herself in the middle of the floor and they began to sway together to the gentle music.

Harvey said, close to her ear, 'It doesn't have to be displayed here, you know, your painting.'

'Do you mean hang it back at Porthdeen?' Alexa asked,

thinking that Jack Fairling's work would look wonderful in the parlour there, if only Eleanor would change the awful beige walls.

'No, I mean in our own home, somewhere else. Would you like to move, Alexa? I know that Ma and Pa have done such a wonderful job at making us welcome, but I didn't envisage our married life here with them. Now that I am ready to qualify, I could look at setting up a practice elsewhere. I feel that it would do us no harm at all to start afresh, move away from Little Porthdeen.'

Alexa smiled, thinking of summers yet to come, of their life together expanding before them. How the mummers on the quayside of Little Porthdeen, each year in the darkness of winter, willed the sun to return. And how they made that promise for all of the village: the fisherman, the farmers, the fishwives; for her and Harvey, and for Sarah, too. For surely, for everyone, the summer will always come again.

'So, tell me, Harvey,' she said. 'What were you thinking?'

'To move not too far, for I would not want to take you right away from your family. I was thinking of the Lizard peninsula.'

Alexa saw a stone farmhouse deep in that pretty, ancient countryside, whitewashed with a slate roof. A little garden, and chickens. A child or two. Boys or girls, she could not tell.

'A country practice?' she asked, enlivened by her little fantasy, itching to tell Harvey that she suspected they had started a child, but not wanting to do so, not just yet. She wanted to be sure.

'I certainly see you as a country doctor's wife.'

'But what about the Mizzen wing?' Alexa countered. 'All that trouble your Ma and Pa have gone to.'

'Ma was itching to redecorate for years. It will be her guest wing. We will stay there when we visit. The Mizzen wing's not a reason for us to remain here. Ma and Pa wouldn't want it to be like that.'

The music stopped, the needle crackling in the grooves, and Harvey went over to reset it, hurrying back into her arms.

'I'm afraid we only have this 78 here. In my haste to get all of this set up, I forgot to bring out my collection.'

'It doesn't matter in the slightest,' Alexa laughed, resting her head on his shoulder.

Harvey said, 'When we got married, I wondered if maybe we would have a ball to celebrate our wedding, but then thought twice.'

'This is so much better,' she said. 'Just the two of us. This is the way I like it. We're dancing our first dance.'

'Just as we did at your birthday ball.'

'But have you remembered the peacocks for the lawn this time?'

'Blast! I forgot.'

Harvey's laugh blended with Alexa's.

She said, 'Did I ever tell you about the dancers I saw in Venice, Harvey, in the square? They were so unusually beautiful. Dancing there in the lamplight. We will go, won't we, and see Venice together again?'

'Soon, yes, soon,' he said.

Alexa rested her cheek against his and they danced as the tune from the gramophone played, as the light in the sky faded and the clouds turned pink.

'Red sky at night,' mused Harvey, 'sailors' delight.'

Alexa followed his gaze out of the open French windows.

A shadow moved, catching the corner of her eye, a fair-weather cloud, surely, teasing the sun. But then a footstep, the tiniest chink on stone and Alexa glanced back to see the breeze pick up the hem of tatty, greying lace. Sarah stepped from the terrace into the ballroom holding Harvey's shotgun, a clumsy dead weight in her hands.

Alexa froze as Harvey's hands clenched around her. She felt his heart pummelling through the fabric of his shirt.

'Hello, Sarah,' he said lightly, his eyes fixed on the gun. 'How are you? Are you quite well?'

As Sarah stepped forward onto the dance floor, the music from the gramophone ended. She had been crying and her face was glossy with tears. Her hands shook; the gun incongruous and monstrous against the rags of her wedding dress.

'Found this outside on your porch. Thought I'd fetch it for you, Harvey. Can't have it lying around like that, can we?'

Harvey put his hand up, gesturing gently.

'Sarah, please put it on the floor. It's very old, belongs to my father.'

She glanced down at the shotgun as if suddenly surprised to see it in her hands. She gripped it tightly.

'Harvey, you did love me, once?' she asked, her voice tiny and plaintive.

He glanced at Alexa and she saw pity for Sarah on his face evolving into sympathy, dissolving into sorrow.

He answered, slowly, thoughtfully, 'Yes, Sarah, I think I did.'

Alexa's breath hissed through her teeth, as if she had been branded. She carefully released herself from Harvey's embrace and folded her arms around her middle, tried to keep still, tried to hold herself together. She must listen to this, she must take this, for all of it was her fault.

'I knew you did.' Sarah's words had an incredible joyful ring about them. 'I shall take that with me to my grave.'

Harvey tried to smile gently and took a step or two closer to her. 'Not so hasty, Sarah...'

Her face lifted to the verge of ecstasy as Harvey stood within touching distance of her, his arms out as if to receive the gun. But her gaze fell on Alexa.

'Do you know what she did in Venice?' she asked.

'Alexa?' Harvey said, giving her the shadow of a glance. 'Yes, I knew that Alexa went overseas for a while—'

'She has been getting letters about it. Solicitor's letters. Ask her. Hasn't she told you? All of the dirty goings-on she's been hiding from you.'

'What letters, Alexa?' Harvey said her name hesitantly, glancing around at her.

Alexa swallowed hard, fear stabbing her like little shocks of electricity.

'Not that it is Sarah's business, and nothing you are not aware of, Harvey,' she said evenly. 'I received some letters from a solicitor's office. I only read one of them. I have destroyed them all.'

'Ask her what they said,' crowed Sarah.

Harvey kept silent, but nodded at Alexa, his eyes wide, brimming with alarm.

Alexa shifted her feet, loath to admit to any of it; the letters had sullied her, had reminded her of her shame, her foolish trust in Guy.

'The solicitor demanded that I tell him about what happened last summer, about the decision I made,' Alexa spoke to Harvey, aware of Sarah's smirking face. 'I was repulsed by the enquiry, the coldness of it. I simply ignored it. Put my head in the sand. Wanted it to all go away.'

Sarah cried, 'She is after a dead woman's money.'

Alexa's anger sparked, broke free. 'And what on earth do you know about it, Sarah?'

Harvey raised his hand, as if to try to soothe the air.

Sarah turned the gun over in her hands. 'Rose Hammett told my mother, and I overheard. It's an easy thing to do in our tiny little cottage... not like this place,' Sarah's eyes glowed like dark stars, her grin slackening her mouth. 'A grand lady has died and Mr

Moreland needs to know if Alexa gave birth to his bastard. Because she could get some of the money if she did.'

If Alexa closed her eyes, she knew she'd picture the look on Rose's face as she picked up the dropped letter, fussed about the spilt tea. And the other, forwarded, letters had looked like they'd been steamed open too now that she thought about it. Rose could have no idea that her idle whispered gossip about Alexa's private trauma had seeped such poison into Sarah's brain.

Alexa said, 'But I didn't carry his child.'

'That's what she says, but look at her, Harvey,' Sarah cried. 'She disappeared for a year or more. Who knows what else she got up to. But I stayed with you. I loved you, stood by you. I bet she still loves this Moreland man.'

'Alexa?' said Harvey, half turning to her.

His unexpected question circulated like a prowling animal. Guy and his machinations, his inert cruelty, had caught up with her to destroy her happiness. He may as well be standing in the corner.

'Harvey, all that has happened is that I have received letters from Mr Moreland's solicitor to find out if I got rid of the child I was expecting. Which of course,' she lowered her voice, 'you know all too well. The way I see it, he must need to write his own will as he has come into a great deal of money from Lady Meredith—'

'The dead woman!' Sarah raged. 'Can't you see what is going on? They have taken us both for fools, Harvey. Moreland and her. Do you want to be with her when she is such a false and secretive slut? It must be a plan. There might be a child yet, hidden away in Italy. She said she was married to him! He must love her and she loves him.'

'But it wasn't love,' Alexa cried. 'It wasn't how we are, Harvey. How we can be for the rest of our lives.' She thought of their unborn child, was so desperate to tell him. She searched his face.

'You know, Harvey. You know. And now, all of this. All of this...' Her despairing sob tore through the air.

Harvey shuddered, gave Sarah a sharp look of pity and walked back across the parquet to Alexa. Sarah watched him, outraged. He stood so close that Alexa could feel the warmth of his body and this gave her the strength to rouse herself, to do something, say something, to try to mend the shredding of all their lives.

'You must see, Sarah,' Alexa began, lowering her voice and sweetening it, as if she was talking to a child. Not Melissa, but a child who possessed not an ounce of confidence or understanding. 'Harvey thought, wrongly, that I was married to this Mr Moreland, that I had married in Venice. And so, when he broke with you it was simply because he felt it was the right thing to do, for both of you. It was nothing to do with me, you see.'

Even as she spoke, Alexa heard her blunder. By trying to explain, she had made it worse than it could ever be.

'So I am not even good enough to be his second choice,' Sarah wailed, the gun swinging precariously from one hand to the other. 'Look at me. Just look at me. I am no one.'

Sarah tilted her head back and gazed up at the ceiling, her glazed eyes travelling down the walls, brushing over Alexa, fixing on the portrait on the mantelpiece.

'Sarah, how many times can I say how sorry I am. So dreadfully sorry,' said Harvey, his voice small and unfamiliar. 'What is it you want me to do?'

Sarah ignored him, peered instead at Alexa. 'She's wearing the same dress she wore at the ball. Bit shorter, but the same dress. But then no matter. She is always so beautiful, isn't she, whatever she does,' she uttered. 'No wonder you chose her over me. That's her, isn't it?' She pointed at the portrait. 'You can see her. Child, mother, grandmother. That's Alexa Rosewarne. You can see her, all through her life. Her beautiful life. Alexa, do you think anyone would ever paint a portrait of me like that? Do you?'

Sarah raised the shotgun, one elbow out, aiming it level and straight at Alexa. Her fear of Sarah had once been a phantom, a curse, an idea stalking her. But now it was physical, this girl with her finger on the trigger; this girl with her piercing mad stare. Alexa could hear her rasping breath.

Harvey said, 'Sarah, the gun is not loaded.'

Sarah shook her head, tears falling, soaking her chin. Both of her claw-like hands, clutching barrel and trigger, were juddering.

'It is loaded,' she whispered. Harvey ran his hand over his face.

'Oh God,' he uttered, glancing fearfully at Alexa. 'I let the rabbits run off. The baby rabbits. But I forgot to empty the gun. I didn't empty the gun. I wanted to give them a chance.'

Alexa reached for Harvey. What possible chance did they have in all this mess? She clung to him with pure, primal fear. He pushed her behind him.

'Sarah...' Harvey said, fear hardening his words. 'Sarah, please lower the gun. It will be all right in the end. Just please put the gun down...'

'All right in the end?' Sarah asked, staring past Harvey, her face twitching to seek Alexa out. 'No, it won't be all right in the end. Not while she's here to live this beautiful life of hers.'

Sarah jerked the gun suddenly and Alexa found herself fixed by its sight, the grotesque double barrel. Her stomach turned to water. Sarah aimed. Inside that dreadful, infinite moment, Alexa's heart emptied of all its blood.

But the gun did not fire. Sarah flinched as if something had pricked her. She broke from her spell, turned and ran through the open French windows.

Alexa subsided into flooding relief, moaning, grasping onto Harvey's arm.

'Stay here, Alexa,' Harvey said, firmly, brutally. 'Where it is safe.'

'You're not going after her—?' He shook her off.

'I've got to stop her. Get the gun. I'll kick it out of her hands if need be,' he said. 'The trigger is probably jammed. It's such an old thing.'

'Please Harvey, no—'

Her scream halted him on the threshold. He turned to her, recklessly stealing one more moment and giving her a smile.

'Stay where you are, Alexa.' He darted out onto the terrace. Standing very still in the centre of the ballroom, Alexa felt a fluctuation in the warm, languid air, as if time was pausing, drawing breath while the glowing candlelight, the sparkling laughter, the ghosts of the Midsummer Ball whirled around her.

When she should have said: 'Yes, yes, yes, Harvey. I will marry you.'

Alexa stared at the portrait. The three generations gazed silently past each other, past the viewer into a void of nothing, while the storm continued to boil outside the painted window.

And still she waited in the dreadful silence, wanting Harvey to come back, longing for the day to continue as it was supposed to, for her life to be as it was, as it should have been. She could not bear it any longer and ran towards the French windows.

The blast stopped her on the terrace. Seagulls shrieked, fleeing the echoing crack of the shot, white wings against the sky. The lawn was strewn with confusion. Sarah was bent over the weight of the shotgun, wielding it, as if she was doubled-up in pain. It was too big, far too heavy for her.

Alexa's idyllic little arrangement had been disturbed: blanket, parasol, book and cushions. All the trappings for the perfect summer afternoon scattered and ugly. And Harvey crumpled on the rug, red spreading over white shirt until white became red and only red.

Sarah stared at the man she had felled, her screams vomiting from her wide-open mouth. She dropped the shotgun as if it burnt her flesh, spun around and hurtled across the grass, towards the rhododendrons. She plunged through the mass of bushes and kept running. But all that was there was the cliff edge and, beyond that, just a few more steps, the endless blue into which she vanished.

Surely this horror was someone else's nightmare. But, as Alexa stumbled forward, it became her own. She ran to Harvey, knelt beside him on the rug, cradled his head on her lap.

'She only shot one barrel,' he whispered, blood bubbling over his lips. 'There's another cartridge.'

'What do I do?' Alexa begged him. 'Oh God, Harvey, what do I do?'

Harvey lifted his head, glanced down at his stomach.

His eyelids fluttered, a sudden stillness, like a shadow, across his face. He tried to smile.

'This is beyond any doctor's help.'

'It can't be!'

'She only fired one shot. Alexa, it's not safe for you.'

But the gun lay inert, yards away. The garden was empty. 'She went over the cliff, Harvey,' Alexa said.

Harvey grabbed for her hands, his blood wetting her fingers. She saw a light rising in his eyes; his last expression of love for her. As warm and as simple as his first had been.

'Then you are safe, Alexa.'

'Harvey, stay. Stay with me,' she whispered, her words failing, her eyes blinded by streaming tears. 'Because everything's only just started for us. We are going to have a baby. We are. We really are.'

'I wanted to give the baby rabbits a chance,' he uttered, as if he had not understood her, his voice diminished. 'And I hurried to you, Alexa. I hurried all the way home.'

When at last she dared to look away – because doing so would mean that it was truly all over and that he was gone – she noticed her mother's book on the lawn. The pages, speckled with the most delicate dots of red, fluttering in the breeze.

EPILOGUE

MIDSUMMER, 1982

Lying alone in her bedroom at Porthdeen, in the first and last house in England, Alexa listened to the bubbling and popping of her breathing. The oxygen cylinder parked by her bed gave off a gentle hissing and she wondered if it was leaking. She squinted short-sightedly at the gauge at the top. Could not make head nor tail of it. She touched the screw valve on the side; thought perhaps she better not. Pressing the plastic-smelling mask firmly over her nose and mouth, she sucked in, gasping on pure bottled air.

Along with Venetian-blue eyes and a Mediterranean complexion, Alexa had inherited her mother's lungs. The pneumonia that had taken her mother with brutal dexterity had tapped into a weakness and she hadn't stood a chance. Alexa, however, developing a propensity for chest colds, had had lots of intervention and lots of chances. Probing, antibiotics, physiotherapy, for goodness' sake, and, now, large bottles of fresh air on wheels. Good old-fashioned emphysema was her lot and the constant questions from doctors over the years were: Do you smoke? Have you ever smoked? And her answer was always: 'Yes, but only once, when Lady Meredith Ainsley stuck a cigarette between my lips and lit it.'

Alexa rested her head back on her pillows ruminating on how she never did find out what happened to milady. Why she died, fifty-one summers ago, in Lake Garda. Illness, or accident, Alexa had no idea. Some people, she concluded, in the wisdom of her seniority, as she watched a trail of the loved and not-so-loved pass away, just simply gave her the slip.

Sometime in the aftermath of the brutal violence of the summer's afternoon at Ferris House, her father had instructed his own solicitor to dispatch with the Moreland solicitor. She never knew the content of the two letters that she'd ripped up, could only guess at the gossip Rose had passed on in the Carmichael kitchen. But months later, when Guy wrote to Alexa himself to privately offer her a slice of Lady Meredith's fortune, she realised, baby or no baby, he wanted to gift money to salve his guilt. He had also added, at the end of his letter, that he'd always known that she'd loved Harvey. She refused him his offer, and heard no more. Alexa adjusted the straps on the mask. Perhaps this was the problem, why the oxygen seemed so thin. The mask was not fitting securely to her face. She wriggled it against her cheeks, the seal dragging uncomfortably on her skin, and peered across her bedroom. Somewhere, over in the cupboard, tucked in a folder in an untidy stack of paperwork was a thirty-seven-year-old newspaper clipping that completed Guy's story.

He had stayed on in Rome when the second great war broke out, his Italian wife securing his residency, and did yet more business with Mussolini. Did up another of his mansions in marble and, for his trouble and his collaboration, the partisans in their heated purge of retribution, executed him.

Melissa found the snippet in *The Times* a month or two after VE Day, just a tiny paragraph on page twenty-three, reporting the event. Alexa did not mourn him –

the ex-patriot marble importer

– she had no space inside her for that sort of luxury.

The coroner's verdict at the inquest for the *Enys Point incident* (as the newspapers tended to call it) was manslaughter and suicide. And Alexa, it was fair to say, had not been a reliable witness. Her father and Eleanor took her straight home, back to Porthdeen where she remained, in exile. She never saw Ma and Pa Ferris again. They moved away to Oban, to live near Aunt Margaret, but they let Ferris House on and off for years. During the war, the house was requisitioned as a hospital for wounded soldiers and, after that, it stood empty and started to crumble. It became the place that the locals of Little Porthdeen whispered about or pointed out with a crack of awe or fear in their voices. Alexa never went back, and neither did Betty and Arthur, for how could they with their son's blood soaked into their lawn.

Alexa's breathing became laboured; she was thinking too much. The past was with her, crouched in the corner. She reached across to her bedside table and plucked a tissue from the box, using it to wipe the tears that were pooling on top of the plastic mask, running down the sides. She glanced at her clock. Marina would be upstairs very soon with a light supper and Alexa did not want her to see an old lady's tears. At least from the window of her room, where she was confined – for walking up and down stairs was impossible – she still had her view. From her window, her widow's watch, she saw the midsummer evening falling, dusty and pink, over the sea, the seagulls wheeling down to roost. The snaking pathway over on the Enys Point headland was, as always, empty.

Here in this bedroom, the spring that followed Harvey's death, Alexa gave birth to Marina and nursed her while, in her broken mind, she walked through sorrow, opening doors onto empty rooms, looking for Harvey, demanding that he talk to her. Telling him that he should not leave her in this appalling place. She was terrified that he had not understood her; had not heard the last words she'd whispered to him.

A tap on the door roused her, and Marina came in with the tray. Like Alexa, she had clear blue eyes, olive skin and dark hair; Marina's now peppered with grey, Alexa's own as silver as moonlight. And just like Alexa, Marina could not cook.

Alexa allowed her daughter to heave her up the bed, pat at the pillows and fuss with the sheet before she peered down at the offering of a rubbery omelette.

'How are you feeling this evening, Mum?'

'As I always do,' she answered, tempted to add disabled by illness and struggling to breathe. 'But I think there may be something wrong with the whatsit. It's making a funny hissing sound.'

Marina had a look at the oxygen tank, squeezed a rubber pipe, twisted at the valve, twisted it back.

'It's fine, Mum. Although I would trust Melissa's judgement over mine. You can't get much better than a hospital matron for your chief carer, can you.'

'Except that chief carer is sunning herself in Majorca as we speak.'

'Yes, lying in the sun planning her retirement so she can lie in the sun some more. But she made your birthday cake before she left. Oh, I must remember to get it out of the freezer.'

Alexa lifted the mask, took a forkful of her supper and slowly, so as not to attract her daughter's attention, put it back down. While Marina's culinary efforts remained below average, Melissa's cake-making skills, she was happy to say, had improved vastly from when she was a little girl.

The one brightness of Alexa's life was that her half-sister and her daughter, with not more than a decade between them, were such wonderful friends. They'd both had their ups and downs, seeing off two husbands and a married lover between them. And they doled out their love for Marina's daughter, Charlotte, in equal amounts. But Alexa had never found anyone to measure up to Harvey. Had never loved in that way again.

'Have you heard from Lotte?' she asked.

'Oh yes, she sends lots of love. I have an airmail letter downstairs, arrived in the second post. Sorry, I should have brought it up earlier.'

'Where is she now?' Alexa asked. 'Remind me.'

'Sydney.'

Alexa chewed gamely on another mouthful of omelette, imagining her granddaughter in another hemisphere, on the other side of the globe, in a country lapped by a different ocean. At night, seeing a different sky. Charlotte – Lotte – lived her life exploring the planet as a travel journalist in a world of freebies, five-star hotels and spa treatments.

Alexa rarely saw her granddaughter but she was always on her mind. For her face was Harvey's. His looks had skipped a generation, missing Marina clean out. But Lotte was a Ferris through and through, with Harvey's height and his stride. Her hair was beautiful: tawny, thick and wavy. She always complained about the front bit flopping forward, and would push it back with an effortless, graceful gesture, unaware of the ecstasy of pain this caused her grandmother. Perhaps it was best that she was on the other side of the earth for, sometimes, Alexa could not bear to look at her.

'Always jetting off, that girl,' Alexa remarked. 'Jetting, I like that.' And her mind drifted over the word. Since Harvey had left her she had lived through the Depression, then the second great war. Then the Cold War, the jet age, the space age, then the Seventies. 'What did we call the Seventies, Marina?' she asked. 'And what do we call now? It's still the jet age, surely, although perhaps Lotte would call it the New Romantic age?'

'I don't know, Mum,' Marina said, clearly not understanding.

She removed her unfinished supper. 'And now we have old age.'

Marina glanced at her as she always did, her face stiff with concern.

'Are you ready for sleep yet? Big day tomorrow.'

Alexa did not answer, for she did not want to tell her daughter how very tired she was. Too tired for another birthday. And that she just wanted to sleep, was so desperate to sleep, but that she did not want to dream. For even her happiest, lightest of dreams shifted into nightmares.

At night, they cruised the backwaters of Venice, or sailed Indigo Moon. Sometimes, in the magical way dreams worked, they sailed Indigo Moon through the canals of an unknown, exquisite eternal city. But *she* would appear, always, in a white dress against black jagged rocks. Sometimes standing, watching them. Other times, lying where she fell, crumpled and broken over ruthless boulders, her head in seawater, the foam pink with her blood, part of the rock and forever part of the sea.

Sarah passed from tragedy into legend and Alexa had briefly, frivolously, wondered if the mummers would ever tell her tale. From time to time, even as late as the space age, the story was referred to in the local newspaper, cropping up here and there. And Melissa and Marina tried to secrete the papers away so that Alexa would not be hurt. She loved her family, all her 'girls' as she called them, but knew that they would never be able to truly know the damage done to her.

Alexa also wondered if Miss Graham had ever seen the news reports. Funny, she thought now, how a simple piece of advice handed out by a schoolmistress could result in such catastrophe, its dismal legacy continuing long into the future.

Marina was heading for the door.

'Seventy summers,' Alexa said. 'That is how I measure my life. Sounds better that way, don't you think? Summers, instead of years. I want to tell you something you don't know, Marina.'

Her daughter stopped, gave a little sigh, sat down on the old wicker chair by the window.

'Yes? What's that?' Marina settled her face into calm acceptance.

'In my twentieth summer, when your grandfather and Eleanor moved me back here, the only things I really wanted to bring with me was my button box and the portrait. And the first thing I did was march into your grandfather's study to telephone Harrods and put an order in for a batch of blue paint. And I redecorated the parlour, all by myself: shifting furniture, sanding, priming, up stepladders, brushes on poles, that sort of thing. Pregnant with you – imagine that. I needed the portrait to look at home and to look wonderful. And it still does, doesn't it?'

Marina nodded.

'I know this, Mum. You've told me before. Now, put your mask back on properly.'

'You have to excuse me, for I am getting on a bit. I forget, you know. What I've said. What I haven't said. But this you don't know…'

Alexa sucked on bottled air. The year after Harvey's death, she visited Nonna in Venice. Her father, Eleanor and Melissa came with her, but she left little Marina at Porthdeen with Aunt Rose, for she was too young to travel.

'That was my mistake, Marina,' said Alexa, 'for Nonna died two years later and she never saw you. She never saw her great-grandchild. But how she loved you.'

'I know, Mum.'

'You don't know. She left me the palazzo in San Polo. I often think of it: that floating palace of the sea.'

'But you never went back,' said her daughter.

'It's yours, Marina.'

Alexa saw tears wetting her daughter's eyes, watched her bravely draw a breath over her shuddering emotion and Alexa knew she must never do what Mamma had done. She must never tell Marina about her own premonition, on the still water of Loch Linnhe, and the tiny voice inside her, warning her.

'Mum, you are getting tired,' Marina said, surreptitiously wiping her cheeks.

'I wonder if you would bring the portrait up, please.'

'Tonight? Here?'

'Please.'

Marina had broken into a sweat by the time she got back up the stairs with it, thumping and cursing a little when she reached the landing.

'It's a fair weight, Mum, I tell you,' she puffed.

'Just prop it over there against the wall,' said Alexa. 'That's it.' The three faces, incandescent in the fading light, told the story of her seventy summers. And how, over time, as the years stretched by, Alexa had moved up to take Nonna's place. 'Would you leave the curtains open, please.'

Marina bent to kiss Alexa on the forehead to avoid the oxygen mask clamped to her face.

'Birthday girl, tomorrow,' she said. 'Goodnight, Mum.'

She left the room with a tender backwards glance, closed the door.

In the stillness of the endless summer evening, Alexa listened to the sighing of the sea, the hissing of the tank. Perhaps it had a leak, after all. The air that she was breathing was depleting, thinning, failing.

Waves of drowsiness, each one stronger, more violent than the last, began to take her. Was this, she wondered, not at all afraid, what it felt like to drown? Was this what it felt like for Luke and Edith and their little unborn soul?

Alexa pulled the mask off and it rested, useless in her hand.

Her nostrils flared instantly to capture more air.

'Tell me the bedtime story again, Mamma. How it was that I nearly wasn't born,' she whispered into the listening room, gazing across at the portrait. 'Please, Mamma, or I will never sleep.'

A spasm gripped Alexa, a horrible, wracking cough. She gasped for air, struggling, could neither breathe in or out. Her throat locked. She pressed her hands to her mouth. The tearing pain eased as suddenly as it started and she rested back into the softness of the bed.

Alexa gazed through hazy twilight at the objects on her shelf: George the doll and the button box; inside, among her collection, the tiny seed buttons from the gold lace dress and one from Nonna's Mary-Jane shoes. All her possessions had fared better than she, apart from the two halves of eggshell, which had disintegrated into dust half a century ago.

She kept her eyes open, would not give in. Not just yet. She watched, with sudden and greedy yearning, the view through her window, the midsummer evening sky a luminous arc over her; the sea, below, her constant friend.

Alexa blinked. Along the distant path on the Enys Point headland, so very far away, but also within her reach, came a figure, head down, striding and determined. For a moment, she did not believe. In the next, she knew.

And she must get ready, for Harvey was a fast walker.

ACKNOWLEDGMENTS

It started in Venice with a painting. While admiring art, marble and Murano glass at the sumptuous Palazzo Mocenigo, a portrait stopped me in my tracks. At first glance, I saw three individual people but, drawing closer, decided it depicted one lady at different stages of her life: girl, woman, grandmother. The portrait (by Domenico Maggiotto, b1713) was fascinating enough until I spotted, right by the girl's bright innocent face, a fierce demon glaring out of the murky depths. I saw inevitable mortality lurking in the background, but also the reassurance of generations continuing.

From here, the story of Alexa and her quest for love and for family began to evolve. I translated the mesmerising triple portrait into a work of art that would fit with the 1920s and 1930s - the era in which I set *The Runaway*, with Alexa, the girl, Carlotta, the woman, and Beatrice, the grandmother, in their own painting. And the demon replaced by a gathering storm.

I'd like to say thank you to the fabulous Boldwood team for all your support, to my editor, Emily Yau, and my agent, Judith Murdoch.

ABOUT THE AUTHOR

Catherine Law writes dramatic romantic novels set in the first half of the 20th century, during the First and Second World Wars. Her books are inspired by the tales our mothers and grandmothers tell. Originally a journalist, Catherine lives in Kent.

Sign up to Catherine Law's mailing list here for news, competitions and updates on future books.

Visit Catherine's website: www.catherinelaw.co.uk

Follow Catherine on social media:

facebook.com/catherinelawbooks
twitter.com/authorcathlaw
instagram.com/catherinelawauthor
goodreads.com/catherinelaw

ALSO BY CATHERINE LAW

The Officer's Wife

The Runaway

Milton Keynes UK
Ingram Content Group UK Ltd.
UKHW041853250923
429376UK00004B/111

9 781837 516018